RED'S 

Satan's Devils MC - Las Vegas Chapter #1

COPYRIGHT

Published 2021 by Trish Haill Associates

Copyright © Manda Mellett

ISBN: 978-1-915106-01-8

All rights reserved. This book or any portion thereof may not be reproduced or used in any manner whatsoever without the express written permission of the author except for the use of brief quotations in a book reviews.

www.mandamellett.com

Disclaimer

This is a work of fiction. Names, characters, businesses, places, events and incidents are either the products of the author's imagination or used in a fictitious manner. Any resemblance to actual persons, living or dead, or actual events is purely coincidental.

Warning

This book is dark in places and contains content of a sexual, abusive and violent nature. It may not be suitable for persons under the age of 18.

PRODUCTION ACKNOWLEDGMENTS

Cover Design by Wicked Smart Designs

Edited and formatted by Maggie Kern @ Ms.K Edits

Proof reading by Darlene Tallman

Photographer: Golden Czermak of Furious Fotog

Model: Andrew Flanagan

SATAN'S DEVILS MC

CHAPTER ONE

"What the fuck is this?" Manny stares in disgust at the piece of paper he's just taken out of the now ripped envelope. As if he can no longer bear to touch it, he chucks it down on his desk. When he looks up, his eyes are narrowed.

My shoulders rise parallel with my ears, then drop. It's self-explanatory, but seeing he clearly needs to hear it from my mouth, I oblige. "My resignation. Two weeks' notice, as required."

"Fuck." Disbelieving eyes meet mine, then lower as Manny picks up the discarded letter and reads it again, as if hoping this time, the words will be different. Then, putting the paper to one side, he pushes his chair out from his desk and stands. Coming around to my side, he puts a grubby hand on the arms of my equally dirty overalls. "Come, son. Let's go get a drink. We'll discuss this. You can tell me what's on your mind."

It might be considered unusual for a boss to take one of his workers to a bar in the middle of the morning, but Manny and I have a deeper relationship than normal between boss and employee. One that goes back seven years to when I first turned up at his garage, an unskilled only-just-adult begging for employment. I don't know what he'd seen in me, but after he'd completed the formal interview—one which had been entirely unsatisfactory, I'd clearly had nothing to offer—instead of accusing me of wasting his time, he'd started to probe. Some of my desperation had gotten through to him.

Manny's was the last of the dozens of places I'd already approached, and no one else had given me a chance. In many cases, there'd been no interview, and those which I'd had were over fast.

But Manny had sensed there was something inside me. Instead of asking what I could offer to him, he asked the simple question why. Once he'd learned of my home circumstances, he'd given me that chance.

He hadn't gone easy on me. He'd pushed me as hard, if not harder than anyone else would have done. But I'd repaid the faith he'd shown in me tenfold. I'd gone from sweeping floors, to completing the apprenticeship he'd sponsored me for, to being, though I say it myself, his number one and best mechanic.

I knew today wouldn't be easy. Of course, he'd be pissed at me for wanting to leave, but I'd also suspected it wouldn't come as a complete surprise.

Removing my overalls and grabbing my jacket off the hook, I put on the warm garment then turn up the collar. Rubbing my hands together and shivering, I step outside into the late autumn chill. Looking up at the sky, I see grey clouds brooding. Rain or snow? The latter isn't forecasted, but what do they know? It feels cold enough for the weather to turn. I grimace. I'm already running out of time.

Alongside a now silent Manny, I cross the street, heading to the bar that's conveniently opposite the auto-shop. I push open the door and hold it for Manny, then follow him as we enter a different world, one that's warm and welcoming, all the elements left outside.

"Manny! Red! Come on in. What can I get you?" Being handily close, we're no strangers here.

I tip my chin toward the bartender while Manny calls out,

"Two beers, Harry." Then my boss waves his hand and indicates a table in the corner. Sure, it's good for privacy, but I wonder why he's bothering. Apart from a drunk in the corner, we're the only customers at this hour. Habit, I suppose.

Manny pulls out a seat, and settles himself, giving out a grunt as he lowers his ass down. His knees creek betraying his advancing age. As I take the chair opposite, he pierces me with his eyes, and barely lets me get comfortable, before he asks, "How did the funeral go?"

I breathe deep and shrug. *How the fuck do I answer?* "As well as these things can, I suppose." Yesterday I'd celebrated a life and buried a body. What more can I say?

Harry arrives and places two beer mats and then the two beer bottles down. Manny takes out his wallet, but Harry shakes his head knowingly, stating, "I'll start a tab."

Barely waiting for the bartender to go, Manny dives straight in. "You're making a mistake, son."

The weight of letting down the man who's done so much for me bears down on my conscience. I didn't expect him to leap at the chance of seeing me gone, but I'd hoped he'd understand. I grimace. "Done a lot of thinking, Manny. I've got no reason to hang around."

He taps his fingers to a rhythm only he can hear. "Is it more money? More responsibility? I can give you that. I was thinking of retiring—"

"Manny, no." Raising my hand, I stop him. "When I started, I only thought it was for a short time. You knew it was temporary. Then weeks became months, months added up to years—"

It's his turn to interrupt. "And you've made something of yourself in the meantime."

Have I? Sure, I've got a trade, a good job, and, if I understand Manny correctly, a chance to take over his business and make it mine. But begging the bank for a loan and committing myself to running an auto repair shop as I ran myself into the ground trying to pay the money back sounds like a fucking millstone I'd be carrying around. It's not the future I'd always longed for.

"I became what I had to," I refute quickly. "Doesn't mean it was my life's plan. Manny, you always knew I was going to move on when…" My mouth twists, and I shake my head. It's hard to put into words even now. "I don't want to let you down, and fuck knows, I can't express how grateful to you I am. But I feel like I've just been motoring, stuck in the same gear, and now I've a chance, I want to take it and move on."

He stares down at his beer. "Yeah, I know, son." His eyes close briefly, then reopen. "I'd thought, hoped, maybe over the years you'd found your place."

"I was never meant to be here," I remind him. I'd had everything planned. I was going to finish school, join the Army with an eye on becoming a Ranger and travel the world. Yeah, I'd had big dreams and had to leave them all behind.

Manny shakes his head sadly. "But instead, life tied you down. Fuck that bitch." He adds the last with more than a touch of malice.

The bitch in question being my mother.

Seven years back, I was set on the path I'd laid out for myself, even had the papers ready and just about to sign on the dotted line when my dad had had an accident at work. A building under construction had collapsed on him, breaking his back, and crushing his skull. He hadn't been given long to live, his injuries considered too serious, but somehow, he'd held on. He'd even recovered sufficiently to be discharged from the hospital.

We'd thought we'd lost him, and it had been touch and go for a while, but he'd survived. I'd been jubilant. What kid wants to lose his dad? But as time went on, I often wondered whether he'd have preferred to have succumbed to his injuries. I'd never find out, as I'd never been able to ask. Left paralysed from the neck down and brain damaged, he'd never come back to himself. Rather than the strong man I'd always looked up to, my dad had become nothing more than a dependent child, unable to understand the world around him, and unable to communicate with it.

When he neither improved nor deteriorated, his wife of twenty years, my mom, had decided caring for him hadn't been something she'd signed on for, totally forgetting the sickness part of her marriage vows. Not content with the man who'd been discharged from the hospital, she'd walked out, expecting me to go with her.

Dad might no longer be the father I'd looked up to while growing up, but I couldn't forget deep down inside he was still that man—a larger-than-life, always-there figure with a loud booming voice he used to praise or admonish a growing boy. Always ready to come cheer when I was playing football or take me fishing and hunting. He'd taught me to drive, and a myriad of other things kids look to their dads for. He might never be that father again, but I owed him a debt and I was going to repay it.

It was then I'd examined my relationship with my mom. She'd provided the basics—food to fill the stomach of a growing boy, a clean, tidy home to return to–but our house wasn't filled with laughter and joy, and the only things that seemed to make her happy had nothing to do with her child, and more with pleasing herself. Having not given me emotional support during my formative years, I'd had none to offer when she'd asked it of me, my loyalty all for my father instead. I'd felt sadness, of course, when she'd driven away, but it was more for a loss for something I'd never had.

Parental obligations meant she'd kept in touch for a while, mainly to see whether her old man was still breathing. She'd never come back.

I'd had no idea what I'd been taking on, my decision made in a rush of emotion. As everything became clearer and my life grew harder, of necessity, I'd shaken off the remaining shackles of childhood fast. I had nothing but hate and abhorrence left for her. Any contact petered out on her side as well as mine.

Dad had lingered far longer than expected—years instead of

the months the doctors had given him. I never regretted not doing what she'd suggested, putting him in a home where he'd be cared for by strangers.

He'd needed expert care, more than I could provide. At least he had a hefty insurance payout which enabled me to employ an experienced caregiver from nine to five but little extra to live on. Hence, my job seeking, which had led me to Manny's door. No one else had wanted an eighteen-year-old with no experience and dying dreams of becoming a Ranger.

Although we could only afford part-time care, Dad had needed twenty-four-hour attention, so that fell to me when the professional wasn't there. Alongside my mechanics training, I learned all about how to look after a man who could do nothing for himself and learned to interpret what little he could still enjoy.

He knew when I was there, beamed when I returned from work and took over from the carer. He enjoyed sports, though it was unclear how much he could understand, and loved it when I filled his sippy cup with his favourite beer. Weekends we'd both sit watching television, me on watch for checking his oxygen, that he wasn't choking, and for when his diapers needed changing.

In essence, I gave up my life to preserve his.

I didn't resent one single minute. But no one, least of all me, expected him to last seven years.

A few weeks back and a massive brain bleed had achieved what his accident had failed to do. I'd held his hand as he'd lain dying, a shell of a man who wasn't my dad anymore. Then, without fanfare, he faded away and was gone.

For seven years, my only reprieve had been working for Manny. Those hours working for him gave me a break which enabled me to hang onto my sanity.

Manny's been good to me, but I don't owe him like I did my dad. I've had enough of giving up years when I could be building a life that I wanted, rather than one duty had forced on to me. It was time to be selfish and be just me. Time to seek whatever it was I was searching for.

Manny raps his fingers on the table, purses his lips, then takes in a deep breath, letting it out on a sigh. "I suspected it was time when your dad went. Knew this was coming, just hoped I had something to offer to keep you here. I'm going to fucking miss you, Red."

"I'll miss you too, Manny. You know I'll never be able to thank you enough. But apart from you and this job, there's nothing to stay here for." Manny's been like a substitute father to me, and I'll never forget him, but I'm fed up with feeling I owe anyone anything. Self-centred? Perhaps. But so much of my life has been stolen.

Before my dad's accident, I'd been a normal teen, partying, getting girlfriends. I'm no twenty-five-year-old virgin, but apart from my hand, my dick's seen no action for the past seven years, all my free time taken up nursing my parent. I want to let loose, make up for those missing years. I couldn't do that staying here working for Manny. Or, if he had his way, taking over his business. Having been forced into adulthood, I want to take a step back. Have my stab at being a wild child, live the life I'd never had.

Not that I want to drift forever. Part of my dream is finding a good woman and settling down—after I've sown my wild oats of course, and I've got a lot of those stored up. Maybe eventually having a kid and teaching it like my dad had taught me.

Manny sits back, brings his bottle to his mouth and takes a few swallows, then replaces the empty bottle on the table, looking up with acceptance in his eyes. "I won't try and talk you out of it, that wouldn't be fair. Christ, I know what you've been through since your mom walked out. So," he leans back, folding his arms, "tell me, what are your plans?"

Instead of the months that in the beginning I'd thought was all I had, I've had years to think about it, gradually revising and refining my plans. Initially, it was a delayed entry into the Army, then as more time passed, an acknowledgment I was too old to subject myself to that authority. Now, I try to voice what my next step is. I acknowledge that even to myself, what I've mapped out sounds vague.

"I'm going south. I hate these winters. I want to go where I can ride my bike all year round." My mouth turns up as I nod out the window where the clouds have finally made up their minds, and a heavy sleet is falling.

"You and that fuckin' motorcycle of yours." He laughs.

She's my pride and joy, the thing that's kept me sane over the years. I'd bought her cheap as a wreck and fixed her up by myself. She's a thing of beauty now, an ancient Harley, but she's still got miles in her, by virtue of being almost entirely new parts.

"So just ride, huh? Where you thinking? California?" He doesn't tell me I'm not being sensible. Instead, there's a gleam in his eyes as if heading out with no destination in mind is something he'd have liked to have tried.

"Nah. California's too crowded." I'd already rejected that state. It also sounds cliché. California or Florida are the main places people tend to head for when they want to move to warmer climates. "I'm just going to head south and see where I end up."

"You're young. In many ways, I envy you." I know his history. Manny had settled down when he was five years younger than I am now. His youngest kid is my grand old age of twenty-five. He and his wife are still happily married, but I sense an unfulfilled wanderlust in his eyes. "I'll fucking miss you." He shakes his head and repeats what he's said before.

And again, it's the absolute truth when I reply, "I'll miss you too, old man."

"Less of the fuckin' old," he growls. I grin. He continues, "You could still sign up."

I shake my head. That boat has long sailed now. Forced to become independent earlier than I liked, I want out from a regimented routine, and have no desire to step back into another one. For too long, my days have been ordered by times to medicate or do this or that for my dad. I want to explore the alien concept of spontaneity.

He moves on to the practicalities. "You want me to store anything for you? Just until you settle down?"

I shake my head. There's little I want to take with me, preferring to make a fresh start. The furniture we had is more likely to go to the dump or to Goodwill, than be something I'd want to keep. The house itself, well, that was forfeited long ago once the insurance had dwindled out.

Truth is, I feel adrift. I have no one to care for now, no reason to get up in the morning. Each day for the last seven years my life has been on repeat, with hardly anything to break the monotony. If I stay here, I will just carry on existing. I want to find out who I am, what I'm capable of, and where my place is in the world. I want to find myself.

Hell, I don't begrudge the time I spent with my dad, not for one minute. I'd do the same thing all over, even knowing what I was letting myself in for. But freedom is going to take a while to get used to.

I'd always known Dad had dreams to travel, to see different parts of the States, if not the world. It was why he'd encouraged me to become a soldier. I almost feel bound to make his dreams real now. Or at least, do what was robbed from him, to enjoy and experience life.

Manny looks up, catches Harry's eye, and holds up two fingers, indicating we want more beer. When we're served, he waits for Harry to regain his place behind the bar.

"I was fooling myself, hoping it wasn't coming, son. Knew as soon as the funeral was over, you'd get itchy feet. Also knew as well as I do the sun sets in the evening that you wouldn't be sticking around. Already put feelers out for a mechanic to replace you."

I'm not surprised. "Found anyone?"

"Maybe. Someone I can call in to give a try." He sits forward again. "So here's the thing. You gave me two weeks' notice, just like you should, but I'm not holding you to that, not if that's not what you want. You want time to get your head around things, you're welcome to carry on. But if you want to take advantage that the winter hasn't really hit yet, then go now. Leave as soon as you're ready to get on the road."

"Appreciate that," I tell him sincerely, casting my eyes back out the window again. "I've been hoping to head out before we get the snow. Just didn't want to leave you in the lurch."

Manny grins. "Don't worry about us. We'll get the jobs done, whether or not you're here to help us. You wouldn't be letting us down."

I take a long swig of my second beer. "You've been good to me, Manny."

"Ain't a thing, son. You've been a fuckin' good worker. The only thing you've never done is have fun. Took a load of responsibility on those young shoulders. Now you've got the chance to live for yourself, you should grasp your freedom and hold on to it. Maybe you'll find a place to call home, get yourself a woman and settle down. Have a few rug rats."

I grin at him. Yeah, that's my plan. Let some wildness out of my system, then become a member of society again. Despite my desire for freedom, I'm too sensible to think my carefree days will last long. Eventually, I'll need to earn money.

Long term? A family of my own is what I aspire to, a job that puts food on the table, and, obviously, the chance to ride my bike whenever I like.

CHAPTER TWO

S aying a final farewell to Manny had been almost worse than watching my dad die. For my parent, it was a welcome release from his suffering, my sadness tinged with relief and the knowledge it was his time. Leaving my benefactor was different, as there was an underlying feeling I was letting him down, even if he denied it. I was also losing an anchor, and conscious of heading out rudderless into the world.

My second thoughts though, didn't last long. If I'm ever going to find that family of my own that I'm looking for, I have to grow up first, and get some experience of living. Christ, apart from the women customers and the nurse, I barely know how to speak to a female. And certainly know nothing of courting one. Hookups in school had been easy. I was a football jock and picking up girls hadn't been hard. Somehow, I think things will be different out in the real world.

A world of which I know barely anything.

I grin to myself. I'm not entirely ignorant. One thing's for sure, if I have kids, I'd never baulk at changing a diaper, or have problems mushing up food.

Maybe it's not the most rational thing in the world to set off into the unknown with nothing more than I can pack into the saddlebags on my bike, but it's the start of experiencing things I've never had the chance to before. To act without simply reacting.

Standing next to my big two-wheeler, I pat my pockets to make sure I've got all I need at hand, and take one last look behind to the house that's already got a foreclosure sign in the front yard. I'd love to say I'll recall it with fond memories, but any happy days are so far in my rearview, it's hard to remember them.

It's a house of pain, of death, of struggles to survive. The last seven years had wiped out any of the pleasure of those that came before.

Move forward, son, don't look back.

The air whispers around me, and I hear the echoes of my father's voice, the one I've not heard for seven years. A fist clenches at my heart, knowing I'll never see him again. *I lost him years ago,* I remind myself. It seems for almost a quarter of my life I've been grieving the man who raised me.

It's time to move on. Deliberately, I swing my leg over the seat, zip my jacket up tight, pull on my full-face helmet and finally my thick winter gloves. I turn the key, then press start. The engine rumbles to life with a thunderous roar, making the ground tremble under my feet. *This is it.* The start of my life, a new beginning, my first step on the road to my future.

What will it hold? Where will the road lead me? As the first cold raindrop falls and lands on my nose, making me pull down the visor, I grimace, then grin. *Somewhere warmer, I hope.*

A lifesaver look behind me to check for traffic, then I pull away from the kerb.

Fuck, but Manny had been good to me, I think as I'm stopped by traffic I can't pass. While my engine sits idling, I cast my mind back twenty-four hours.

After drinking the second beers, my now ex-boss had told me not to bother returning to work, but to go home and get myself ready for the next chapter of my life. His other instruction was to make sure I swung by at the end of the day to collect my final paycheck. When I'd done so, I'd been astonished when I found he'd given me a hefty bonus. To top that off, my fellow workers had done a collection and had pulled together a nice wad of cash as a going away present. If I'd had to turn away to rub at my eye, it was only because I'd had a speck of dust in it. That's my story and I'm sticking to it.

It had made me question why I was so determined to leave all that behind. For a moment, I'd wavered. But interpreting my hesitation, Manny had given me the best gift of all—a security net with his insistence I'd always get a warm welcome, and my old job back, should my plans not work out. When we'd embraced, I knew I'd miss the old fucker more than I'd realised.

Finally clearing the jammed-up traffic, I drive through the streets I've known all my life, and with a sigh of relief, reach the city limits. Stopping off only to top off my bike with gas, once back on the pavement, I twist the throttle, determined not to look in my rearview.

As if they understand the gravity of the occasion, the elements seem to be with me. Like a welcome onto the road, the rain eases off and the ominous clouds part to let weak rays of the sun through, lighting my path. With every mile under my wheels, I start to leave doubts and regrets behind me. Instead, my head fills with thoughts of excitement and adventures ahead.

Where should I go? It's a thrilling thought that the whole of the United States, if not the world, is my oyster. Florida? Too humid and full of alligators. California? Nah, in addition to the reasons I'd rejected it before, they have earthquakes. Texas? Maybe. New Mexico? Louisiana? Strange as it may seem, I've no preference. No real experience of other states than the one where I've lived all my life. As I'd told Manny, I'll head south, and when I see something that appeals to me, that's when I'll stop.

If I never find it? Well, I'll return, not with my tail between my legs, but with a sense of satisfaction that I'd at least tried.

The wind muffled by my full-face helmet buffets me, and

my exhaust sings its grumbling song as the road flies by beneath my tyres. The emotion of the pain of my dad dying, together with the twinges of guilt that it had been a release for us both, the writing of the final page in his story of preparing for and attending the funeral, and even the weight of the last few years all gradually start to fade and are replaced by anticipation.

I can reinvent myself. I'm going where no one will know me. I've no past to either live up or down to. This is a chance to discover myself.

I ride on, relishing even the monotony when the scenery offers nothing of note, wanting to put as much distance between myself and my old life as I can in as short a time as possible. The only times I stop are out of necessity, to top off my tank and fill my stomach until daylight begins to fade. Then, when a motel appears in front of me, I pull in.

My muscles, unused to such a long journey, complain as I kick down the stand and protest the weight I put on my legs. I bow my spine, putting my hands to the middle of my back and then stretch. It's good to feel a physical pain rather than the mental anguish. Honest aches, like those gained through a good day's work.

I'm pleased to find the sign advertising vacancies hadn't lied as I head inside and question the woman sitting behind a reception desk. Inwardly I smirk. To me, I'm on an adventure, to her, I'm just one in a long line of guests passing by.

Have I ever stayed in a motel before? I'm fucked if I can remember.

"One night?" she queries in a bored voice.

"One night," I agree, scrawling my government name in the book she pushes over to me. *Colt Masters.* It's a name that's alien to me. Due to the colour of my hair, I've been known as Red all my life and can't remember ever being called anything else.

Having dumped my saddlebags in the allotted room, pleased to find the room is light, airy and clean, I set off for the adjacent restaurant. I treat myself to a couple of beers and a steak, then return to my abode for the night.

The bed's comfy enough, and tired from the long hours of riding, I fall asleep fast, and sleep through the night for the first time in forever. As Dad had often needed me during the night, I'd always slept with my ear alert for alarms alerting me he required assistance. After he'd gone, the habit had been hard to break, and even after the funeral, I was still sleeping light. When I wake with the dawn, I realise that this trip is already providing the necessary healing.

Day two starts the same, but without the same sense of urgency. I stop earlier in the afternoon, and after finding a place to stay, I do some sightseeing. It's strange to just be me, having no one else to think about, no reason to keep an eye on the clock, or think about being there to give someone their medication or do one of the numerous personal tasks I'd stoically performed but would prefer not to think about.

I feel free. Even the air seems easier to draw into my lungs. Quickly, I realise how I relish that feeling.

Enjoying that interlude so much, on the third day, I deliberately start taking the journey more leisurely. I'm in no rush. No demons are chasing me. The only thing I'm keeping an eye on is the winter weather that's approaching all too fast. Having checked the forecast, finding it predicting high pressure and no sign of clouds forming, I break my journey at midday and pull up in a small town. Leaving my bike parked outside, I enter a mom-and-pop diner.

Obviously dating from the fifties, it doesn't look like it's changed much since. Grinning at the nostalgic elements scattered around, I seat myself on a red plastic seat and eye the jukebox. Currently, it's playing some early Rolling Stones. Is it an omen? That record was one of my dad's favourites. Tapping my fingers to the beat, I wait for the waitress to come over.

There are a couple of other tables filled, but not many, and I suspect there's only one person waiting on them. Curbing my impatience, it's not like I have to be anywhere, I let my eyes roam around, taking in the details of the small place, my eyes captured by the black-and-white photos on the walls, all showing patrons past, and how the place used to look from the outside. It doesn't seem to have changed much. It's as though it's stuck in a time capsule.

To pass the time, I watch the busy waitress as she picks up an order at the counter. All I see is her back, and wow, she's got a shapely ass. My eyes seem drawn to it, and my cock, which doesn't usually have something in the flesh to perk up to, gives a twitch. I've watched porn, of course, but none of the women I actually meet in real life have been so tantalising, or not during my limited existence over the past few years. I even start thinking I wouldn't mind tapping that. Nah, not in the least.

The chances, however, are extremely unlikely. When she expertly balances three plates and swings around, she's pretty, but in a homely girl next-door type of way. A good girl, one that probably goes to church each Sunday, and certainly wouldn't be up for a roll in the hay.

But hey, I can look, can't I?

When she leans over to deliver the food, I notice her breasts fall forward—not overly large, and not too small. Definitely natural, I can see by the sway. When she stands though, she massages the small of her back, and gives a little stretch and a roll of her shoulders. Then, she seems to shrug her tiredness away. Spinning around, she spies me waiting, and plastering a welcoming smile on her face, she comes straight over.

"Well, greetings stranger. I've not seen you in here before." She taps her pencil against a notepad she'd taken from a frilly apron that exactly matches the 1950s vibe. "What can I get you?"

"I'm just passing through." My lips curve naturally as I address her statement, noting while she probably wouldn't grace a magazine cover, her face is full of character. Big hazel eyes rimmed with long artificially blackened lashes, a nose that could possibly be thought a little too large, and blonde hair pulled back into a ponytail which makes me want to see what it looks like down. Her lips? Full and soft looking, just right for sucking a cock.

Yeah, my thoughts went straight there, which is decidedly odd. In high school, I hadn't found many girls willing to take a dick in their mouth, and the intervening years had been a desert. I wouldn't have expected my first thought about a woman to be other than sinking my cock into the hole built for it. But while I continue to drink in her appearance, my nose twitches in anticipation of how she might smell, and what her essence might taste of. *Are women different from teenage girls?* Guess I've got a whole lot of education to catch up on.

As if she can read my thoughts, her smile broadens. Hoping to fuck she's no mind reader, the pale skin I'm cursed with starts to flush. My freckles must be blazing like beacons as my cock gets into the act, swelling, luckily hidden, under the table.

Christ, I haven't felt this way since I was a teenager. *Is it her who's responsible for the state I'm in? Or has my new freedom meant I've shaken off the shackles of respectability and I'm likely to get hard when faced with any female?* Which would be decidedly awkward.

"What can I get you?" she repeats, with a hint of amusement in her voice.

I come back to my senses. "Sorry, darlin'," I drawl. "Been riding too long. Coffee, please. And I'll have your special." I nod toward the board hanging over the counter.

"Coming right up." She rewards me with one of her dazzling smiles.

"Thank you… Cheryl." I read her name tag. *Cheryl*, my mind echoes. *Oh yeah, Cheryl, that's it, suck my…*

I give myself a mental slap to snap me out of my daydream just in time to hear her tell me, "I'll be right back."

What the fuck has gotten into me? Of necessity, sex has been the last thing on my mind for a very long time. It's going to be mightily inconvenient if I start looking at every female as a potential partner in bed. Giving my libido a lecture, I tell my dick to behave.

Nevertheless, my eyes are again drawn to her as she goes to the counter, shouts out my order to someone named Joe, then raises the coffee pot and brings it back over. I push my cup toward her, and she fills it.

Multi-tasking, she jerks her head toward the parking lot. "That your two-wheeler out there?"

I'd deliberately sat by the window so I have sight of my bike outside, which means I don't have to turn to check. When I grin, and respond, "Sure is," I don't miss the look of longing in her eyes. But seeing it's directed at my bike, not me, I suppress a snort.

"You ride?" I doubt it, but I've learned not to jump to conclusions. There had been a few women bringing in their rides for a service where I'd worked.

"Huh," she snorts, and shakes her head, making her ponytail fly. "No way. But I've always wondered what it's like to go on the back." She sounds wistful.

I could make your dreams come true, sweetheart. In exchange for a ride of a different sort. Not being stupid, I keep those thoughts to myself. She's a good girl, probably loves horses and Jesus, and would be horrified if let the words escape my mouth.

"Order up!" a loud voice shouts grumpily from the kitchen.

Immediately, Cheryl spins on her heels, goes to the counter and exchanges the coffee pot for a loaded plate. She returns quickly, and offers a practiced, "Enjoy your meal," before she strides off to deal with another customer who's trying to attract her attention.

Relaxed, in no hurry to be anywhere, I take my time to relish the offering that's actually quite good. By the time I've cleaned the plate and downed my second coffee, I notice the few other customers have left. There seems to be a lull in trade, so when Cheryl returns to clear the table, I point to the seat opposite. While eating, I've become annoyed with myself that I've been looking at her as a potential sex partner. I should be better than that. While I only have a vain hope that could be on the agenda, getting to know her better could only help. If nothing else, having a conversation with a fellow human being will counteract the self-imposed loneliness of the past couple of days.

I make a suggestion, "Why don't you take the load off for a bit?"

Startling, as though she hadn't expected the invitation, she casts a glance around, noticing, as I had, there's no current call on her services. With more elegance than I expected, she pulls out the chair and sits on it. Her sigh of relief as she takes the weight off her feet doesn't go unnoticed.

I'm not even sure of the name of the place I've stopped at. It's just another Podunk town, just like many others I've driven through. Her, though, for some reason, she's caught my interest. So much so, now I've got her full focus, I'm tongue-tied.

She, however, has no such problem. "What's your name?" she asks, picking up a napkin and twisting it between her fingers. I notice she's a sociable girl, clearly feeling no awkwardness talking to a stranger. Whether it's learned because of her job, or her natural inclination, it's hard to tell.

I supply the required information. "Folks call me Red."

Her eyes widen a little. "Nickname?"

"Yeah." I chuckle. "Been called it all my life. Barely remember the name I was born with. I have no idea why." I wink at her.

She gives a soft laugh. With my features, the answer is obvious. I'm pleased she refrains from testing my memory on my legal name. *Why should she? We're not starting a relationship.* "So, are you passing through, or staying for a while?"

I shrug while my eyes assess her. Could she have something to tempt me to break my journey? I'm attracted to her, but hell, I'm a man. I suspect she gets chatted up on a daily basis. "Passing through," I tell her eventually. While I'm intrigued by my physical reaction to her, it would only be a whim to stay longer.

Again, she glances outside at my bike, her eyes lingering on it for a moment before she brings them back to me. "Where are you heading?"

"I've no idea." I grin at her, replying honestly. "Right now, I'm going where the road and the wind take me."

Her eyes widen. "Oh?" Seems she hadn't taken me for a drifter. She bites her lips as though she wants to ask more.

For some reason, I've a need to satisfy her unspoken curiosity. Sighing, I tell her much the same as I'd told Manny. "I'm heading south. Got me a hankering for a warmer climate."

Her mouth opens in an O, and her eyes become unfocused as a look of longing comes over her face. "California?"

"Maybe." I shrug. "I've got no real plans. I'll ride until I find somewhere I like and some place I can settle down."

Her gaze sharpens again as she shakes herself, and her voice sounds dreamy. "I wish I could do that. Just take off."

"Why can't you?" I've glanced at her finger. She wears no ring.

"I…" she starts, then frowns. "It's not what normal people do, is it."

It's a statement, not a question. I grin widely. "Fuck normal people."

Giggling now, she glances outside once again, and I see the look of hunger in her eyes. Fuck knows why, but I hear myself saying casually, "Got a pillion seat if you're interested."

A bark of laughter comes from her. "Yeah, right. Just like that? I couldn't possibly."

I raise an eyebrow in challenge.

"And anyway," she starts to justify herself, "I haven't got any riding stuff. I'd need a helmet to start with."

I don't know why I just don't leave it. For some reason, her riding behind me is something I'd like to experience. I've only taken one of the other mechanics on the back before in an emergency, and he was hanging on to the hand grips, obviously struggling to keep his junk well away from my ass. But her?

She'd be up close, her soft breasts pushing into me, her hands around my waist… And just like that, I harden as much as I had before.

Damn cock. Behave.

"You wouldn't need a helmet while we're in Illinois." And anyway, I've got a spare. I've also brought along the half-helmet that I wear when it's warmer.

A spark comes into her eyes, a slight flush warming her cheeks. Her lips purse as though she's really thinking. Then she snorts and mumbles under her breath, the words meant for herself, "Don't be stupid. This is crazy. I don't know anything about him."

"Cheryl? Those tables clean?" a loud voice booms.

My eyes look in that direction to see a middle-aged man wearing a chef's hat leaning on the counter, his narrowed eyes glaring in our direction. I give him a polite raise of my chin, and he, clearly not wanting to offend a paying customer, gives me a slight nod back.

"Yeah, Joe," she answers.

He slaps the counter with his palm, but only lightly. "Get your ass back here and give me a hand then."

"Sure." Immediately, she sends me an apologetic look and starts to stand, placing her hands on the table and wearily pushing herself up.

Reaching out my hand, I place it on her arm, halting her progress. "Anywhere you'd recommend to stay around here?"

Her eyes widen slightly. "You sticking around?" At my shrug —as yet I'm undecided, I may have unexpectedly found a nugget of gold in this godforsaken town—she confides, "Momma Branston has a place down the road. Just carry on that way." She waves with her hand. "You can't miss it. It's basic, but clean. She's usually got vacancies."

CHAPTER THREE

Out of Cheryl's sphere of influence, I wonder what the hell I'm doing as I ride about a mile further down the road and come to a cheap-looking motel set back from the road. Damn woman must have cast some kind of spell over me. If I had any sense, I'd stick to my plan and continue riding. But a sense that I might be missing something important pushes me into making the turn.

Huh. I might have no choice. The unkempt parking lot makes me suspect the place is closed and that Momma Branston might have gone out of business. All I can see is a beat-up car outside one of the rooms, and the rear of a truck of some sort parked around the back. Part of me thinks fate might have stepped in and given me a reason to keep heading south. But seeing as I'm here now, I might as well explore my chances.

The door I expected to be locked, opens when I push on the handle. Still unconvinced, I step into the reception area which clearly has seen better days, noting there's not a speck of dust or dirt even though the decoration is shabby.

There's no one in sight, and no sounds come to me. Dubiously, I press the bell on the counter, hearing the ring echoing down the empty corridor. Then, there's a shuffling. Widening my eyes, I purse my lips. *Seems they might be open after all.* Part of me is disappointed. I wanted an excuse to get back on the road.

A woman who looks like she's in her eighties comes slowly along the corridor that leads to the back of the building, heavily leaning on a stick, the tip of which she lifts and places down deliberately, then allows her slipper-clad feet to catch up, before lifting and positioning the stick once more. When she reaches the desk, she takes her time easing herself behind it, and only looks at me when she's seated on a stool.

She pulls a register toward her. "You after a room?" Her voice is gravelly as if she's smoked too many cigarettes.

Raising and lowering my chin, I give her a response, "Sure, if you've got one."

She gives a semi-smile. "Honey, you can take your damn choice." She opens the register, flicks to a page, then turns it around, and pushes it over at me.

Noting the last guest seems to have checked out two days ago, I enter my name and the required details. "Business slow?" I ask, conversationally.

"You could say that." She doesn't seem particularly bothered about it as she checks what I've written.

Turning, she reaches for one of the keys hung up on the wall behind her. "Room eight, at the end of the row." Leaning forward, she points to the door, then waves her hand to the right. "That do you?"

"Sure." I shrug. As long as it's got a bed, I'm not particularly bothered. "And it's for just one night."

"Payment in advance."

Unperturbed, I take out my wallet and pay her, take the key, raise my chin, then disappear back outside. There's an elderly ice machine I notice as I walk to my room, and a machine with a few sodas and waters in it. From the clanking and clonking, I gather they're both turned on.

Room eight is, as Cheryl had promised, basic but clean. I note the ancient television sitting on a chest of drawers and check out the bathroom which has a few broken tiles, but even they've been scrubbed and there's an odour of disinfectant in the air. The bed might have a sagging mattress, but the sheets look and smell recently laundered.

Returning outside, I paddle walk my bike until it's parked directly outside, then remove my saddlebags and carry them in. Shrugging out of my clothes, I enter the shower with the intention of washing off the dirt of the road. The stream of water is powerful and nothing to complain about.

As I stand, letting the water beat down on me, I bow my head, wondering why the fuck I decided to stay. *I could have been miles along my way before nightfall.* There's only one answer. The waitress who seems to have bewitched me.

Am I so hard up for female company that I'm turned on by the first girl's pretty smile?

Sure, my dick could do with some action that wasn't supplied by my hand, but I've managed seven years, I can wait some more. There's sure to be plenty of pretty women along the route that would make my cock perk up. *Why does it want her?*

There was something about her. Some sense of longing when she looked at the bike, as if underneath her practical façade she was a kindred spirit, drawn by the freedom of heading out on the road with no restrictions, no rules, and no one to tell her no.

She intrigues me.

Uh-uh, I scoff at myself, trying to dismiss my impulse to stay over having more to do with the stiffness in my legs and ass rather than the woman I just met being responsible for the delay. It's just me needing a break from being on the road. Even a biker can have too much of a good thing. A chance to rest and recharge my batteries. But as I talk to myself, even I know I'm lying. *She got to me.*

Stupid asshole, Red. Even if you want her, chances are your paths won't cross again. Plenty of women get the hots for a biker, drawn by the machine rather than the man. It doesn't mean they're going to act on it.

I try to remember her critically. On first sight, there's not much there. Her ass is great, her tits, well, more than enough to satisfy me, but she's not model thin or anything near. I'm sure if I touch her, softness and curves would greet me. *I could do better.* But could I? Her at-rest face didn't resemble a barn door, but when her features rearranged themselves to show pleasure, amusement, and that sense of longing I'd noted before, she transformed into a thing of beauty.

My kind of girl. Which is odd, as I'd never gone for that type before.

Of course, that's not unusual. I'm a man. It doesn't take much to make my dick perk up and pay attention—just decent legs, tits and ass. I've seen girls in bars, girls I pass in the street who've fuelled some of my night-time fantasies. I've never been tempted to follow up, feeling they were out of the league of a ginger-haired reject like me. Most women, I've found, want the myste-rious dark stranger type, or the blond surfer dude. My pale skin, freckles and red hair don't attract many women to me. And anyway, for the last few years, I've had fuck-all chance to do anything about it.

Wanna come over to my place, doll? Oh, hang on, I've just got to change my dad's diaper…

I'm free. Free to do what I want when I want to. Free to explore. Why settle for the first girl I've come across? Of course my dick's fucking interested. It knows I've not got the same restrictions anymore. If it gives me the signal and the girl's up for it, I can act on my impulses now.

Was it my bike, or me she was interested in? I huff a laugh at the thought it could be the former.

My issue is, I muse as I turn off the water and rub myself down with a towel, *is if she does have a reciprocal interest in me, the question is, whether I'm going to act on it.*

I'd thought one-night stands were not my thing. Even in high school, I dated. While then knowing a happily ever after was unlikely, I'd be faithful to my current girlfriend, and willing to hang on for the ride until it, hopefully amicably, ended. I was brought up to respect and be respectful to women. Despite how my mom walked out on my dad, I'd stayed that way.

If you want to get off, son, you've always got your hand. Women, my dad had told me, *deserve more than a quick fling.*

Just say I got together with Cheryl, I won't be changing my plans. I'm too invested in finding my future. *Could she be part of it?* Could her place really be on the back of my bike? Fuck, I may be wary of one-night stands, but I'm even more concerned with jumping in deep with a woman I've only just met.

If, and it's a fucking big if… If she was up for a night in my bed, could I walk away and feel right about it? On the other hand, on such limited acquaintance, could I take her with me?

Just say Cheryl and I were physically compatible. What's the alternative? To stay here? I snort. From what I've seen of this town, there's nothing to attract me. I still want to follow my dreams and head south, and I've gone nowhere near far enough to make this my base. A god-awful town in the middle of nowhere? *No thanks.* It's worse than where I've come from.

Okay, I tell myself at last. *I'll enjoy the elongated stay here, rest up my sore muscles from the long hours of riding, then tomorrow I'll move on.* I'll forget all about Cheryl. I'm bound to find someone else at some point.

Cheryl could be the one. There has to be a fucking devil on my shoulder. When I decide to stay well away from that diner, he perks up and gets in my ear. *Cheryl could be the one I'm searching for.* The other half of my soul.

Unlikely.

But who's to say where or when such a woman, if she exists, could turn up? What if I left without knowing, would I always look back with regret?

If I got to know her more, would I be able to ride away?

Damn it. How could one woman get to me with so little conversation between us?

I take out one of my few clean tees, brush the tangles out of my hair, and ask myself, what the fuck is it about her? Am I so starved for female companionship I give the first woman I meet a second look?

I'm fooling myself, but there's something that calls to my inner soul, a sense she's unfulfilled, in the same way I'd been while working for Manny. It's so damn stupid from just one meeting where we'd exchanged so few words, but I want, *need*, to know more about her.

Crazy idea.

I sit in my room, venturing out only for a soda, trying to distract myself with a suspense novel I'd picked up at one of my stops for gas, trying to tell myself winding down for a few hours is all I need. *Tomorrow, I'll ride on.*

Bored with the words on the page that don't seem to make sense and restless, I go outside to my bike. In preparation for the morning, I check the tyres, oil and eye the chain critically. In the last few days, I've put more miles on her than I have since I've had her. Don't want to break down where there's no help for miles.

Almost without realising what I'm doing, I grab my helmet, zip my jacket up and pull on my gloves. Almost in surprise, I find myself riding that mile in reverse, back to the diner.

Just for dinner, I tell myself. *A man's gotta eat.* I know I haven't explored further, but why should I? Here I can expect dinner to be just as good as lunch. And it's inexpensive and I don't even know if Cheryl's working, and—

"You're back!" Cheryl's eyes come alive as I walk in the entrance. "I thought you'd be miles away by now." She glances around, trying to spot a spare table.

The restaurant this time is indeed busier, and I realise I won't be able to monopolise her time as I had before. Even though she's not the only waitress serving, she looks rushed off her feet.

Worried about losing my chance to speak to her, I find the words coming out of my mouth, "What time do you get off?"

Her eyes widen, but she replies, a little breathily and without hesitation, "Nine."

"Come ride with me?" I jerk my head to my motorcycle parked just outside, the same as earlier.

Her eyes look larger than ever. For a moment she looks shocked, then her lips start curving until a huge grin splits her face. As if her expression wasn't enough, she adds the words, "You bet."

Is she so fast to say yes to every stranger? As she leads me to a table that's just been cleared, I worry for a moment, wondering whether I know what I'm doing. She could be the town slut for all I know about her. *And if she is…* Nah, I won't be one of a long line to use her. I'm just not programmed like that.

Unobtrusively, I spy on her as she goes from table to table. For the kids, with whom she's clearly familiar, she has an easy smile as she ruffles their hair or bends down to admire their colourings with much oohing and ahhing. She does what she can to calm an obnoxious toddler, quickly finding him something to keep him amused and isn't fazed when faced with a screaming baby. With a nod from the kid's tired-looking mom, she lifts it out of the highchair and cuddles it to her. Within a moment, the tiny girl's all smiles. *She's got a way about her.*

Her interactions with the customers make me smile, an expression I hide behind a menu.

Until she approaches another table, then my lips firm and form a scowl. This one is full of farmhands, obviously in after a hard day's work. Now they are more of a problem for her. I growl softly as I see a hand fondle her ass, and half rise, for some reason feeling possessive. But before I can estimate my chances against the four brawny men, she evades his touch with an expert twist of her hips and puts him in his place with a few well-chosen words, spoken loudly enough to draw attention.

"Brad, what have I told you?" Her tone's one that would be used with a naughty child. "I'm a good girl and I don't appreciate you getting familiar."

There's a growl from a couple of the dads whose kids' drawings she'd admired, and the baby's mom is frowning with disgust.

When she leaves the group and heads back to the kitchen, I listen brazenly to the farmhands' conversation. "What's gotten into you, Brad?" the largest of them hisses. "This place has the best fuckin' food for miles. You know Joe would ban us if you upset his best waitress."

Brad looks uncontrite. "Girl's got to give it up sometime."

Not to you, fucker, I just about stop myself saying out loud.

"Keep your hands to yourself while you're in here," one of the other men warns him, then looks around him with an uneasy smile, lifting his chin toward the men still frowning.

Relieved that his friends have him under control, and the object of my obsession has removed herself from my sight, I start perusing the menu in earnest, trying to make up my mind between the ribs and meatloaf. In the end, I order the latter. The only problem is, the waitress I give my order to, isn't her, and my service, unlike earlier, isn't fast.

As I eat, I continue to watch Cheryl. She's rushed off her feet, a total contradiction to the other waitress who seems to take her time about everything, leaving Cheryl to do twice the work. But she makes no complaint, even though I can see her shifting from foot to foot as though her feet are aching. Despite her tiredness, she continues to have a pleasant word to say to everyone.

Though I linger as long as I can, I finish far too early with still an hour to go before her knocking off time. Cheryl's busy and customers are still coming in, obviously wanting my table. So I stand, leave my money and a generous tip, but pause before moving until I catch her eye. Mouthing, *later,* I wink.

She blushes beautifully, grins and nods. With that, I leave.

On my bike, I take a ride through the shut-up-for-the-night town, noticing most businesses have something to do with farm machinery. *This place isn't for me.* It's too small, too insular, and, as I saw from the diner, everyone knows everybody. *I couldn't be happy here.*

What the fuck am I doing? I ask myself again, parking my bike, this time at a discreet distance from the diner where Cheryl works. Settling in for a wait, I flick my lighter and apply it to the end of a cigarette. As I draw in smoke, I question whether the better thing to do is take off and leave her. I'm already itching to get moving. There's a restlessness inside me that says I've already tarried too long. But vying with that equally powerfully is the thought that I'll lose something if I don't stick around. There's just something about her, a notion that it could have been fate that made me stop at that exact place in time. A fear of losing an opportunity if I don't take this further.

One night, I remind myself. It's all I can offer. As long as she knows the score, what's the harm?

So I stay. Slowly the number of patrons entering are exceeded by those coming out. Through the lighted windows I can see more tables empty than occupied, and then, I see no customers at all. I get a glimpse of Cheryl wiping down tables, then, at last, the lights in the front flick off. Getting off my bike, I walk closer.

As I suspected, a back door opens, and she emerges, calling behind her, "Night, Joe. I'll see you on Friday."

Friday's two days away. Has she got time off? Hmm. Interesting. But I'd made a bargain with myself. I'll stay here no longer than one night. That ride through the town had convinced me apart from her, there's nothing to make me linger.

"Red," she exclaims excitedly as I emerge from the shadows, her delight telling me she half-expected me not to be there.

"Promised you a ride, darlin'." She's not to know I'm a man of my word. Stepping forward, I hold out my hand. "Are you ready?"

She glances at me, then at my bike, hesitates only a moment before, with a delightful little shiver, she puts her palm against mine. I take a moment to check what she's wearing. Jeans, a heavy coat, and walking boots.

"I like your boots," I tell her, grinning, not having expected her to be wearing sensible footwear just right for my bike.

In the parking lot's lights, I see her blush. "I don't have a car and I walk home in all weathers."

Does she? I frown, then realise this is her hometown, and maybe the crime level is low here. Or maybe it's simply she's got no choice. Whatever, it's not my place to admonish her. It's not my business and I shouldn't interfere.

Keeping quiet, I lead her toward my bike, open the saddlebag and take out my spare helmet. Placing it on her head, I help her to fasten it. I then take out my safety glasses which I don't wear with my full-face helmet, and hand them to her.

"Ever been on a bike, sweetheart?

"No." Her face tightens as she eyes the machine with some trepidation.

"You're going to be fine," I reassure her, then take a moment to explain the basics to her. "We won't go far. Just enough to let you get a feeling for it."

I've rarely had anyone on the back of my bike before, and certainly not a woman. As she gets on behind me and tightens her arms around my waist, I realise how intimate the position is. Even more so, when moments later, I brake, not even sharply, but it has her sliding closer. I swear I can feel the heat of her pussy against my ass. My cock goes from half to full mast.

The road is quiet. There's not much traffic this time of night, but I keep my speed low in view of her inexperience. After a couple of miles, her death grip around my waist begins to relax. She's still holding on to me, but seems to have lost her fear of sliding off the back. I twist my throttle, raise my chin and head into the wind.

Her being behind me is a new sensation. Her slight weight doesn't unbalance the bike, but there's something different about riding with a passenger. I'm responsible for the safety of someone other than myself which seems to sharpen me. As much as I'm aware of the road, I'm conscious of her—the warmth at my back, the touch of her hands even through the leather jacket that I wear.

The engine rumbles beneath me, always an aphrodisiac, tonight even more. While my breathing remains steady, my heart rate speeds up as I wonder how easily I can persuade her to stay with me tonight.

A ride on my bike might be all that she wanted. I'd be disappointed, but alright with that. There could be more danger if she agrees. *What happens if I want more?*

I wonder how I'd feel about sex without any commitment, without promises or thoughts of a happily ever after. I'm not sure. I've listened to my fellow mechanics talking about their one-night conquests, wondering how they could be bastards like that. How they could lead a woman on, bed her and leave her. Now, it seems, I'm proposing to do just that.

As long as she knows that's all that can happen, what could be wrong with it? Cheryl intrigues me, so much so, I'm willing to give it a chance. But after, would I really be able to ride on and forget her?

I tell myself I haven't had her yet. She could be a disappointment, or me to her.

Above us, stars gleam, and the moon peeps out from behind a cloud. My Harley rumbles on, as she leans into me. Her now more-confident hands pressing against my abs.

We might not be compatible, but hell, I'd like to find out.

Fuck tomorrow. I'll take tonight.

CHAPTER FOUR

We've been on the road for about almost an hour when I notice the air is chill and she's huddling closer, either for comfort or warmth. In case it's the latter, I turn and head back. I'm also conscious she's not been on a bike before, and that even after that short distance her ass will likely be sore.

I pull up at the motel I've booked into for the night, letting the sound of the engine fade until all I can hear is the ticking as it cools. In the sudden silence, I raise my visor and turn my head.

"Your choice." I nod to the room I've been allocated. "I'll take you straight home if you prefer."

She sighs, rests her helmet-covered head against mine, and clearly takes a moment to think about it. Her comment when it comes sounds wistful. "I don't want this evening to end."

"Neither do I," I admit. It's the truth. I'd thought I'd enjoyed riding solo, but with her it's been different. It might not have been for long, but I already know I'll miss her presence when I ride on alone. *What if she agreed to be there forever?*

My eyes widen. I'm an ass, we've only just met. What the fuck am I thinking? I don't believe in love at first sight, and definitely not when I haven't even kissed her, let alone anything else. What I'm feeling is lust, that's all it could be. Possibly a reaction to the newfound freedom that's been opened on me, a reaction to the fact I no longer have responsibilities or places to be. *Maybe I'm lonely.*

"I could do with a smoke," I tell her, buying myself some time to make sure I want this, and allow her to consider whether she's sure. "Let's talk for a while. We don't need to do anything more." I hold out my hand in invitation.

She takes it in her left, placing her right on my shoulder, and dismounts the bike more gracefully than I'd expected as she's never ridden before. Standing next to me, she unclasps her helmet and grins widely.

"The ground's vibrating," she tells me, handing me the head protection she'd been wearing.

The corners of my mouth turn up. I get that. It still happens to me, but nowadays only after I've been riding for a few hours. I kick the stand down then swing my leg over the saddle, bending to place her lid in the saddlebag. I then look around. There's a low wall surrounding the parking lot. I lead the way to it. Once I'm there, I take out the pack of cigarettes and offer it to her. She shakes her head.

Unperturbed, I flick my Zippo and hold the flame to the tip. I breathe in deeply, then turn my head to blow out the smoke. The evening is clear. The few clouds have dissipated, revealing even more stars than would be visible under the streetlights a mile or so down the road. The moon is full, making me wonder whether some madness has got into me.

She sits, and I copy her, placing myself so close our thighs rub together. For a few minutes, we sit in silence. It's not awkward or uncomfortable. Quite the opposite, it's companionable. I can appreciate a woman who doesn't need to fill the quiet with conversation.

I smoke my cigarette down to the filter, stub it out on the brickwork, and place the dog end in my pocket to dispose of later. Turning to face her, I place my hand against her cheek. My face lowering is her warning, but I hover with my lips an inch against hers to give her time to protest. Instead, she tilts her face upward, bringing her mouth within range.

I hope she doesn't object to the taste of cigarette smoke, I muse, as I bring my lips down, noticing immediately how soft hers are, and how quickly she yields to me. I angle her head for better access. When I apply a little pressure, she opens to me. When I tentatively press my tongue inside, hers meets mine.

If my taste offends her, she shows no sign, but enthusiastically starts responding. A little moan comes from her as I deepen the kiss. My arm goes around her, bringing her closer to me.

Snuggling her hands under my jacket, she places them on my chest. A little mewl fills my ears as she responds when I intensify the kiss, noticing she taste of sweetness and coffee. *I could get addicted to this.*

I've kissed girls before, but I can't remember any I've enjoyed quite as much. *Maybe I'm just out of practice?* Ask me to explain why and I wouldn't be able to answer. Maybe her perfume contains pheromones that attract me, I don't know. All I can say is there's something about her that makes me want to make her mine. My body seems alive for the first time in forever, and my balls throb in time with my heartbeat.

Even if I get lucky, it will only be one night.

It is what it is.

I'll etch her into my memory and then move on. I'll have to, even if one night won't be enough. It's all I can offer. I start to hope she'll turn me down, so I don't have to go through pleasure followed by torture. *She could break me.*

Could I stay with her? Nah, that's ridiculous. That would be too heavy a load for her to bear. If I allow her to upset the route I've got planned, I'd come to resent her. My future's not here in the land of winter cold and snow.

The sensible thing would be to draw back, take her home, ride away and forget her. But I'm not feeling very sensible tonight, and the more we kiss, the more I know, I have to have her. Part of me starts to hope we're not compatible.

Any future regrets are put to one side as I tear myself away from the delights of her mouth, placing my palms on each side of her face, staring intently into her eyes and letting her know exactly what I want, and where my limits are. "I want more from you, baby. I want you in my bed tonight." I wait for a pause, delighted to see that flare of passion in her eyes and hear the hitch in her breathing. Then I'm honest. "But that's all I have, all I can offer. Tomorrow, I hit the road again."

"One night," she breathes out, covering one of my hands with her own. "I'll take it. I've never met someone like you. I'd be a fool to give up this chance."

Fisting my hand in her hair, I turn her head up. "You sure?" I stare into her eyes.

"Red, I've never done anything so impulsive. There's just something about you…"

As her voice trails off, I take a deep breath, knowing she's not the only one who's affected and acting out of character. Somehow, I believe her. I know in my gut, she doesn't jump into bed with every stranger who passes by her door.

She's offering me something, the same as I'm offering her.

"You gotta be sure," I repeat, hesitant to take advantage. If I have to live with regrets, it will be the same for her. "You going into this with your eyes open?"

"I am. And I'm sure," she says without hesitation. Her eyes fix on mine, showing me whatever doubts she might have later, she has none now. "Make me yours, Red. If only for a few hours."

If I were a good man, I'd walk away now. But it seems that I'm far from having good intentions. I could no more take a step away from her than I could stop taking air into my lungs. I stand, take her hand, then try to slow my steps to match hers, almost forgetting to compensate for her shorter legs as we head for my room. Once inside, I push her back against the door and start kissing her again.

Our tongues meet, twisting, turning, advancing and

retreating as our passion heightens. Urgency rushes through me as I almost tear off her coat, then slide my hands up under her sweater, feeling her luscious tits through her bra, groaning as I get my first touch of them. Have I ever felt any so perfect before? Fuck, if I have, I can't remember.

She gasps and shivers, and I realise my hands are cold, but hell, they'll soon warm up. I could no more remove them than a starving man could put down his first plate of food in forever. Her breasts are every bit as amazing as I thought they would be —plump, firm, and barely fit into my hands.

Pulling her lips from mine for a second, she gasps out, "I want to see you, Red."

I know I'm no fitness model. I've muscular arms from the work I used to do, but a six pack? Not there. I'd even admit my stomach isn't firm due to the junk food I often consume. But as my fingers touch the rolls of excess flesh under her bra, I realise we're probably well matched, and expect nothing spectacular of each other. So I only have a moment's hesitation before letting her go, letting my jacket drop to the floor, then ripping my t-shirt over my head.

Her cheek falls forward, and she rubs her face against the red curly hair on my chest, just as if she were a cat seeking affection. Then, she makes the next move, releasing me and taking off her sweater.

Her stomach is pudgy just as I expected, but fuck, it looks good. She's soft everywhere and all woman. Nothing I see turns me off. So what if neither of us is perfection like the models in magazines? We're real. We're typical human beings.

My eyes glance at her bra, then up to meet hers, and my mouth twists in a grin. She reads my unspoken question, reaches behind her and undoes the clasp. The offending item drops, revealing her breasts to my eyes. They're goddamn fucking perfect, teardrop-shaped orbs topped with dusty pink nipples.

I push her back to the bed. With one arm behind her, I help her down, encouraging her to shuffle back until her head meets the pillow. Lowering my body, I pause to take her lips once more, before dropping my head and feasting on those nipples which have already formed peaks. Her hands come between us. She's touching me, learning the contours of my body just as I'm learning hers.

My cock is swollen and uncomfortable in my jeans, but I make no move to free it. If I've learned anything in my previous encounters, it's that the woman should always come first. I know if I let it out to play this early, my years of abstinence will mean it will be over too fast.

I let my hand wander, making short work of the button and zipper on her jeans, then I slide my fingers inside her panties, and reach down to her clit, that bundle of nerves I'd ignored the first time I'd ever had sex. That, I remember with embarrassment, knowing I'd left my equally naïve partner unsatisfied, and remained in ignorance until I was schooled on the omission by a girl who was more direct and unashamed to give me pointers on what a woman needs.

I now pride myself on knowing I should scoop up the copious moisture she's produced, use it for lubrication, then find which moves work best—a circling around, direct pressure on it, or a strumming effect. It takes me a moment, and a few wriggles from Cheryl, as well as a couple of instructions; *up a bit, down... oh yeah, right there.*

Obeying her guidance, I grin as I feel her muscles start to tense. I redouble my efforts and shortly am rewarded by her drawing in a breath, going rock still, then a cry comes out of her mouth as her body jerks. *I made her do that.* A man's pride settles in me as I continue to let my fingers move, gently bringing her down, feeling her muscles continue to spasm.

It's my turn. Leaving her panting, trying to catch her breath, I move off the bed, toe off my boots and slide my jeans down over my hips. She's watching me intently, licking her lips, the sight making me groan. Without waiting for me to do it for her, she sits up, tugging her own pants down and off her legs, taking her panties down with them.

I draw in air. *She's fucking beautiful.* A natural blonde, I notice. Her pubes are only a fraction darker than her sun-bleached hair.

As I can't tear my eyes away, a little coy, she lies back and presses her legs together. I let myself drop on top of her, breaking my fall by bracing myself on my forearms. Then, using just one arm to support me, I move the other down.

Now I'm no longer staring at her there, she raises her knees and parts her thighs, making a cradle for me in between them.

"You ready for me, darlin'?"

"Red." My name is all she says, but her tone is half-chiding, as though asking why I'm waiting. She adds in a wriggle for encouragement.

With that permission, I line myself up, and start pushing forward. She's tight, and it takes work. My brow is creased in concentration, and glancing at her, so is hers. But I make way by pushing and retreating until I'm completely inside. She feels fucking amazing, better than any of the girls I remember having before. We're a good fit, and I can feel her muscles rippling as she tightens her Kegels.

I start to move in and out, commencing slowly, then speeding up. She makes encouraging noises and pushes back against me. I think she's enjoying it, but know from my previous experience that a lot of women enjoy the closeness, but don't necessarily get off from the invasion of a cock.

"Yes," she cries out, spurring me on.

I'm panting, sweat dripping off me, and a tingling starts in my spine. "I'm coming," I warn her.

"Yes," she gasps out again.

I can no more stop coming inside her than I could halt an oncoming train. I lose rhythm as cum shoots out of my cock, flooding into her. I press myself in deep, holding myself inside her, my head rolling back as I let the sensations fill me and inadvertently growl. *Christ, that was good.* In fact, it was perfect.

As my cock deflates and I roll off her, pulling her into my side, I feel our combined juices leaking onto the bed. I sigh with satisfaction and plant a kiss to the top of her head.

She takes hold of my hand, writhing against me, and pleads softly, "I need your fingers."

Ah, I realise, as I manually help her reach the peak that had evaded her before. Our mouths meld together as I make sure she's satisfied. After that, she waves toward the bathroom. When I give an understanding nod, she goes to clean up, then I use the facilities after her.

Staring into the mirror over the basin, I shake my head. *That was too good.* I clench my fists. *I am not going to get addicted to her pussy.* I renew my vow that in the morning, I'll get back onto the road.

"You're amazing, Red," she tells me softly when I return to bed.

What man wouldn't preen at that pronouncement?

"So are you," I reciprocate truthfully. "You gonna stay the night, or you need me to get you home?"

She smiles sweetly. "I can stay, if that's okay?"

"Sure it is," I reply, again totally honest. I'm certainly up for doing that again.

As I lie back down beside her, I try to stifle a yawn, but I can't. The long ride, the good sex, and I'm sorry to say, I drop off.

When I awake, I take advantage of the naked body lying beside me, my cock once again gets its relief—after I make sure she comes, of course—and once again I fall back asleep.

When dawn breaks through the flimsy curtains, I yawn. Feeling the warmth of her body, I realise it's the first time in my life I've woken with another body in my bed. I smile, knowing how much I like it, then frown, realising nothing will come of it and sit up. *Best get this day started.* Goodbyes are better said fast than drawn out.

A little wriggle at my side warns me Cheryl's awake. I lean down to kiss her, but she covers her mouth.

"Morning breath!"

Chuckling, I stand, stretch, then go into the bathroom to rectify that, piss and get cleaned up. When I've finished, Cheryl's waiting to take my place.

When she emerges smelling of toothpaste, she approaches with an upturn to her mouth. "You can kiss me now."

Smirking at the permission, I do just that, pulling her into my embrace. She responds, clutching at my arms, clinging to me even after my lips leave hers. I return the caress with the same desperation. *Nothing can come of this,* I remind myself.

Her forehead comes to rest against my chest. "You leaving today?"

"Yes," I force out. Last night was more than I'd expected, but I'd promised myself it could only be a one-night stand. I know I wouldn't be happy staying. I'm single focused on heading south before winter really starts to take a hold. Even now, I should be miles on from where I am. A temporary interlude might upset all my plans. A few more days and snow might be settling.

She's quiet, and still she's holding me tight. *Did I raise her expectations?* Hoping not, I try to think back on any promises I might have made in the throes of passion, but I decide I hadn't misled her. I'd been clear all along.

I stand still, idly rubbing my hand up and down her back. *Could I stay?* Fuck no. This isn't my kind of town. I might not know precisely what I'm looking for, but I know I won't find it here. *Would I like to get to know Cheryl better?* I try to block that thought from my mind, as the honest answer is yes. The sex had been great, and she's got a way about her and a spark about her that I find captivating. My cock sure would be willing, but I'm sensible. I know that's not enough to upset the plans which have been months and years in the making.

She pulls away, wrapping her arms around her. Going to the window, she stares out wistfully at my bike, making me wonder if she's seeing it as another woman who's taking me away from her.

Is she going to make this hard? I hope not. I'm a sucker for tears. I hate seeing them. I frown. If she begs, will I change my mind?

Running my hands through my hair, I try to think of what I could say to her. *It's been good, babe. Thanks, but I'm moving on now.* That seems cold, and while I'm nowhere near ready to express my undying love for her, I do have regrets leaving her behind, and already suspect what-ifs will come back to haunt me.

She's still staring away from me when she makes her request. "Take me with you."

The words, spoken so softly, take a moment to filter through my mind. Even so, I have to question whether I've heard her correctly.

"Say again?" My eyes are wide open, and I forget to breathe.

She spins around, half-smiling, half-frowning cautiously, as if worried about my response. "Take me with you," she states firmly. "There's nothing for me here. I like the idea of just heading out on the road, not knowing where I'll end up."

I approach and stand right in front of her, my heart leaping at the solution she's proposed. But she has to see sense. One night isn't enough on which to base a future, however good it had turned out. "Cheryl, babe. I can't make any commitments. You and me? We had a great night together, but I'm not in a position to pledge anything to you. I don't even know which state I'll land in or what I'll do for work. Some people might say I'm throwing my life away on a whim, and I don't want to interrupt yours."

"What life?" she huffs. "I'm a waitress in a dead-end town. I was born here. I didn't choose it. I work, sleep, get up and repeat. What would you have me do? Sit around twiddling my thumbs and waiting until another stranger comes through?"

My gut suddenly clenches at the thought of another customer taking a liking to her, and just like me, taking her back to a motel and using her for just one night. *Maybe he'll see the treasure I'm tossing aside and marry her.* Fuck no to that.

It's fucking stupid, but my thoughts become possessive, and I don't like the idea of her ending up in another man's arms.

It's that that makes me rash. "There's not much room in my saddlebags, but just enough for you to bring a few essentials." Then I force myself to be sensible. "Cheryl, we've known each other one night. I can't promise you a happily ever after or anything like it."

"I like you, Red." She fixes her eyes on mine, then shrugs. "But who knows where the road will take us. I'm prepared for us not to work out. I… I just like the idea of freedom, of heading out of this no-hope place. Sun on my face rather than snow? Yeah, I like the sound of that."

I study her intently. *Does she know what she's getting into?* But there's determination in her face, the set of her jaw, and the stubborn twist of her mouth that tells me that. Why shouldn't she be a kindred spirit just wanting to seek out her own future instead of waiting for it to come to her? There's absolutely no reason.

"O…kay." I draw out the word, hoping I'm not making a mistake.

Her eyes brighten. She gives me a wide smile, and dances on the spot with unbridled excitement.

I know in that instance, she's my kind of girl.

CHAPTER FIVE

I'd said yes, but it's not long before I start to wonder whether I'm doing the right thing as I sit on my bike waiting for Cheryl to emerge from the house where she apparently lives. I certainly hadn't planned on having a companion on the road. There's one advantage for sure, good sex on tap. But am I being led by my dick? And if I am, has he my best interests at heart or just looking out for himself?

What if I get bored? What if she thinks I'm making more of a promise to her? How, if I wanted to, would I get out of this?

Ride away now. Before she comes out. A sensible option, but fuck knows I can't do it. The thought of her riding behind me as she had last night has me rooted to the spot as I wait for her.

Giving her time to pack, a difficult task as there's a limit to what she can bring, I light up a cigarette. As I blow smoke out, I consider what I know of her. Not much is the answer. What I've seen of her I like well enough and can't deny there's a connection between us. We haven't spoken much, haven't confided in our pasts, but for some unknown reason, we've clicked. Well enough, that we're both prepared to upend our plans to be together.

Is it because she's the first woman I've been with since I had my freedom returned to me? Should I be more cautious? Yes, I probably should. But how could I ride on, never knowing if there could have been a relationship between us?

I like her, her easy smile, her approach to life which seems to coincide with mine, her ease with people, and her sense of humour. For all I know, I might have found my elusive life partner, literally picked her up by the side of the road.

Well, this road trip will certainly show whether we can make a go of it or not. Riding for miles isn't easy, and who knows what trials and tribulations will face us? It's a good way of discovering whether we're compatible or not.

Although I continue to think of all the pros and cons, inside me, there's a kernel of excitement at the idea of having her along on this adventure. To see the sights, to share new experiences, and not the least, to share my bed at night. Yes, it's sure going to have some advantages.

I've smoked the cigarette down to the stub by the time she comes out of the house carrying a rucksack that's not overly large. She approaches the bike and starts to put the straps over her shoulders.

"Hey, give me that." Getting off my bike, I beckon to her. "You can't ride with that."

"It's okay." She hugs it to her as if not wanting to part with it.

From the way she's having difficulty hefting it over her arms, it's not light. "Darlin', it might be okay now, but you're going to feel that weight after a hundred miles." I delve into my saddlebag to get out the spare bungee hooks I'm never without.

She grins and releases the bag once she sees I wasn't asking her to leave it. I strap it tightly onto the rack, then offer her the helmet I'd lent her last night. As the day's chilly, I also dig out a bandana and give her that. Ideally, she needs a full face like mine, at least until the weather gets warmer.

I nod with approval, seeing her pulling on a pair of thick gloves.

"Said your goodbyes?"

She shrugs. "I left a note. Mom's at work. I'll call her later." Her mouth twists and I wonder about her relationship with her parent that she can walk out so casually. Aren't girls normally close to their mothers? Deciding to question her more at some point, I let it ride for now.

"What about work?" I didn't take her as someone who'd just walk off the job.

She grimaces. "I've got a couple of days off. I'll call Joe later when we stop."

Ah, yes, I remember. Perhaps she doesn't want to call while she's still in the same town in case someone might dissuade her, as most sane people would. For all she knows, I could be a murderer.

That thought makes me want to reassure her. I place my hand to her cheek. "You're safe with me, Cheryl."

Leaning into my touch, she confides, "I know I am, Red. Maybe it's stupid, but this feels so right."

I pause only a moment before getting on my bike, kicking up the stand, then holding out my hand. Taking it, she slides on behind me as though she's been doing it forever.

Before I start the engine, she yells into my ear, "Where are we heading?"

I grin at her over my shoulder. For an answer, I point my hand in the direction I was heading yesterday. "Thatta way."

She throws back her head and laughs. "You really don't have any idea of your destination, do you?"

"You know it, babe." And it's *our* destination now, I remember. The thought puts an even wider grin on my face.

I start the engine, pull in the clutch, kick into first and ease out onto the road, then we're on our way. Soon, I've moved through the gears, have exited onto the highway and am cruising in top. Her body behind me seems right. Her hands around my waist squeeze me gently. While I've no intercom and we can't speak while moving at speed, it's still companionable. *I could get used to this.* There's nothing about her being here that bothers me.

I ride straight for a couple of hours, then pull into a rest stop when her tap on my shoulder suggests she needs a break. When she comes out of the bathroom, she's rubbing her backside.

She grins at me ruefully. "I've got a sore ass."

Well damn, I should have thought of that. We've only covered about a hundred and fifty miles. I'd been planning to more than double that before stopping for the night. Now I'm worried she won't be able to make it. "You okay to go on?"

I get a sharp look sent my way, and the haughty response, "Of course I am."

Seeing she's serious, and thinking, *thank fuck for that*, we get back on the bike. I do, though, plan to stop off again a little more often.

We ride across plains, miles and miles of open land as far as the eye can see. I settle in to enjoy being one with the road, but have to admit as entertainment, it's boring. When I feel her slump against me, not wanting her to fall asleep during the ride, I know we have to make another break.

Although I'd get more miles under my belt if I were alone, the upside is her company. When we stop off to top off the gas and our stomachs, I enjoy her quick wit at the expense of some of the customers. Soon she's got me playing the game too, as we make up imaginary histories for the men and women around us.

"He's a salesman," she whispers, shielding her mouth with her hand. "Got a different woman in every state."

"You think?" I spy her target out of the side of my eye.

"Oh yes. Ill-fitting suit and look how tired he is. He keeps texting, probably trying to keep his story straight with all his women."

I snort. To me, he seems no catch for one woman, let alone many.

"She's a nurse." I jerk my head at the twenty-something

who's just passed us. "Has a man, two kids, and works nights to get away from them."

"Hmm. Kids, yes, I can see that. But a nurse? How d'you get that?" She creases her eyes.

"I'm imagining her in candy stripes," I respond, waggling my brows up and down. She bats me on the arm and giggles but doesn't take umbrage. So I chance my luck. "She can check my temperature anytime."

"You can see how hot you are from just looking." She pretends to fan herself while giving me a compliment. "Oh, him, now." She pretends to swoon. "He must be a fitness model or a wannabe film star."

I take a quick glance behind me. Sure, the guy is cut, and his swagger oozes arrogance. I turn back to her. "Hey, I thought it was me you said was hot."

Placing her hand over mine, she gives me a smile and says, "Of course you're the hottest man here, Red." She rolls her eyes, making me laugh.

"Brat," I tell her, grinning widely. "You done?"

She drains her coffee and starts to stand. "I've just got to visit the bathroom."

After I've paid and taken the opportunity to empty my own bladder, we're back on the road again.

If I were by myself I'd have carried on until the daylight meets dusk, but as the miles pass, I can feel her shifting behind me as she tries to ease her sore muscles. When we come to the outer limits of a small city, I spy a motel and turn in.

I tap her leg to get off. She eases herself off the bike, then stretches and places her hands on her backside, rubbing vigorously.

"Cheryl," I start, reaching out my hand and cupping her cheek.

She smiles and catches my fingers. "I'm alright. Just not used to riding. I'll get better."

I grimace, thinking she might be too sore to ride far tomorrow. Maybe I should have cut her first long ride shorter. Still, I'm further south than I was, and every mile puts the risk of a harsh winter behind us.

Jerking my head toward reception, I dismount. "I'll get us a room. Want to wait here with the bike?"

She rolls her neck to get the kink out of it and nods. Leaving her, I stride inside. When I enquire with more hope than expectation, I find they've got just what I'm looking for, a room with a tub. After I've fetched her and moved my bike as close as I can get it, I open the door to our room. When Cheryl spies the open bathroom her face lights up with delight.

Knowing I've scored points, smirking, I tell her, "I thought you could do with a good long soak after that ride."

"I think I'm in love," she gasps.

"With me?" I tilt my head to one side, not knowing how I'd prefer her to answer.

She laughs loudly, and she bats my arm. "Not you, you big oaf. With the tub."

Well, that's put me in my place. I chuckle, brushing off the brief disappointment, then go past her to turn on the taps. I look around, but apart from soap, there's nothing to add into it.

A groan from behind gets my attention. Turning, I see she's taken off her pants and her hands are rubbing the now visible globes of her backside. Going to her, I replace her hands with my own, digging in my fingers as I try to massage away her soreness. Of course, as I do, my cock begins to lengthen. It becomes fully erect as she takes off her t-shirt and bra, and her gorgeous tits fall free.

"Hey, babe, I could do with a soak myself. Think we could get in together?" Eyeing the tub, I work out the logistics.

When she grins, I test the temperature of the water, then carefully step in, easing myself down and stretching out as far as I can, my legs bent to accommodate my size. She eases in, lying as I wanted, her back to my front.

As the warm water laps around her, she sighs deeply. "Bliss."

I'm not going to argue with her. I might not be as saddle sore as the woman in my arms, but there's something to be said for hot water easing tight muscles. Gently, I rub my hands up and down her, and hey, I'm a man, so I concentrate on her chest.

"Better?"

"Mmmm."

I feel her relax, one hand rising and moving so she can cup the back of my head. Turning her face, her lips are within tasting distance, so I take what she's offering.

Fuck, this feels good. Predictably, my dick again starts to rise to the occasion. As if of its own volition, my right hand slides down her body, and I start playing with her clit.

"Oh, so good, Red."

I grin as she lays her head back onto my shoulder. What man doesn't feel good when he's pleasing his woman. *His woman?* Sure, Cheryl's mine, for the moment, anyway.

Things just come so naturally when we're together, like parts of a puzzle that are meant to fit.

Her orgasm causes the water to ripple wildly, and when I tell her I want inside her, she sits up and turns around to ride me. It's a novel experience for me. Though the position might be awkward, the sight of water streaming off her, forming droplets which run from her nipples down her body make me want to lick them off her. When she positions me, I thrust up, my movement sending water sloshing all over.

"Red." She uses my name as an admonishment for the mess we're creating, as well as an exclamation as I surge up inside her.

"Hold on, sweetheart." Raising my body, I place my hands on her hips, helping her to ride me.

It's awkward as fuck. The tub's narrow, my hips are wide, and Cheryl is inelegantly perched above me, but somehow, we make it work, even though I have doubts there'll be much water left after.

Christ, she feels so good. I surge up, my hands keeping her anchored to me, then raise her up, pulling her back down.

"Red! That's so good, don't stop."

I've fuck-all intention to. My head rolls back as she squeezes my dick. My balls churn, tingles like lightning run up and down my spine. When I feel something against the root of my dick, my eyes snap open and looking down, I see her fingers strumming her clit.

Her mouth is open, her eyes squeezed shut, her jaw locked in concentration then, *fuck me*, she gets herself off. My dick's being strangled in time with her convulsions.

"Fuck, Cheryl. I'm gonna come."

I yank her down, push myself in, and then hold us still as the aftershocks running through her body finish me off. As cum shoots out of my dick, I struggle to catch my breath.

Never been so good. Ever.

When our breathing returns to some semblance of normal, I sit up, pulling her to me, taking her mouth, trying to show her what she means to me without being able to put it into words.

As predicted, most of the water that was in the tub is now on the floor, luckily soaking away through the drain hole in the middle. What's left is decidedly on the cool side, as evidenced by the goosebumps on her skin.

"We need to get out," I tell her, a chuckle in my voice. "Think you need to go first, babe."

She giggles and placing her hands on either side of the tub, pushes herself off my body, managing to get purchase on a foot without squashing my balls in the process. Taking my hand to support her, she swings her leg over, placing her other foot on the floor.

Water streams off her, and I can't help but feel masculine pride as our combined juices leak out of her.

As soon as she's out, I follow, grabbing a towel and wrapping it around her. Then, I get the second for myself.

"You less sore?" I'm grinning at her.

"I'm less something." She winks.

Every movement she makes is erotic. As I towel myself off, I watch her. As she dries herself, flicking her wet hair over her head, then reaching for a hand towel and making a turban of some sort. She returns to rubbing the water off her body–her breasts, her ass, between her legs—and my cock starts to come back to life.

Bath sex might have taken the edge off, but it won't be long, on my part at least, before I take advantage of my traveling companion again.

I could get used to this.

I know something else as well. However cautious I'm trying to be, *I want to keep her.*

CHAPTER SIX

"Yeah, Mom." Cheryl smiles into the phone. "All's good." She grimaces. "I know Joe's not happy, but..." There's a pause, then she's back to grinning again. "Yeah, I know. He'll get over it."

I leave the room, taking my saddlebags out to my bike, looking up to the sky with a practiced eye, noting the darkening clouds above. *Looks like we might have a wet ride today.* Well, wet for me, I'll make sure to lend Cheryl my waterproofs.

It wouldn't hurt to put fewer miles on the clock today. Despite the hot soak, Cheryl's ass is still sore. I can tell by the way she's moving. But I do put some of her bow-leggedness down to how many times I couldn't resist her last night.

Hearing footsteps behind me, I turn to face her. "Everything okay?"

"Uh-huh."

I eye her for a moment. "Your mom's the bomb, you know that?"

I'd been worried the first time she'd spoken to her mother that she'd have been pressured to return home. It wasn't the case.

Cheryl laughs. "My mom's an aging hippy. She was always a

'follow your dreams' type of girl. That's how she ended up in our town with my dad. She met him at an agricultural fair and followed him home."

I'm genuinely curious. "It work out?"

"Yeah." She smiles at the memory. "They were really happy together." Her face falls slightly. "Dad died a few years back. Mom stayed faithful to his memory. He was her one and only."

"I'm sorry to hear that. How old were you?" I lean back against my bike, folding my arms, wondering how it is we still know so little about each other.

"I was ten." She shrugs. "He was a larger-than-life figure. Mom kept him alive for us both, never letting me forget him. She's so fucking strong." A look of admiration crosses her face.

It sounds like they were close. She must hate me for taking her daughter away. "Doesn't she miss you?"

"Of course, she does. But she knows what it's like to be swept off your feet. In her eyes, it's my time now."

I realise I've never asked. "How old are you, Cheryl?"

Another woman might have been coy and asked me to guess, but she gives it to me straight. "Twenty."

A little younger than I thought, but old enough not to be tied to any apron strings. I'd been imagining a poor home life that she'd wanted to escape from, not probing as I didn't want to open any wounds. But instead, it turns out, she's a true kindred spirit and comes from the same stock.

She glances at what I've laid out on the seat of my bike. "What are those?"

"Waterproofs. Put them on, darlin'."

Picking them up, she snorts. "They're going to drown me."

"Better that than get drowned by the rain." I raise my eyebrows, then point to the sky.

"What are you going to wear?"

"I'll be fine," I tell her, optimistically.

Shrugging, she steps into the pants and pulls them up, bending down to roll them up a few times. Then she slips into the jacket and all but disappears. I help her sort herself out and do up the zip as she's struggling to extract her hands from the too-long arms.

The material is thin, so I slip the hood up over her head, planting the skull cap on top of it. Once I'm satisfied she'll survive whatever the elements throw at us, I step astride the bike. Like an expert, she gets on behind me, with only a slight groan as she does.

I take the predictable route out of the city, the interstate heading south. For the first hour it's good riding, then, as I'd predicted, those clouds join forces together, and let loose on us humans below. When light rain turns heavy, then into sleet, I wonder what I've done to earn the gods' vengeance.

My gloves, which should be waterproof, seem no match for what's being thrown at us. Fixing the throttle, I alternate hands on the handlebars, but gradually both become numb. My body's so wet, I'm shivering.

Despite her having the benefit of my wet-weather clothing, as Cheryl pushes herself closer behind me, I can feel her tension as if she too is frozen.

By midday, even I've had enough. I pull in to stop outside a diner.

"I-I-I'm fr-fr-free…zing," she stutters, as she gets off.

"Me too." I take the saddlebags off the bike, then grab her hand and pull her with me as we head for shelter. We enter, looking like two drowned rats. At least she's dry once she takes her outer clothing off. Me, I'm soaked through to the skin.

The waiter looks at us dubiously.

Raising the saddlebags I'm holding, I ask him, "Mind if I change in your bathroom?"

A grin starts to curve his lips. "Go ahead. I'll get your lady seated."

I wait only until I can see where he's taking her, then go find the men's room. Grabbing a handful of paper towels, I head to a narrow cubicle where I contort myself to get my clothes off.

Every part of me is saturated, right down to my boxers. I strip off, vainly trying to dry myself, before struggling to get some clean clothes on over my wet skin. I swear I've bruises on each elbow and knee before I'm finished. Finally, I scrunch my wet clothing into my saddlebag, which immediately becomes ten times heavier.

The whole process has taken several minutes. By the time I've finished and am heading back into the restaurant no longer dripping water everywhere, I'm feeling semi-human again. Deciding I'll treat myself to a bowl of hot soup, I approach our table.

Instead of glancing up to greet me, Cheryl's staring blankly down at the table as I slide into the seat opposite her.

"Have you ordered yet?"

"What?" Her eyes are glazed as she glances up. I notice her phone's on the table in front of her.

"Food," I clarify.

"Oh, no. I was waiting for you."

Something seems off. I narrow my eyes. "What's up, babe?" Reaching my hand out to take hers that's lying conveniently on the table, I notice she's still shivering.

"I was thinking soup to start with," I tell her. "Warm us both up."

Even those words seem alien to her, as she looks at me with no comprehension. Then suddenly she blurts out, "I can't do this, Red." She whips her hand away from mine.

I frown at the menu. "Okay then, not soup. What do you want?"

"Red." My name is spoken with more than a slight amount of anguish. Putting the menu aside, I give her my attention. "What?"

"I want to go home."

What the fuck? What could have happened in the short time I was in the bathroom? "What the hell are you talking about?"

Shaking her head, she looks down at her hands. "I can't do this, Red. This thing between us, well, it's not working."

My brow furrows. It's working fine from where I'm sitting.

She gestures toward herself. "I'm wet."

Not so much as me.

"Cold," she continues. "And sore. I thought travelling with you would be an adventure, but we're just going from motel to motel, with lots of boring scenery in between."

I don't think I promised her anything more, but I force myself to look at it her way. I'm a man on a mission, my ride to go south before winter hits. My goal, a new life in the sun. to me, the journey is something to be undertaken. It's a means to an end, not an end in itself. Sighing, I reclaim her hand.

"I wanted to travel as far as I could to outrun the risk of snow." I've told her that already. "But what if we take it slower? Ride less, stop off and sightsee more." I know I don't want to lose her. Just the thought is turning my insides sour.

Her lips thin. "I've got three changes of clothes, Red, and a few toiletries. I suppose I was naïve, expecting it wouldn't take long to get to where you wanted to go."

"A few more days, a week, not long," I assure her.

Again, she takes back her hand, and pairs it with the other as she throws both into the air. "And where is there? You don't even know that."

I don't. But I'm banking on knowing what I'm looking for when it's there. Suddenly, I realise there's a real risk that Cheryl won't be with me. "I need you," I tell her earnestly. "Fuck knows how or why, but you've become important to me."

Her shoulders rise and then lower. "I get the feeling any woman would do for you, Red. What are we really, but fuck buddies?"

She's far more than that to me, but maybe she's describing what I am to her. "How compatible we are is just part of it," I hiss, trying to keep my voice low. "I respect you, like you, love like fuck having you at my back on the road."

"I'm giving up everything for you, Red, and I don't even know who you are." I go to open my mouth, but she gets in before I can summon up any words. "When we get to wherever, what am I supposed to do? It's far too soon to commit to living together. I've been an utter fool."

"I thought you were a free spirit like your mother—"

"At least she had a home to go to," she spits. "My dad had somewhere to take her. She wasn't going to a strange town, expecting to live in a hovel or sleep rough."

"Neither are we. We'll stay in motels—"

"For how long?" she cries out and interrupts. "How long until the money runs out?"

"I'll find a job."

"Like that's going to be easy." She scoffs.

I stare at the woman sitting opposite me. For a moment, I can say nothing, just try to gather my thoughts so the wrong words don't blurt out of my mouth. As I sit speechless, the waiter stops by.

She gives her order of coffee, and a sandwich. Still feeling cold, now emotionally as well as physically, I go for the same drink, and add in a request for soup, but my appetite has fled now. I can't understand this change in her and dread the thought of riding on alone.

It's only been a short time, but I'm already used to her riding behind me. In my head, she's been with me all the way, sharing my excitement when we choose a place to stop, if not permanently, then at least for a while. I may not have been quite at the point of drawing hearts with Red and Cheryl forever written within, but I've gotten pretty close to it. *How could I have misread the situation so badly?*

A hundred things come to me, solutions for the practicalities at first. The offer that we could ride slower has already been made. Clothes, well, they can be purchased anywhere. I've planned to do that for myself, hoping to swap jeans and sweaters for shorts and t-shirts as we get further south. A home?

Well, I doubt I'll have much trouble finding a job. There's always a call for good mechanics, and Manny would give me a glowing reference.

I'm confident that I could make a comfortable life for her, but maybe, on our short acquaintance, that's too much to ask. Even this, the fact she's surprised me, makes me realise how little I know her. And while I wouldn't have expected it, how fickle she is.

Her phone buzzes on the table. She picks it up, listens for a moment, then tells the caller, "Yeah, Mom, I'm coming back. No, it's okay, I've got money for that. Yeah, I'll see you soon."

The one-sided conversation lets me know she's already spoken to her mother and that the decision's already been made. There's probably nothing I can say to change it. That she hasn't given us a real chance to talk this out, to consider our options, suddenly makes me furious. I look out of the window, staring at my bike. *Just you and me again, old girl.* Perhaps as it was always meant to be.

Our drinks are delivered, and we down them in silence. Then when the food comes, despite not thinking I would be able to eat, I inhale my soup, while she nibbles her sandwich. Outside, the sleet's still falling.

"I'm not driving you back," I tell her, having decided. It's one thing to stay with her when I thought we'd have a future, quite another now she's decided we don't.

"I'm not asking you too," she retorts. "I've already checked. There's a Greyhound that passes through here. I'll hop on that."

Now I feel a bastard. And selfish. I reach my hand over the table, leaving it lying in invitation, palm up. "Give us one more night?" I ask, with a hint of desperation in my voice.

She gulps, swallows, then shakes her head. "I can't, I'm sorry."

"Has anything happened?" Suddenly, I'm sure it has. This morning she was happy and smiling, and I didn't think the admittedly cold ride would have changed her this much.

Her mouth opens as though she's going to confide in me, but then she shakes her head. "Nothing. I just realised I wasn't made for this."

So, it's no more than that. She'd had me fooled. I thought she was something more than she was. I'm angry I've wasted time when I could have gotten more miles under my belt. What an idiot I've been, falling for the first woman who let me into her bed, or joined me in mine, more to the point.

My coffee cup is empty, my soup all gone. With an air of finality, I suddenly stand. Extracting a decent handful of dollars, I throw them down. "For the food, for your journey, and for whatever else I owe you."

I'm treating her like a whore, but my temper's come out on top again. Normally, I can control my rage, but when it bubbles up, I'm a typical redhead. "It's been *nice* knowing you, *sweetheart.*"

I ignore the way she flushes, and how her eyes widen in disgust. I ignore the whimper of protest that comes out of her mouth.

I leave her there, seated at that table, as I return to the entrance. Pointedly, I turn to look at her as I put on the water-proofs she'd borrowed. Then, I storm toward the door, only just managing to avoid the man who'd served us.

It's only when I get back out to my bike and start strapping my saddlebags back on that I see her forlorn rucksack still tied to the back. For a second, I've the impulse to take it off and leave it sitting there in the mud, but I'm not that much of a bastard. With a sigh, I start to undo the bungee straps, recalling the pleasure and anticipation from this morning when I'd tied her belongings on.

I've completed my job when she hurries out, sheltering under a borrowed umbrella. I'm still holding her bag, as she runs up. Wordlessly, I hand it out to her.

"Red," she starts, almost pleadingly, then stops.

Unless she says she's changed her mind, and in truth, it's

probably already too late if she has, there's nothing more we have to say to each other.

"Look after yourself, Cheryl," I tell her, as I step my leg over my bike, the one thing I know will never desert me.

"You too, Red."

I don't miss the look of longing on her face, as I press start and allow the engine to roar. But it's too late now. Vowing to look forward and never to look back, I ease out the clutch and move forward.

The last thing I see as I glance in my rearview before turning out onto the road, is her standing right where I left her, huddled under the umbrella, with a look of sadness in her eyes.

I raise a hand, and she lifts one back.

Then I'm off, riding alone, as I was always meant to be.

CHAPTER SEVEN

Cheryl would have loved this I think to myself as I wind my way up into the mountains. The air is still cool, but the day is bright, and the sun glistens off the snow already settled on the tops. The scenery is wonderful. If she were still with me, we could have stopped off to explore, but alone, I have no impulsion to do anything but ride.

I've changed direction slightly, gradually making my way west. I'm now in Colorado, and somehow headed to the very state where I didn't want to end up.

It's time to head south again, I tell myself. Well, tomorrow in any event. As the light is fading, I need to find a place to lay my head for the night. I'm not fussy, and soon find a place to stop.

As I take off my saddlebags, my eyes flick to the empty rack. *Hope you got home safe, Cheryl.* Hell, we hadn't even exchanged phone numbers, and I'm still berating myself. How could I have just left her? Anything could have happened to her alone. *Should I retrace my tracks and go back to check on her?*

Part of me says yes. I've stopped off two nights since I'd left her, and each night slept alone in my bed. I miss her like fuck. I miss a warm body to slide my cock into, but so much more than that. Until she abruptly decided my life wasn't for her, she'd been such an easy companion, one I'd have had with me out of choice. I miss our discussions, even though they'd not been of substance. I miss hearing her voice.

Fuck it! I can't go back. She had her reasons for leaving, shit she hadn't told me about. I could tell there was more to it. What would I find if I followed her home? It might be to discover an ex-boyfriend who had reconsidered his loss and persuaded her to return to him. It could simply be that she wasn't the girl I thought she was.

But still I worry about her, whether she got home alright. *Maybe I could ring the diner where she worked?* But I'll be fucked if I can remember what it was called, or even the name of the Podunk town where I'd stopped.

Nah. That chapter's closed. The sooner I put her out of my mind, the better.

Leaving my bike parked outside my room, I wander to the building next door. It's a bar and if true to the sign outside, should still be serving food.

It's one of those places you enter a stranger but aren't made to feel one for long. As soon as I've a drink in my hand, a man approaches.

"Was it you I saw ride in on that bike?" He nods over to the motel where my bike is standing in plain sight.

I confirm that it was. It's not the first time my older model has attracted interest. Soon, he's regaling me with stories of bikes he rode in his youth. When a couple of his friends come over, we're soon debating the virtues of Harleys and Indians, and agreeing that anything not made in the US isn't worth our time.

I order a bar meal, just fried chicken, but when it turns up, it's delicious. We get off the topic of bikes and onto my journey. Being weekend warriors, the trio of men find my long ride admirable and of interest, and also my indistinct plans for the destination at the end of my ride.

"California." One smashes his meaty hand onto the table. "LA, that's where I'd go."

"Why, Brett?" the man who originally approached me, and who I've since learned is called Frederick demands.

Brett wiggles his eyebrows. "Think of all those wannabe actresses. They'll be gagging for some cock."

The third man, Les, rolls his eyes. "Firstly, they're all called actors now, whatever the sex, and secondly, I doubt your cock has worked for years."

Fred laughs loudly, and Bert just shrugs. "It's the principle. I bet this young'un here doesn't need any blue pills."

Grinning, I avoid agreeing with his assumption, and try to get the conversation back on track. "Cali's okay, but it's too crowded. I'd like to go somewhere quieter. And LA's such a big place, I'd get lost there."

"Vegas!" Fred offers triumphantly. "If I was your age, that's where I'd go."

I have visions of *CSI* and films showing the strip. "Does anyone take themselves seriously in that town?" And avoid getting murdered in a myriad of nasty ways. I've always wanted to visit, but choose it as a place to live? Nah, doesn't appeal to me.

"I'm going to retire to Miami," Brett puts in.

"You are retired!" Les points out, with a sideways look toward Fred.

Brett waves his hands dismissively. "Well, when I retire from being retired—"

"Then you'll be dead."

I snort at Fred's comment.

"Arizona," Les suddenly puts in.

Arizona? My eyes narrow. "Is anything there except for desert?"

Les snorts. "There's Phoenix for a start, that could be a good place. Or," he taps his nose as he thinks, "what about Tucson? Great place that. Winters are mild, and there's a mountain range where you can go skiing if that's what you like."

Tucson. Despite the fact I've no impulse to go speeding down a mountain on two wooden sticks, I consider it for a moment, but all I can conjure up are the westerns I've watched in my life.

"Tucson's good," Brett agrees. "Knew a girl from there once."

Fred throws a beer mat at him. "You knew a girl everywhere, or according to you anyway. Doubt there's much truth in it."

"Fuckin' is," Brett growls, sending a heated look toward his friend. I brace myself to separate these old codgers if they start fighting, but now ignoring him, the offended man turns back to me instead. "Tucson's a city, but not one big enough so you'd get lost. Friendly place too if I remember rightly."

"Don't mind him," Les leans in and confides to me. "He can't remember shit. We have to remind him of his name half the time."

Dutifully, I chuckle. But the old man has made me think. Couldn't hurt swinging by to look at what Arizona has to offer. The climate is right, and from what I can recall, it's not on a fault line, and it's not a place I associate with hurricanes or tornados. I could land there, see if I can find work and just see how it goes. Doesn't mean I have to commit to staying there forever.

Brett nudges Les and jerks his head toward Fred whose eyes have closed. "Best get this one 'ome."

Les grins, grabs his car keys out of his pocket and stands. "Nice meeting you, Red. Hope you find what you're looking for."

"Yeah." Brett stands and takes one of his friend's arms while Les takes the other. "And if you run into a big breasted woman called Betsy, give her my best regards."

I snort, wondering how many elderly Betsy's I'd have to come across to find the right one. Especially when Les barks a laugh. "That's if he's even remembering the correct state, let alone the right town."

With his free hand, Brett shoots Les the bird. Then, gently, the pair raise Fred to his feet. He snaps awake looking bleary-eyed, but as he doesn't protest their help, I gather they've done this a time or two before.

As I go to the bar and get another beer, I wonder where I'll be and who with when I reach their age. Hopefully, I'll have friends who'll have my back, just like Bert and Les had Fred's. And who'll yank my chain and not let me get away with shit, just as I'll yank theirs in return. And when I've had too much to drink, will help me find my way home.

But between now and then, I've a whole lifetime to live.

Which brings me back to the conversation I'd just had. Tucson? Why the fuck not? Might be time I started heading for a particular point on the map rather than just dallying around.

Yeah, Tucson. I start to like the sound of it.

Wonder whether Cheryl would have been happy there.

I grimace, staring down into my beer. Whether she would or not is a moot point. I've divided my journey into two segments, that with and that without her. I know which I prefer. Having someone to share shit with had been better than being alone. That she hadn't been the right woman for me is obvious, seeing how easy it was for us to part. Perhaps I could find a replacement?

But it's her I miss, not just a female to keep me company. Having parted like we had, it felt unfinished. Maybe it's that I've no way of contacting her that I can't get her out of my mind. I can't reassure myself she's safe. I'd give anything just to speak to her one last time. Perhaps if she could better voice her justifications for leaving me as she had, it might make me realise that we'd just come to a division in the road.

Maybe I'm putting her up on a pedestal, but she's become all that I want. While I tell myself how stupid it is, something tells me that she was my one and that I'd lost her.

I should have done more. Gone back with her. Maybe stayed for a time. If I could have explored what I was beginning to feel for her, maybe I could have settled down.

But I didn't and wishes and second thoughts won't resolve one damn thing. Tomorrow, I'll head for Tucson. I might be able to make it in one day if I push on. Consulting a map, I see it's darn near eight hundred miles to Tucson from where I am now. Doable if I leave early.

With that thought in mind, I leave the bar and start walking the short distance to the motel. When I reach my bike, I hear the sound of multiple motorbikes. Pausing, I turn my head, then sink back into the shadows.

Hardened men in formation ride past me. A motorcycle gang by the looks of them, all wearing leather cuts. *What do they say?* Ah, yes, *Satan's Devils MC*. I shudder. I've heard about biker gangs and never had any inclination to join them. They treat their women abysmally from what I've heard and earn money running drugs and guns. Not the kind of group I'd want to be associated with, even if I do admire some of their bikes. I wait until they've all gone past, then emerge into the light and take the room key out of my pocket.

I might ride a bike, but I'll never be a member of an outlaw club. Uh-uh. No way.

Once secure on the inside of the door, I strip off, venture into the bathroom and stare into the mirror. *Tucson,* I remind myself once more, the thought of where I could be this time tomorrow erasing thoughts of the probably murderous bikers from my mind.

Feeling I'm truly beginning my future, I go to bed with a smile on my face for the first time since Cheryl and I had parted. Now I've a place to head for, there's no room for regrets about her anymore. Or that's what I tell myself.

Tucson.

I might be out of my mind, but for some reason the place I've never been and which I know nothing about, doesn't just start calling to me, it's screaming into my ear.

It's early morning when I awake and rise. Shivering in the chill of the morning, I treat myself to a scalding shower, then venture out to grab some breakfast. It's only seven by the time my stomach and bike are both topped off. A quarter of an hour later, I'm leaving Pueblo in my rearview.

And wouldn't you know I've made it just in time? There's a light snow falling, not settling, but not boding well for those bikers I saw last night.

I grin, face into the wind, and think that by the end of the day, I'll be in the desert, and winter riding a thing of the past.

Shoving down the thought that I miss having warm arms around me, I twist my throttle and settle in for the ride. When I finally cross into Arizona, for some inexplicable reason, I feel like I'm coming home. I grin as a hawk swoops down, flying alongside me for a moment. It seems like an omen. When it tilts its wings and soars away into the heavens above, it's as though I've been welcomed. This is my time now. A chance to live for myself, to do things right.

I feel lighter than I have in months, scrap that, years. Although I still regret not having Cheryl beside me, I vow to put thoughts of her behind me. The world's my oyster as the saying goes, and there's no one but me to fuck my chances up.

Hey! *Will you look at that?* I grin as I see one of the cacti that must have formed the backdrop for numerous westerns I'd watched with my dad. What are they called? Ah, yes, saguaro. The sight's certainly not like any I've seen in the flesh before and represents the warmer climate I've been seeking.

Yeah, that old guy was right. Arizona's warm, bike friendly, and a good place to stop.

CHAPTER EIGHT

After a long day on the road, my only thought when I finally reach my destination is to find a place to crash, quickly followed by somewhere to eat. Tired and aching after my longest ride to date, I stop at the first chain motel I find.

It's cheap, basic, but will do the job. This time, however, I book myself in for a few days. Apart from visiting the nearest place to fill my stomach and wet my throat, I don't take much notice of my surroundings, and am almost asleep before I drop into bed.

It's different when I wake the next day with feelings of excitement and anticipation throbbing inside me. *What will I find when I step out of the door?*

Before I leave my room, I flick through some leaflets which have been left for tourists. I grin when I see there's the Old Tucson film studio here, especially when I read on and find a lot of the programs I used to watch as a kid were filmed there. *Little House on the Prairie,* would you fuckin' believe it? Loads of films too. That's somewhere I'd like to go and explore. Then there's Tombstone, not too far from here. A desert life museum, well, I'm not too certain I want to get up close and personal with some of the native creatures, but whatever, it looks like I won't be at a loss for entertainment.

But first, I've got to get my priorities straight. If I don't get employment, I won't be staying here long. *I'll be returning with my tail between my legs to Manny.*

Back home, everything that had seemed easy feels daunting now. A moment's hesitation hits me as I go out to my bike. Will I really be so lucky as to walk into a job? Good mechanics are needed everywhere, aren't they?

Of course, they are, I reassure myself.

As I treat myself to a fortifying breakfast, I decide to drive around, stop at any auto-shops I come across and see if any have an opening. I prefer to work on bikes rather than cars if I have my choice, but beggars can't be choosers. After I've got a steady paycheck in my hand, I can look around for something else. Once nourished, I head down into the city. The temperature is in the low seventies. *T-shirt weather,* I think with a grin. As I ride through the streets, I realise my pale skin will stick out like a sore thumb. Everyone I pass has a decent tan.

Tucson isn't an intimidating city, there are no huge skyscrapers, and the business area seems to be concentrated in just a few blocks. Housing developments, many single story, sprawl out into the surrounding area. Leaving my exploration for later, I spy a sign to an auto-shop, and head off in that direction.

Having made my enquiries and having had no success, I tell myself I'd be too lucky to walk into a job immediately. The second's also a bust, and the third, and I start to have misgivings about just how easy it will be to find work. I didn't even have a chance to offer up my credentials. However impressive they might be, it's no good if there are no vacancies.

Maybe I need to rethink my plans. It's money I need, not necessary fulfilment in the short term. Surely, someone, somewhere will be hiring. Even if I end up stacking shelves, it will help boost my dwindling money.

I've cash in my pocket to last awhile, all thanks to Manny,

and I've only been looking for one morning. Maybe I should just relax and enjoy myself for a few hours.

Ah, look there. It's a Harley store, a mecca for all things biker. I don't need anything, but maybe they'll have an opening, or at least know someone who's hiring. I can while away some time looking at parts. Maybe a lightweight jacket for myself. The one I brought with me is far too heavy.

Pulling up in the designated area for customer motorcycles, I turn off the engine, take off the half-helmet I'm now wearing, slide off my gloves and place my shades in my pocket. Looking up at the unbroken blue sky above, I remind myself, this is what I travelled so many miles for. It was worth it.

Under my feet, the ground is dusty and dry. *My kind of place.* In more than one way, winter has been put behind me. I start swinging my leg over the seat when a massive roar reaches my ears. Completing my move, now standing on two feet, I see half a dozen bikes pull in around me.

Oh fuck. What hits me first is the cut they're all wearing, and the swagger that comes from a familiarity between men. A bonding, a suggestion that no one can touch them. They park and the roar dwindles to nothing, then with back slaps, laughter, a few ribald suggestions, and, with only a quick glance toward me, five of the bikers walk toward the store entrance.

One half-turns and calls over his shoulder, "Watch the fuckin' bikes, Prospect."

Said prospect gives a mock salute, his face showing no umbrage with the order.

I'm hesitant about going into the store now. With their backs turned to me, I can see they are members of a gang called the Satan's Devils MC. *Wasn't that the crew that passed me in Colorado?* I'm sure it was. They seem to be fucking everywhere.

Are they here to rob the store? Or just to innocently shop like me? Whatever, I'm considering whether to leave it for now and come back later, when the lone biker they left outside, talks to me.

"Nice ride you got there."

One on one, he seems no threat, and he sounds friendly. "Restored it myself," I tell him proudly.

"Yeah?" He walks around it. "I like your pipes."

"I was lucky to find them," I respond. "Took me a while to find originals in a decent enough state. All I had to do was have them re-chromed."

"Nice job." He takes out a pack of cigarettes, taps one to the fore and offers it to me.

Gratefully, I take it, and also the offer of a light when he flicks his Zippo. Drawing in smoke to my lungs, I think I might as well stay for a moment. Deciding to pick his brains while I'm here, I ask, "Know any places that might need a mechanic?" I shrug. "Bike, cars, anything. Though I'm not into heavy machinery."

He looks at my bike again, focusing for a moment on the out-of-state plates. "Vermont? You're a long way from home."

Deciding the truth always works, I grin at him. "Got fed up with the cold weather, thought I'd give it a try somewhere warmer."

"Yeah?" He chuckles. "Can't say I blame you. Been here long?"

"Arrived yesterday."

Suddenly he remembers his manners. "I'm Wraith by the way."

Wraith has to be a road name. It's surely not one a parent would have chosen, but then, neither is mine.

"Red." I hold out my hand, noticing his firm grip as he shakes it. "So, a prospect, huh? You miss out on all the fun times?" I refer to his motorcycle-sitting duties as I nod toward the store's interior.

"Something like that," he replies with a grin. "But it's worth it."

I draw in smoke and breathe it out again, turning my head up a moment to enjoy the warmth of the sun. "What does prospecting entail then?" It's just a question to pass the time, not that I'm particularly interested.

"It means I do all the shit jobs and get hazed." Wraith sends an easy grin toward me.

Fuck that. "Why do you put up with it?"

"Because I want to earn my patch." Seeing I'm not comprehending him, he adds, "To become a full member."

He wants to be a criminal as much as that? I finish my cigarette, stub it out, and place it in the receptacle provided. As I do so, I see the other Satan's Devils exiting the store, one proudly carrying a package under his arm. From the satisfied grin on his face, I gather he'd gotten what he'd come for.

One of them has obviously made some kind of joke, as they're jostling and play thumping each other, just like schoolboys. Their easy relationship and obvious friendship make me envious for a moment. Had I ever had that? Sure, I'd had school friends, but none that had followed me into adulthood.

"Hey, Lefty." Wraith steps up to my side. "This here's Red. He's a mechanic, and he's looking for work."

I suppose I should be grateful, he's obviously asked for a reason, but I'd rather have not drawn attention to myself. What's the protocol when a biker meets members of an MC? I'll be fucked if I know.

The man he'd spoken to steps close enough I can see the name, *Lefty* on his patch, together with one carrying the letters VP. *Vice president.* Warning myself I need to watch my words, I raise my chin to the biker.

"Red, eh? Any experience?" The VP looks at me quizzically.

"Seven years," I tell him. "Got all the certificates that I need."

"He rebuilt his bike," Wraith puts in, pointing to the ride beside me.

Another of them breaks off and goes to look at my bike, quizzically eyeing everything as though trying to find fault with it.

"Whatcha think, Blade?"

Blade stands, puffs out his chest, and gives me a grin that looks quite evil. "Could do with more hands, 'specially those that know what they're fuckin' doing—"

"How long are you going to blame me?" Another man throws up his hands and turns his back.

"Ah fuck, you've hurt Viper's feelings," one of the two men who are standing, arms over each other's shoulders, says in a joking voice.

"Can it, Rock." Lefty swings around and glares at them. "You too, Beef."

"Could give him a try," the man called Blade, the one who actually scares me, remarks.

One of the jokers steps forward. "Drummer wanted members only as it's inside the compound."

Lefty presses his lips together. "He did that."

Wraith enthusiastically bumps my shoulder. "He could prospect."

What, me? Never. How the fuck do I get out of this?

"You just want to palm off the shit jobs on someone," the other one of the pair now speaks.

"True," Wraith replies, unapologetically. "You lot keep me run off my feet."

Lefty looks thoughtful as he eyes me. "You in any trouble, Red? See you got out-of-state plates."

They're questioning me about legality? I suppress my snort, thinking it would be impolite, and not wanting to get on the wrong side of them as they heavily outnumber me.

I decide the truth will suffice. If they know I'm squeaky clean, they probably wouldn't want me anywhere near them. "I've not so much as a speeding ticket. I left Vermont because my dad, who was sick for a while, died. I'd been his caregiver."

"Sorry, man." Blade's demeanour has changed. "Must be hard. You wanting a fresh start?"

"Prez said—"

"I know what Drum said, Rock." The VP rounds on him.

"But there's nothing to say Red here can't come around as a hangaround. He might see something he likes."

"Er—" I open my mouth to thank them and somehow tell them I'm not interested, but I'm not given the chance.

"He could come back with us. Take a look around. Talk to Prez if he think's he'd be a good fit."

I so do not want to go back with the bikers to their lair. Fuck knows what it would be like. A grotty warehouse comes to my mind.

"You mind getting your hands dirty? Ever thought of being a prospect?"

I need to shut this down fast. "I'm not the man you want. Hell, no criticism intended, but I walk the straight and narrow. Can't see me stepping off."

Wraith slaps his hand on my shoulder. "No worries, man. I'll do the burying of the bodies myself."

Spinning, I turn my wide eyes on him. *He's got to be joking.* But I can't tell from his expression whether he's serious or not.

Lefty's having a private conversation with Blade which seems to consist of grunts, chin lifts and waves of their hands. After a moment, he turns to me, and thank fuck, he uses words.

"You got something you need to be doing?"

Quickly I try to think of something fast. "I was going to go inside and see whether they had any jobs going—"

"Well, we might," he interrupts. "Get on your bike and follow us."

Oh shit, no. Visions go through my head of them abducting me, stealing the bike they seemed pretty interested in and no one ever finding my body. But how can I politely refuse?

I'd had a fucker try to mug me once, and I managed to fight him off. I'm certainly not afraid of sticking up for myself, but that's one-on-one. One against six? Hell, the way these men hold themselves show they're no strangers to violence. The VP has a scar down his face that I suspect was caused by a knife.

The one called Blade has his namesake out and is cleaning his fingernails with it. *A threat?* "Thought you wanted a job," he says, lazily.

I do. But how can I say, *but not with the likes of you?*

"Offer's legit," Lefty states, then shrugs. "It's up to you."

If they had genuine work like wanting me to keep their bikes in running order, sure, I could do that. Tune them to get the best from them as well. *But join their club?* That's what they seem to be asking of me.

I shudder. I might ride a bike, but I'm not a biker, or not in the way that they are.

I try to back out gracefully. "Look, I'd love to come back with you, but I really need to search out employment."

"Which I've already said is what we might be able to offer you," Lefty states, as he narrows his eyes. "You turning us down without giving us a chance?"

I can feel the tension around me, and it's not lost on me that these men are all armed.

Fuck.

Swallowing hard, I manage to sound firm as I capitulate. "I'll follow you."

CHAPTER NINE

What the fuck am I doing?

I'm riding behind five patched members of the Satan's Devils MC, with the prospect Wraith riding alongside me. Before, I've only ridden with one of the other mechanics from work, and only know from television shows that groups of bikers ride in formation. I'm nervous as hell. My biker pride wants to show I'm no weekend warrior. Hell, I've just ridden close to three thousand miles what with the detours I've made, my bike an extension of my body. I shouldn't fuck this up, but the men around me ride with practiced ease, looking like they're taking part in a choreographed dance as though they've ridden together a thousand times before which undoubtably they have.

Along with my fear of keeping myself and everyone else shiny side up, I'm concerned about what I'm heading into. *Is this some sort of press-gang, a way to find new members?* Fuck. I don't want to join a motorcycle club. I hadn't lied when I'd told them I'd never stepped the wrong side of the law. Doing so hadn't even occurred to me. I'd never taken anything that I'd not earned, nor solved arguments with my fists. One thing for certain, I won't fit in with this club.

Feeling like a kidnap victim, and for once, not enjoying the feeling of my bike under me, knowing if I'd had any other kind of transport they wouldn't have given me a second glance, I dutifully ride on. When Lefty makes a hand signal showing he's going to make a turn, the gesture clearly for my sake, I tap down through the gears as I slow. Instead of some broken down building, we turn onto a track.

It was clearly at some time a well-maintained road, but the elements have taken their toll. I follow the others as they move into single file, and watch carefully as they wind their way around potholes and cracks in the pavement. It seems to go on for miles as we cautiously head through the desert, but from a glance at my odometer, it's only half a mile before we eventually draw up at some steel gates.

Lefty waves Wraith forward. The prospect dismounts his bike, pulls the gates open, letting the rest of us pass. Blade pulls to a stop just inside the entrance, indicating to me I should do the same, while the other bikes peel off and continue on. Not far though. As I turn off my engine, the noise of their engines also soon stop.

The first thing I notice is the silence. Birds, unfamiliar to me, squawk and chatter, but there's no noise of traffic reaching up from the freeway. It seems an isolated spot. *They could kill me and bury my body.* Grimacing, I realise, even Manny doesn't know which state I've stopped in. If I go missing, there'll be no one searching for me.

For once, I'm pleased Cheryl didn't come with me. It's only me who's gotten myself into trouble, and no one else. Wondering whether the future I've promised myself is about to come to an abrupt full stop, I kick down the stand, swing my leg over the saddle, and get off.

The scary man called Blade is standing expectantly. A slight curve to his lips comes as he waits for me to take in my surroundings. Having analysed the sounds, I now take in the sights.

We've parked outside what looks like a hastily thrown up

building. Inside, there are a few bikes and a couple of cars. A hand-drawn sign is slowly swaying in the gentle breeze, announcing *SD Auto Repairs and Servicing*. Inside, I can see tool benches, a mechanic's pit and a ramp, and a man lying under a car.

They hadn't lied. They've got a shop. But it's not one I'd ever have approached for a job.

Blade tilts his head, indicating I should look further, in the direction in which the rest of the bikes have gone.

I do, creasing my eyes to make sense of what I'm seeing. Burned-out hulks of what seems to be accommodation, and beyond that, some buildings which look new or restored.

"What the fuck is this place?" I find myself asking.

Blade gives a real grin now. "It's our compound. We moved here a couple of years back. Well, I didn't, as I wasn't part of the club then. It's something, ain't it?" He smiles with pleasure as he stares around. "It was an old vacation resort that got wiped out by a fire. Club bought it cheap."

Yeah, very cheap, I expect. There are hulks of structures that look like they'd be better torn down.

"So," he turns and indicates the ramshackle building behind me, "this is our auto-shop. Hey, Tongue. Get out here and meet our new mechanic."

Hell, I haven't said yes.

"Mechanic? Fuck yeah," a muffled voice comes from under the car. "'Bout time we had someone that knows what they're doing." Feet first, the man begins to emerge.

"Shut your mouth, Tongue. I ain't chopped liver."

"Never said you were, Blade, but we kind of picked it up on the job." He's standing now, and as he talks, I get glimpses of a gold stud in his tongue. He turns to me. "You know anything about carburettors?"

Well, yeah. I resist the urge to roll my eyes and just answer with a shrug and one word, "Sure."

"Hired," Tongue tells me with a smirk.

"Who's the fuckin' manager here?" A knife has magically appeared in Blade's hand as he steps forward, making me hold my breath waiting for blood.

But Tongue's not fazed, just brushes the hand and knife away. "You won the toss, Brother." His words seem to appease Blade, while I'm left wondering what the hell kind of business they're running here if no one seems to know what the fuck they're doing.

Run a fuckin' mile, I think to myself. I even eye my bike to assess my chances. But as the prospect's pulled the gate closed again and has been busy applying a padlock to it, I guess I'm kinda stuck.

"What d'you work on? Bikes or cages?" Tongue asks me.

"Everything," Blade answers for me, doing some weird movements that look like a happy dance. "He's got certificates and everything."

"Ooh." Tongue wiggles his, well, tongue, making that stud catch the sun. "I'm fuckin' impressed."

I'm not. It seems an amateur outfit. I wonder how they get anyone to trust them with their vehicles. *Maybe they tune getaway cars.* Well, probably only other criminals would come here.

Blade shares one of those silent conversations with the man he called his brother—though I can see no familial resemblance —then with a chin jerk, comes back over.

"Guess I better take you to see Drum."

He's still holding that fucking knife, twisting it around in his hand like someone else might a stress ball. Straightening my back, as it appears I have no choice, I raise my chin. But I want to know what I'm getting into.

"Who's Drum?"

"Our Prez," he replies, then adds, "Come on."

Only just biting back a comment to *take me to your leader,* I walk alongside him as we make our way up a paved track, better maintained than the road to the compound, I notice. As I do, I can't help but look around. If this was anything other than a biker compound, it would be a stunning location. Mountains are all around. A forest is in the near distance, and to the sides stretch miles of desert. Ignoring the evidence of the burned-out buildings, there's beauty all around. Despite my misgivings, I feel a kind of peace here.

A bend in the path, then a row of motorcycles comes into sight, all parked in front of what makes me recall this was once a resort as it indeed looks like the entrance to a fancy hotel. This is where they've clearly focused their reconstruction attentions.

Blade leads me up to a door, pushes it open, then ushers me inside. There's a bar where I'd half expected to see a reception desk. Mismatching tables and chairs are strewn around, and there's a pool table off to one side. New woodwork shows in abundance, and some recent brickwork is exposed showing where they've done some renovation. It's clearly been patched up to be usable but isn't completely finished.

Lefty and the other bikers that had been at the store, along with a couple of others I don't recognise, are milling around the bar area, demanding drinks from the prospect who's hastily changed roles from bike minder to bartender.

When the VP spies me, he raises a bottle and shouts at Blade, "Drummer's in his office."

"This way," Blade tells me, marching me through the large room and into a corridor. He knocks at the first door, and a growly voice tells us to enter.

I'd had preconceptions of what I expected to find when I walked through that door, but the reality was different. From the president title, I expected a middle-aged man at least, but the one sitting behind the desk looks like he's only got a couple of years on myself. Sure, there's some grey in his temples, but his face is youthful looking and virtually unlined.

"Blade," he acknowledges, nodding at the man who's entered after me.

Then, steely grey eyes land on me, piercing through me, making me want to admit to a crime I'd never committed just to get his focus off me. He might not have many years more than mine, but there's just something about him that shouts power, and that he's not a man to be crossed.

"This here's Red. He's a mechanic," Blade explains. "Thought he could prospect for us."

What? I never suggested such a thing.

As I frown at Blade and go to refute his proposal, Drummer growls, "And why do you want to join the Satan's Devils?"

It's time I stuck up for myself. "I don't want to join a motorcycle gang at all," I hiss.

His fist slams down on the table as he rears forward. "We're a club, not a fuckin' gang. Why the fuck are you here if you don't want to join us?"

My temper flares. "I wasn't given much choice in the matter. I was basically kidnapped and brought here."

Drummer narrows his eyes at Blade. "What the fuck?"

"Lefty was there." Blade sounds like a petulant schoolboy and presses his lips together. "We need new members, and a mechanic. Thought he looked likely."

"I've got a bike," I spit out. "Just because I ride doesn't mean I want to join a fuckin' … club."

"You're not local," Drummer says sharply. "Where you from? How long have you been in Tucson?"

"I'm from Vermont. I rode down, arrived yesterday."

Astute eyes zoom in on me. "So, what are you running from? Or are you running toward something?"

He's shrewd, I'll give him that. "I'm looking for something new, something different." I add in a shrug. "Tucson was just a pin on the map. Doesn't mean this is where I'm staying."

I feel like I'm under a microscope, or a butterfly pinned to a board for someone's entertainment. I can't move away, can't move my eyes from his. I'm tense, my muscles flooded with fight-or-flight endorphins. *This man is dangerous.*

"His dad died," Blade puts in, as I inwardly wince, regretting sharing my history with him.

Slowly, very slowly, Drummer moves his eyes from me, fixing them instead on the man beside me. His lips begin to curve, though only slightly, as though he's not a man used to smiling.

"You may be on to something, Blade," he says at last. Then to me he states, "You don't just join an MC. Any man who wants in has to prospect for a year or so to show whether they're a good fit for us, and us for them. Works both ways, you see. No commitment on either side until a patch is offered, or it's not. You've apparently got skills I'm needing, and maybe there's something we can offer you in return. A home and a family, which I suspect you're lacking."

Has he got a crystal ball hidden somewhere? I startle as he's read me right. Drummer might not be far off my own age, but he's far more mature than I. I wonder how he got his experience and suspect his life might have been hard. He clearly hasn't let the world pass him by for seven years of his life.

He turns back to Blade again. "Get the prospect to show him around. If he sees anything he likes, then bring him back to speak to me again. Oh, and Blade, you might be wearing that brand-new enforcer patch but that doesn't mean you can go around picking up strays and forcing them here at knifepoint."

Blade eyes me, one eyebrow rising as he studies me, and his mouth curves. "Had a feeling about this one, Prez. And I'm pretty sure he doesn't have fleas."

"Get out," Drummer growls, but without malice. It occurs to me it's probably just the way he normally sounds.

CHAPTER TEN

The prospect and I have reached the top of the compound. I stand for a moment, gazing out at the forest beyond, noticing an area has been cleared in front of it.

"Firebreak," Wraith points out. "They say lightning doesn't strike twice, but we wanted to make sure of it."

That makes sense. I turn, looking down at the rest of the compound. Wraith's been a good guide. From what looked an absolute shambles when I'd first entered the gate, now is starting to make sense. The old resort was made up of several guest blocks, each housing two suites. A number of these, apparently the least damaged, have been done up and now serve to house members of the club. Wraith had let me in to his to show me an example. I was impressed with his balcony and the view from it, and that they've kept the facilities meaning every man has his own bathroom. The suite next to his was vacant but looked like it was ready to be occupied.

To my astonishment, he'd also shown me a swimming pool, shimmering with bright blue clear water and ready to be used. Apparently, there used to be three, but two have been filled in now.

At the top of the compound, where we are now, the foundations for three houses have been laid. He'd told me, one will be Drummer's, one for sweet butts—whatever they are—and one for visiting members from other clubs.

"There's a hell of a lot to do." I indicate the start of the building work behind me, and then on down to the burned-out blocs waiting to be restored.

Wraith nods. "Viper and Bullet are slowly getting around to it. As we're down a mechanic, Viper helps out at the shop when he can, but he and Bullet spend most of the time at SD Construction in town. It's like everything. Building takes time and money, and the civilian work brings the money in. They can only work on the compound part time. Most of it, evenings and weekends. But we'll get there."

"I notice the clubhouse wasn't finished."

"It's got walls, a roof and a bar." Wraith grins at me. Then he shrugs. "But yeah, it'll be done eventually."

"How long's the club been here?"

"A year or so, eighteen months?" He seems uncertain, but a precise answer doesn't matter. I suppose in that timescale and given the constraints, they've done quite a lot.

It's certainly not what I would have expected as a biker compound, the area around for one. As had struck me when I first arrived, it's so peaceful here. The scenery is to die for. I don't think I've ever seen a prettier spot.

For a second, I wonder whether I could find a place here.

I like Wraith. I think we could become good friends. Lefty seemed okay, Tongue a bit of a clown. Blade, hmm, on him, the jury's still out. I'm not sure how much I'd trust him. Then there's Drummer. Now he's a man who commands respect. In some ways, he reminds me of Manny, and I wonder whether there are similarities. A man who runs a tight ship, but underneath the exterior beats a heart of gold. There must be some of that. One thing I've picked up is these men's loyalty toward him.

But they're criminals. They're outlaws, living outside the law.

"Apart from the construction business, how does the club

make its money?" I wonder whether Wraith will tell me. Or, if he does, whether he'll need to kill me afterward.

Wraith indicates a pile of bricks and goes to sit on it. I take a spot beside him.

"The club's cleaned up its act since the old days." His eyes, unfocused, stare out at the horizon. "As a prospect, I only know what's general knowledge of course. But in Bastard's day—he was Drummer's dad, and president before him—the club was into all kinds of illegal shit. Prostitution, gun running, drugs, you name it. Whatever you can think of to bring in money, well, they did it."

"What happened?" I sense a story.

"Raid by the feds. Half the club were gunned down. Bastard was killed, along with his old lady, and several other members. The Satan's Devils were almost no more. Drummer pulled what remained of the club together, took on this place and moved the club here. As well as physically rebuilding the compound, he's rebuilding the club. He doesn't want the feds to have excuses for coming after us anymore."

Puffing my cheeks and blowing out air, I revise my opinion. "You're telling me everything they do is legal?"

Wraith snorts. "I wouldn't say that. But the legit side outweighs the other. As well as the auto-shop and construction, we have a restaurant in town, and a strip joint that we run. Together they bring in a decent income."

"The auto-shop?" I give a snort of my own.

He looks at me sharply. "SD Auto Repairs had a good rep, even in the bad old days. Got lots of loyal customers knowing we do a good job and never rip them off. Problem is, the shop's having to be rebuilt from scratch, and our best mechanics were killed by the feds. Blade, well he patched in just when I came on board a few months' back. He at least knows which wrench to use, so he's the manager."

And hence why he jumped at the chance of a qualified mechanic, I suppose.

"Why did you join, Wraith?"

Again, he gazes out in front of him. "I did two years in the Army. Joined at eighteen. Saw all kinds of shit I can never unsee. I got out, but one thing I'd learned was the benefit of having men at my back. I kind of missed that. I'd heard of the Devils from a man in my unit, so I sought them out. Liked what I saw and decided to join them. That was three months back."

I crease my eyes. "Don't you have to sign on in the Army for like eight years?"

He shrugs. "Technically, I have. I'm a reservist for the next five years. The Army could call me back." He shudders as if he really doesn't want that.

"I wanted to enlist," I confide. "Wanted to be a Ranger."

His eyes widen in respect. "What happened?"

"Life." I don't go into details.

"Sucks, man." He goes to pull out his smokes, but this time I'm ahead of him, getting mine out first. He takes one with a chin lift, then cups his hand to the flame from my lighter.

As I draw in smoke, I consider what I've heard. A little voice in the back of my head asks whether it could suit me. But there are drawbacks, of course. "A year prospecting sounds like a fuckin' long time."

"It's not all work, man." Wraith grins at me. "What's better than riding your bike along with your friends? I may only be a prospect, but I'm club, and as much as I'll have their back, they'll have mine. Sure, some of the jobs are fuckin' irksome, but you say you wanted to be a Ranger? How d'you think you'd get through the hazing if you weren't prepared to smile and ask how high when you're told to jump? Prospecting's hard, there's no denying that, but it's also fun. And at the end of it, there's that patch. Still, it may not suit if you're scared of hard work."

"I'm not fuckin' scared of working," I growl. No, it's the being at everyone's beck and call I'm worried about. I'd had enough of that when I first started at Manny's and began washing cars and sweeping floors.

Like Wraith, I stare into the distance as I think back. I kind of had gone through the same thing at Manny's, hadn't I? But then as I progressed, I got more interesting jobs, and when I became qualified, it had made it all worthwhile. But I've moved on from that now. I've got a trade and should be able to walk in anywhere as a mechanic.

They want my skills here too.

"I best be getting back." Wraith stubs out his cigarette, pockets the end and stands. He turns to me as I do likewise, a serious look on his face. "Club isn't for everyone. It attracts many, but only a few get a chance. You should think yourself lucky to even be asked, and that's only because you've got something they want. This chapter has had a rough time and is trying to crawl back out of it. They lost good men who are hard to replace. We need a mechanic who knows his shit. Blade and Tongue do well enough, but they're run off their feet. We bumped into you, or you to us, at the right time."

"Hey. Some Satan's Devils passed me when I was in Colorado. Was that you?"

"Pueblo?" When I nod, he shakes his head. "Nah, that was more likely the Colorado Chapter. There are others around— Vegas, San Diego and one over in Utah. Tucson's the mother chapter. Drummer rules over the lot."

Bigger than I expected then. Once again, I'm impressed that Drummer's got so much power, not just Tucson, but four other chapters under his control. I wonder how he managed to hang on to that role seeing the trouble and decimation of this club. Only a very strong man could have done so.

A man I could respect and learn from? Perhaps.

I follow Wraith back down toward the clubhouse, casting my eyes around me as I go. Sure is a pleasant place to make a home here. If it wasn't for the types I'd be living with, that is. But what type is that, exactly? Men who love the freedom of riding bikes, men scraping together a living. Men, like Drummer, who I could grow to admire.

Maybe I could give it a shot?

I grin to myself. I can just imagine a conversation with Manny. *Yeah, man. I'm doing fine. I've joined an outlaw motorcycle club.* My father, meanwhile, would be turning in his grave. Or would he? He might well have a smile on his face. As long as I was following my dreams, he'd be cool.

But are they my dreams or am I scraping at the bottom of the barrel? Have I given anything else a chance? It's like there's a magic spell being woven around me, drawing me in.

I'm still undecided when we reach the clubhouse. Wraith leaves me immediately, taking his place behind the bar. I hover just inside the doorway, not entirely certain what to do. The most sensible thing would be to return to my bike and ride away. If they'd let me.

Something keeps my feet tethered, the camaraderie in front of me. It's easy to see the affection between the men. Even Wraith, trying to catch up with the drink orders, is laughing and seems happy.

"You born in a fuckin' barn, boy? Either come in or go out!"

The shout is directed at me. Glancing over, I see a tall, heavily bearded man. He's glaring in my direction. Sheepishly, I step inside, wondering why when I'd been given the option to leave.

The man who called me boy—like Drummer, slightly older than me, but not by much—beckons me over. As I move toward him, he closes the gap between us. I notice him limping heavily and leaning on a crutch for support.

"Name's Peg. I'm the sergeant-at-arms." He says it so sharply I have to suppress my immediate impulse to salute.

"Red," I tell him, locking my hands at my sides.

"That I know. You looking to join us?"

My mouth forms a no, but for some reason, the word out of my mouth is a cautious, "Maybe."

"Need to get some muscle on you." He's examining me critically. "You seen our gym?" *Gym?* I shake my head. "Boys here finished it recently. It was put in for me. Lost my fuckin' leg overseas." He glances down, presumably at said leg. As he's got two boots on, I presume he's wearing a prosthetic.

"We'll soon have you back on your bike, Brother." It's Drummer who's approached and has slapped Peg's back.

"Sooner the better," comes another voice loudly. "He's even more of a grumpy motherfucker since he's come back."

"Shut your trap, Viper. I'd like to see you deal with a fuckin' stump," Peg roars back.

"Could be arranged," Blade mutters mildly, while picking at his fingernails with his ever-present knife.

As I wonder whether a fight's going to start, Peg cuffs Blade round the head, and the enforcer gives a good-natured snort. I start to gather this is how they behave together. *Like family.*

"Come, sit," a deep voice instructs from behind me.

Turning, I see it's Drummer and that, expecting me to follow, he's heading for a table in the corner. When I join him, he holds up two fingers. I guess Wraith must have been watching out for him, as he comes straight over to us, two opened bottles of beer in his hand. He places them on the table, then makes himself scarce.

"So, Colt Masters, have you decided?"

I lean forward quickly. "How the fuck do you know my name?"

For an answer, he pulls out my wallet and puts it down. *What the fuck?* Even though it's right there in front of me, I pat my pockets. Once I'm assured it is indeed mine, I quickly grab it, open it, and check. I had a few hundred dollars in there, and from what I can tell, still have the same amount. *I could have been robbed.* I wasn't.

Drummer smirks. "Lefty's got his uses." He nods over to the bar at the older man, who's looking back at us, grinning widely. "Need to know who I'm dealing with. Got Token from San Diego to put out some feelers. Young lad, but he knows his shit. Apparently, there are no warrants out for your arrest, and your employment history stacks up. Far as I can tell, you're no fed plant." His steel eyes darken. "Just warning you, if I'm wrong on the latter and you are, they'll never find your body."

His tone makes a shiver run down my spine. "No need to worry, Drummer. No fuckin' way am I joining your club." Angrily, I pick up my beer and swallow half of it down.

Ignoring me, he simply continues, "We work hard, party hard. Live and ride free. We don't give a damn about citizen rules, but that doesn't mean to say we set out to break them without good reason. I'm trying to turn this club around, not just this chapter, but Satan's Devils wherever they are. You want to be a part of this, I'll give you this one chance." He breaks off. Not once have his piercing eyes shifted from my face. "I think you're a man that we want, and that we've got something to offer in return. There's only one way to find out. You come on board as a prospect and prove your damn fuckin' self. You'll help Blade and Tongue in the shop, get that business off the ground. We'll give you accommodation—there's a spare suite next to Wraith's, and a wage enough to live on." He pauses as if to give me time to let that sink in. "Ask yourself what you have to lose, man, and then give me your answer."

"You're asking me to prospect?"

He nods his head.

"For twelve months."

"Maybe more, won't be less unless you don't live up to your promise, or you decide you don't like the club."

"You know nothing about me." My brow, by now, is creased.

He grins, picks up his own beer and takes a swig. "Don't I? See, I spoke to a man named Manny. Ring any bells? He gave me glowing references. You're dependable, smart, and a darn good mechanic. You, according to him, are destined for better things in life."

I'm sure he was thinking of me managing my own shop, not prospecting for a motorcycle club.

"Doesn't seem much of a career progression," I toss back.

"Doesn't it?" Drummer sits forward. "You'd be surprised,

Red. See, in the Satan's Devils, a man can pretty much go as far as he wants, and what he's got the aptitude for." He drains the bottle, and the moment he puts it down, Wraith comes over and offers him a new one. He declines, demanding a whisky instead. Then his attention comes back to me. "Manny had a lot to say, Red, and pretty much summed up what I can see with my own eyes. You got potential. I'm wondering just how far you'll go in this MC. After you've done your prospecting time, of course."

I've no home. No job. No family. The woman I could have seen myself with had turned me down. What have I got to lose? Drummer seems to think I might have something to gain, but quite frankly, for now, a roof over my head and money in my pocket would go a long way.

"I can walk away at any time?"

Drummer's mouth quirks as though he knows he's reeling me in. "If you want to, you wouldn't be right for us, and we'd never give you a patch."

I finish my beer, place the bottle on the tabletop, then sigh. Wondering what I'm letting myself in for, I tell him, "Okay, I'm in."

"Somehow I don't think that's a decision you're going to regret, Red." His reassurance is strangely comforting until he adds, "And if you want a fresh drink, you better go get it yourself. And while you're there, hurry Wraith up with my fuckin' whisky."

And, as I quickly find out, he's not the only one who needs a drink. There's no doubt they're already testing me when I get orders shouted from all directions.

Standing behind the bar, I'm already beginning to wonder if I'm going to regret my hasty decision. Especially as I'm asked to mix up a *Sex on the Beach*, only to discover, when I do find someone who knows the ingredients, that yeah, there's vodka but no fucking Peach Schnapps and certainly no cranberry juice. I grit my teeth and take the ribbing good-naturedly.

CHAPTER ELEVEN

S *ix months later*

"Fuck! How many did the brothers get through last night?" Wraith directs the net toward yet another condom in the swimming pool, while I kneel with a water testing kit, making sure, despite the amount of semen probably floating around in it, the water won't actually kill anyone.

A feminine snort comes from beside me. "Quite a few as I remember." Pussy, lazing on a sun lounger, stretches lazily with a grin the size of a Cheshire cat's on her face. "Just a shame you boys can't get any action."

"Won't be much longer," Wraith growls, and promises, "Then you'll know what a real man feels like."

Pussy snorts. "Hope you can live up to that boast, little boy."

I shake my head at them. I'd been horrified at first to discover the club kept a couple of women just for the brothers' use. But once I'd seen both Selina and Pussy were one hundred percent up for it, never complaining when they serviced multiple men in one night, and often, more than one together, I'd revised my opinion. The girls love sex, the more of it the better. And for their services, they live comfortably in the now finished house at the top of the compound, with pocket money provided for any expenses.

But Wraith and I being prospects, the girls are off-limits to us.

I have to admit, I've not got Wraith's confidence. These girls must be experts on fucking by now, how can he assert he can satisfy them more than the others? I suppose it's here my lack of experience lets me down, but as I remember, I hadn't heard Cheryl complaining.

Though my exposure to what goes on in the open in the clubroom makes me have doubts. Some of the positions the brothers have the girls in, I hadn't imagined were possible.

Much as I'd like to experiment, I haven't had a chance. As the club girls aren't available to us, I could only get my dick wet if I went into Tucson on the prowl. Doing a full-time job as a mechanic, then performing my club duties, meant I had very little time off. Even if I'd had the inclination to seek out a woman for a one-night stand, doing what I do for the club, I could offer no other commitment.

The always present odour of sex in the clubroom from the live porn shows doesn't make abstinence easy. I often think it's just one more trial set up for prospects. Letting our dicks shrivel for lack of use from anything other than our hands being just one more way to prove our loyalty to the club.

Wraith's fucking lucky. He's done nine months. Not too long before he'll be up for his patch, and I suspect he's a shoo-in. They'd be crazy not to want a good man like him in their ranks. Me? Well, I've got a bit longer before I'm considered, but I'm hopeful. I'm doing my hardest not to fuck this up.

Any regrets I thought I'd had about becoming a prospect hadn't lasted long. My room is comfortable, homey now I've put my own stamp on it. As a mechanic, I'm respected, already treated not so much as an employee, but an equal partner. Blade, Tongue, Beef, and I pick the jobs we want to work on depending on our abilities. None of us shirk the hard stuff either or leave it for anyone else. Manny was a good boss, but I was always conscious of working for him. Now, I quickly discovered, being part of the club meant I was working for myself. It serves as a good boot up the ass when you know what you put in will be coming back to you.

I've come to respect the men here and like all of them, even though most yank my chain whenever they get the chance. There's only one man I know little about, a man called Digger. He's ancient and appears from time to time, and then only to prop up the bar, until he can't stand anymore and summons a prospect to drive him home. According to Wraith, the excuse Digger's bike always breaks down on Friday's isn't even offered or sought anymore. Drummer knows the old guy is no longer capable of riding, but to admit it out loud would lose him his patch.

Blade? Well, he doesn't scare me anymore. There's a darkness inside him, that's for certain, but no different from a number of the men. Having seen how the club pulls together, I can see how he fits in. The brothers are like pieces of a puzzle going together. Peg looks out for the good of the club, and Blade is ready to enforce the rules when anyone steps out of line. Drummer and Lefty are the glue that pulls us together. Beef and Rock, both steady, are prepared to give their all to the club. Rock has done so already, in Bastard's time, having done time for a crime he didn't commit to keep another brother on the outside. Dollar counts the money. Viper and Bullet, with the rest of us helping where we can, are slowly making something of the compound. Tongue? Well, he's the joker, the man always ready to make you smile even at the worst of times.

Tongue's also popular with the sweet butts and the hangarounds who come up for the regular weekend parties. It seems that stud in his tongue can work wonders. I'd never realised how much oral goes on, that sex involved more than fingers and a dick. Maybe I should have. I've watched enough porn, but thought they'd just been acting, and people were far more circumspect in everyday life. Seeing the girls' appreciation of Tongue's talents makes me wonder what Cheryl would have tasted like. I regret I've never tried it, and vow to rectify that at the earliest chance.

"Think that's the lot of them," Wraith shouts, eyeing the growing piles of used condoms with disgust. "But who's getting that?"

Pussy is convulsing with laughter. "That's what I was wondering. Why do you think I'm here, boys?"

That is a beer bottle lying on the bottom. Wraith's trying to scoop it up with the net, but it just keeps rolling away from him.

Shooting Pussy a look which speaks volumes, I strip off my clothes, right down to my boxers, and dive in.

When I surface, trophy in hand, shaking my hair making water drops fly from it, it's to her slow hand clap.

"Hmm, I like what I'm seeing there."

She stares at my groin, teasing her nipples with her hands while doing so. Predictably, my underworked cock perks up. It's hard to hide a hard-on with sopping wet underpants clinging to every contour.

"Want to take a moment to deal with that?" Wraith's chuckling and pointing.

"Shut it," I growl, picking up my clothes. The hot sun will dry me quickly, and hopefully my other problem will recede just as fast once Pussy stops playing with herself and taunting me.

If the dip hasn't cooled my ardour, it's been refreshing for everywhere else. I'd wanted to come somewhere warmer, and Tucson is hot. Too hot at times for a northern boy, but I'm slowly getting used to it.

Putting the net and other equipment away, Wraith comes over. "Prez wanted us to check the perimeter."

Of course, he did. Cleaning the pool in one-hundred-and-ten-degree temperature isn't an unpleasant task, but walking around the whole of the compound with the sun beating down? Yeah, that's not what I signed up for.

Brushing the last few droplets of water off my legs, I pull my jeans and boots back on, then put on my t-shirt.

"Here!" Pussy might be a working girl, but she looks out for us in other ways too.

Gratefully, I reach up my hand to catch the bottle of sunscreen she's just thrown over to me and slather it all over my face and bare arms. Another drawback of my colouring, I easily burn.

"Want some?" I offer the lotion to the man who's fast become my best friend.

Wraith glances up, shielding his hand from the blazing sun and nods. He's Tucson born and bred, and far more used to the climate, but on hot days like this and the make work task Drummer has come up with, even he needs to take care.

"You smell like a couple of pussies," Pussy gets in, doubling over as she laughs.

"Rather that than looking like a lobster." Wraith goes to hand her the bottle back, and adds, "Thanks, babe."

"You're welcome," she answers, staring appreciatively at his male form.

Yeah, these girls are here to work, but another thing that made that easier for me to accept is that they're treated respectfully. Everyone has their place in the Satan's Devils MC. Even whores.

There's a definite hierarchy. Officers, then members, then prospects and finally sweet butts. It's harder to decide where Sandy and Carmen, Viper and Bullet's old ladies should be placed. Above the sweet butts, definitely. Although they can't order prospects around, heaven help us if Wraith or I upset them. Still, it's no hardship being polite to them. If it wasn't for them organising the kitchen, if left to me and Wraith to cook, we'd all starve or get food poisoning.

When Wraith and I set off to walk the boundary, checking for non-existent breaks in the fencing, I can't stop my eyes examining my surroundings. It never gets old—the welcoming coolness of the Coronado Forest stretching up into the mountains, the desert extending around, littered with saguaro and other cacti.

"Hey." Wraith pulls at my arm, pulling me to a halt.

There, just beyond our boundary, is a family of javelinas. Nasty brutes if you get up close, but good to see from a distance. We watch for a moment as the mother and piglets snuffle around then wander off.

The heat might be a little more than I wanted, but this spot? I wouldn't swap it for the world. It's fast become home, and I've got a chance to make it that forever. As long as I don't fuck up and do what I need to get my patch.

We walk the boundary, reporting back there's nothing out of order. Lefty comes up with another job, getting us to ride down to the strip club, Satan's Angels, to pick up his lighter he left there. What a way to spend a Sunday. But a ride out with my friend never hurts, and I know better than to do anything other than plant a smile on my face and look enthusiastic. It's all these little ways of testing us. If we protest, suggest he borrow a light from someone else until he gets back there himself, it suggests we won't obey orders when it comes to important shit. I may not have gotten the point when I'd first arrived, but I sure do now.

A man's got to prove he's got his brother's back, even in little things that don't much matter.

"Hey, you hear about that hangaround, Jeff something?"

"Jeff Andrews?" I ask, pushing my safety glasses up my nose and pulling on my gloves. I've gone without wearing a helmet for months now. It might not be safe, but sure is one thing less to worry about. I straddle my seat. "What about him?"

"He's going to be voted on as becoming a prospect."

"Is there a vacancy?" I ask, raising an eyebrow.

Wraith smirks. "I'm kinda hoping there will be."

"He's a good man," I tell him. "I got to talking to him a week or so back. Got a background in explosives. Useful if we ever want to blow shit up."

Wraith raises his chin and we set off, me opening the gates, and then closing and locking them behind us.

When we arrive at Satan's Angels, we park around the back. The building is empty, but Wraith's got the keys. It's not the first time I've been here during non-working hours, and it amuses me how under the harsh lights, the place looks nowhere near as magical as it does when the girls are dancing on the stage.

It's one of the club's major money earners, but hadn't always been that way. Back in Bastard's day, the members saw the strippers as an extension of their sweet butts, club pussy they could use anytime with the result the dancers were only those who were desperate for money. Drummer cleaned that shit up. Members are now one hundred percent hands off, and the girls trust us to protect them. While, for most, it was never their childhood dream to end up earning their living taking their clothes off, the fact that they get good money and are protected means the dancers we attract are top notch. Our earnings have gone up as a result.

"Where the fuck do you think he left it?" Wraith's completing his third circuit of the main room.

"It's not in the office or the heads." I take my phone out of my pocket and stare at it. Then, taking a breath, place the call.

"Lefty, we've looked… Right?" I swear under my breath and send a fierce glare in Wraith's direction. "Oh, that's good then. We'll be right back." Ending my call, I answer Wraith's unspoken question. "Fucker had it on him all the time."

Wraith snorts. It's par for the course. No point getting worked up.

CHAPTER TWELVE

Three months later

Wraith's beaming like the cat that's gotten the cream, and I don't blame him. I stand, leaning on the bar, pleased as fuck for my friend as he gets back slaps all around. I envy him for getting his patch, but fully expect my time will come.

I even keep a smile on my face as he approaches and demands with a huge smirk, "Beer, Prospect."

I bump the fist he's holding out. "Coming right up, sir."

The new prospect, a good-looking bald-headed man who's picked up the name Slick, after having unfortunately had an encounter with oil on the road resulting in dropping his bike on his first ride out with the club, nods at me as he reaches past to get Drummer's favourite whisky from the top shelf. Wraith's patching-in party is going to be a busy night.

Beer in hand, Wraith turns and surveys the room. As he does, the new sweet butt, Raquel, who'd come to one of our parties a month back then stayed on, approaches him with a practised smile on her face. When she's close enough, she slides her hands under his cut and pouts those overpainted lips.

"Want to have some fun?"

I expect he does, but her fake tits would put me off. I prefer them real myself. There's something about her I don't like, but pussy's pussy, I suppose, and anything is welcome after you've been wandering in a desert for months.

Slick nudges my arm as he sees the pair walk off. "She's a bitch," he tells me, quietly. "Pussy's already talking about getting her chucked out. She's getting above herself. Proper patch chaser there."

"She won't get that from Wraith." In the moment's lull, I lean on the bar, watching the new member walk off with the sweet butt toward the crash rooms.

"Nah, but she'll try. They think all newly made-up members are fair game. Did you see Carmen slap her yesterday?"

"No?" I turn with my eyebrow raised at that tidbit of gossip.

"Yeah, she was coming on to Bullet, wouldn't take no for an answer. Carmen had to shut that shit down fast."

Bullet and Carmen are tight as thieves. I've never seen him unfaithful to her, and as a prospect, I've seen quite a lot. Viper, for instance, swears he isn't unfaithful to his wife, or not as he sees it as he never shares his cock, but he's not averse to getting blow jobs from the club girls. Whether Sandy's aware of his proclivities, I don't know. No one here would tell her.

I stay sober, it's expected. I might have a couple of beers, but that's my lot. I get my amusement watching the action going on around me.

Peg, a man who rarely, if ever, takes advantage of the sweet butts, walks over to me. I have a beer at the ready, but he shakes his head, holding up the one he's only half drunk.

"You and Slick ready to give us some entertainment tomorrow night?"

Drummer likes his men to be fit. Not only are we encouraged to train regularly, and under Peg's instruction I've certainly muscled up, there are regular spar nights in the gym. Prospects aren't allowed to be matched against members, so up to now, I've been limited to fighting Wraith. At the beginning, he'd had a definite advantage, but over the months I'd started to level things up.

"I'm up for that. I'd like to see what he's made of." I half-turn the other prospect's way.

"I'll pulverise you," Slick murmurs into my ear, having overheard.

"In your fuckin' dreams," I retort.

Having got fed up with bruised ribs and black eyes, I'd taken benefit of Peg's pointers and Wraith's willingness to let me use him as a punching bag, and now keep my skills topped off. I'm confident in my new skills and enjoy using them.

It's not as if we actually want to kill each other, I muse as Peg, now more comfortable with his prosthesis, walks off. A busted nose or broken rib is about the worst of it, and that's only a lesson to be sharper the next time.

Knowing we all have the ability to protect each other's backs, understanding the weakness and strengths of the men you ride with, is what this brotherhood is about, and why I so much want to be a part of it.

A sudden scream, a loud slap, and a screech of protest pulls me out of my reverie. As my eyes search the disturbance out, I see Wraith looking bemused, with Pussy standing over Raquel who's lying on the floor.

"Bitch fight!" Tongue yells out. "Oh yeah."

Slick raises his eyebrow at me as he catches my eye in a *told you so* kind of way. Yeah, there does seem to be trouble in the club girl's version of paradise.

But as prospects, we're then overrun with orders for drinks. To our disappointment, neither of us see the outcome, and we lose any interest in finding out what it was all about.

The next day, Slick and I work side by side in the auto-shop, each helping the other out when necessary. When evening comes, our personalities undergo a change and we're ready to beat the hell out of each other. As we march back into the club-house, our camaraderie put on the back burner for now, I'm amused to see Raquel sporting a black eye, but as I'm not talking to Slick, I don't bother pointing it out.

Peg does the honours, calling us into the ring and announcing the bout, warning the brothers to stay back if they don't want to get splattered with blood. He's beefing it up, trying to scare the shit out of us, but Slick catches my eye and I don't miss his wink.

If it's a show the club wants, a show is what they're going to get. We come together, at first just circling, bluffing, trying to get the measure of each other. Then my first punch kicks the shit off. As it turns out, we're evenly matched. In the Satan's Devils version of MMA, when time is called, we've each picked up a few bruises, but nothing to write home about. I'm declared winner on points, which I think is right, and Slick's magnanimous handshake suggests he's not too disappointed.

But he does point his fingers at my eyes then his. "Next time," he warns.

"Bring it on," I respond, dancing on my heels and throwing a few practise punches.

"Good job, Prospects." Drummer walks up. I swear both Slick and I stand taller. "Got a run tomorrow. Want you in on it, Red. Slick, you stay here on the compound."

He's gifted with two sharp nods. We've got our orders and will obey them. Me? I'm over the moon that while no doubt I'll be kept out of the action, for the first time since I put on my cut, I'm going to be involved in club business. This is no pleasure run, I've heard brothers talking, though they've kept the details to themselves.

As a prospect, I know fuck all about the workings of the club, other than what I've been told or what I pick up from standing behind the bar. Tending bar has been quite an education. By watching and listening and examining body language, my knowledge has expanded. Now with an extra personal interest, when Drummer, Lefty, Peg and Blade get into a huddle, from their expressions and gesticulations, I gather whatever we'll be heading into the next day is serious.

Slick, also proving himself not slow on the uptake, shoots me a look of envy, to which I respond with a raise of my chin.

I've heard the brothers discussing the Hell's Damnation MC, a rival club who I'd have had to be both blind and deaf not to have gathered aren't friendly toward others. When Beef and Rock had come in hot last week, it was hard to miss the name that was sworn about in several quarters. And a few days later, when a truck tried to run Dollar and Bullet off the road, blame was assigned to the same MC. Although I've been told shit, I'm certain the Devils are planning retaliation, and I'd put good money down that that's where we'll be heading.

Bring it on. Mess with my club, mess with me. Yeah, my thoughts on the Devils have done a one-eighty.

Despite my misgivings when I first met the Satan's Devils, I no longer regard them as violent criminals. Instead, I know this lifestyle is worth protecting, and if others hit us, then we need to hit them back. This compound alone is the envy of many, and having enjoyed its facilities and amenities, I wouldn't be giving it up without a fight. The same goes for our businesses and property.

The thought that I might be called on to take up arms for my club no longer worries but excites me. Society might think the lengths we'll go to protect what we own is criminal; however I no longer feel that way myself. We're just a subset of society and deserve to keep what we've got.

I go to bed determined to make a good show of myself. Whatever Drummer calls on me to do, I'll perform to the best of my ability.

Early the next morning, the brothers, their numbers now swelled by Wraith, are huddled behind closed doors in the meeting that they call church. I, like any grunt for centuries over, just wait for my orders, and for now go to the shop and get on with my work.

"They're expecting there could be trouble here tonight," Slick confides in me as soon as he sees me. "Blade told me I'll be on guard duty."

"Know who's staying with you?" One man can't defend the compound on his own, so someone or someones are bound to be left with him.

"Not yet." Slick doesn't seem overly concerned. "Know what you're going to be doing?"

I start shaking my head but am interrupted.

"Red? Lefty wants you." Blade's hanging off the doorframe that leads to the shop's office.

"Guess I'm about to find out." I wink at Slick, slip off my overalls, wash what oil I can off my hands, and then head up to the clubhouse.

"In my office." Drummer waves in that direction as I appear.

Giving him a chin lift, I notice Raquel and Selina are peering on interested, and hence respect the need for privacy. As a bartender, I've observed those girls don't seem to limit their curiosity to the brothers' sexual preferences.

Entering the office, I find Lefty standing, but he gestures me to a seat. He remains upright and folds his arms over his chest.

As I sit, he starts, "Red. How long you been with us now?"

He knows without asking, but I answer anyway.

"Nine months."

He gives a slow nod. "Hmm. Seeing that patch just over the horizon, are you?"

Trick question? "I'm doing all I can to get it, VP."

There's a pause, then his hand comes down on my shoulder. "And it shows, Prospect. It shows." He takes a step toward the desk that's in front of me, opening a map and anchoring it with a cup and a paperweight. "There's a club called the Hell's Damnation who are based here." He points to a particular spot. "They've been causing some trouble for us. Fucked up a few of our runs."

I know that the Devils run guns over the border to Mexico.

It's a lucrative business. While as a citizen I'd have been uneasy with it, I've settled my head on the matter by accepting if it wasn't us, someone else would do it. Putting a weapon in someone's hands doesn't make anyone else responsible for what they do with it.

"They took a delivery that was meant for us," Lefty continues. "Today, we're going to get it back. Want you along, Red. You'll drive the crash truck, and park up here," he taps a particular point, "and watch over the bikes. You got that?"

I've got that. Although I might want to be part of the front line, I'm also conscious of the trust he's showing me by letting me into this much of his plan. That patch seems more likely.

My response comes from the heart. "I won't let you down, VP. When do we go?"

"Tonight. We'll approach under the cover of darkness."

He talks to me for a bit, making sure I understand what I'm doing and that I'm not going to fuck things up, and does so without sharing too many details.

I return to work. Slick doesn't ask questions. Then I go to my room and change and prepare myself for the evening. I'm excited as fuck and feeling ten feet tall when I enter the clubroom.

The first thing I notice is that the sweet butts are missing, banished to their house at the top of the compound, I expect. The second is that also absent are the two old ladies, Carmen and Sandy. Usually at this time of day, the women are in the kitchen working their magic, but today they must be at their homes off compound. Slick's in their place, trying hard to make edible sandwiches.

The atmosphere is different—no music is playing, and there's less talking. Men are more serious than usual, and weapons are being cleaned and prepared, and occupying spaces on the tables where drinks would normally appear.

I help Slick out for a bit, then go back to my normal place.

But bar duties are slight— the odd beer is requested, but in the main, alcohol in large quantities is being avoided.

In a particularly long lull, Slick, now back beside me, thumps my back. "You be careful out there, man," he tells me quietly.

My sense that this is a serious situation grows and along with the excitement at being included, I also feel apprehensive. *If I want to join the club, I'll be expected to give my life for it.* There's a chance I won't be coming back.

This is the turning point, the time I throw in with the Devils.

If I die for the club, so be it. Somehow, over the past nine months, these men, their way of life, has become important to me. Looking around, I assess the men once again, seeing how close they are and knowing I'd give anything to be part of this family, even if I have to give my life for it.

It's now I realise while I might still have a prospect's patch on my back, already I'm a Satan's Devil at heart. That I've a real chance at it is solidified as Lefty's trusted me with the knowledge that tonight there will be a hit on the Hell's Damnation compound.

It's close to midnight when Drummer gives the signal we're heading out. Raising my chin at Slick, I follow the brothers, noticing Peg, Beef and Wraith give back slaps and receive them, but stay in the clubroom. Guess I now know who's going to be with Slick protecting the compound.

"You got a gun?" Lefty's hand shoots out to stop me as I go past him.

I open my cut and show him I indeed have, in a shoulder holster. I might never have handled a gun before arriving on the compound, but Peg's got me up to speed, and I pride myself on being a good shot. Not that I've ever shot at a human target before, but if it's them or us, I think I can handle it.

"Good man," the VP mumbles, before doing a final check on everyone else.

I head to the crash truck, just as I'd been instructed. I wait until the bikes pull away, then follow them out of the compound.

My last sight in my rearview is of Slick sliding the gates closed behind us.

I don't envy him staying safe at home, no, I feel privileged to be going along tonight. Even if it's only to guard the bikes and transport home injured or captured.

Not having been given the route details, I carefully follow the bikes ahead, my hand occasionally patting the gun in my cut. It feels so alien, so different from everything I knew before. The Red Manny knew would have been horrified to see me.

I'm surprised at myself. I'm ready for violence, ready to defend my brothers. Over the past nine months, all the morals I thought I had have become turned upside down and resorted. What use would cops be if they were called in when a brother was run off the road? No fucking use at all. In our dog-eat-dog world we have to get justice for ourselves.

Prospecting has shown me this outlaw life is worth living. If no one fucked with us, we wouldn't fuck with them. Hell's Damnation brought trouble to us. We didn't go asking for it. If we don't retaliate and hit them back hard, they'll just go on picking away at us.

The old Red would have looked away in horror.

I may not have joined the Army as I had planned, may not have served my country, but hell, the Satan's Devils stand for all that I am. Individual freedom and a lifestyle worth dying for.

The bikes pull over to the side. Drummer gathers the brothers around him. When I hang back not sure of my place, Blade takes my elbow and pushes me forward.

"How the fuck will you know what to do when the time comes if you don't bother to listen to instructions?" he hisses, and I think it's a little unfairly. But sensibly, I keep that thought to myself.

Listening, I hear them plot how they're going to surround the compound, approaching on foot rather than loud exhausts announcing their arrival. That it will include traversing some rough ground explains why they left the sergeant-at-arms out of it. Peg's coming on in leaps and bounds since he got his new prothesis, but stealthily walking long distances is probably not where his strength currently lies.

My duties are simple. Stay with the truck, watch no one tampers with the bikes, and keep my phone at hand. I'll only be called on to come closer if I'm needed to pick up any injured, or if they've taken a captive.

Once the plans are finalised, the brothers waste no time heading off. Although I regret not being in the forefront of the action with them, I know being their backup is an equally important job, so I go back to the truck, position myself behind it, and light up a cigarette, shielding the light and glowing tip just in case anyone's around to see it. Unlikely, as we've parked well off the road, but my new skills have been drummed into me.

They've given themselves thirty minutes to get to the Hell's Damnation compound. The brothers have been gone for less than half that time when sounds reach me. Easing out from behind the truck and walking to where I can see down the road, still staying hidden so no one can see me, I spy three trucks heading my way. It's hard to tell from the first two, but the second has men crammed into the open back, leading me to suspect the other two are also packed.

Fuck. I make the obvious assumption.

I take out my phone and dial a number. "Lefty? Yeah, I've seen three trucks come past. Think they might have come from the Hell's Damnation compound."

He quietly laughs. "Love your fuckin' enthusiasm, but no, Red, they can't be the Damnation. They haven't a clue we're coming. We've eyes on the compound, and no one has left it. Lights are all blazing inside. They're having a fuckin' party." He chuckles in anticipation of the way their celebration will be ending.

I stare at my phone. I should be reassured, but something in my gut is niggling at me. But Lefty says things are alright, and he knows better than me. "Okay. Yeah. Just thought I'd mention it. Shiny side up, Brother."

"Not going to criticise you for keeping your eyes open, Prospect," Lefty says magnanimously, then ends the call.

I try to settle but the uneasy feeling inside me doesn't abate. I've heard my VP, *but...* I stab at a few more digits and call up a different number. A guy can't lose his chance at a patch just by being cautious, can he?

"Peg? Yeah, it's Red. Look, Lefty's certain this is nothing to worry about, but I've seen three truckloads of men heading past me. Bit of a push, but it makes me wonder whether the Hell's Damnation could have gotten wind of our attack and are thinking to catch us with our pants down."

Peg's quiet for a moment, then says, "Good thinking, Red. Even if it's nothing to do with them, I'd rather be prepared. If Lefty asks, I've got the compound covered."

Like Lefty's going to ask a prospect anything at all, but I feel better having made my call. If I've raised an alarm for no reason, then no harm done, maybe suffer some jokes at my expense. But I'd rather be thought overzealous than risk my home and the people I've come to love, only to have them come under an unexpected attack.

CHAPTER THIRTEEN

Having done all I can, I settle back to wait. A second cigarette is smoked down to the butt before I hear gunfire. *It's starting.*

But the brief burst is soon over, and long before I expect. I know Blade's an expert with a knife, and had hoped to get up close and personal with some wet work, but surely the resident bikers would have put up more of a fight?

My phone rings while I'm still thinking what to make of it.

"Get the fuck down here now, Prospect," Lefty shouts.

My immediate response is to jump into the truck, start, then gun the engine. It's a mile on foot or as the crow flies, two by road. I cover that distance in only a couple of minutes, making the rear of the truck swing out and spit gravel as I slam on the brakes.

Gun in hand, I leap out, ready to bolster the ranks should that be needed.

But instead of a fight going on, brothers are running out of the Damnation's clubhouse and heading for the truck. So many pile on all seats are filled, as is the cargo hold. Rock and Beef end up hanging onto the open doors as Lefty shouts at me to get moving and head back to the bikes.

Glancing in my rearview, I see flames flickering around the building they'd just vacated. Driving slower than I had on the way down, if only to not dislodge Beef and Rock, I still reach the bikes in good time. As I'm starting to brake, I hear an explosion, but it seems I'm the only one not expecting it.

Without a word to me, all the men flood out as soon as the truck slows without waiting for me to stop completely. One by one, they race for their bikes, then head off into the night forgetting about formation, just in a hurry to get where they're going.

"Follow us!" is Drummer's only terse instruction my way.

The swift end to the fight, the desperation to get back to the bikes can surely only mean one thing.

Fuck, I was right. They're attacking the compound.

Putting pedal to the metal, I haul my ass out of there fast.

The truck's no slouch, but even I can't keep up with the bikes who are able to easily pass slow-moving traffic. Not that there's a lot at this time of night, but an irritatingly slow eighteen-wheeler gets right into my path.

The others have got a good few minutes start by the time I turn into the track leading up to the Satan's Devils' compound. As I draw close, smoke and flames fill the air, as well as the sound of gunfire.

I do an emergency stop when I come upon the bikes parked haphazardly halfway up the track and make a quick assessment. By the orange glow I see, the gates are still locked tight, and the fire is one of the old outbuildings burning on this side of the fence. By its light, I see the Hell's Damnation crew are pinned between those inside who are doing a fucking amazing defensive job from what I can see, and those freshly arrived. Two of their Damnation's getaway trucks are lying on their side, seeming to have been blown up in some kind of explosion.

A lull in the bullets and Drummer's voice booms out, "You're surrounded. You've got no fuckin' chance. Give yourselves up."

"Go to hell," comes back, along with a hail of bullets sent in Drummer's direction.

"Put this on, kid." Lefty hands me a Kevlar vest he's dug out of the back of the truck. "Can you swing out to the sides, take out any stragglers that try to get past you?"

"Dead or immobilised?"

"The latter if possible, but the former if it's a choice between you and them. Just don't fuckin' shoot anyone with a Satan's Devils cut on."

I would bristle at the suggestion, but I know I've not been tested yet. Unlike many of the brothers, I don't have military training. All I've had has been the likes of Peg and Blade teaching me to shoot and their tips on how not to get shot. Hoping I'm a quick learner and won't freeze the first time a gun's pointed at me, I sidle around the truck, and using the scrub and bushes, try to get closer to the action.

Huh. A man comes straight for me, running as fast as he can, his weapon held loosely in his hand as he tries to get away from the fray. All I need to do is stick out my leg and he goes right over, knocking his head on a rock and splitting it open. Confident he's out, I kick away his gun, then use the zip ties that Blade had told me to always carry on me, and have his hands and feet trussed. Then, picking up his weapon as an extra might come in handy, I crouch and move forward again.

Their last remaining truck having been surrounded, it seems our attackers have decided to flee rather than take more punishment or surrender. It's immediately clear the truck I drove has become their target. I grin as I pat the keys in my pocket and vow to stop them reaching it. As another decides to make a break for it, this time, I make my move with less finesse involving swinging the acquisitioned rifle at his head rather than relying on nature to help me. In the end, I take three of them down while being hidden, all without wasting a single bullet.

By this time the rapid exchanges of gunshots have died down, and the firing is now just sporadic.

Seeing no more of the Hell's Damnation heading my way, I

move closer, leaving my three zip tied captives behind. I've become overconfident and forgotten I have no six.

The first warning I have of there being someone behind me is the bullet hitting my back. I fall forward, agony blasting through me, gasping for breath, thinking for a moment I'm dead until I remember it hit the Kevlar. But fuck me, that hurt, and it got me right in the kidneys. Suspecting I might be pissing blood for days, I play dead.

They might not have had my back, but at the sound of the shot, they're all there for me. A gun fires followed by the sound of a body falling, and the man who tried to take my life drops to the ground only a short distance from me.

The ensuing silence is eerie, populated only by the cries of night owls, and the odd sound of somebody moaning. I'm still alive. That the Devils have won, and the battle is over is confirmed when I hear Drummer yelling, "Prospect?"

Damn it. I get to my knees, then my feet. Agony floods through me, making me want to vomit and fall back to the ground, but I remind myself I'm bruised not dying and start to stagger toward the prez when a heavy hand on my shoulder stops me.

"Slick's with Drummer. You fuckin' take it easy."

I turn at Blade's voice, to see, for once, he's grinning at me, and not evilly. "Thank you," I tell him, earnestly, my words needing to be aided by a few shallow breaths in between. My back feels like it's on fire, but I try to show no weakness as I take account of my surroundings. There are bodies on the ground, some still moving, some clearly not breathing. "Three more back there that I took down," I tell Blade, jerking my head in that direction.

In the light from the flames, I see him grinning at me. "Come on. We're heading on up to the clubhouse. Seems you've got a pass on cleanup."

"I can help," I insist, trying to straighten.

"Not tonight, son." Lefty appears out of the darkness. "Wounded warriors get a pass."

"Did we lose anyone?" I ask, anxiously.

Lefty looks at me strangely, a look I can't interpret, then exchanges a glance with Blade who shrugs. "Nah," he eventually replies, shaking his head. His mouth opens as if he's going to say more, but then thinks better of it.

Thank fuck, I think to myself, ignoring his strange reaction.

Blade helps me until we reach the gates. When I tell him I'm fine, he gives me an assessing look, then leaves me to slowly head on up under my own steam to the clubhouse. On the way, Wraith joins me, a hand clasped to his arm.

"You okay?" Blood is dripping from his injury.

"Yeah, fucker just winged me." He doesn't look too happy about it, but seems more put out than hurt.

Hearing more footsteps behind me, I turn to see Rock bare chested with his t-shirt held to his head, and Beef cursing beside him, limping. Considering the number of the Damnation who were down, the Devils seem to have gotten away fairly lightly.

I enter the clubroom. My one wish is to collapse on the nearest flat surface, but I force myself to ignore the pain and head for the bar. I haven't my normal speed, but I set out beers on the bar top just the same. Having done that, I lean against the counter heavily. My back's throbbing and on fire with pain.

Some of the uninjured, followed by Drummer, enter soon after. Prez's gaze falls on me, then he frowns, his steel eyes going hard. *Fuck, what have I done wrong?* Despite my back aching, I try to stand straighter, ready to do whatever is asked of me.

Drummer shakes his head, then his attention turns to the injured and bleeding. "Doc's on his way."

"I'm fine," Rock tells him dismissively. "Just saw stars for a moment." But each time he takes that t-shirt away, blood streams from his head.

"Beef?" Drummer enquires.

Beef holds out his leg and grimaces as he rotates his ankle. "Sprained I think, not broken."

Wraith, knowing he'll be facing an inquisition next, pulls his hand away from his arm which is still obviously bleeding. "Just a scratch, Prez. But I might need a stitch or two."

Gritting my teeth, I load up a tray, and carry five bottles of beer over.

"What the fuck, Prospect?" Drummer rounds on me. "Get your ass seated, Red. Doc may want to look at you."

"I'm fine, Drum. And the men will want drinks. You want your whisky?" I'm proud how strong I make my voice sound.

"If I do, I'll get it my fuckin' self. I'm not helpless. Sit your fuckin' ass down!"

If I sit, I doubt I'll be getting up again, but with his sharp eyes on me, I place the tray on the table, and allow my ass to settle on the nearest seat. As I sit with a drawn-out shuddering breath, I muse this portion of the clubhouse is like a hospital waiting room.

There's the sound of a motorcycle arriving outside the clubhouse, and in walks a man I've not seen before. He's wearing leather, but no cut, and has a military hairstyle.

"Doc." Drummer approaches and shakes his hand. He waves back at the three members. "Fix them up first, I need them in church. Leave the prospect 'til last as he's making out there's nothing wrong with him."

True, I did imply that. I feel my lips curve.

Having issued his instructions, Drummer starts to walk past, glaring at me as he passes. "You want that patch, brother? Then you stay there on your ass."

I think I'd need help getting back on my feet, so I'm quite inclined to obey. Who am I to argue with the president?

Doc seems to know what he's doing, though as he tends to the other men, he explains to Wraith and me that he's only an ex-Army medic. Still, he seems expert at field dressings and basic first aid. Wraith, indeed, has several, not just a couple, of stitches, and Rock gets some glue. Beef gets his foot bandaged tightly.

As they are being treated, the rest of the men come in. Slick, raising his chin at me when he sees me sitting with the walking wounded, takes position behind the bar. As I suspected, his services are in great demand.

Slowly, the men start to move toward the meeting room. I watch them in envy. Sure, I've been a part of this today, and have got the bruises to show for it, but from hereon in, I'll be told nothing.

I want my patch, I remind myself. I'll be asking no questions. I'll just have to wonder about what went wrong, and what happened at the Hell's Damnation clubhouse.

It's not long before the medic has finished and has left, and the clubroom is empty except for me and Slick.

"Wanna beer?" Slick calls out to me.

"Water." I wave the packet of painkillers Doc has had left with me. "I'll get a beer later."

Slick grabs a bottle and brings it across. As there's no immediate call for his duties, he flops down on the couch opposite the one which I'm sitting on.

"That was some shit," he starts, shaking his head.

"What happened here?" Putting the tablets in my mouth, I wash them back with a huge gulp of water. Fuck knows what I've been given. I'm not allergic to anything, and if it takes the edge off the pain, I'm not going to refuse any medication.

"Peg got a phone call and suddenly started to go ape shit. He sent Wraith and me to the fuckin' armoury." Slick shakes his head, perplexed. "I didn't even know they had one, let alone where it is."

I've learned of it recently; it's hidden beneath one of the filled-in swimming pools. But it's not my place to enlighten him, nor tell him the phone call that got Peg so heated was one that came from myself.

"So, we came back with rifles and grenades. We were loaded

down with all types of interesting shit." Slick's eyes gleam at the memory. "Peg sends me out with some explosive, so I set that and a timer. Soon as the trucks appeared, we disabled two of them with the fucking grenades, and I blew the old barn up, setting light to it. Then, well, the rest's a blur. It was all fighting the enemy."

"Were they all killed?"

"Nah." Again he shakes his head. "About half are dead. The others were taken to the storeroom."

Ah, the storeroom. I might not have witnessed Blade at his work, but I've got no doubts on what goes on there. Only a month or so back, us prospects had been tasked with fixing more soundproofing.

"You okay?" He tilts his bottle toward me.

"Just feel like I got a kick from a mule in my kidneys. I'll be fine. You?"

He shrugs. "Not a fuckin' scratch. But I think I've still to come down from the overload of adrenaline."

"You and me both." I salute my own bottle toward him.

"Hey, Red." Bullet appears in the hallway. "Prez wants you in church."

"Uh-oh." Slick grins at me. "You're in fuckin' trouble."

Shit.

CHAPTER FOURTEEN

The only times I've been in the meeting room before is when the table needed a polish, and cigarette ash swept up. It always amuses me that some joker had put up a sign reading, *When the ash tray is filled, please use the floor.* Unfortunately, some of the members seem to have taken that to heart.

As I enter, I ruefully think I'll be back in here soon to clean up. The air is thick with smoke, and it seems Beef and Dollar are the only ones who haven't lit up. I breathe in the tainted air, letting the second-hand smoke fill my lungs. Nervous as I am, I could do with a smoke myself, but being a prospect, I keep my cigarettes in my pocket.

All heads turn to me as I enter. Drummer's stare is as steely as I've ever seen it. Lefty's wearing his VP's version, not quite as scary, but nerve-racking enough. Wondering which way the wind is blowing, I surreptitiously look toward my friend. Wraith, though, seems like he's trying hard not to meet my eyes.

The others though? Well, they're looking my way scowling and frowning.

How have I fucked up? I called Peg without waiting for permission, but surely that was for the good of the club? *I hadn't waited to help with cleanup, but it had been Blade who had ushered me away.*

Fuck, fuck. Fuck.

Whatever it is, all I can hope is that I haven't blown the prospects of getting my patch. Cast adrift from the Devils? I don't think I could bear it. For a brief moment, my mind wanders. *I want to be a member. I want this chance. I can't think of anything more that I want out of life.*

But somehow, I might not have lived up to their standards.

Fuck, fuck, and a hundred more fucks.

Hovering at the back of the room, standing behind Tongue who's sat at the bottom end of the table, I clasp my shaking hands behind my back, and trying to ignore the pain in my bruised kidney, stand up straight. *I won't fail now.* If I get kicked out, I'll man up and take it.

The room's deathly quiet. All eyes, except for Wraith's, who worryingly still won't look my way, keep staring at me.

I bite back any nervous words that threaten to spill out of my mouth.

Finally, after I'm sure I can't stand much more of this, Drummer crashes his hand down onto the table.

"What the fuck were you thinking?" he bellows.

My brow furrows. *What is he talking about?* I cast my mind back, but I'm certain I'm innocent of any wrongdoing.

"Answer me, Prospect." The prez bangs the table again. If I didn't know, or had seen for myself, that Drummer earned his name by banging every female in sight, I'd have thought his use of his fists against the wood had given him his moniker.

Completely unnerved, words start tumbling out of my mouth. "I'm sorry for anything I've done. Any disrespect," I offer, uncertain what I'm apologising for.

"Too fuckin' right," Peg growls in his gruff low voice. "I should think you are fuckin' sorry."

"Fuckin' prospects," Blade murmurs, spinning his knife on the table. I don't feel any better when it comes to a stop pointing right toward me.

Drummer's eyes darken, and I swear a cold blue light flashes from them, like he's some kind of demon. It makes me want to curl up and beg for forgiveness. "You're a fuckin' prospect. You do what you're fuckin' told. All these months that's been drummed into you, and yet you still have the fuckin' nerve to think for yourself?"

"I apologise for any wrong action I've taken, and for any disrespect." I know I'm repeating myself, but it's hard to keep the shaking out of my voice, let alone speak words which make sense. I've gone from fear of my future to appreciating there might be a threat of a beatdown or death. If I've done something that's fucked up the club, I've no right to be a member. *Could they think I betrayed them? That I was the reason the Hell's Damnation chose this night to attack the compound?*

Hell, I didn't even know that's where we were heading until this afternoon. *More than enough time to place a warning.* Fuck, that must be it. *How can I prove my innocence?*

"Too right you fuckin' apologise." Drummer casts a look to his left. "You disregarded what the VP said."

What? Dragging my mind back from how to defend myself against an accusation of treachery, I have difficulty catching up. *When did I disregard anything Lefty had told me?* Ah, yes, I remember I had. I'd called Peg.

I could argue it had saved the club, but maybe they'd already had a plan in place. Maybe Peg had been ready and was expecting it. Maybe I'd fucked up, and while I thought I'd shown initiative, I'd shown a lack of respect for, and confidence in, the VP.

Will an apology cut it? Might as well try. I'd sell my soul at this point if I thought it would save my future patch. "I apologise, Lefty. I—"

"Shouldn't have called the sergeant-at-arms?" Lefty cuts in and states it bluntly. "Shouldn't have fuckin' tried thinking for yourself?" He shakes his head, but for some reason not at me, but at the brothers sitting around the table. "Too fuckin' right an apology is needed."

I look down at the ground, wishing it would open and swallow me up. I've broken the cardinal rule for a prospect. *Do what you're told and don't question it.*

How can I word an apology that would be accepted? After the long, hard nine months, is this the thing that will have me kicked out of the club? Moisture pricks at the back of my eyes as I realise this might be it. Like my dreams of being a Ranger were brutally destroyed as a result of my dad's accident, likewise my hopes of joining the Satan's Devils ranks look equally set to be flushed down the toilet. And this time, there's no one to blame, but myself.

Lefty takes a deep breath. "As I said, an apology is needed. So, I give it to you, Brothers. I misread the situation, and darn near lost us good members, and possibly our compound."

Rock taps out another cigarette and lights it. "You called it as you saw it, Brother. Up to then, all signs were that the Damnation were all in place. I was fuckin' there. I agreed with you."

Slowly, I raise my face, seeing the attention is on the VP, and not on me now.

Drummer raises his chin. "I was convinced myself." He shoots a look at his VP. "Though some element of caution could have been expected and information received, acted upon."

While I try and interpret what he's saying, Lefty holds up his hands. "Want my VP patch, Prez?"

Fuck. Now my fear isn't for myself. *The VP's holding up his hands to a crime so serious it threatens his VP status?* I try to appear disinterested while rapidly trying to work out what's going on and why the attention has been removed from myself.

Drummer picks up the gavel and bangs it. "Let's bring it to a vote. Lefty to lose his VP spot. Aye or nay."

"I'm abstaining," Lefty states as the prez looks to him first, then stares down at his hands on the table, as if not wanting to look.

"Nay," Dollar says to his right.

"Nay," Beef agrees.

"Nay," Viper states.

"I was convinced we'd gotten them pinned down." Bullet shakes his head and then adds, "Nay."

One by one, the brothers give their votes. Not knowing how this works, I'm not sure if it has to be unanimous, or whether a majority vote counts. When the whole table's spoken, it's clearly up to Drummer to cast the final vote.

Before he does, he raises his head and his steely eyes have me firmly in his sights. "What say you, Brother?"

Brother? "I, er… I don't have voting rights," I remind him.

Drummer frowns, the expression he's perfected would send an icy chill through anyone's veins and has that effect on mine. Then he thumps his hand, yet again, on the table. "Well I'll be fucked. Guess we've forgotten something. VP?"

Lefty, presumably reassured his position is secure, reaches under his seat and picks something up. He slides whatever it is down the table. My eyes widen as I catch sight of what Beef, Bullet and finally Tongue, pass along, finally pushing them in my direction.

My hands fucking shake as I reach down and pick the patches up. The Satan's Devils full colours.

Tears prick in my eyes, and I wipe the back of my hand across them unsurprised when it comes up wet. Trembling, I gaze at them in disbelief and then raise my head, wanting to say something to the assembled men, but have been rendered speechless.

"Get the brother a fuckin' chair before he falls down," Drummer snarls.

I'm only vaguely aware of the door opening and closing, of Tongue moving his seat along, and of Wraith placing a new chair beside him. It's only when Wraith puts his hands on my shoulders and applies pressure that I eventually sit down.

"But I've got another three months," I say, completely bewildered as I take my place.

Drummer, my *prez*, snorts loudly. "If it wasn't for your observation and quick thinking, *Brother*, there might not be a fuckin' club to give you those months. Welcome aboard, Red."

As though a switch has been thrown, fists hit the table, feet stamp, and cries ring out. "Ride Satan's Devils. Satan's Devils Ride together."

They'd been stringing me along. Wryly, I grin. "You fuckin' assholes." I speak my first memorable words as a full member. "I thought you were going to throw me out."

"Fuckin' love this," Peg roars, chortling.

"Couldn't make it easy on you," Rock agrees.

"You fuckin' knew." I turn to Wraith, knowing why he couldn't meet my eyes when I'd first entered. "Motherfucker. You fuckin' knew."

Wraith slaps my back, a gesture that makes me exclaim in pain, "I got the same treatment, Brother. You weren't singled out."

They're all assholes, I realise, unable to stop grinning despite the grumbling pain in my kidney that Wraith had re-awoken. *But they're my assholes. My brothers. My family.*

Choked, I finally raise my eyes to Drummer whose mouth is curved in an unfamiliar smile. "I won't let you down."

"Fuckin' right you won't." Then Drummer's smile fades. "Back to business. Back to the vote. What say you, Brother?"

He's asking me whether Lefty should lose his place. "Nay," I respond without hesitation.

Prez, *my prez*, slowly nods. "Vote carried. You'll be at my right hand a while longer, VP."

No one seems particularly surprised at the outcome, but Lefty grimaces, and raises his chin toward me as if acknowledging the little I did saved his ass.

Drummer raps on the table again and his whole face darkens. "What we've got to work out is how the fuck they knew we were coming for them."

"Someone betrayed us," Rock states.

"Slick's the newest arrival," Dollar observes.

Peg snorts. "Slick was responsible for blowing up the barn. He threw one of the grenades into the trucks. Saw him take out a couple of the Damnation crew. If he was part of them, he was going a funny way about showing it."

Blade points his knife toward me. "Red took out three himself. Impressive as fuck."

I feel my all-too-pale face redden. *Fuck my complexion, it always gives me away.* But him bringing attention on me gives me an opening. "Slick's solid. He'll make a good brother when he's done his time. He's no fuckin' plant."

Drummer's glance lands one by one on the men sitting around the table. "I trust each and every one of you. If it wasn't the prospect, who the fuck could have known of our plans?"

Not knowing the protocol, I raise my hand. At Drummer's raise of his chin, I let him into what I was thinking. "Working behind the bar I got to learn a lot. Like that the Hell's Damnation have been instigating the recent problems." When several faces turn toward me, I continue, "See, I gathered all that from listening. I didn't need to come into church to hear it. The Hell's Damnation have been needling us, trying to get us to respond. They'd have known we wouldn't have let it ride or go on too long. They've been waiting for us to make a move on them."

"Which is what we're all fuckin' thinking, Red," Lefty all but snaps.

"Just gathering my thoughts, Brother." *Fuck but it's good to call him that.* "They've either been watching the compound, or they've got a plant." There's only one person who's always around the club and who I don't trust. I drop her in it. "Could that plant be the new sweet butt?"

There's an intake of breath. "Raquel?" Rock's mouth drops open. "Sweet butts don't get to know anything that's going on with the club."

"She wouldn't need to know much, just how to make a phone call when she saw we were all headed out. Hell, just being confined to her residence would have been indication enough if she was on the lookout for it."

"Oh fuck." Tongue's head drops into his hands.

Drummer lurches forward. "What the fuck, Tongue? You been loose-lipped around her?"

Without raising his head, Tongue just looks up through his long eyelashes. "Bitch stopped me when I passed her going up to the house, moaning at why she was sent away and saying she wanted to suck my cock. I told her she'd have to wait until we all came back."

I take pity on him. "She needn't have been told anything, Tongue, other than what all the sweet butts knew, that they were banned from the clubhouse for the evening. It was pretty obvious something was going to go down."

"Fuck it, we've been played." Drummer still glares at Tongue even though I gave him an out. "When are we going to get someone who can properly vet hangarounds? Who vouched for the bitch?"

The table is quiet. It's Lefty who dares open his mouth. "She seemed straight, Drummer. Said the right things, was annoying enough we all assumed she just wanted a patch."

"She wanted a fuckin' property patch alright," Peg snarls. "Just not one of ours."

"She still on the compound?" I ask, casually.

Drummer, the only man who's allowed to bring a phone into church, gets out his device. He hits a pre-programmed number. "Pussy? Raquel there?" His eyes widen. "Did she? Nah, it's alright, sweetheart. I don't want anyone else." Ending the call, his eyes meet ours. "She had an emergency. She took off a few hours ago."

<hr>

CHAPTER FIFTEEN

<hr>

Rock gets up and kicks his chair. Beef runs his hands through his hair. Again, fists hit wood, but this time in anger.

This is one coincidence too many. It's clear where the leak had come from. *Fucking bitch.* I'm just glad that as a prospect I hadn't fucked her lying ass.

Prez bangs the gavel. "Meeting over. Time to find out if Red's right, and we did indeed let a snake into our camp. Let's get up to the storage room and get that, and other questions answered."

It's on the tip of my tongue to ask whether I'm invited, but those patches I'm still clutching in my hand tell me I automatically am. *I'm a full fucking member.* It's going to take me more than a minute to get used to that.

"Brother?" Wraith stops by my chair, laying his hand on my shoulder. "You coming?"

"You bet." I stand, slowly, admittedly. "Just getting my head around the idea of this patch."

"You did fuckin' good, Brother." Wraith squeezes his fingers. "We'd have been sitting ducks without your phone call."

"Just did what anyone would, Brother."

"No," a voice growls. Once he's got my attention, Drummer,

who's also hung back, continues, "Takes a good head to put two and two together. You made the call, Brother, despite your VP telling you it wasn't no matter. You're the type of man that's the future of this club. And, that we've still got one, is quite possibly down to you."

A patch and a compliment? Can this day get any better?

My pit stop on the way to the storage room morphed my pleasure from getting my patch into anger. What man likes seeing pink-tinged urine coming out of his dick? It's the fuckers we had contained in the storage room who were responsible for it and I, for one, was seeking vengeance.

It was my first time seeing how the Satan's Devils treated their enemies. Blade, as I already know, has a darkness within him, a yearning for doling out pain and retribution. His methods of making the captured Hell's Damnation members talk were like nothing I'd witnessed before. Effective, I'll give him that, even though it made my stomach turn over.

Watching him at work was a revelation. The Hell's Damnation didn't put up much resistance and held little back.

Along with my brothers, I learned they were a small club, their numbers roughly the same as the previously decimated Satan's Devils' mother chapter and were new to the area. They were lazy fuckers though. Instead of building their businesses from the ground, full of impudence, they thought they could take us out and take over.

Their prez and VP were young, with no military experience, nor anything much more than the ability to ride a bike. Instead of respecting the brotherhood, they were out for all they could get from it. If you wanted to join the Damned, you didn't need to prospect for the club, just show a willingness to kill and maim for it. They were fucking amateurs compared to us.

Encouraged by Blade's knife skills, they didn't hold back. Raquel? Well, she was the VP's sister. Once he'd lost one eye and his other was under threat, the VP gave an address for her.

I stood stoic alongside my brothers when the three rank-and-file survivors were given bullets to the head. I stood my ground as the VP and prez pissed themselves in fear. I watched on, swallowing down vomit as their Hell's Damnation tattoos were burned off, then the two screaming, begging for mercy fuckups of officers were put down like the animals they were.

Instead of disgust, all I could think of was that no one should do this to *my* club. No one tries to take something from the Devils and gets away with it. They signed their own death sentences when they admitted that no Devil, woman, or man, would have been left alive on the compound.

Instead of them cleansing Devils from this town, there were no remaining Hell's Damnation members left to deal with.

As it should be, I think with satisfaction, heading at last for my suite, and my all-too-welcome bed.

Would Manny have recognised me? Would my dad? *Would Cheryl?* For once, I'm glad she hadn't come with me. She wasn't cut out for this life. It's a dog-eat-dog world, and while civilians might not understand, I'm more than happy to be part of it.

My bruised back got me out of having to help dispose of the bodies. Wraith, too, had a pass because of his injured arm. I do, however, become aware of what use the club puts the forest behind the compound to. It's a burial ground for our enemies.

As for the one person we hadn't yet dealt with, the betrayer who swallowed secrets as readily as cum, Peg and Blade set out to pay her a visit. When they returned, it was with the news that the ex-sweet butt wouldn't be troubling us anymore. She'd met with an unfortunate accident.

The day after we'd taken the Hell's Damnation down is a strange one for me. Instead of running around, being at everyone's beck and call, I'm allowed to sit on the couch, my only task sewing the new patches on my cut. A task I do with much pleasure. Slick, looking on obviously envious, but with a grin on his face, can't do enough for me. A needle? Thread? Anything I ask for magically appears.

"Hey." Wraith flops down next to me. "There's your patch-in party later."

"Yeah?" Usually that comes after the vote in church, but last night we were all somewhat distracted.

He nudges me. "You know what that means, don't you?"

"We get drunk?" I wince as I prick my finger and hold it away from the patch not wanting to get blood on it.

He snorts. "Pussy!"

"What about her?" I'm sucking my finger, hoping the bleeding will stop.

"No, not *Pussy*." He laughs. "Pussy." As he spread his arms out wide, I catch up with him at last.

"Oh yeah." I try a lecherous wink, but it doesn't quite work.

He narrows his eyes at me. "You don't sound overeager. After nine months of using your hand, thought you'd be all up for it. You haven't got a woman in town, have you?"

Truth be told, I've not been near a woman since Cheryl. Damn woman is still on my mind. It has to be lack of opportunity that I've stayed faithful to her. How can you carry a torch for a woman you're never going to see again? My one attempt at a casual relationship had failed at the first hurdle. *I'd fallen for her.* Fuck the woman for still, after all these months, being on my mind. Getting laid might be a good way to forget about her.

Multi-tasking and my finger finally stopping bleeding, I sew the last few stitches, admire my cut, then ease myself forward to slip it over my shoulders. A sense of fulfilment comes over me.

Wraith's still waiting for my answer. Going with a sweet butt? I frown. They can, and do, have any man here. A fact I point out to Wraith.

"So, they know what they're doing." He wiggles his eyebrows. "Take Pussy." He chuckles. "There's not a lot you could do that would surprise her." I doubt it myself. I'm not the most inventive lover. "Hey, get a few drinks inside you, Brother. You won't care how many other fuckers have had her. Or Selina, now her cunt's tight as fuck. And as for head?" He leans back and adjusts himself. "She's like a fuckin' hoover. You'll see stars, Brother."

Men start to flood in. More than one has mud on their boots which gives me a clue as to what they've been doing, and I now suspect our enemies are safely six feet under. When Peg enters, he heads to the bar and going behind it, stops whatever's been playing and puts his choice of music on. A collective groan goes up, but I just grin. I can listen to Bob Seger anytime. It reminds me of my dad and his eclectic taste in music.

When he's sorted out the songs, Peg grabs a bottle of Jack and a few shot glasses and brings them over to where Wraith and I are sitting. Placing them on the table, he slaps his hand down on my shoulder. His jolt makes me lean forward.

Peg whistles softly. "That patch looks fuckin' good on you, Brother."

Wraith sets out the three shot glasses and pours the spirit out. "To Red." He lifts his drink. "May he always stay shiny side up."

"And dirty side down." Peg adds his salutation, raising his glass in a similar manner to Wraith.

"Hey, what's it like to be a fuckin' hero?" Rock grins as he joins us and meets my eye.

Damning my skin once again for making my flush obvious, I shrug. "I just did what anyone would have done."

Beef appears from behind. "Nah, not at all. You had an inkling and ran with it. Others might have ignored it. Hey, Prospect?" He turns, beckoning at the bar. "Another bottle here, pronto. And more glasses."

Fuck but this feels good. I'm not drunk—yet—but am pleasantly buzzed. I feel part of something, knowing I've earned my place in this club. I begin to feel like a king seated on my throne as one by one, every brother comes up to offer congratulations. Soon it seems every member, including the prez and VP, have shared a glass with me.

When the others have faded away, I'm left with Wraith. I smile a dopey grin at him. "Fuckin' love you, Brother."

He snorts. "Love you back." His eyes narrow. "Hey, 'bout time we got you initiated." He nods toward Pussy who's standing at the bar.

A flood of self-doubt comes over me. "Nah, not tonight."

"What?" Incredulous wide eyes turn to me. "You gay?"

My mouthful of Jack splutters out of my mouth. "No, I'm fuckin' not."

He eyes me carefully, then shakes his head. "Don't understand you, Brother. First thing I did when I got the chance was get my dick wet."

It's the drink talking, I surmise as I surprise myself with the next words I utter. I lean in so I can speak in little more than a whisper, "I'm fuckin' embarrassed, okay?"

Eyes narrowing in confusion, Wraith chuckles quietly. "You've got a small dick? Hell, we can't all be well endowed." He palms an impressive bulge in his jeans. "And it's not what you've got, it's what you can do with it. Or that's what I'm told."

"It's not what I've got," I hiss. "There won't be any complaints about that. It's more the other part."

Wraith's wrinkles deepen. "You don't know what to do with it? You a fuckin' virgin, man?"

"Keep your fuckin' voice down," I snarl, looking around to make sure no one's overheard. "Look, I've got experience, just not too much of it. I haven't disappointed a woman before, but the sweet butts?" Breaking off, I eye Pussy who's openly fondling Rock's dick. "I think they expect a greater repertoire than what I've got to offer."

Wraith's eyes go wide, then he gives a broad grin. He gets up and goes toward the bar. I expect him to get a drink, but instead he whispers in Pussy's ear, and pulls her away from Rock. Rock growls, but then shrugs good-naturedly, and wanders off to Beef who's got his arm around Selina.

"Hey, Red," Pussy greets me, leaning down and putting her arms around me. "Wraith suggested you wanted some company."

"I'm okay." I try to shrug her off, but she's not letting go of me. "My back's hurting and—"

"No need to worry, I can do all the work, lover." Her husky voice right in my ears sends a tingling through me with a direct link to my cock.

Wraith shoots out his hand, wraps it around my arm and pulls me up. "Come on, let's use a crash room."

My brain tries to process. Is he setting me up with Pussy, or himself? But stumbling a little from the alcohol I've consumed, I just go along. When we get to the crash room that only yesterday I'd restocked with condoms as part of my prospecting duties, Pussy opens the door, and Wraith drags me in.

As soon as he closes the door behind him, he whips off his shirt.

Hold up a minute. My inebriated self leans up against the wall. In my experience, sex is a one-woman one-man game, unless it's porn of course. I have no desire to see another man's dick, or heaven forbid, accidentally touch it.

"Er, I'll leave you alone—"

"Don't be so hasty, lover." Pussy's right in front of me, her hand slipping up under my shirt. "Wraith asked me to make sure you enjoyed yourself."

"Seems like the room's a bit crowded."

"Not to me." She accompanies her words with a wink. "Looks like I'm going to be one lucky girl tonight."

"So…" Shirtless, Wraith flops down on the king-size bed, linking his hands behind his head. "You do your thing, Red, and I'll give you pointers."

"Oh, I'll let him know if he's doing that shit right," Pussy purrs.

What? No. There's no way I can perform with an audience, and that's in addition to the nerves I have already.

"I'll leave you to your fun—"

But Pussy's relentless. She's rubbing against me, and despite myself, my cock hardens again. Her hands push up my t-shirt, and when my chest is bared, she licks at my nipples, her talented tongue moving in swirls, making my pecs quiver and nerves in my body alight.

"Can I help you with this, lover?" She gently pushes at the sides of my cut.

Ignoring Wraith's smirk, I take off the precious leather, and lay it down on a chair, then, my decision probably influenced by the alcohol I've consumed, I remove my shirt. Over the last nine months under Peg's stern eye, I've muscled up, something Pussy seems to appreciate as she rubs her cheek against the ginger hair that peppers my pecs. Then she turns her head and starts to lick instead.

____

CHAPTER SIXTEEN

____

I've never been with such a forward woman who knows what she wants and sets out to get it. Strangely, my nervousness about how I'm going to measure up begins to dissipate, as I get the feeling she won't allow me to disappoint her.

She sinks slowly to her knees, reaching her hands to my belt. As she starts to undo the buckle, I remember my manners. "Let me take care of you first."

Glancing up, she winks. "Well, that's not an offer I'm going to turn down."

Using my belt to balance herself, her fingers brushing against my dick, she pulls herself up, steps back and commences to do a strip tease. Not that she's got much to remove, but she shimmies her hips as she eases her shorts down. As she's dispensed with panties, her bare waxed mound is quickly revealed.

Her tank top follows fast, allowing her generous tits to bounce down. I all but forget Wraith is in the same room as I push her back to the bed and encourage her to lie on it.

Falling to her side, I inch my fingers down her skin, confident that all women like to be fingered.

But just before I reach her clit, Wraith helpfully chooses that moment to speak up. "Pussy prefers your tongue, brother."

I startle at the reminder he's there. *What's he talking about? Does she want to be kissed?* I open my mouth to tell him he can get lost along with his unhelpful comments when he gets in first.

"Women always do," he continues. "Don't you like the taste of pussy?" When he raises himself up on his elbow and catches the expression on my face, he barks a laugh. "Christ, you don't know, do you? Brother, you do not know what you've been missing. Of course, if she's already had a man bare, you won't want to taste fuckin' cum." His mouth twists in distaste. "But everyone here uses condoms."

"Ain't going to be no taste of rubber tonight, honey," Pussy lazily smiles at Wraith. "I've been saving myself for our newly patched member."

Embarrassed, knowing only from porn how this should go, but not wanting to admit as much to Wraith, awkwardly I ease myself down the bed while trying to pretend I know exactly what I'm doing. Pussy, with no such discomfiture, bends her knees and lets her legs flop open, and I get the first three-dimensional image of a bare pussy, immediately knowing the ones on the pages of magazines don't compare.

I start to salivate in anticipation.

She's wet and glistening. Gingerly I lower my mouth and get my first taste of a woman. She's a combination of salty and sweet, and my cock throbs in interest.

"Feels good, Red," she encourages.

Tentatively, I lick her slit, relishing her copious juices, then I slide my tongue up to her clit and hit the jackpot when she jerks. Immediately, I mimic what I'd be doing with my fingers, trying to make her come. She responds, her body writhing, her fingers clutching at the sheets.

"Hey, man. Slow down. It's a marathon not a sprint."

Raising my head, I growl to show Wraith's commentary isn't welcome. As soon as I get her off, I can get my cock inside her and relieve the growing pressure in my balls.

Wraith's undeterred. "Use your fingers, put them inside her."

I do it as much to shut him up as anything else. Keeping my tongue playing with her clit, I put one, then two fingers inside her, pushing them in and out, mimicking what I'd far rather be doing with my dick.

"Found her G-spot yet?"

What the fuck? That's a myth, isn't it? But Wraith seems to think it is not, as he starts to issue instructions for finding a certain place inside her, describing that it should feel spongy when I've got the right spot.

"Oh fuck!" Pussy's head falls back signalling I might actually have found it. Well, fancy that. I didn't think it existed. "Red, oh, Red…"

I suck on her clit and press with my fingers. God, it's like a rocket going off. Pussy bucks, her muscles go tight, her head presses into the pillow and she seems to stop breathing. Wondering whether she's acting, I've never seen a woman come that hard.

When her chest again starts heaving, getting oxygen into her lungs, she clasps at me with her hands. "Red, that was amazing." She seems totally genuine. Then she turns to Wraith with a grin. "Thank you for your help."

He bends and places his lips to her forehead. "Red should think of me as his own personal GPS."

For some reason, I'm outright laughing. Seems like I needed that assistance.

"Now, are you two boys going to get your pants off and get down to business?" Pussy, now propped on her elbows, raises an eyebrow.

"I like your thinking, darlin'." Wraith wastes no time rolling off his side of the bed. Oblivious to my presence, he kicks off his boots, shrugs out of his boxers and pants, and in just his naked glory, turns and gets a condom out of the drawer in the table beside the bed.

"Er, I'll be off then."

"What the fuck?" Wraith asks. "Nah, you're part of this,

Brother. Think of it as your initiation."

"Oh, for fuck's sake, Red. Lose the clothes," Pussy demands, licking her lips. "I can't wait to see what you're packing."

Shaking my head, acknowledging I wouldn't be doing this sober, hoping the drink will make me forget by morning else I'll never be able to look Wraith in the face again, I, less smoothly than he, slide my legs off the bed but keep my ass firmly on it. Bending, I undo my boots, then raise my ass an inch, and divest myself of underwear and jeans. Then I cover my junk with my hands.

"Bottom or top?" Wraith asks, then corrects himself. "Fuck, you're new at this. You take her pussy, I'll take her ass."

Is he saying what I'm thinking? Or have I suddenly forgotten how to interpret English? My face must have gone blank, as Wraith barks another laugh.

Dubiously, I look at Pussy.

Reading my expression as a question, she responds, "I get two for the price of one. Mmm mmm." Then she turns to Wraith. "Think he needs GPS guidance again."

Snorting, Wraith doesn't seem the least disconcerted when he chucks me a condom than waves his hand at the bed. "You lie on your back. She rides you. I ride her ass. That enough directions?" He smirks.

Well, the first part's not much different from what I've done before. Still covering my man parts, I ease myself into position to lie down on my back, wince, and shift my weight off the bruise.

Pussy takes hold of my hands and lifts them, revealing my eager cock underneath. At least one part of me isn't at all perturbed with the proceedings. "Ooh, big fella. I'm going to feel you, aren't I?" She leans down and takes my dick into her mouth, so fast and unexpected it makes me gasp and my eyes squeeze shut.

I hear a light slap and Wraith instructing, "Come on, Pussy, you know what I want."

Cracking my eyes open, I see her pout like her favourite

lollypop has been stolen, but she edges herself forward and up. Expertly, she covers my cock with a condom, then lines me up and lowers herself. She's so wet, all it takes is a couple of thrusts and I'm inside her.

She squeezes her Kegels or something, making me gasp. "Fuck, you feel good."

"She'll feel even tighter in a moment." Wraith pushes her down onto my chest. For a moment, I'm distracted by her boobs pushing into my skin and my hands automatically hold her to me. Then I notice he's holding a tube of lube, and I feel Pussy quiver as he starts applying it copiously presumably to her ass, then clearly has no shame at all when my eyes are drawn to watch him lubricating his dick. Quickly, I look away again.

He leans over her, one hand balancing himself, one guiding his cock home. Unashamed, I again watch, fascinated as he lightly slaps her ass, demanding that she push back.

Fuck. I can feel him. My eyes widen as my cock seems to have to fight for space, but hell, what a feeling. My manhood isn't threatened. I'm surrounded by everything woman, but another cock inside her at the same time, makes this intense.

He pushes in, and automatically, I pull out, then I return to my previous position. It's almost automatic how we get into a rhythm, our cocks alternating in filling her.

The room's full of the scent of sex and sweat, the sounds of men grunting and Pussy's gasps of encouragement.

In, out, in, out. My thrusting becomes more urgent, and Wraith also speeds up.

"You there yet, Pussy?"

"Close," she breathes out.

"Finger her, Red." Wraith's back to giving instructions. "Get her off." There's urgency in his voice as if he's struggling with himself.

When I do, with some slight hesitancy as I don't want to touch his cock, Pussy tenses. It doesn't take long before her body goes taut.

"Fuck, man. You there?"

I'm about to blow. All I can do is utter a harsh, "Yes."

Pussy screams and convulses, the movement setting me off. Wraith shoves his dick in as far as he can go as cum squirts out of my cock.

It's been the most intense experience of my life. Best sex ever. I laugh at myself. Never thought I'd say that when a man was involved. *But I don't need to give up my straight card, all my cock and hands touched were her.*

With a groan, Wraith pulls himself up from where he's collapsed over her body, turns his body sideways, and slips off the condom, tying it carefully. He throws it at the bin in the corner. As a prospect, it was my job to clean them up. I'd rather be on this end.

Pussy, chest heaving, starts to sit up. She gives me a brilliant smile. "That was great, Red." She turns and grins her gratitude at Wraith, then carefully raises herself off my body.

My hand's there, holding the condom to me. Then I copy his actions, tie it off, and miss the bin when I throw it. Yeah, as a prospect, I'd found that a lot.

Wraith stretches, arms held high over his head, and yawns widely. He seems in no hurry to get himself dressed.

Pussy, though, she's already pulling on her shorts, followed quickly by her top. "Hmm, thanks, boys. Now, I wonder what Beef and Rock are doing?"

With a kiss blown our way, she's out of the door before I can say anything.

Wraith snorts when he sees my expression.

"That was a joke, right? She's not going straight to them from us?"

"Haven't you learned those girls are insatiable?" Wraith reaches for his jeans and chucks me my shirt. As I pull it over my head, he continues, "They want dick. They don't much care who it belongs to."

In my experience, women want to be held in these circumstances, not jump into another man, or men's, bed.

I sit up, grasp my pants from the side of the bed, and slip into them, feeling better now my cock's not swinging in the wind. "Just sex, huh?"

Pulling on his boots, Wraith shares some of his wisdom. "Make sure it is, Red. Some whores or hangarounds take anything more, kissing or cuddling, as a sign you're going to weaken. If you give in, you'll have a woman wearing your property patch before you know it. Pussy knows the score and won't try anything. But you get a girl who wants romance or intimacy, take it from me, run a mile."

It's like going with a prostitute. I frown, then reconsider. What happened just now was nothing like that. It wasn't a man paying to get off. There was definite mutual benefit, or more geared toward Pussy, she was the one to have two orgasms.

"Oh, and while I'm sharing shit. Those condoms, Brother. Always wear them. Even if a girl says she's on the pill, never trust her. Last thing you want is a paternity suit. Don't think there wouldn't be a girl out to trick you. Now you're wearing that patch, they'll be running after you."

"Of fuckin' course, Brother."

Though as I assure him in a tone that suggests I don't need advice, my mind goes back nine months. *I hadn't worn a condom with Cheryl.* I hadn't broached the subject and she hadn't asked me to. I assumed she was protected.

But what if she wasn't?

My brows knit together. Not much I can do now. But from hereon in, I'll take Wraith's words to heart.

"Don't know about you, Brother, but I need a fuckin' drink." Wraith slides his cut on and passes me mine.

I give him no argument. A drink sounds fucking good right now.

Another few shots of Jack later, and my fears the relationship with Wraith would now be different are long behind me as it's immediately back to where it was all along.

As it turned out, it certainly wasn't the last time we shared a girl, or girls, together. Wraith, while younger, hadn't spent seven years celibate, looking after a disabled parent. No, he was out getting an education I'd clearly missed out on.

It becomes my life's mission to take advantage of all that he'd learned.

CHAPTER SEVENTEEN

Being a full member was everything and more than I'd expected. I'd seen the camaraderie and brotherhood from the outside looking in, but it was so much more from the inside. The patch on my back makes me more than just a member of this club, it makes me family, and that includes with brothers from all the other chapters.

I work, play, drink and fuck beside these brothers. Sometimes I think on what led me to here, my journey to leave my past and make a fresh start. Never in my wildest dreams had I imagined I'd end up in Tucson and a patched member of an outlaw MC.

A year has passed since Wraith and I were patched in, and we're still firm friends. We still share a club girl or one of the hangarounds who come to the club from time to time, but nowadays, I certainly don't need any pointers. I could fill my bed most nights of the week with a girl who's heard of my reputation. You could say I've been making up for lost time.

Yet however many women I have in my bed, only one remains memorable.

Sometimes I look back at my short time with Cheryl, realising how naïve I'd been then. *Would she have stayed if I'd delivered more than bland vanilla sex?* It might not have changed the outcome, but it might have made her want to stay with me longer.

When she invades my head, I tell myself it was all for the best. Whether Cheryl would have fitted into this life, there's no way of knowing. But if she'd come with me, prospecting would have been ten times harder, and I might have failed. I may not have seen it that way at the time, but her going home had done me a favour. I certainly wouldn't have gained my sexual prowess, and in time, either for her or for me, our sex life would have become dull.

So what if I still dream of her some nights? Dream of doing to that perfect body the things I've learned since we've parted. I might have been twenty-five at the time, but in sexual experience, I'd been little more than an awkward teenager. Now I'm all man. If I knew then what I know now, I could have had her screaming instead of softly crying out my name.

I haven't forgotten her. She's a memory I take out and dust off from time to time. The problem is, I've met no one like her. There's often a niggle at the back of my mind which says I'd made a huge mistake in not making her mine, of not taking her home and not giving her more time.

My introspection comes to an end when the seat next to me bounces as Wraith flops down and wipes a hand over his sweaty brow.

"Hot out there?" I grin at him.

"You know it, Brother."

A rumble of thunder sounds, making me add, "At least you got back in time."

Tucson's summer monsoons aren't for pussies. I've learned to keep wet-weather clothing in my saddlebags as the storms seem to spring up from nowhere and aren't conducive to riding bikes. If it's not the sandstorm that blinds you, it's the floods from the washes that only a fool would attempt to drive through. Many's the time I've had to wait out a storm, stuck on the road unable to get anywhere.

Taking out my pack of cigarettes, I offer him one. When he takes it, we both light up.

"What time is the Vegas crew getting here?" he asks, drawing smoke into his lungs. His eyes close as though to better appreciate the nicotine hit.

As lightening lights up the clubhouse, I glance up then back down, and wryly offer, "A little later than expected, I suggest."

He gives a booming laugh. "Too fuckin' right, Brother. You know what Brick wants?"

"Not a fuckin' clue. Just a sit-down with Drummer is all I've heard." Brick is the prez of the Satan's Devils chapter in Nevada. He's riding in later today with Rainman, his VP.

It's not unusual for the mother chapter to have other clubs visiting, but normally we have a heads-up as to why and have already discussed our response around the table. On this occasion, if Drummer knows, he's keeping the cards close to his chest.

"Whatever it is, it won't affect us, Brother," I tell Wraith confidently, flicking ash into the ash tray.

"Fuckin' weather." Slick announces his entrance by flinging the clubroom door open so hard the frame shudders, and he comes in shaking rain off his shoulders while running a hand over the drops of water dripping from his bald head. "Hey, Prospect? Get me a fuckin' beer and a towel."

"Coming right up!" Dale, our latest prospect, a clever guy who seems to have a good head on his shoulders, jumps to comply.

Slick sits down beside Wraith, dripping water all over him.

"Asshole," Wraith remarks, shifting along. Then he eyes the prospect as the required items are delivered to Slick. "He was a good find," he remarks quietly as Dale walks off, and Slick polishes his head with the towel.

He's not wrong there. Dale's got the right attitude and I suspect he'll go far in this club. At first, I suspected he was far too soft. He wears his emotions on his sleeve, but he's proven he's got the backbone needed, and isn't not slow to stand up for himself.

"Whatcha gossiping about?" Slick starts drying his arms and hands.

"We're wondering about the reason for Brick's visit," I tell him.

Slick pauses, holding the towel to his face, his eyes peering at us over the top. "You don't know? He's recruiting."

Wraith and I glance at each other. "What?" we both ask at once. "And you know this how?" I narrow my eyes.

Slick gives his easy grin and looks not at all contrite. "Blade was on the phone to Drummer. I might have overheard him."

"Well, I'm going fuckin' nowhere. Vegas isn't for me." Wraith leans back, kicking out his long legs. "Too full of fuckin' tourists following their get-rich-quick dreams."

"Too noisy," Slick agrees.

"Yeah, I don't much fancy the place, too full of suckers." My mind goes back to the days when my only goal was to get somewhere warmer, and how I'd decided not to give Las Vegas a try. My reasons haven't changed. I love Arizona and will be quite content to stay here until I die.

"Who do you think would go?" Wraith creases his brow.

"Who do we want to get rid of?" I chuckle in response.

"Dart?" Slick suggests, mentioning our newly patched in member. "Last in, first out?"

"I like the fucker," I protest. In truth, I don't want anyone to leave. I've gotten too used to calling them brother.

This time it's Wraith who gets out the cigarettes and offers them around. Both Slick and I take one. After we've all inhaled smoke into our lungs, Slick lets out a slow whistle.

"Who the fuck's that with Pussy?"

Of course, Wraith and I turn our heads so fast we almost get whiplash. In the time that I've been here, two sweet butts have gone. Raquel, of course, and Selena, who'd decided she was never getting a property patch and had decided to move on. Jill turned up not long after, but I can immediately see who Slick's talking about. There's a stunning woman who's entering alongside Pussy–big boobs, long legs, hmm. Might be worth giving her a try. The clothes she's wearing suggest she's here for one reason only, to get laid.

Wraith's adjusting himself, Slick too. If I wait too long, I'll have missed my chance. Before they can get their brains into gear, I get to my feet, Wraith belatedly makes a move, and with one hand, I push him violently back down.

"Fucker," he breathes out as his ass meets the couch hard.

But I don't hang around. I'm at the bar in the few steps it takes my long legs to reach it. "Introduce me to your friend, Pussy?" Close up, she's as much a stunner as I'd thought from afar.

Pussy gives a knowing grin. "Red, meet Allie. Allie, Red. Allie's going to be staying with us for a while to see if she might like it here."

"Prez know?" I raise an eyebrow.

"He knows," she confirms.

I turn my attention to Allie. "You know what you signed up for, darlin'?"

She looks me up and down, then says shyly, "I know what I'm letting myself in for. And," her eyes gaze around, landing on Wraith, Slick, then back to myself, "I'm sure it won't be a chore."

"Oh, honey," I respond, smirking. "You'll be in for some hard work." Which will start right now. I start reaching out my hand to take hers when I'm interrupted.

"Red?" My name is all but snarled.

Swinging around, suppressing the annoyed growl that threatens to come from my throat because the voice is that of the prez, I respond, "Yeah?" Hopefully it's a simple enquiry and I can proceed with my plan to put this new sweet butt through her paces.

"Need you in my office now."

"I'll take over." Wraith's sidled up and is beside me with a lecherous grin slitting his face. He starts to reach for Allie.

"You too, Wraith," Prez adds with an amused grin. That man rarely misses anything.

Wraith groans loudly, and slaps Slick who's wasted no time taking his place and, who's annoyingly ended up with the girl. Then, with a grimace toward me which I return, makes his way over to the prez.

Issuing a quick, "Later," to Allie, I follow him over. Drummer precedes us into his office, pointing us to the two chairs in front of the desk while he goes to sit behind it.

Prez makes himself comfortable, then links his hands in front of him. As he seems to be gathering his thoughts, I seethe inwardly about his bad timing. *Now Slick will get the first turn at the new girl.* Jeez, what's so important to drag me away? My dick's still at half-mast just thinking about trying her. She's going to be a success here, I already know, which means fuck knows when I'll get my chance. This time of day, it won't be long before all the brothers return, and they'll be all over her. It was the same with Jill when she first appeared. Poor girl walked bowlegged for a few days.

"Got something to discuss with you boys," Drummer begins at last.

Still hoping the others won't break her or chase her off before I can give Allie a try, I raise an eyebrow and try to focus on what he's going to talk about.

Wraith sinks lower in his chair and folds his arms over his chest. "You got a problem with us?"

Drummer smirks. "Nah. The opposite in fact. You've both been here, what, two years?"

"Thereabouts," I agree.

As Prez nods, he reaches behind him, takes a bottle of his top shelf whisky and three glasses, and places them on the desk. He then pours three shots and pushes two of them over toward us.

I cast a sideways glance at Wraith. This is not what I

expected. Drummer's stingy on who he shares his best whisky with.

After taking a few sips, licking his lips as though relishing the expensive spirit, Drummer places the glass down, gets out a packet of cigarettes, takes one, then slides it over to us. He smokes, like almost all of us, but doesn't often share them around. Who can blame him? Unable to show favouritism, his pack would be emptied in no time. Mind you, unlike Blade, he doesn't pilfer them from anyone else.

The small room soon becomes filled with a haze of blue smoke. *Christ, I'm getting nervous.* Looking again at Wraith, I see him shifting uncomfortably.

Prez is normally a *what you see is what you get* man. If he's annoyed, you soon know it. Conversely, if a member deserves praise, he's equally forthcoming to say a good job's been done. This delay, this buttering us up, is causing me to be anxious.

What the fuck has he called us in here for?

When Drummer stops examining the end of his cigarette, he taps ash off into the ashtray. "I suppose you're wondering what I wanted to talk to you about." As it's a rhetorical question, neither of us answer. "You know, of course, Brick's coming in later."

"With Rainman," I state, confirming I've not been caught napping.

Wraith's more direct. "And they're the reason you wanted to talk to us?" He takes a long drag on his cigarette, blows out smoke, then asks lazily, "And there's a purpose you wanted to talk to us outside of church?"

Singling us out from the other members, he means. That's what interests me. Allie forgotten, my curiosity increases.

Drummer's mouth twists. "You two wandered into the club and found your places here. I couldn't ask for two better members."

"Aw, Prez, you're making me blush." Wraith has to state it while I, of course, simply go red.

Drummer raises an eyebrow at Wraith's interruption, but otherwise ignores it. "For a while, I've been concentrating on building the mother chapter up. Still got a ways to go, but I've been reminded recently that I'm the national prez of the Satan's Devils, and that means I can't be selfish." He pauses, takes a swig from his glass, then carries on, "I can't keep all the best members to myself."

Fuck. I recall Slick mentioning Brick coming here for a recruiting drive. Could this talk be anything to do with that? *Is he going to ship Wraith and I off to Vegas?* I suppose going together wouldn't be too bad, but hell, I'd miss this club. I love all the brothers. I particularly love the location of the compound and its unusual facilities. Wraith's eyes catch mine. He seems equally worried.

Another drag on his cancer stick, then Drummer stubs it out. "Brick's lost three members recently."

"How?" Wraith asks when Drummer comes to a stop.

Prez shakes his head. "Fuckin' gambling. They got in over their heads. Needing money, the stupid assholes tried to fuckin' rob one of the casinos. Got caught, and heat's come down on the club. Brick's been fighting to get the police to accept it was nothing to do with any of the other members. Feds were all over it."

"Jesus," Wraith breathes out. "He succeed?"

"Eventually. But not until after a few good men ended up behind bars. Oh, they all got out, but the club's taken a hit, were searched far too often to be comfortable. It's blown over now but at the loss of three members who quite rightfully have been banged up." I suppress my smile, knowing it's not the crime that will have gotten Drummer rattled, but the unwanted attention they brought on the Satan's Devils. "Morale's rock bottom," he continues. "Brother looking at brother, wondering who will be the next to fuck up. Spending nights in cells and lawyers having to be brought in to defend the club. It was only pure fuckin' luck no one, except for those guilty ones, were stitched up."

"And Vegas has now got the cops looking at them closely."

"You got it, Brother." Drummer raises his chin at me. "We all got out of most of the hard stuff some time back, but we still dabble when there's money in it."

We do. I've been on a few gun running trips myself. But someone's going to be moving those guns across country, why shouldn't it be us? If someone wants a weapon, he'll get it one way or another. We might put it in his hand, but we don't aim or pull the trigger. It's a good money earner.

"Brick needs to clean up the club. Make sure everything's legal." Wraith continues my line of thought.

"Exactly." Drummer nods first at Wraith, then at me, as though we're his star pupils. "Money's coming in short, and ideas on business ventures are coming up lacking."

"Which means there's discontent in the club."

Drummer raises and dips his chin once again.

"And you want us to go there, help them out?" Wraith startles as I sum up what I think Drummer will say next. My brother's expression shows he thinks as little of that as I do, and his body stiffens as though readying for a fight. "Why us, Prez? Why not bring this to the table? We're still new. Why not send someone experienced? Dollar would be good, or Viper or Bullet, they know about setting businesses up, or—"

Wraith interrupts, "Is this because we're still finding our place here? Are we dispensable?" His eyes flare.

"Why not Dart?" I suggest. He's not long been patched in.

Prez raises his hand, stopping our protests and suggestions mid flow. "It ain't nothing to do with the length of time you've worn your patch. And you're only half right. I don't want you both to go, I'm only prepared to lose one of you." He waits a beat for that to sink in, enough time for Wraith and me to exchange worried glances with each other. Then, tugging on his beard, he again takes up the thread. "I've some members I won't see leave this club. Some, I know, would go if asked, but they haven't got the skills Brick's in search of. You two? Well, I've been fuckin' impressed with you both. You're both officer material in the making."

I flop back on my seat. That, there, is some fucking praise from the prez. It's also something I've never considered.

"I'm not saying now," Drummer quickly adds. "For a start, there are no vacancies. But hypothetically, if there was one to come up, I don't doubt either of you would get sufficient votes to take it."

Wraith seems lost for words, as am I, myself. I recover faster. "Well, thanks, Prez, but I don't know what the fuck I've done that's anything more than any other brother."

Having also absorbed the compliment, Wraith backs me up. "Same goes here, Prez."

Drummer's lips curve. "And that, right there, is what makes you so fuckin' good. Red, you came up with some ideas for the strip club, as well as the auto-shop. Didn't seek praise or thanks, but it didn't go unnoticed. Wraith, you've input a lot into the running of this club. You speak one fuck of a lot of sense at the table, and don't get side-tracked by the jokers."

In Wraith's case, he's right. I could see him with an officer patch. But me? "I'm just your run-of-the-mill member," I protest. "I do no more, no less, than anyone else."

"No? I disagree, Brother."

Well, hot damn. What can I say to that? My skin says it for me as again I blush.

It's Wraith's turn to take out his cigarettes. I need one. Hell, I need another few stiff drinks to process Drum's commendation. This time, Prez doesn't join us in lighting up.

"Say you lose one of us." Wraith draws smoke into his lungs, then blows it out. "If we give so much to Tucson, not saying I agree with you on that," he adds fast. "But if that's your thinking, won't it leave the mother chapter short?"

"Initially, yes. But Dale's doing well. He's got a business degree and we'll be able to put that to use. And the hangaround working on his bike with Blade, Tse, the native American, he's got some mean computer skills. There's talent emerging here, Brothers." He pauses and rubs his hand down his cheek. "Won't say we wouldn't miss you, but we can make do. Vegas though..." Again, he pauses. "I don't want to see a chapter wound up."

"That's not where it's heading, is it?" I freeze, holding my cigarette halfway to my mouth.

"Brothers don't like their takings being short each month." Drum states the obvious and shrugs. He leans forward, bringing his two fists down, gently for him, onto the desktop. His action still makes the papers on it jump. "So, like it or not, I've got to lose one of you. Question is, which should I choose?"

CHAPTER EIGHTEEN

I turn to stare at Wraith. He looks at me, and I can see my expression of horror mirrored on his face. Neither of us want to relocate, that's for certain, and being such good friends as we are, neither wants the other to go either.

Lowering my gaze, I look down at my hands. *I don't want to leave Tucson.* After Vermont, it had become my home—more of a home than I've ever had if I'm honest. Sure, prior to my dad getting injured, I'd thought my parents to at least have had an adequate marriage. To me, my mom was okay, making sure I was clothed and fed. My dad, though, he'd been my rock until that fateful accident that had taken them both away. Mom, by choice, Dad, through no fault of his own. Looking after the shell of the man meant I'd grown up fast, and home became somewhere I'd had to be by design not by choice.

It might have been an accident the way I'd landed in Tucson, but I'd stayed because I'd found a family I wanted to be part of. Tongue, Rock, Beef… all of them up to and including Wraith were the friends I'd always have chosen. It was no chore or formality to agree to give my life for theirs when I was voted in as a full member. I belong here.

I know all the brothers in Vegas would have my back, simply

because I wear the same colours as them. But it's not easy knowing I'd have to trust them, without knowing the type of men that they are. And from what Drummer is saying, the club's in a mess. How could I be so arrogant as to think I might be able to help sort it out? Drummer's got the wrong man. Sure, he might not want to lose an officer, but Beef, to my mind, would be a great choice. He could bang heads together if needed.

I'm not saying I'm a slouch in the brawn department—Peg's made certain of that—but I prefer to use my head rather than my muscles, and sometimes that just doesn't work. Some people need to have sense knocked into them.

Wraith's the same, which is partly why we're such friends. He prefers to use reasoning without resorting to fists, or at least, at first.

Maybe that's what Drummer's looking for?

Wraith's head is in his hands as he seems as deep as I am in thought. If I don't volunteer, he will. I know that. I've no doubt our friendship will transcend the miles between us, but what kind of kindred spirit would I be to let him go somewhere he doesn't want to go just so I can stay comfortable?

His base has always been Tucson. For me, it's only been a couple of years. I found my place here, maybe I can do that again with a new bunch of brothers beside me. Is it fair to expect him to move on?

It's not.

Raising my chin, I open my mouth and let out the fateful words, "I'll go."

Problem is, I've said them at exactly the same time Wraith has reached his own, and similar conclusion. We've spoken together.

Drummer snorts. "'Bout what I fuckin' expected." He reaches for the whisky and tops up our glasses again. His eyes actually twinkle. "We ride, live and die together. I thought you'd have each other's backs."

"So let us both go," Wraith states, almost pleadingly.

Being a solution I can get on board with, I nod.

"No can do," Drummer states. "I think you've both got great futures in front of you, and I'm not letting Brick have two of my best."

"What do you want us to do?" Wraith snaps. "Fight it out?"

I smirk toward him. It would be far from the first time we've been matched in the ring. The outcome has always been fairly balanced between us—sometimes he gets a lucky shot in, sometimes I get there first. We always provide the brothers with good entertainment, and money put on us are even bets.

"While that would be fun," Prez starts with a grin, but quickly his face becomes serious, "that's not how I want this to go down. A move like this has to be permanent. I can't have you going, thinking you'll give it a try for a few months and then come back home. That wouldn't be fair to Brick, or to the Vegas members. Whoever goes can't go in half-hearted. This is why I'm talking to you. You've got to decide between yourselves who's the most prepared to make this move."

I have to admit, I'd been thinking along those lines. *Go to Vegas, help get them on the right track, then return to Tucson.* Now Drummer's ruled that out, I need to give it more serious thought.

"Drummer, I respect the fuck out of you," I start, having to stop when Drummer purses his lips.

He pretends to blow me an uncharacteristic kiss, and states, "Love you too, Brother."

It makes us both snort and relieves some of the tension.

"As I was saying," I attempt to be stern, "I know you, but I don't know Brick. Can we meet him before we make up our minds?"

Drummer's always been fair. Not an easy man at times, but you know where you are with him. If Brick's equally deserving of my respect, maybe it won't be too great a change. But I'm wary, seeing as the reason he's seeking support is that he's finding running his club difficult. I can't give my all to a man who has done nothing to earn it.

His moment of levity passed, Prez nods, and again his steel eyes become hard. "Brick wants to talk to each of you individually."

"He know he's only got a pool of two to call on?" Wraith asks, his jaw tightening.

Fixing him with his famous stare, Drummer retorts, "I ain't getting rid of my rubbish to Vegas. I'm the mother chapter prez. It's to my benefit all clubs run smoothly. I can't send him my best, they're already in the officer ranks. But either of you would adequately represent me, and I've already told Brick that. We talked through the others but discounted them."

"Shouldn't you give them the chance? Bright lights might attract one of them."

"Red, I'll bring this up at church, but I can fuckin' guarantee not one brother will stand up and volunteer." He smirks. "You all have too good a life here."

Ain't that the truth.

"I'd still like to see it offered to them," I insist, my jaw set.

Wraith turns to me. The raise of his chin tells me he agrees. Time ticks on in silence for a few beats until Drummer slowly nods his head.

"Speak to Brick, make your decision, then I'll raise it at church. If I'm wrong, and someone is willing, then we'll reconsider. But I need to be in a position that one of you will step up."

That's fair, I suppose. Drummer's eyes fall on our half-filled glasses. Both Wraith and I pick them up, raising and draining them together. When Drummer jerks his chin at the door, we both take the hint, stand, and walk out.

When we enter the clubroom, there, at the bar, are Brick and Rainman. *My future prez and VP if I make this leap.* From here, they're typical bikers, downing a beer after a long hot, dusty and wet ride on the road. Rainman says something to Brick which makes him chuckle, but I can't make a choice based on a man's ability to laugh.

The prospect looks at his phone, then, politely, attracts the attention of the two Vegas members. He whispers something which has them turning, and beers in hand, they walk past, obviously on their way to a meeting with Drum.

Wraith nods his head to an empty table, away from prying ears. When we're both sitting, he leans forward. "What the fuck do you make of that?"

"That this beautiful relationship between us is ending." I lower my head into my hands. Wraith drew me into the club, showed me how to fuck for fuck's sake. I owe him so much. Where would I be if I hadn't met him? And if I don't go to Vegas, he'll go instead. How could I do that to him? But one way or another, our friendship won't continue, or not in the same way that it has.

"You found your place here, Brother. I don't want to upend you. I'll go to Vegas." He sits back and folds his arms.

"No fuckin' way," I growl, sitting forward. "This is your home, Brother. Me, I'm prepared to move on. Landed here by accident and not desire. Not to say I haven't found what I want, but I can more easily start over somewhere."

Wraith looks down at the table, then glances up with mirth in his eyes. "Look at us, each offering to fall on the sword for the other."

I chuckle. Not that I think it will come to something as drastic as that, but I shudder at the thought of Wraith not having my back and having to depend on a so far unknown brother.

How the fuck can we decide? I come up with one answer. "Let's meet with Brick. You know him, Wraith?"

"Not much more than you. Never been to the Vegas club, though I've met him on runs, and when he's visited. Seems straight, a bit old-school like Drum. Would I want to ride with him? Can't really tell."

"Do you think there's a pay raise to go along with the move?" I idly wonder out loud.

Wraith snorts. "From what I heard, it's more likely a pay cut. Vegas sounds like it has problems making bank. Wanna beer?"

I consider then nod, knowing I should limit myself as I don't want to make a decision I'll come to regret when I'm drunk. But one beer on top of the whisky shots won't hurt.

When Wraith turns to get Dale's attention, I lean back in my chair. There have been a few good men who have proved a steering influence on me. My father when I was a child, then Manny, who'd given me a chance and direction when I was flailing. Drummer, well, he's someone all would look up to. I need that in my life. I've not worn the patch for long and I've still a lot to learn. I only need to look at Peg, Blade and Lefty to realise that. Running a club is more than having fun riding around on a bike. If Brick is someone I can respect, this might work. If he's going to leave me to flounder for myself, then I don't think I'd have anything to offer. I don't think it's weak to admit I need guidance.

What the fuck is Drummer thinking by putting my name forward?

Dale arrives with our drinks. When Wraith lifts his beer, he changes the subject. "Most of the brothers are lusting after the new girl. Think Pussy's feeling neglected." He points to where she's standing alone. "How about we play with her later?"

She was our first together, might as well be our last. Mentally, I slap myself at my macabre thought, and steer the direction in a different way, one that doesn't harp on about the forthcoming change in our living arrangements. Soon, we're having one of our heated discussions about the virtue of different Harley models, Wraith insisting I should upgrade, and me being perfectly happy with my old Harley girl. The mods I've made have increased her speed, and I can see no reason to get something different.

Overhearing, Beef joins us, and where he goes, normally too so does Rock. Soon, we're all debating until Rock pulls out a deck of cards. He deals us all in, and I end up, as usual with him, losing my money.

But before I can lose my shirt, Drummer bellows from the hallway. "Wraith? Got a moment?"

Our eyes meet. I signal good luck with a waggle of my eyebrows. As he leaves, Beef looks up puzzled.

"What's going on? Drummer seems to be coming down hard on you boys."

Shrugging, I raise my chin to Rock. "Deal me some better fuckin' cards this time," I growl.

I try to concentrate. Maybe Vegas isn't for me if I can't win a simple poker hand. This time my cards are better, and I expect to beat Rock's suspected straight flush. I'm already grinning when I lay my hands down, but he just smirks and sets out a full house.

Damn the man. Not for the first time, I check the cards, looking for any mark on them. But of course, find none. He's just *that* good.

Sighing, I watch as he slides his winnings toward him.

"Red?" Drummer's voice bellows again.

"Uh-oh." Beef looks up and shakes his head. "Looks like it's you in trouble now."

He isn't wrong, I think, standing and pushing my chair into the table. For a moment I stand, eyeing my brothers and the cards, wishing I could just sit back down and carry on, maybe learn a few tips from Rock. It's hard to think this might be the last night I'll have in the Arizona chapter.

I'm not ready to move on.

There's a lump in my throat as I leave the table and I go for my meeting with destiny, and with Brick.

CHAPTER NINETEEN

Following Rainman and Brick, I take one last look in my rearview as we turn out of the track leading to the compound that's been my home for the last two years and head off into an uncertain future.

Am I doing the right thing? Fuck knows.

I'd met with the Vegas prez and VP and had liked them. Their vision for the club tallied with my own, and their honesty that their chapter had veered away from it had impressed me. They'd asked for my ideas and listened. Who was I, a lowly member, to bring up suggestions for the direction of their club? That they'd given my ideas credence had encouraged me to offer more.

Riding with Drummer had obviously influenced me, but so had my time from before. I'd started with Manny as a youth who washed cars and swept floors, worked my apprenticeship, and, had I stayed, I know he'd have offered me the manager role. I drew off the experience I had of keeping mechanics in line, and with the basic knowledge of bookkeeping, and how money flows.

It was clear that they wanted me, and I'll be fucked if they hadn't offered me something that I hadn't realised I'd wanted. A chance to be more than just one more man in the pack. Oh, there was no promise of an officer spot, how could there be when all positions were filled? And as I didn't wish death on anyone, I might never be given such responsibility in Vegas, or Tucson, come to that.

But they told me the members would respect me for what I could bring to the club. That they were waiting for a man to bring fresh insight, to drag them out of the depths to which they had sunk.

Brick was clever, more open than Drummer, quicker to acknowledge his faults. Easier to get along with, but there was a hardness there too. A suggestion that he'd be your best friend for life until you crossed him. Then the kid gloves would come off, and you'd better have somewhere to hide, or they'd never find your body.

Rainman reminds me of Peg in a number of ways. Direct, no nonsense, and a hardness born from the realities of life. He was the quieter of the pair, but I could tell he missed nothing.

At the time, I hadn't known how Wraith's own interview had gone. I suspected he'd, too, impressed them, and they him.

I'd been hesitant meeting him later.

"You finished with them?" He'd been waiting for me to exit the room. "Vegas sounds a fuckin' mess." He visibly shuddered.

"It does," I confirmed. "But there's a kind of challenge in wanting to have a hand in sorting it."

"Rather you than me, Brother." Then he realised what he'd said. "Oh, fuck. You actually want it?"

I'd slowly raised and lowered my shoulders. "Not sure I want it as such, staying here is more enticing. But there? Yeah, I think there might be a place for me. Unless you...?"

He closed his eyes briefly. "Brother, I'm going to miss you like fuck. Hell." He broke off, and wiped his hands down his face. "Kinda expected we'd be riding together forever."

My gut clenched. This was almost as bad as leaving Cheryl in my rearview. It fucking hurt. Wraith was my kindred spirit. "We'll still be here for each other. And we're still in the same club."

He opens his eyes again and narrows them. "Bet Drum would have you back if it doesn't work out."

But Drummer had been right. Whether he would or not is not the point. If I'm going, I've got to give it one hundred percent, and not depend on a lifeline. "It will work out, Wraith. I'll make fuckin' sure of it."

At the hastily called church, with Brick and Rainman in attendance, the brothers looked away when the opportunity was discussed. As Drummer had predicted, none of the fuckers had wanted to switch clubs. My raised hand was the only one, and that was met with disbelief, and enough conversation to make me satisfied I'd be missed.

When the decision had been recorded, and Drummer banged the gavel for my final appearance in the Tucson church, there was a party. As Wraith had suggested, he and I had spent a few hours with Pussy, a light-hearted moment when they both told me at least I'd now be able to show the assholes in Vegas how to fuck.

Then, this morning, the final farewells and enough back slaps to bruise my spine, wishes from Beef and Rock to keep the shiny side up and the dirty side down, and advice from Wraith to ensure I always wrapped my shit up, I headed out to my bike laden with saddlebags just like I'd arrived three years back.

If I had to wipe moisture from my eye, it was only the dust in the wind making them water. Or so I told myself.

Then I'd metaphorically straightened my back as I'd kicked up my stand, and at a sign from Brick, I'd knocked down into first. Then let out the clutch, twisted the throttle and commenced on the next chapter of my life, heading into the unknown for an uncertain future once again.

During the first few miles, I let memories wash over me, recollections of all that I'll miss from the club that I've just left. The club girls, the wives, and every fucking one of my brothers. The great accommodation, the swimming pool and the gym. Until we reach the point where we stop to remove our Satan's Devils cuts, replacing them with sweatshirts carrying the more discreet SDMC lettering, I wallow in regrets for what I'm leaving behind.

We top off our bikes, then Brick steps to my side. He eyes me for a moment, then without speaking, lays his hand on my back and taps it twice. He returns to his ride and his engine roars.

It's at that point I make the conscious decision to stop looking back, and as I follow my new prez and VP again, I begin wondering what Vegas will have to offer.

With each hour of the journey behind us, my sadness fades and excitement takes hold. Will Vegas be the end of the journey or just another stopping off place? Whichever, and wherever my road will lead me, I'll give it my best shot.

I haven't spent all day on the road for a while, not nonstop, only breaking for gas, since I headed south from Vermont, so I'm stiff and my hands need flexing to get some of the movement back by the time we slow down on the outskirts of Vegas and outside a not so promising looking warehouse. As I ride through the gate, I have an immediate pang of homesickness. Instead of forest and mountains and an ex-vacation resort, this place is industrial, and set against the backdrop of harsh looking desert. No saguaro, I notice, noticing the surroundings lack character.

I'd always thought Las Vegas a noisy place, but here, away from the bright lights and strip, it's at least peaceful.

Letting my engine idle for a moment before turning it off, I try to fortify my nerves. In Tucson, I had to work to get accepted, here, I was going to have to do it again but this time without the benefit of wearing a prospect patch. Prospects are meant to fuck up, it's all part of the process. At this club, I'm coming on board as a full member. Of course, I prefer it, but I'm not sure how I'm going to work it.

Rainman comes over and offers me a cigarette. Lighting it, I leave it between my lips as I take off my saddlebags and hoist them over my shoulder. Removing it, I tap off the ash. "Lead on, MacDuff," I say with a grin.

"You look like a fuckin' Christian being thrown to the lions." He smirks.

That pretty much sums up the way I'm feeling. When he slaps my back, I stub out my cigarette, and step toward the heavy wooden door. It creaks as it opens which is par for the course. I wouldn't be surprised if I walked into the set of a horror movie.

Instead, I'm pleasantly surprised. The odour hits me first, smoke, stale beer, and male sweat, but alongside that is the hint of polish. I blink for a moment as the interior is dark compared to the bright evening light outside, but as my eyes begin to adapt, I see the layout is familiar, as if there's a blueprint for Satan's Devils' clubrooms. A long bar stretches along one side, a few game machines are dotted around. There's the obligatory pool table, and in the centre, there are tables and chairs, many of which are occupied.

The men seated stand as I enter, and the heavy metal music is immediately turned down. I'm the subject of their attention while they wait as if they are a tableau in a painting. I take a deep breath, then another, and then do what any biker does, head straight for the bar.

"Any prospects around here?" I knock on the bar top.

"Yeah. I'm here." A tall, stout but muscled man pops his head up. "What can I get you?"

"Beer." I notice his prospect patch as he turns.

"Got your priorities right." A man comes up to my side. "Make that two, Josh. I'm Crash, by the way. Sergeant-at-arms." He turns his body slightly. "Twister? Come meet our new member."

"Hey, pleased to meetcha." Twister holds out his hand and smirks. "Don't have to ask who you are, that hair would give you away anywhere."

I grin. "Yeah, it's hard to go incognito."

"You know anyone?" Twister gestures to the prospect that he, too, needs a drink.

I raise my own to my lips, wet my throat, then answer, "Nah. Been a while since the chapters have met. I think I've seen you at a ride out—"

"Yeah, that was about twelve months back. Fox was with me. Hey, Fox. C'mere."

The man I vaguely recognise comes over with his arm around a pretty girl. She's cute, good figure, but not dressed like a sweet butt. Still, it's probably the reason she's here. I let my eyes roam over her.

I feel a sharp pain around the back of my head. "Show some respect," Fox growls, being the culprit who slapped me. "This 'ere is my old lady, Tiffany. And keep your fuckin' eyes to yourself."

Seems like I should learn how the land lies. "No disrespect meant. Nice to meet you, Tiffany."

"None taken," she says with a wink. "From your expression, at least I know I still have it."

"Tiff," Fox warningly growls, but he manages a smile with it. Guess he trusts her—well he patched her—so he must be sure of her.

"Anyone else taken?" I eye the two who do look like club girls who have just entered. They look young, barely legal.

Twister looks where my attention has settled and barks a laugh. "Nah, that's Pixie and Angel, our club girls. We did have another…" As his voice trails off, Fox again growls, and this time distinctly with displeasure.

I don't ask questions, just bank that for later. I'm sure all the club secrets will gradually come out.

"Just don't come on to Rosa," Fox warns me. "Unless you don't value your balls. She's prez's."

Twister gives a snort which I don't immediately understand as two kids, both boys, come tearing into the room. They're screaming and laughing, using the legs of one large, older biker, to hide behind. They're quickly followed by a woman, who has to be at least forty.

"Tristan, Thomas. You come here right now." She wiggles her finger. "And don't think Titch will protect you." She pauses and points a finger at the old man. "And don't you encourage them."

"Hey, Rosa," the grey-haired and bearded biker holds up his hands. "I ain't doing shit." At her raised eyebrows he chooses another word. "Anything." He rolls his eyes, and more quietly but equally audibly complains, "Fuck this watching my language."

"Fuck! He said fuck!" One of the boys who have to be twins they look so identical screams out, then covers his mouth with his hands before collapsing in giggles.

"Want a hand corralling the little f… devils?" Another biker steps up, grabbing the backs of each of the boys' shirts. They wriggle but can't get free.

"Thanks, Cobra," the tired and frazzled woman replies. "They need their showers."

"We don't," one says, obviously speaking for the other.

"Pooh." Cobra bends down and sniffs. "I think you do. You don't want to chase off the girls, do you?"

"A little less about girls, please, Cobra." Rosa rolls her eyes. "Think I've got enough to worry about before we get to that problem."

The boy who hadn't as yet spoken wriggles out of Cobra's grip, turns around and places his hands on his hips, then says, authoritatively, "Girls suck."

I'm not the only one who can't suppress a snort. *Yeah they do, kid. If you ask them right.*

With one boy in her grasp, and Cobra bringing the other who's trying unsuccessfully to wriggle out from under his arm, the two walk over to the industrial metal staircase and drag their unwilling captives to the top.

Twister watches until they disappear from sight. "Guess you've now met Rosa, Brick's ol' lady, and their two obnoxious brats." He says it in a friendly manner, with no malice. Especially when he adds, "Keep your eye on them, they get up to all manner of shit in the club."

"How old are they?"

He answers with an expression between a grin and a grimace, "Four. Going on teenagers already."

"Where is the prez?" I look around, not recalling seeing him since I got off my bike.

"In his office, I expect." Fox frowns once again. "He'll have shit to catch up on having been away for two days."

At least he takes the club seriously. A part of me wonders whether we'll see more of him once his two terrors are in bed.

CHAPTER TWENTY

Two hours later, I've got a decent buzz on. My saddlebags are still at my feet, but I've spent the time socialising, and getting to know my new brothers. The Vegas club is smaller than Tucson, with ten members and two prospects as far as I can tell. The three that had gotten themselves arrested and locked up appear not to be spoken of, so I don't ask.

Sometime back, I propped my ass on a bar stool, as I got into conversation with Titch. Brick, I'd place in his early fifties, and Titch probably a couple of years older. A real old-timer, I note him as someone to talk to if I want to learn more about the background of the club.

I spend a few minutes talking to Keys, their computer expert, immediately realising why Drummer thought Tse was a good find. Though more than half the talk of technology goes way over my head, the kind of shit he can do must come in useful at times.

Hammer, well he seems solid. It doesn't take me that long to discover I've met most of the club, with the exception of the second prospect who's already picked up a road name of Shadow, as he can creep up unawares on almost anybody. Inadvertently, he'd given me an example, and I'd nearly dropped my beer from my hand.

When there's a natural lull in conversation, I ask where my room is as I'm well past needing a piss and a chance to freshen up.

"Prospect?"

At Hammer's call, Josh runs up. "Take Red up to the room prepared for him. Check he's got everything he wants."

A quick up and down bob of his head shows me Josh will do the task and happily, just as any prospect should. Inwardly I grin as that was me not so long ago.

Sliding off the stool, I pick up my saddlebags. Carrying them in one hand, I follow the prospect across the clubroom and over to the metal staircase I'd noticed earlier. It clangs under my motorcycle boots with each step that I take. When we're at the top, I find we're in a long corridor with doors off to the left and right.

A suspicious aroma exudes from one, my hunch proved correct when Josh pauses, points and says, "That's the heads. There's another at the other end of the corridor."

Heads? My eyes narrow as I prepare to lower my expectations.

At the fourth door along, the prospect comes to a halt, pulls out a key and turns it in the lock, then pushes the door open. "This is you."

I glance in, taking in the meagre decoration and the dark intimidating interior, feeling my spirits sink. *I left Tucson for this?* A wave of homesickness goes through me, and I have the sudden desire not to unpack, just to pick up my bags and run back home. Only, it's not home anymore. Drummer had made it clear, if I made the move, I was gone for good. *Unless I fuck up.* I start wondering what it would take for them to kick me out.

Josh leaves. I close the door and step inside, laying my bags on the at least clean-looking king-size bed. Then I go to the small window and glance out. Darkness has fallen so I can't see much, but I doubt I would anyway. There's no balcony, nowhere to sit in the fresh air and take in the night. Worse, as I turn, I see my suspicion was correct, there's no other door suggesting I have my own bathroom.

Fuck.

Running my fingers through my hair, I recall that apart from living with my family, I've never shared a bathroom before. Even the motel rooms where I've stayed have all come with en suites. Maybe it wouldn't matter to the vets who've lived in barracks, but to me? Hell, I like a bit of privacy when I shower, particularly when I rub one out. As for crapping, I don't even want to go there. Or brushing my teeth when someone's taking a dump in the stall behind me? I shudder at just the thought.

My first impulse is to get onto Drummer and beg him to take me back.

Man the fuck up, Red.

Oh, I'll try. But… *no bathroom?*

I can barely bring myself to unpack, but I force myself to. I've made my bed and have no option but to lie in it. *Maybe Vegas will have something to compensate.* Right now, I'm not sure what. *I could rent my own place in town.* Approaching the age of twenty-eight, maybe it's time I put down roots. I baulk at turning down free accommodation but know I can't have it both ways. *I was spoiled in Arizona.*

Putting my belongings away, I place a photo Carmen had taken of the Tucson club on the bedside table, then check the drawer. Stocked up with condoms, I note, realising some things, at least, are the same.

I grin as I remember Wraith's last admonishment to me. *Always wrap it up, Brother.* Hell, I never forget. Then I grimace as my mind goes back to the time when I didn't bother, when I was naïve enough to trust a woman to take care of herself.

My fingers press into my temples. *Cheryl would have loved the*

Tucson compound. Here, not so much. More than two years later and that woman still resides in part of my head. I give myself a shake, hoping to clear her from it.

When I've stowed my shit, I take a deep breath, and pay an overdue visit to the heads. As I piss long enough to represent my country, I notice they're clean enough, but even the strong smell of disinfectant can't completely cover the odour of urine, and the aromatic evidence that someone's recently used one of the stalls. I check out the showers, basic, with just a plastic curtain for privacy.

Oh well, that's a no then to shower sex. That place in town starts to look rosier.

My phone rings as I hang my last t-shirt in the closest. Picking it up, I wince when I see the caller, but answer anyway.

"What's up, Wraith?"

"Just checking you got there safely. What's the club like?"

I don't want him to know I'm having regrets, nor feeling guilty he should have been here in my place. "They seem a solid group of brothers."

"And the accommodations?"

I can't lie, but settle for, "Basic, but okay."

"Already miss you, Brother."

I miss him like fuck. All of them. "Miss you too, Wraith. But I think this was a good move to make." That's for his benefit. Personally, I can't see how this is going to work, or how I could be happy here. It's too strange, there's nothing familiar.

"Fuckin' ace, Brother. I've been worried about you. I keep thinking maybe I should have gone instead."

I snort and lie. "Fuckin' glad you didn't. Else I'd have missed out on everything Vegas." In truth, I think I could have lived my whole life without regretting that. I realise if we talk longer, he'll figure out I'm stretching the truth. "Gotta run, Brother."

"Take care, Red."

"Shiny side up, Wraith. Shiny side up."

I end the call, glance around the room with a look of disgust, then make my way back down to the clubroom. I'm an object of interest to the club girls and end up taking the voluptuous Angel back to my room. I don't disappoint her, and I get my own rocks off, then dismiss her.

After one more visit to the hated heads, having to exchange pleasantries with Cobra who's pissing into the urinal next to me, I take myself off to bed.

What have I done? I ask myself, as I toss and turn on the unfamiliar mattress. *Looks like I've made a fuckin' big mistake.*

Morning comes, not with the gentle birdsong or the chirping of cicadas outside my window, but with the clumping of heavy boots out in the hallway, and the loud clanging as said boots stomp down the staircase.

When I open my door, it's to greet Hammer wearing only his boxers and carrying a towel over his arm as he heads for the showers. I, too, was going that way, but was proceeding there fully dressed. I step back into my room, not wanting to get into a queue. After a few minutes, I try again, this time only clad in my jeans.

Someone whistles. "Nice ink!" Turning, I see Keys heading my way. He nods at my tats then eyes my towel. "There's a shower free if you hurry."

Raising my chin, I take his advice.

I've been naked in front of Wraith more times than I can count, and with others when we've shared the club girls. But I'm still self-conscious having my dick swinging free as men come in and out to use the urinals and the cubicles. Needs must be attended to, however, and unless I want my personal hygiene to go to shit, I've got to suck it up and get showered.

I survive the first indignity of the day, then descend the staircase. At least a welcome and recognisable aroma meets my nostrils, the smell of cooking bacon. Following my nose, I enter a kitchen area behind the bar. Rosa's at the stove and she seems to be cooking for everybody.

She grins widely when she sees me and points to a seat. Then she fills a plate and brings it to me. Angel, with a wink to remind me of last night, brings me a cup of coffee.

Titch is watching me, his brow creased. "Eh, Rosa. What we got to do to get personal service around here?"

She points her spatula at the old biker. "He's new. I'm trying to impress him and show some of us have got manners."

I raise my eyebrow and shrug. Digging in, I find the breakfast is more than edible and there's plenty of it. At least I won't starve.

Rainman comes in and gives me a chin lift. "Church this morning."

"Is that your normal meeting?" It seems an odd time.

"Nah, it's normally Friday evenings, but Brick thought it useful to get you properly introduced."

Makes sense, I suppose. Members wander in and out as I finish the food, then drink a second cup of coffee while exchanging pleasantries with Keys and Cobra.

Needing a moment to myself, I leave the kitchen and exit the clubhouse, going outside and taking in my surroundings properly for the first time. Lighting a smoke, I walk around the building, noticing there's a large enough yard of sorts out back, and a children's playset on which the twins are currently having a good old time. Smoking himself, and watching them, is Brick.

"Prez." I greet him politely, while wishing I was addressing Drummer.

Turning, he gives me a chin lift. "Red. Sleep well?"

I nod. I had. When I'd eventually dropped off.

He eyes me carefully. "The clubhouse isn't Tucson, but I hope you'll be comfortable here for all of that."

I shrug, not bothering to deny the obvious.

He glances at his watch, then yells, "Come on, boys. Daddy's got to work."

There are the predictable protests, but when Brick growls, the boys realise he's serious, and reluctantly leave their play and come running across. Taking hold of one twin—hell, I can't tell them apart—he launches him into the air and then catches him.

"You be good for your mom, today, promise?"

Two sincere nods make me hide my smile. Sure, I reckon these little hooligans will run Rosa ragged. It's strange being around youngsters, there were none in the Tucson club.

The one Brick isn't holding is standing in front of me, hands on his hips, and pouting. When I stare down, not knowing what I'm supposed to do, he huffs, "Up."

I raise an eyebrow toward Brick. "Not wary of strangers, are they?"

"Not if they're wearing a Satan's Devils cut. Makes you part of the family." He tilts his head toward the boy still demanding to be picked up.

More used to hefting heavy boxes of motorcycle parts, I put my hands down and lift him up. There's not much finesse in it, but it makes him giggle. *Oh fuck.* I just about manage not to drop him when he leans back and waves his hands about. *Don't kids have any sense of self-preservation?*

Brick's chuckling, seeming not to find it odd a stranger is carrying, or trying to carry, his wriggling son. He just takes his own bundle of dubious joy and marches into the clubhouse expecting me to follow him.

"Got you roped into babysitting duties already?" Tiffany laughs when she sees me walking inside, holding the kid awkwardly.

But she takes pity on me when she sees me struggling, holding out her arms and taking him from me. She balances him on one hip and looks quite expert about it. "You been good for your Uncle Red, Trist?"

At least she can tell which one he is. And how the fuck did I pick up the uncle title?

Brick, having rid himself of his twin, returns. "Ready to head for church now?"

Too right I am. Time for some adult conversation and topics which I do know something about. Kids? Maybe it will happen in my future if I find the right woman to have at my side, but right now? You can keep 'em.

CHAPTER TWENTY-ONE

The Vegas meeting room is much the same as Tucson's, enclosed with no windows and no way for peering eyes to see in. Brick indicates I should drop my phone in the box Josh is holding. Being one of Drummer's dictates as well, I have no aversion to following his rule.

The large table is oval, with the Satan's Devils' insignia carved into the top. The seating arrangements are peculiar. Some chairs are next to each other, but there are definite gaps. As I take the seat the prez waves me to, I watch as the rest of the members come in, intrigued when the chairs are left in the same positions. It looks like the seats have been removed, but spaces are still left. I realise these are for the three members who have recently left.

Are they expecting them back? My brow creases in thought. As far as I'm concerned, they broke the Satan's Devils' rules, maybe the unwritten ones, but they'd brought the eyes of the cops down on the club. While Devils don't always walk the right side of the line, committing a crime for personal gain which brings blowback on the MC is not something I believe Drummer would have tolerated.

I want to know answers. I've committed to moving to Vegas, but surely I won't be held to my word if this chapter isn't what I could have anticipated. Keeping the door open for the traitors is not what I expected.

Brick bangs the gavel once all members are seated, and then stares straight at me. "We're here, Brothers, to formally welcome our new member. Let's introduce ourselves. I, and the VP need no introduction, but…?" He tilts his head toward the man on his left.

"Crash, sergeant-at-arms. We've met," he adds as an afterthought.

Indeed we have. I incline my head.

"Fox. I take care of the money, collect dues and give out your pay."

I grin. "I'll be extra nice to you."

"Keys. If you need help from technology, I'm your guy."

I know that already as we'd spoken last night, but it seems Brick wants to go through the formalities.

"Titch," the old biker growls. "Don't ask me for anything and we'll do okay."

A few chuckles follow his statement.

Cobra and Hammer introduce themselves next, followed by Twister, who gives me an evil look as he adds his rank of enforcer. He can't intimidate me, not after Blade.

Brick picks up the conversation when all have introduced themselves. "Red comes highly recommended by Drummer. He proposed him as a useful person to have around."

My damn skin betrays me yet again, as I suffer through the praise of my ex-prez.

"Yeah?" Titch doesn't seem convinced by the prez's words. "What you got to offer?"

"I'm a darn good mechanic," I tell him. Not adding Drummer expected me to be here for anything else.

Titch's face brightens at that.

"Know much about this club?" Rainman asks. Then, without waiting for me to answer, he continues, "We still, er, used to, run a few guns. Not that we can do that any longer." His face momentarily tightens. "We've got the auto-shop as you're aware. Titch runs that. We've a strip joint, but that's having to compete with the big clubs nearer the centre. Hammer's trying to make that work, but it's tough."

Hammer grimaces and nods as he adds, "Used to be a cover for a prostitution ring, but Drummer wanted us out of that shit."

Rainman's face brightens. "And we've started a security business. That's Keys' baby. Looks like that could be a money spinner if we play our cards right."

"Don't forget the pawn business," Twister pipes up. "That's where we do any money laundering."

"Offering a service or washing our own?" I ask, interested.

"Bit of both," Twister replies.

Brick clears his throat. "Fresh eyes on things never hurt. Before we assign Red to Titch's tender mercies at the auto-shop, I suggest he checks out all our businesses. Might find some opening or shit that we've missed. You up for that, Brother?"

I'm up for it. But will my new brothers resent me for poking my nose in? Most have worn the patch far longer.

"Couldn't fuckin' hurt," Fox states. "Fuck knows we're going round in circles."

"'Specially since the tattoo parlour closed."

Cobra's words initiate a period of dead silence. It's only broken by Indian's rasp, "Fuckin' Tide and his shit." His jaw is tight.

Tide? Creasing my brow, I realise I hadn't heard the name, and wonder if he's one of the incarcerated members. Which reminds me, no one's addressed the elephant in the room, and by not doing so, there's a big fucking gap in my education.

I decide to man up. Pointing to the three empty spaces, letting my hand dwell on each one for a second, I frame my question carefully. "Who's gone, and what hole have they left? Will they be coming back around the table?"

If the silence moments earlier was deafening, it's even more so now. I watch the reactions. Some look up to the ceiling as if trying to divorce themselves from the discussion. Crash and Twister share grim expressions with each other. Rainman raises his eyebrows and sends an amused look toward Brick. Fox's face is tight, and Cobra lowers his head into his hands.

Brick just stares at me. After more than a minute has passed, he wipes his hands down his face. "'Bout time we faced up to this, Brothers." He adds in a chin lift my way.

Titch glares at me. "Who's he to fuckin' walk in and dictate how we run our business?"

I raise my hands up as if surrendering. "Hey, no offence meant, but I'm coming in as a fuckin' outsider and I'd like to know what I'm stepping into."

Titch opens his mouth as if to respond, but Brick is faster. "He's right, Titch. He needs to know, and we need to come to some decisions." He stares at his oldest member, his expression not having quite the same impact as one of the cold looks of Drummer's, but effective enough, as Titch sits back.

"Fine." He folds his arms over his chest.

I wait, but no one starts speaking, so I decide to prompt the discussion myself. "As I heard it, three members got into debt gambling."

"We're in fuckin' Vegas," Titch blasts at me. "What would you expect?"

My redheaded temper rises. "I'd expect brothers to know their limits, and at the fuckin' least not do anything to bring attention down on the club."

"He's right, Titch." Fox nods at me. "We all know the risks."

Rainman sighs heavily. "We knew Tide, he was our road captain, well, we knew he had a gambling addiction. Thought he had it under control. What we hadn't realised was the extent of his losses, nor that Townie and Bass were likewise afflicted. They'd all been at the same casino, one of the smaller joints off the strip. Tide convinced them the house was stacked against them—"

"As normal," Cobra butts in.

"Sure, but Tide couldn't understand how he was losing so much."

"What, they decided to rob the place to get their money back?" I breathe out air. *Fuckin' morons.*

Brick's face grows hard. "It wasn't planned. Tide was drunk off his ass, lost his last dollars so pulled out his gun. Bass and Townie were with him and thought they should back him up. Things got out of hand."

My eyes widen. "Anyone fuckin' shot?"

"Tide winged one of the dealers." Keys meets my eyes. "The other pair didn't go down without a fight, so the place was busted up."

"What did they get?" I ask, looking at Brick.

"Tide went down on a felony charge, got twenty years. Bass and Townie weren't carrying so they got away with misdemeanours and are inside for twelve months."

"And you're keeping their spaces around the table for when they get out?" If I sound disgusted, it's because I am. Addiction is an illness, I know that. But the club can't harbour men who don't put the Devils first.

"We haven't actually discussed it," Rainman explains. "We've been dealing with the cop raids, having our guns confiscated, and having our businesses searched. They've been looking to pin something, hell, anything on us."

"Which is why we're cleaning our shit up, and why we no longer have a fuckin' tattoo business. Bass ran it."

"Be honest," Keys suddenly states, leaning forward. "It was never the best. None of us would have our tats done by Bass."

An incompetent tattoo artist and gambling addicts, men who felt they were entitled to rob and shoot just because they lost at the tables. They don't sound like brothers I'd want at my back. My jaw tenses.

"Coming in as an outsider, for what damage they've done to the club, I'd have their patches." My judgement is harsh, and I know it. I'm talking about their family. Well, if they give me a beatdown and send me packing, so be it. I'm not sure I want to be a member of this chapter if they put up with shit like that.

"Oh, for fuck's sake." Indian slams his fists down. "Those three were problems before they fucked it up good and proper this time. We gonna ignore the fuckin' obvious? Does it make us feel better keeping our heads in the sand?"

Keys mouths a word at me, *drugs.*

Fucking great. I glance around, wondering whether any others are meth heads or addicted to other hard shit. That wouldn't fly under Drummer's rule.

Brick's having one of those prez/VP silent conversations that I've often witnessed between Lefty and Drum—slight movements of their eyebrows, nods of heads and shakes. Rainman wiggles his hand a couple of times, but in the end, they both raise their chins.

Brick bangs the gavel. "The club's taken a hit since the three of them went down. We're constantly walking on eggshells, waiting for the cops to arrive, and we all know we've come close, if not actually to the attention of the feds. It was pure luck they didn't push to find club sanction for what went down. A RICO indictment is not what we fuckin' want, yet our former brothers brought us too fuckin' close for comfort. As it is, we've had to cut back on our trades, and get out of anything with a whiff of illegal. Relying on legitimate business ventures, when one of those has had to close, has meant we've all felt the result in our pockets. I know hearing Red's views is uncomfortable, fuck, those are our brothers we're talking about." He pauses and wipes a hand over his brow, then takes out a pack and lights up a cigarette.

Others follow, me included. When both our lungs and the room is full of smoke, Brick continues again, "If Bass, Tide and Townie walked back in now, how would we greet them?"

"With a fuckin' beatdown," Crash growls.

Twister bangs his fist on the table. "We don't know what the feds are planning. We could still be facing a RICO charge and won't get out of the eyes of the cops for some time. For that, I'd take their patches."

"Hey," Titch objects. "I visited Tide last week. He's having trouble inside. We take his patch, we remove his protection."

"He show remorse?" Rainman asks.

"Like fuck," Hammer says. "Or not when I saw him. The only remorse he showed was about not getting his money back."

I decide to state the obvious. "Declare him out bad, and he's likely not to get out alive." That's the truth, albeit a harsh sentence.

"What's the alternative?" Keys asks. "He was a liability, let's admit it. How many times has he let us down on a ride as he was too high to take part? As a road captain, he sucked."

So why hadn't Brick done anything about it earlier?

"Abandon our brothers? Might as well take my patch while you're at it," Titch growls.

"So don't abandon him." I shrug. "Let him keep the protection while he's inside. Fuck knows, twenty years is a long time. He might have overcome his addiction by then." And someone else is likely to be sitting in Brick's spot.

"We keep his account topped up?" Fox asks me directly.

"Could be the minimum, just to get by. But he doesn't get the full amount owing to him. That's split between us. Only fair compensation for the mess he left us to clean up."

Brick raises the gavel and bangs it. "Tide retains our protection, for now. Once he's out, we'll vote on taking his patch. That's the vote in front of you. Who's for?"

The ayes are unanimous, and I'm not surprised. Always easier to put off a decision until later, and by that time, there could well be a different set of brothers around the table. I'm happy with that. It could also be useful having a brother inside, as long as he can get off the drugs while he's in there.

"What about Bass and Townie? They're likely to be around in less than a year's time. Titch, you want to speak up for them?"

Titch looks down at his hands. Having been put on the spot,

it seems like he's struggling. "Ah fuck, Prez. If they were solid brothers, then I'd say wait, and have them back once they've done their time. But they're not inside for doing something on behalf of the club. I've gotta ask if I can now trust them."

"And can you?" Cobra asks. "'Cause I'm fuckin' sure I can't."

Titch meets his eyes. "Honestly? No."

"Anyone want to speak for them?" Brick asks.

"Who can?" Twister challenges. "Neither have been pulling their weight for a while. Half the time, they're stoned out of their minds."

"So, they're out. That's the vote, Brothers."

As if they've realised the decision has to be made, again, every vote is an aye. At the end, Brick stares my way with a wry look in his eyes.

"Seems you've made us face up to the shit that's invaded the club. I thank you for that, Brother."

Some of the glances sent my way suggest not everyone is so grateful, but that still leaves one thing on my mind.

Wanting to get on to something positive, I ask another question. "How are the prospects coming along? Either of them close to getting their patch?"

"You're suggesting we should build up our ranks?" Rainman raises his chin toward me.

"Only if they're a good fit," I clarify.

Twister replies, "I got no problems with Josh except he can be a bit of an asshole. Shadow needs longer, he's only been here a few months."

"I got two hangarounds who come to the auto-shop," Titch remarks. "Strange guys, but solid. Spend their off time in a BDSM club."

Keys snorts. "They'll have us converting the basement to a fuckin' dungeon."

"And that would be bad?" Indian's got a glint in his eye.

Hammer snorts.

Brick's shaking his head, but grinning. "Feel them out, Titch.

See if they're up for prospecting. Tell them to come around the club to see what we're about. But Red's asked a question and I'd like an answer to it. Are we ready to patch Josh in?"

"I like the man, he's solid. Apart from those lame jokes of his." Rainman dips his chin up and down.

"I'm an 'aye'," Fox says.

"I'd vote yes, with the suggestion we give him the road name, Joker." Indian's grinning. His suggestion raises a few laughs, and no one offers an alternative.

"Okay, let's vote."

At Brick's suggestion, it goes around the table. When I'm asked, I truthfully reply, "I barely know the man, so going by the rest of you, I'll vote, aye."

CHAPTER TWENTY-TWO

"You made your mark." Rainman raises a glass my way that evening after church.

I've spent the day touring around the various businesses. The auto-shop is good, well positioned, but could do with some updated equipment. Titch is old-school, failing to recognise cars and bikes are increasingly being driven with electronics. To give him his due, the old biker seemed interested when I'd pointed it out and had given me the go ahead to have a word with Keys on my return about getting the computer shit updated, and purchasing diagnostic equipment.

The strip club, well, what can I say? Lacklustre and rundown. If it wasn't dead cheap to enter, it would probably get no patrons. The pawn shop was exactly what I'd expected and seems to be running just fine. I'd even stopped off at the locked-up tattoo parlour. The location was good, but no other brother had inking experience. I wondered whether we could tempt an artist to work for the club and decided to raise my idea at the table.

Keys' security business interested me the most. He's a whizz with alarms and cameras, and had a growing clientele. The only room for improvement was bringing other brothers in on what he was doing. He'd tended to play it close to his chest, but I thought he'd benefit from help in some quarters.

It was obvious all the legit businesses had to be beefed up to make up for the loss in other income.

I realise Rainman is waiting for me to address his statement. "Have I?" I belatedly answer the VP.

"Well, for a start, you forced us to address the situation. In one meeting, the club lost three members and gained one." He grins as if that wasn't unwelcome. "Then those observations about the businesses are spot-on. Do you know just how fuckin' tactful you had to have been to make Titch consider changes? The old guy's never wanted to move on, despite what we've been telling him. In one fuckin' day, you got him to agree to computerisation."

Despite our clashes in the meeting, I'd gotten on with Titch on his home turf, probably as we spoke the same language. He had been impressed with the rebuild on my bike and understood why I didn't want to part with it.

"You've got a way about you." Rainman raises his chin as he assesses me. "Cool, calm, but firm, and likeable. I can see why Drummer recommended you."

Yet again my face glows. *Damn complexion.*

I shrug off his compliment. "I just call things as I see them."

He tilts his bottle toward the bar where Josh—no, *Joker*—is demanding Shadow's attention. "Patching him in was a good move. Gave us something positive to focus on."

I grin, remembering how we'd mentally tortured the poor man. I think Joker had thought we were throwing him out of the club, but fuck knows why he'd think that. He'd appeared cowed and acted as though he'd been expecting to be kicked to the kerb. When we'd relented and passed him his patches, he'd damn near broken down.

He's over that now and making the most of it. If he's like any other newly patched in member, I'll place bets where he'll be heading next.

Standing, I rest my hand on Rainman's shoulder for an instant. "I'm going to get some private time with Pixie before Joker decides to get his dick wet."

"Good idea, Brother." The VP offers me a smirk.

Pixie's hovering close to Joker with Angel by her side, both ready and waiting for the newly patched member to remember he's allowed to fuck them now. I'm certain I can offer something better. Joker won't have fucked a woman in nearly twelve months, yet I'm in top form.

Approaching Pixie, I put my arm around her shoulders. "Wanna fuck." It's a statement, not a question, and without a good excuse, Pixie won't be able to turn me down. Not that I think she'd want to. I'm confident enough that when I look in the mirror, I see a good-looking man staring back. I don't make young kids run screaming, nor pick my nose or scratch my ass and try my best not to fart, but hell, that shit happens to the best of us.

Pixie's obviously not disappointed to be pulled away from the newly patched man. She turns, slides her hands under my cut and rests them against my t-shirt covered chest. She glances up, her lips curved, and in a voice that sounds breathy, replies, "Well, let's see what we can do about that, big boy."

As I place my hand against her lower back and guide her toward the stairs, I lean down a little and breathe in deeply as my nose touches her hair. She smells clean and freshly showered, just as I like my girls. I've got a greater repertoire when I get in first.

I unlock my door, let her walk inside, follow her in, then turn and relock my door.

Sweet butts need no flirtation. They know exactly what they're here for. She starts stripping immediately, though the loss of her short skirt and cropped top let me see hardly any more skin than I had before.

She hesitates at her underwear, but I nod my head. I'm

already hard and unwrapping her myself won't have much of an effect.

When she stands naked in front of me, I wave her back to the bed.

"Open your legs."

She pulls up her knees and lets them flop to the side. Raising her head so she can see my reaction, her mouth twists into a smirk. She's bare as a fuckin' baby, just as I prefer. And for that, she gets a reward.

"I'm fuckin' hungry," I tell her, with a wide grin on my face as I remove my cut and place it over the back of the chair. "And I see something I can eat right here."

"God, yes, Red."

It's no hardship to go down on a club girl, as long as they don't taste of rubber or semen. I've acquired quite a liking for the sweet yet salty taste, and for how out of control a woman becomes when I'm licking her there. I also like to refine my technique for when I meet that elusive woman I'm searching for. If I ever come across her, I'll have made sure she'll have no complaints or think my technique is lacking.

I nibble, suck, and bite between her thighs. When I curl my fingers inside her, she half comes off the bed. It's not long before I have her convulsing and bucking into my face. When she comes down and pulls away, I wipe the back of my hand against my mouth.

"How do you want it, big boy? Want me to return the favour?"

Considering a blow job for a moment, I dismiss it. She'd felt tight and today my cock wants in her cunt.

I strip out of my t-shirt, shuck off my boots, then undo my zipper. As Pixie looks on and licks her lips in anticipation, I issue another instruction.

"Hands and knees, sweetheart."

I love doing it doggy style, when I can feel luscious breasts bounce into my hands and can hammer into that cunt without mercy. Club girls can certainly take a good pounding.

Pixie winks before she obeys, then, once in position, wiggles that luscious ass. I gaze on, all but salivating as I use a condom to cover my cock.

She's already wet, my beard can attest to that. Kneeling behind her, I line myself up, find the position and then thrust in. My hands go to her hips, pulling her back against me as I sink in to the root. Then with one arm anchoring her to me, I use the other to fondle the soft tissue of her breasts, soon finding she responds to having her nipples pinched.

Then I let myself go. The room is filled with the sound of flesh slapping against flesh, her moans and exclamations, along with my grunts.

She's a perfect fit for my cock, her tight muscles trying to hold on to me as I hammer in and out.

When I swivel my hips, I hit her sweet spot, so I do it again, then again. It doesn't take long before she's tightening, squeezing my cock to death. As she convulses, I lose it myself, shooting cum into the condom.

"Jeez." My lungs heave for breath as I lie down over her. "That was good." Slowly, I pull out, holding onto the condom.

Once I'm free of her body, she rolls over, and throws her arm up over her face. Her chest is heaving as she struggles to get her own breath.

"Red, you're something else, lover."

What man wouldn't feel pride, even though she probably says that to everyone. But for a second, I'll believe it.

"You're not so bad yourself, Pixie." She deserves my praise. What more could I ask for but a warm, willing body? "Want a smoke?"

When she nods, yes, I pick up my jeans, and still naked get out my pack. I offer her one, then take another for myself. I lie back on the bed propped on the pillows. She inches herself up, so she's lying beside me.

"I think I'm glad you transferred to Vegas." She sighs in contentment. "Love you fuckin' me, Red. Wanna do that again."

"Maybe we will." It's a certainty, but I'll be making no promises. Don't want a club girl getting ideas that we're exclusive or some such shit. Though Pixie's been here a while by all accounts, and probably knows the score.

I close my eyes, relaxed and at peace, mechanically putting the cigarette to my lips, taking a drag, then huffing smoke out. If I were to grade myself, I reckon I'd given a good performance, maybe an A.

Opening my eyes, I grimace, flick ash into the ash tray, and think with regret. *With Cheryl, I was probably a D minus.* I've improved a lot since then.

Would it have mattered? Would it have made a difference?

Finding myself thinking of one woman while another's in my bed, I slap Pixie's butt. "Time to go now, sweetheart."

Without complaint, she stubs her cigarette out, slides into her meagre clothing in seconds, then with a wink, shows herself out.

My good mood has evaporated. *Why did I think about Cheryl again?* Sometimes I hate the woman who appears to have rented space in my brain. It's not as if I'll ever see her again. Despite the time that has passed, often something will send me back to that short time I spent with her. Though I like the way things turned out, I'm always left wondering, what would it have been like if she hadn't left? Would my ride through life have been better? Or would she have brought me down? Would I have joined the Devils? Or found something to keep me content in civilian life? Unanswerable questions.

One thing's for sure, I've never found a woman quite like her in any respect, and none that have held my interest for any length of time. *It was the timing, the death of my father, the excitement of heading into a future unknown. It wasn't her. It was circumstance,* I reason with myself.

So why, when I breathe in, do I imagine her scent in the air? Why do I compare all pussies to hers and find them lacking?

As I hear Pixie's high-heeled footsteps tapping against the wooden floor, I grimace, wondering when I became the man who'd be satisfied with casual sex. I'd originally thought by now I'd be married, have a couple of kids, be the example to them just like my dad had been to me. Instead, I'm in an MC, and unlikely to attract the woman of the sort I'd thought I'd be looking for.

Maybe Cheryl would have left anyway as soon as I put on the Satan's Devils' cut.

Or maybe, she would have stayed and maybe she'd have made a great old lady.

Fuck!

There's only one way to get her out of my head. That's to get dressed, go downstairs, drink with this new set of brothers and maybe find another sweet butt to sink my cock into.

CHAPTER TWENTY-THREE

"That fuckin' gang is coming on strong," Rope states, his worried eyes meeting Cuff's. "They were waiting for us last night."

In the two years since I've been in the Vegas club, some things have changed. The two BDSM-loving hangarounds became prospects, and after serving their time, had been patched in, picking up the fairly predictable handles of Rope and Cuff. Subsequently, we got a new prospect by the name of Sarge. An ex-Army dude who's not without his own baggage. But we make allowances for his PTSD, and in return, it's already clear he'd die for the club. There hadn't been many places for a vet who can't sleep at night, but instead naps during the day. Oh, and he can't cope with loud bangs, and an engine's backfire can leave him catatonic for a while. But once all allowances are made, he's a fucking good guy, and he'll be patched in before long.

The other change has been the security business, which I now concentrate on along with Keys. There's a gang who're running a protection racket, and we've stepped up to protect the businesses from them. We'd thought the message had been received

—they were messing on the wrong side of town—but apparently, according to Rope, we were wrong.

"They want a meet," Cuff states.

"You talked?" Brick questions, then turns his head away to cough.

"Couldn't do much else. We were fuckin' surrounded," Rope confirms. "Ten against two ain't good odds. Luckily, they wanted to parley more than shoot us down. Think they want to take a cut."

Keys is frowning. I know our security cameras had picked the gang up, but he couldn't get brothers there in time to help. They'd sprung Rope and Cuff as soon as they'd arrived to start their patrols for the night.

"We're lucky they didn't get violent," the VP states, his brow furrowed.

"Think they're declaring war?"

Brick looks at Twister but shakes his head. "Ten men were the whole fuckin' gang. That's not enough to take us on."

"Apart from the kids they use to throw bricks and shit," Crash points out.

I think about the problem for a moment, sensing the brothers are out for blood, as am I for the issues they're causing us. I just want to do it smart. "We just want them off our patch." I tap my fingers on the table as I think. While we charge peanuts to protect the businesses compared to the gang's extortion, we don't want to lose the income nor the reputation. Our side of Vegas is getting a good rep due to our protection. "They're greedy, untrained, but I don't think we should underestimate them."

Their idea of violence is arson, filling windows with bullets, or damaging vehicles. It's Brick's view they're all bluster, and we'd slaughter them in a fight. He could be right. We're a team, a family, we fight for each other. The gang members are more likely to run than take a bullet for one another. That's his theory, but I'm not sure I want to stake my life on it.

Titch settles back and crosses his arms. "We're damaging them. Our business is expanding. The sex shop owner was telling me the other day he's been recommending us."

"Yeah," Cobra says. "That's how the tattoo parlour came to hear about us."

Brick taps his fingers against the table. "Who are they expecting—" A fit of coughing interrupts him. It seems to go on forever. His face reddens, and Twister opens a bottle of water and passes it his way.

None of us say anything, though more than one glance is exchanged. At first, we put it down to the flu, but Prez didn't fully recover, and for the past year has been steadily worsening. We've learned, though, sympathy or probing is not taken kindly. I make a mental note to talk to Rosa later. Maybe she can get him to see someone. I see Cobra taking out a pack of smokes, catch his eye and shake my head at him. With a look toward the prez, Cobra nods, and puts away his cigarettes.

Having managed to get himself under control, Brick continues what he was saying. "Who are they expecting to talk to?" Now the flush has gone from his face, I notice how pale he's looking.

"You," Cuff states.

Brick snorts. "Fuck that. Ringo's not going to get the top man." Ringo being the gang's leader, and I agree with Brick's assessment. We can't give in to them or let them believe their leader carries the same weight as our prez.

"Send them a fuckin' prospect." Joker laughs, and there are a few sniggers at his suggestion.

"You want me to go?" Rainman asks, shooting Joker a look.

Prez thinks for a moment. "He won't be happy without an officer, so yeah, you go. Take Red, Cobra, Rope and Cuff with you."

"Prez," I start, then pause, having to wait for him to finish coughing again. "I don't like this. I'm not so sure they just want to talk. What if we're heading into an ambush?"

"Nah, Red," Brick says patiently. "If they wanted a fight, they wouldn't have let Rope and Cuff go free. I know these boys. They can bully the innocent but would run from an actual fight. They wouldn't want to take any of us on."

But it won't be him that's staking his life on it, and I kind of like mine.

"Prez is right," Rainman states. "We pushed them out of the area pretty easily. They're strong against civilians but won't take on the likes of us."

I don't agree, but who am I to argue with the VP and prez?

Crash catches my eye. "Want me and Twist to go to provide cover?" Turning his head, he shows his question is for the prez.

"Would put my mind at ease," I admit.

Indian leans forward. "I don't trust those assholes." I raise my chin to him, liking that we're on the same page.

Brick grimaces, then capitulates. "If it will make you feel easier, put snipers in place."

A few hours later, I'm riding behind Rainman, heading to the rendezvous, wondering if I'm wrong to give any heed to this impending sense of doom. Sure, Brick's view of the gang is that they're kids, but kids grow up and become men. Prez thinks these are just some upstarts making noises, seeing how far they can push before we shove them back.

I hope he's right. But in case he's not, I'm tooled up, and won't be lowering my guard.

Our orders? Make Ringo know he hasn't a chance at getting us to give up ground. To achieve that, all Brick thinks we need to do is show up and flex our muscles.

Thanks to the sergeant-at-arms though, we've a backup plan in case they come to talk with guns instead of their mouths.

The meet's around the back of a casino that had been built too far away from the strip, only lasting a few years before it went bust. Crash, Twister, Indian, and Joker are already in strategic positions, hidden with high-power rifles.

The decaying casino is bordered by a high steel fence aimed to keep out intruders, but there's a gap where druggies, pushers and whores have long since broken through. To suit all nefarious purposes, that modified entrance is out of the way and in an area not covered by CCTV cameras. It's wide enough for us to ride our bikes through. We're expected so there's no reason to hide our presence. Our approach is in no way covert. The gang are already here waiting for us, as Twister had already informed us. Our snipers had gotten here first.

We draw up just a few yards shy of the group standing around the back of the building, kicking down stands and cutting engines. I remove my helmet, hanging it over the handlebars, then place my gloves and safety glasses inside.

Rainman glances around, checks we're all in position, then gets off his bike and takes a step forward. Cuff, Rope, Cobra and I line up behind him. We're outnumbered, but some of the punks move backward at our approach, making me stifle a smile. *Fucking cowards.*

"Ringo." Rainman nods his head coolly at the man who we know leads the gang.

"Rainman." Ringo steps forward, his eyes flicking back toward his men as if to make sure none are going to start running.

The VP reaches into his pocket and gets out his cigarettes. Without offering them around, he takes one out and lights it. Only after twin plumes of smoke have come out of his nose, does he speak. "I ain't got all day, Ringo. What do you want to talk about?"

"Er," Ringo starts, then closes his mouth. When his men shuffle uneasily behind him, he clears his throat. "We need you to stay out of our business." His words are spoken so fast they almost run together.

Rainman shrugs. "You've come into our side of town. You were warned to stay out."

"Yeah?" The little punk puts his hands on his hips. "Well, we warned you not to try to take over."

"Not taking over, man," Rainman says easily, blowing smoke out again. "You've got your own territory, just stay out of ours."

"It was fuckin' ours until you lot chased us out." A man behind Rainman breaks ranks and steps forward. Behind him, others are getting noticeably agitated.

I share a look with Cobra. How did they expect this to go? We just shake hands and agree to take a cut in our payments? No fucking way.

Cuff's eyes meet mine. He widens his eyes, and shakes his head, then slightly turns his body, pulling my eyes in his direction of sight. It doesn't take a genius to work out what's caught his attention. Several of Ringo's men are fidgeting, and their hands look like they might be going for their guns.

I give a slight raise and dip of my head to show that I've gotten his point.

"Rainman," I say, softly. "Think both messages have been delivered. Why not allow Ringo to think on it?"

I've got a feeling this will be a fucking blood bath if we rile them up further. It's time to shut this shit down, and resume when we've got more of an upper hand.

"Think on fuckin' what?" Ringo asks, his body actions awkward. "There's nothing to think about. We need that money."

Rainman half turns to me and raises his chin. *Message received and understood.* "I'll take your requests back to the prez," he offers.

Brick won't change his mind, and neither will the club.

"Why the fuck isn't your prez here? It's him who I wanted to meet with tonight, not his fuckin' trained monkeys."

"I can speak on his behalf."

"Then why don't you?" Ringo is getting more riled. "Agree to pull your men out and let us take over."

A voice rings out, "Told you, you couldn't trust fuckin' Devils."

"You can trust Devils," Rainman contradicts, keeping his voice calm. "We're just sticking to the agreed boundaries. You stay out of our territory, and we won't go into yours."

"Ringo? Whatcha going to do? You gonna let them get away with this?" Another voice, this one high pitched and desperate.

As murmurs of discontent go around, Ringo leans in, lowering his voice. "Give me something or I'm going to lose this crew," he desperately confides.

"I've nothing to give," Rainman tells him apologetically. "Can't help with your problem, man."

Ringo's face contorts. He looks angry, upset, a man at the end of his tether. Then, he suddenly launches forward, closing in on Rainman before I can get my gun out.

Rainman gives a sharp cry and folds to the ground.

For a split second, I don't react, not sure what's happened, or how Rainman was hurt. Then, Ringo steps back, an evil looking flick knife that had been concealed on his arm, the blade dripping with blood.

Then I'm moving. "Take them the fuck out!" I scream, while extracting my gun and placing a bullet into Ringo's skull.

I don't have time to check on the VP, we're fighting for our lives. But we've expertise, organisation and snipers on our side. As bullets fly, the gang members are mostly mowed down, a couple trying to escape into the locked building, firing to cover their backs.

"Fuckin' assholes!" Cobra yells out. Swinging around, I see him clutching his arm.

"All clear?" I scream out.

"Clear!" Crash's loud voice comes back down from the rooftop.

I drop to my knees. "Rainman?" Then finding him unmoving, repeat with more desperation, "Rainman?"

"Red?"

Ignoring Cuff, I search for a pulse, unbelieving when I'm unable to find it. Gently, I turn Rainman over. Jesus Christ. It was a lucky strike, between the ribs and straight into his fucking heart.

"He's gone," I tell Cuff and Cobra softly, shaking my head in disbelief. Then my voice hardens. "He's fuckin' gone."

"What the fuck do you mean?" Rope asks, crouching and checking for himself.

As I just look at him, sadness shining out through my eyes, there's the sound of running feet.

"The VP's dead?" Crash sums up the situation fast. When I nod, he looks around. "Anyone else hit?"

"Me, got winged. I'll live." Cobra makes it out to be no big deal. At least he knows he'll be riding again, unlike our VP.

The loss of Rainman has hit us hard. No one seems to know what to do next and since the enemies are down, no one remains to face our anger. I look to the sergeant-at-arms, but he seems at a loss as much as anybody.

It's not my place, but as Twister and Joker approach, I take charge.

"Twister?" I raise my head, pointedly looking toward the dead bodies. "We've got to get Rainman home and them out of here."

For a moment, he looks like a man seeking a solution to a problem. "Fuckin' gangs. Always taking each other out." He looks around at us. "Rope, call Sarge, get him to bring the crash truck here. Everyone else, wipe your prints and get ready to say goodbye to your fuckin' guns. I want them all handed to me."

I nod in approval. He'll get rid of them, no way to link the shootings back to us.

Indeed, he takes it a step further, when the first guns are handed to him, he goes around the dead, seeking similar firearms and swapping them out. Now the cops, like Twister suggested, will simply think they've taken each other out.

As the adrenaline brought forth by the fight for our lives has started to fade, anger rises to take its place. *I knew we could be walking into a trap.*

But my objections had been overruled. And heaven help us, for that mistake, Rainman has lost his fucking life. Thank fuck Brick had agreed on sniper support, else we'd all be dead.

CHAPTER TWENTY-FOUR

Funerals suck. The last one I went to was for my father, and this one is no better. All my ears hear are expressions of sympathy for the man who was no doubt not the angel he's being painted to be, mentions of a better place to which he's heading when I'm sure if he's anywhere, he'll be looking up and not down. Not that I believe either option is available, dead is dead to my mind. A whole lot of nothing for the person concerned, but it's those he leaves behind who bear the brunt of it—a loss, a hole incapable of being filled.

And the what-ifs, such as why did I let Ringo get so close?

"I'm sorry, Brother."

As a familiar voice reaches my ears and a hand lands on my shoulder, I let out the breath I've been holding, feeling some of the tension that's been with me since the night of Rainman's death start to fade.

Turning, I clasp Wraith's hand, pulling him into me. The customary back slaps completed, he holds me at arm's length. "You doing okay?"

"Shouldn't have fuckin' happened," I tell him quietly. "Waste of a goddamn life." To him I can say the words I've up to now had to keep to myself.

"Brick's not on the ball." His reply is also sotto voce. "And, Brother, you're not the only one saying that."

"Vegas is tight with Brick." My statement contradicts his words. Rainman has been mourned, and now buried, without any admonishment for the orders that got him killed. Or, not in my hearing.

"Vegas has been on this path before, remember, Brother? Brick had to pull it back together. Who'd admit the man who gave them purpose in the club was losing his touch?"

My eyes narrow as I consider his words. Could it be that an outsider could see what was happening better than those looking from the inside?

"I tried to warn him—"

"I'm sure you did." Wraith pauses to raise his hand in greeting to one of the Colorado brothers who's walking past.

Rainman, a VP of the Satan's Devils, has had his funeral with full honours. As a prior forces' member, the Patriot Riders were also out in full force, as was representation from all our chapters.

He was a good man, he will be missed. *But why hadn't he stood up to Brick?* I'd seen doubt in his eyes that night and his blind obedience had led to his death.

"Red!"

This gruff voice I certainly recognise. "Drummer." We clasp hands, but the man hug is shorter than that from Wraith.

"Bad fuckin' business." My old prez stands with his arms folded across his chest, shaking his head.

Spilling my thoughts to my old prospecting partner is one thing, being critical of my present prez in front of Drummer wouldn't do me any favours, so I restrict myself to a simple response. "It sure is."

"Prez? Brick wants a meet. Hey, Red."

"Lefty," I greet him, going through the handhold back slap thing all over again. "Good to see you."

"And you, Brother. But I've gotta pull this one away."

This one, namely Drummer, narrows his steel-grey eyes

clearly messaging he'll be following Lefty in his own sweet time and only if it suits his purposes. But, nevertheless, he follows his VP away.

"I better be sociable." Wraith's staring at the members from the other clubs, in particular my brothers wearing the Vegas patch. "Offer my respects and all that." He goes to move off, then turns. "Any word on who I should suck up to? Who's going to replace him?"

"Truth, Bro? We haven't yet discussed it." In my head, I'm reckoning Twister or Crash will step up, the sergeant-at-arms being my best bet. I catch sight of someone. "Hey, who's that wearing your colours?"

"That?" He turns to look. "Oh, that's Adam. He's newly patched in. And with him are Mouse and Heart. Best day ever when we came across Mouse."

Translating Mouse as the man I knew as Tse, and Heart as Dale, I nod my head. "Yeah, Keys has been singing Mouse's praises." Mouse apparently knows his way around a computer like no one else in our chapters.

"I'll catch up with you later." Wraith lays a hand on my shoulder again, then walks off.

I raise my chin, feeling easier now I've caught up with my old Tucson brother. My brow creases as I ponder what he'd said earlier, about people seeing Brick wasn't at his best. That cough of his? Could it be something serious?

With Rainman's death and Rosa's preoccupation with organising his send off, I'd never had a chance to speak to her about encouraging her old man to see a doc. Fuck, if Brick was incapacitated, what would that mean for the club? Sooner we get a new VP voted in to be a strong second just in case, the better. If nothing else, Brick might need to rest up for a bit.

In my opinion, Rosa's an amazing asset for the Vegas club, or would be in any club for that matter. Since I've been here, it's easy to see how she balances out Brick, tempering his impulses and calming him when needed. She keeps the club running, makes sure we're fed, takes on the mantle of preparing for events such as this funeral, keeps the girls in line, and directs the prospects who do her bidding without complaining.

She's a quiet presence, always in the background. The relationship between her and Brick is sound, and both adore their kids. Looking at them at times, I'm envious. This is what I would have wanted, a strong woman by my side, one who'd complete me, and would take no shit while doing it.

Knowing today's not the time to broach the conversation with Rosa, I concentrate on raising my glass and sharing stories of our dead brother. Of course, most here have ridden beside him much longer than I, so my role is more of a listener, and to laugh in the right places.

Rainman was thirty-eight, far too young to die.

The day grows dark. Tables previously laden with food have been emptied, drinks flow freely, and more than one brother has passed out while those still capable of thought start talking revenge.

I'm tempted to join them but remember vengeance has already been taken. Ringo and his crew are dead. I'm also wary, for some reason, of fingers being pointed in the right direction. It would destroy the club were it to openly be acknowledged that Brick sent a man to his death, and that if it hadn't been for parts of the plan that had gone right—us having snipers in place—me, Cobra, Rope and Cuff could well be in our coffins lying alongside him.

"Kevlar." A familiar voice breaks into my reverie.

"Blade, Brother." I turn fast. After I've properly greeted him, I raise my eyebrows.

"Get yourselves stocked up with body armour. Doesn't protect against a head shot but will stop a bullet headed to the heart or a stabbing."

He's right. It would. I raise my chin in appreciation. "I'll bring it to the table."

Blade nods. "Yeah, Peg's made sure we're stocked up." He

pauses, and his eyes narrow. "You had enough of the bright lights yet?"

Is he suggesting if I have, I could go back to Tucson? I turn away, watching the people around me. If the option was there, would I take it? Go back to where a prez is fully fit and won't send his men into danger? Go back to having a suite with a bathroom all to myself? For a moment, I seriously consider the idea, then dismiss it.

"Nah, Sin City's okay, once you get used to it." And there's work to be done here. Whoever the next VP is, he'll need support. I'd held back from approaching Rainman, not thinking it was my place, but it irks me that as I hadn't tried hard to dissuade him, I bear some guilt in his death. Whether it's Twister or Crash who steps into his boots, I'll step out of the shadows. They'll get my views whether or not they want to hear them.

But any future plans have to be put on hold as I spend long hours socialising. It's good to catch up with my Tucson counterparts, then making myself known to brothers from our other clubs. Sarge, bolstered by help from prospects from other chapters, is run ragged trying to keep glasses topped up.

Funerals are emotionally draining, and I feel myself flagging. My bed starts calling me loudly when I notice I'm not the only one looking tired. Pixie, Jinx and Angel have been in high demand all evening, and spying Angel now, I see her eyelids are drooping. I'd seen Drummer go off with Pixie earlier, and Jinx is missing, probably servicing one of the visitors.

It's not unexpected. Death seems to want to be celebrated by acts of procreation, or at least, fucking, if only for a celebration of those still breathing, an affirmation they still have a life they're living.

Passing Angel, I give her a pat on the shoulder as I walk past.

Being one of the few hosts remaining upright, I forgo the temptation of my bed and stay until the clubroom begins to empty, or rather, people drag sleeping bags in and crash on the couches, and when those are filled, make do with the floor. A few of the visitors go to motels in the vicinity, but most have decided it's cheaper to bunk down at the clubhouse.

Brick looks dead on his feet, I notice, when the lights dim, and the music turns off completely. Rosa's got her arm around him, and I read concern in her eyes as she encourages him across to the metal staircase.

He grabs onto the handrail and pauses as he passes me. His chin lift seems to suggest he's pleased I'm still around. "Church tomorrow once our visitors have left."

I raise my chin. It's what I expected. "I'll be there."

"Red—"

Seeing his eyes full of regret, I shake my head. I want no apology, no acceptance that had he listened to me, Rainman wouldn't be dead. I don't want that shit brought out in the open. I want us to learn and move on from it. If Brick accepts responsibility, we'll have to talk about whether he's the right man to lead this club, and that's a topic I don't want to have to address yet.

He blinks, tightens his jaw, then starts pulling himself up the staircase, pausing halfway as a coughing fit makes him struggle for breath. I stand, watching Rosa help him to the top, unable to stop myself worrying about what's wrong with him, and how it will affect our chapter, when I hear a familiar voice.

"I've got faith in you, Brother."

I spin around. "Drummer." He's holding a bottle of water and is obviously making his way up to bed. We'd be accused of poor hospitality if we were unable to find room for the visiting mother chapter prez. But his statement unnerves me as I've no idea what he's referring to, or what response he might expect. So, I simply settle for another chin lift, and then stepping back, allow him to go ahead of me.

Then, with a final glance around that everything's quiet, I take myself off to bed where I fall into an exhausted slumber.

My sleep is broken by the sound of loud voices, boots stomping, and groans and cursing, then thunderous roars as bike after bike leaves the Vegas compound.

I'd said my goodbyes last night. Not being an officer, I'd had no duties to see our visitors off this morning. Instead, I roll over, closing my eyes, but I can't stop my mind from thinking.

A funeral should be a new beginning, a final goodbye then eyes turn to the future. But I can't get the desire for justice out of my head. *Rainman shouldn't have died.* I should have done more to prevent it. But would saying more have had any effect?

I'll speak to the new VP. He'll share my concerns about Brick, won't he?

By the time I've gotten to the front of the line to use one of the showers and have returned to my room and dressed, the clubroom is virtually empty of anyone but Vegas members. There are only a few stragglers.

Rosa and Tiff are bringing out fresh cups of coffee, so I grab one, and also a bagel from a tray which has been organised.

I drink, munch on my inadequate breakfast, eyeing Titch in the corner holding court with a couple of the other old-timers who'd hung back.

Then Brick appears from his office, announcing himself not with his familiar whistle, but with a hacking cough which serves well enough to get our attention. His arm wave in the direction of the meeting room is the only instruction.

Titch says his goodbyes. I put my used cup on the bar top, then along with the rest of my brothers, answer the summons.

We file into church, as if paying homage, each of us in turn looks at the empty chair to the left of the prez, knowing it won't be left vacant for long. There's only one reason for this meeting. To vote in the next VP. A club is vulnerable without the full quota at the top, unbalanced like a car running on only three wheels.

As I sit, I glance at the two men who I believe are in the running, wondering which of the pair I'd vote for if they both are contenders. I settle on Crash. He's the steadiest. Twister's okay, a good enforcer, but I'm not sure he'd handle the VP's role quite as eloquently as I'd expect from the sergeant-at-arms. I wonder which way the others will be voting.

Brick coughs but takes out his pack of smokes and lights one. He draws in the smoke deep, and it seems to calm his lungs. I frown, a temporary reprieve I would expect, they can't be good for him.

Nevertheless, most men, including myself, follow his example and light up.

Brick bangs the gavel and taps at the papers he's placed in front of him. "There's only one reason why we're here today, Brothers, and that ain't no secret. It's to vote in the man who can fill the shoes Rainman had walked in." He pauses, takes another drag, then continues, "I need a man to be my second, a man capable not only of leading, but being able to get others to follow him. The club needs a man who can think on his feet. Each of you might have ideas as to who that man is." He takes another pause as he examines their faces.

"It's up to each of you to put forward the name of who you'd most like to see in the seat next to me." He slides half the blank pieces of paper toward Fox and gives the other half to Crash. "Put the name of the man you think is right for VP on the paper. We'll see where we are when that's completed."

I'm surprised he didn't put forward the name of the man he wants as his number two, but maybe there's a reason for giving everyone a chance. The main problem is finding a fucking pen to write with. Most of us have knives, but Joker's option for stabbing a name out or Cuff's for writing it in blood was turned down.

Fox, at last, produces a pen and we pass it around. I deliberately don't try to look at what the brothers beside me are writing, and I see more than a few cupping with their non-dominant hand to protect their chosen name from prying eyes. Inwardly I grin. I'd place good money only two men would be named, it's just a question of who comes out on top.

I double over my paper in half, then for good measure fold it again, and push it into the middle of the table, then sit back and fold my arms. Sooner we get this over with, the sooner we can move on.

"Fox. You up for counting?"

Fox nods and reaches out his hand, pulling the stack of folded paper toward him. Meticulously he takes the top one, straightens it and smooths it out. He perches his probably unneeded glasses on his nose and reads out, "Red."

What the fuck?

I glance around, wondering who the fuck could have proposed me, but not one face gives anything away. I nevertheless feel I have to defend myself. "I didn't write that."

"That was an option?" Joker's eyes open wide. "Fuck, I'd have proposed myself."

There are snorts all around. Joker's a good sort, but VP material he is not. Much like myself.

Fox has the second paper straightened. "Red."

This has got to be some kind of fucking joke. I narrow my eyes, waiting for the laughs, then watch as he takes another vote and opens it up. Now, surely, we'll get one of the serious contenders.

"Red."

My eyes go to Brick, expecting to see him frowning, but one side of his mouth is turned up.

"Crash."

Thank fuck. That's a rightful vote. Now there'll be more to come.

"Red."

"Red."

"This is getting boring." Rope slides down in his chair.

I growl at him. *Boring?* It's anything but. I'm just pre-occupied trying to work out what the fuck's going on.

The next few votes are opened and for each the same name is pronounced. *Every one of the fuckers voted for me.* The one vote for Crash had to have come from myself.

Stunned, I don't know whether I can believe it. Me, VP? The words don't compute. I can't fucking comprehend. I'm not counting my chickens yet either. There were two names, now we'll vote on them both. Crash should get his rightful place, the one he's worked for and earned.

As the final vote has been counted, Brick picks up the gavel. "Red's VP."

As the men around me start hollering, I slap my hand down. "Hold up. There are two names put forward—"

Crash raises his hand. "I'm happy where I am. If need be, I withdraw my nomination."

"Get your ass up there, Brother," Twister shouts, pointing to the empty chair.

"Congrats, VP!"

"Fuckin' ace, Brother."

As the shouts ring out, Brick uses his foot to kick out the chair at his side, and grins widely in my direction.

Cobra, moving behind me, pulls out my seat so fucking hard, if my reactions hadn't been fast, I'd have ended up on my ass.

In a state of total bemusement, I stand, cuff Cobra around the head, then walk the couple of steps needed. I pause for a moment, feeling it's all wrong taking the chair that Rainman sat in last, then, at another prompting from Prez, sit my ass down, still shaking my head.

I'd left Vermont hoping to find a future. I never expected to end up in an outlaw motorcycle club, let alone be appointed to an officer role. It blows me away that all my brothers think I'm right for this club.

Can I do it? For a moment, I think about all the problems I was going to lay in the new VP's lap and realise now they'll be my responsibility. I frown, then slowly, my face relaxes.

Fuck yes. This is my chance. If I see something wrong, I'm now in a position where I can do something about it.

I'm the VP, one step down from the prez.

It's going to take more than a moment to get my head around it.

CHAPTER TWENTY-FIVE

When the extraordinary meeting is over, I want to talk to Brick, if for nothing more than to talk about how our new partnership is going to work. But when a brand-new VP patch is passed over, and the gavel finally comes down, I'm yanked out of my chair by at least two sets of arms.

"Party!" Keys shouts.

I try to pull away, my eyes meeting Brick's. "Prez—"

Brick's eyes sparkle as he waves his hand. "Go. Enjoy yourself. We've plenty of time to catch up later."

"First duty as VP," Joker yells. "Join us in getting drunk."

I open my mouth to protest but shut it when I remember every one of these assholes just voted me in as VP. Every. Fucking. One. How the fuck did I deserve that? And how am I going to live up to it?

I could be coy, could say I've done nothing to warrant such support, but that would be deceitful. I'm confident I'm the man for the job. I just hadn't expected anyone to recognise it, nor held out any hope that I'd ever be able to contribute from anything other than a lowly member's seat. I won't let power go to my head, but it's a heady rush to know I've now got a chance of stopping useless deaths like Rainman's in the future. When I have my say, my new role means I'll be listened to, even by the prez.

As Cuff drags me out by the arm and Rope's somehow got his hand on my back steering me toward the bar, I feel overwhelmed by just how much faith this club has in me. It's not until I have a beer in my hand that Drummer's words of last night come back. *I've got faith in you.*

The wily mother chapter prez had known what was going to go down, he had to. He'd been ensconced with Brick yesterday. Maybe it had been his plan. But how had they got one hundred percent of the members on board in such little time? There'd been no closed-door meeting that I'd been told about.

It's a question I ask Fox later, as I've got what must be the fifth beer in my hand. "How did Brick persuade you?"

"Persuade us about what?" Fox sways, reaches out his hand to hold the bar for balance, misses, stumbles and would have crashed to the floor if not for my somewhat quick thinking, automatically blocking his fall with my arm.

Once he's righted himself, I elaborate, "Persuade you to vote for me."

Fox's glazed eyes clear, and he gives a vehement shake of his head, after which he takes a moment to get steady again. "He didn't. Well, not to me. As far as I'm aware, we all made up our own minds."

He's lying, isn't he? But one look at the confusion on his face assures me he's not.

"Look… look…Bro…ther." He's starting to slur. His finger comes out and digs into my chest as he punctuates his next words. "You've sorted our businesses, got us on the right track. Pulled this fuckin' club together by just believing in us. Your advice about Rainman's last ride should have been heeded, but it wasn't. We love you, Brother, and we need you."

Well, doesn't that just give a person a fuzzy warm feeling inside? One that's amplified when Rosa walks up, reverently carrying my cut she'd offered to sew the VP patch onto. For a moment when I take it, I just hold it, trying to focus my eyes. My lips curve as I read over and over, *Vice President* and underneath that, my name, *Red*.

"Stop admiring it and fuckin' wear it," Titch, coming up behind me, growls.

Chuckling, I do as he says, realising even this old man had lent his support to me.

Titch orders another round, this time with chasers. Well, I'll be fucked if I remember much more after that.

My back is slapped until I fear I'll be bruised later, and my head spins with the amount I've drunk. When I can barely stand any longer, I'm escorted to the stairs. Cuff steps up alongside me and takes my arm. I shake him off.

"I've got it from here, Brother." I eye him suspiciously, my alcoholic haze bringing doubts to the fore. He's a kinky asshole, and he's not getting into my bed. *Uh-uh.* I'm heterosexual, thank you very much. Dicks really don't do it for me.

"Nah, come on." It seems I can't shake him off. Nor Rope, who's stepped to my other side.

"Leave me alone," I growl. But in shrugging them off, I lose my balance and would have fallen if it hadn't been for Hammer standing one step beneath me.

"Brother," Twister drawls, sounding amused. "They ain't gonna jump your bones. Just want to see you get to bed okay."

For some reason, it seems pertinent to hold on to the belt on my pants, my drunken mind telling me if I keep them secure, I won't get molested.

With my free hand, I grip tight to the banister, taking the steps carefully one at a time. My head is spinning by the time I reach the top, so I pause for a moment getting my equilibrium back into balance. Glancing around suspiciously, I realise Keys, Shadow and Joker have also come along, and for some reason seem to be waiting for me.

I just want to crash on my bed. I won't bother getting

undressed. I push on, this time using the wall for support until I'm in front of my door.

"Night," I manage to get out, then turn to find the door handle which seems to evade my hand.

"Nah, this way, VP." Cuff again gets a hold of my arm.

I shrug him off. "Not sleeping with you, Brother." I think for a moment, and then add, to be polite, "No offence."

He chuckles. "None taken."

But the asshole still won't let go. Hammer's behind me, helping Twister push me along. Fuck knows where they're taking me.

My head is spinning, and my stomach is threatening to rebel. "Come on, Brothers. A joke's a joke—"

Suddenly Cuff throws open a door. Hammer and his helper push me inside. I stop, one step over the threshold, looking around in shock.

My bedding is on the bed, and it's all made up, not left the way I'd rolled out of it hours before. My books and laptop are on the desk, my riding gear hanging over the chair. *But it's not my room.*

It's Rainman's.

Sadly, he won't be needing it anymore. And there's nothing here left of him. That picture by the bed is of my dad, along with the one of me and the Tucson brothers. The one hanging up, a Harley I'd admired. And if I'm not mistaken, were I to open the closet and drawers, I'd bet good money they'd be stocked with my clothes.

"Fuck, man, you stink," Cuff helpfully points out. "Think you better take a shower."

I grab onto my belt buckle again, half suspecting he'll offer to help, when I suddenly realise what he's making a fuss about. It's the door that's in the middle of what was, in my room, a plain wall. A door that's open, revealing a basin and a stall, and behind that I know I'll find a cubicle containing a shower.

My own en suite.

"Think we'll leave the officer to get acquainted with the room his new status brings." Hammer chortles behind me.

I'd taken the VP patch incredulously, but that was its own reward. I'd never expected there to be any other benefits connected to the rank or to be moved into the officer accommodation, or, if I had thought about it, not so fast or so soon. No wonder I'd seen little of Sarge today, he'd had to have been working his ass off.

"We'll leave you to it." Twister slaps my back hard.

"Unless," Rope pokes me in the ribs, and inclines his head toward Cuff giving an exaggerated wink, "you'd like us to stay?"

"Get out of here!" I roar, turning and manhandling all of them out, losing my balance in the process and all but falling against the door.

When I'm alone, I concentrate hard and manage to turn the key in the lock. *Can't be too careful.* Even though I think it was just drunken sport, I'm not sure I'd put too much beyond the reach of Rope and Cuff.

Still needing the door to balance me, I lean against it as slowly a smile comes to my face. I might not have the balcony or the view of the forest, but I've got my own head and a shower. What more can a guy want?

"Look at me now, Ma," I say to no one but the empty room.

Then, unable to support myself any longer, I slide down to the floor and pass out.

Sometime during the night, I must have crawled my way into bed, but when I wake, I can't quite remember. *Fuck, I laid one on last night.* My first waking thought is the overwhelming need to vomit.

Fucking grateful that I've my own bathroom now, I manage to get to it in time, leaning over the commode and purging my stomach, grateful there's no audience. It's bad enough puking without one of your brothers giving a running commentary, and yes, I've been there and done that.

Once I've gotten over the feeling I'd prefer to die, I wait a moment for the room to stop spinning, then flush, and try standing upright. When my head stabilises, I try the shower. It's powerful and hot, and probably thanks to Sarge, my toiletries are at hand.

My head's all over the place, trying to process this sudden and unexpected change in my fortunes.

I'm the fucking VP.

It's not that I'm afraid of the role or fucking up. I know I can do it. It's just while I've committed to give my all to the club, I've never had dreams or visions of rising through it. The only officer I know of who left his role while still breathing had been Tide, our road captain, and that was only because he landed himself in prison.

Road Captain. The club had never replaced him. Maybe I'd broach the subject now. I know previously no one had wanted the job, but I've a feeling Joker would be up for it. Despite the drums banging in my head, I smile to myself. *I've got power now.* It wouldn't hurt to use it.

But other than Tide, once an officer had the support of the club, they were in the role unless they seriously fucked up, or until they left it for a coffin. Even when Rainman had been laid in the ground, I'd had no inclination that I'd be chosen to replace him.

Brick could have easily already had a name in mind, one of the longstanding members.

They all chose me.

Sure, for the past three years I've put my heart and soul into this life. I've no family, so the Devils have become mine. I've nurtured the relationship and the club as I would have a wife and child, done my best for them, advised, cajoled, suggested... I suppose thinking back, most of my ideas had been acted upon, but I hadn't wanted thanks for it. Why should I? When our income went up, I'd benefitted from it.

Being VP is going to heap responsibility on my shoulders, but hey, I'm up for it. *I'm so fucking up for it.*

Normally, I'd leave the bathroom dressed in at least a towel, but today I stride out naked knowing there's no one to comment. I stretch, fart, scratch my balls, relishing the freedom of the basic human necessity, *privacy.* Something I'd gotten used to not having, and never expected.

Now if only the thumping beat in my head would stop.

I go to my bedside table, and hey, Sarge has worked his magic again. The inevitable pack of condoms is there, and under it, a pack of Advil. I take two tablets and swallow them dry, then pause, my hand on my stomach, willing it to settle.

Today's a fresh start.

Dressed in my usual uniform of black jeans and black tee, I slide on my cut, glancing down at the fresh patch with pride. I run my fingers over it. *Might not have been what you expected of me, Dad, but I hope you're proud.*

Perhaps it's lucky I don't have an old lady. Carrying no baggage means no distractions. I vow in that moment to be the best fucking VP this club has ever had. Well, when I get rid of my headache.

Lighting a cigarette, I take a drag, then, when satisfied it doesn't make me want to throw up, open the door and step out. When I reach the clubroom, the state of the men around me suggests I wasn't the only one to have overindulged last night.

Sarge, wiping down tables, looks cheerful, but Crash and Twister both have their heads in their hands. Keys doesn't look much better, and Cobra blinks then slides shades down over his eyes.

At that moment, the door bangs open and two rowdy boys rush inside.

"I said play outside!" Rosa shouts, her voice piercing my brain. "Go on, take those water pistols back out." Trist and Tom's faces fall, but they thankfully obey her sharp demand. Then, as peace mercifully descends again, she notices me standing there, and beams a welcoming smile. "Breakfast, VP?"

Fucking hell. Her use of that title sounds good. I have to fight from keeping myself from grinning and punching my hand in the air.

Yeah. Something to eat might settle me. I nod, wince, then follow her into the kitchen. There I find Brick, nursing a coffee, but looking remarkably unscathed. As I recall, he'd left the party early.

He lights a cigarette as I stub mine out into an ashtray that's already overflowing, then drains his coffee cup and stands.

"Eat, then come talk to me." When I raise my chin, he goes to his old lady, and enfolds her in his arms. She relaxes into him briefly, then turns her face to his. Her eyes soften, and her hand cups his cheek. They stay like that for a few seconds.

I feel like an interloper. They're close, I already know that, but such open affection between the pair is unusual. It almost makes me jealous for a relationship I don't have. *Would Cheryl have looked the same way at me? With such love and concern?*

Berating myself for being maudlin, I take my eyes off the prez and his old lady and approach the stove. But Rosa, having dismissed her husband, gets in front of me and bats away my hand. She then proceeds to heap a plate with bacon, eggs, waffles and sausage links.

Three coffees, two more cigarettes and a big breakfast inside me, I feel human enough to go meet the prez.

CHAPTER TWENTY-SIX

As I approach Prez's door, I hear him coughing. When I enter, he's popping tablets out of a strip and washing them down with water.

He glances up, examines me carefully for a moment, before chuckling and raising his chin. "VP. You've got a bit more colour than you had earlier."

"Yeah. It was a good night." I grin back.

"That it was." He leans back in his chair, linking his hands behind his head. "So, you and me." He waves his hand between us as he wastes no time getting down to the matter at hand.

Our new partnership. "I've got your back, Prez."

"Never doubted it for a fuckin' minute, Brother. And before you ask, I had no hand in how the votes played out. Drummer did Vegas a solid when he sent you to us. He fuckin' knew what he was doing."

I frown. "He couldn't have predicted how things would play out." Unless he'd a crystal ball that I'd not been party to.

Brick nods. "Yeah, no one could have foreseen Rainman's death." He grimaces slightly. "Though you did try and warn me."

I had. But what's the point of rehashing things now? Shrugging, I tell him, "I didn't envisage it would play out to that extent."

"I think you did," Brick challenges, and levels me with a gaze that's not quite as effective as Drummer's but chilling all the same. "You tried to tell me, I didn't listen. I was too quick to dismiss those pricks."

"No one blames you, Prez. You've known Ringo far longer." Though I do think it's his fault, what's the point of making him feel worse? Sure, he could have done something to prevent it, but nothing's going to bring Rainman back. And now I'm his second, I can speak more forcibly when I don't think things are right.

"Which means I should have known." No longer looking relaxed, he leans forward, his fist meeting the table, making paperwork on it jump. He then wipes both hands against his cheeks, pulling at his skin and drawing down his eyes which I can see are tinged with red.

He looks tired.

A wave of sympathy goes through me. Well, I'm here now to share the weight. "What do you need me to do, Prez? I mean, I get I'll take on what Rainman was doing, but what more do you want me to do to help?"

He shakes his head. "Straight to the fuckin' crux of the matter," he mumbles, half to himself. "There's no beating around the bush with you, is there, Red? And no hiding that I've not been myself."

"Prez—" I go to deny it, but he holds up his hand.

"You ask me what I need you to do, Red? I'll be straight with you. This isn't going to work if there are secrets between us." He pauses, takes a deep breath, then announces, "I need you to learn how to run this fuckin' club."

My head dips and rises. "Sure, that's the VP's job. To back you up and act on your behalf when necessary."

Brick's lips open, but before he can speak, he's overcome with a coughing fit. Taking a handkerchief out of his pocket, he holds it over his mouth. It takes him more than a minute to get himself together. When he finishes, he's flushed and breathing heavily. Instead of speaking again, he takes out his cigarettes, lights one, then slides the pack toward me.

"Should you even be smoking?" I ask, taking one, placing it in my mouth, then leaning forward to accept a light.

He gives a nonchalant shrug. "Won't make no difference whether I do or do not. Which brings me to the conversation we need to be having."

I start to get a bad feeling in my gut. Brick's got health problems, no one needs to tell me that. Apart from his coughing, there were those tablets he'd swallowed when I walked in. At least he's on medication.

Jumping to a conclusion, I take a drag on my cigarette, then state, "You're ill. You need me to step up for you? Just tell me what to do and I'm there."

The smoke, strangely, seems to have calmed his lungs, at least for now. He takes a deep breath, shudders as he lets it out, then states, "I trust you, Red. What I'm going to tell you is just between us for now. I got your word on that?"

"You've got my word." He doesn't need to ask me. I suspect there's quite a lot that needs to be kept tight between VP and Prez.

"Rosa knows. No one else. Not even the kids." He pauses, but realising it's more to gather his thoughts than expecting me to say something, I stay silent. I'm rewarded when a few seconds later he resumes. "Not going to pretty it up. I've got lung cancer."

I'm a problem solver. "Right. Give up the smokes for a start. Hell, I'll be right behind you." I stub out my half-smoked cigarette to make the point. "You need time off for treatment? Then I'll step right up—"

"Whoa, there, Brother." Brick stops my flow. He grimaces. "I've been a fuckin' fool, or maybe it wouldn't have made a difference, but I ignored the signs. Brushed it off as a smoker's cough. Rosa," another pause as his face softens, "Rosa finally got her way and pushed me to see a doc. Seems I left it too late, it's already spread. I've only got a few months."

I draw in a breath and hold it, trying to compute what I'm being told. I'd come here expecting to talk about our long-term partnership, and he's hitting me with the suggestion our time working together will be short. "Jeez, Brick. I don't—"

"There's nothing to say. It is what it is." Brick stares at me. I take that moment to examine him closely. Now I'm really looking at him, now his flush is fading, his skin's not only pale, it looks grey. But his eyes are still sharp as they focus on me. "I'm going to die in harness. I'm not going to give up and fade away. I'll stay in this chair as long as the Devil lets me."

I'll be beside him all the way. "I'll do whatever I can."

He wipes his hand over his mouth. "This isn't fair on you, Red, but I want you to start planning. You'll have to be my shadow, ready to take over. I… I just don't want anyone else to know. I don't want pity or sympathy, or people taking it easy on me. And I don't want to upset the members."

"Shouldn't you plan for a successor?"

Brick snorts. "What the fuck do you think I'm doing? You think anyone would accept someone from outside the club? Nah, the only man they'll look up to is their VP."

VP? But that's me. "Brick, no. I've not been in this role for a day. If you're suggesting what I'm thinking…"

"I'm suggesting when I'm gone, you take the title of Prez." He puts it so bluntly it leaves me stunned.

A few seconds pass before I can speak. "No way, Brother." VP is hard enough to get my head around. I'm pretty sure I know what it involves, but Prez? Leading the club? Answering to no one but Drummer? I'm not ready for that. Give me a few years and maybe, but it seems I haven't got years, only a few months.

"Yes, way, Red. Either you work with me on this, or you can get out of my club."

Leave the club? I sit back, fold my arms, lower my chin and start thinking. I'm ambitious, seems odd to say as people would see me ticking along in an outlaw motorcycle club just getting by and having the time of my life. They may be right, but it doesn't mean I don't want to make that endeavour the best that I can. I'd hoped to maybe run a business under the SD umbrella, but run the whole fucking club? Be responsible for its members?

"I'm not leaving the club," I tell him, my voice calm and measured. "You've just laid a lot on me. I'm gutted you're going through this, Brick. If there's any way to help, I will. I'm not even sure I'm cut out to be prez." In my head, I'm thinking of Drummer or Brick himself. Could I be like them? Firm, fair, taking no shit from anyone, having decisions that lead to the life or death of the members? Something occurs to me. "The whole thing got fucked when Rainman died."

"Stop there, Red. If this is to work, we need to be straight with each other. Rainman was a good second, but I had my doubts about him leading the club. I never told him my diagnosis." His brow furrows. "I think I was putting it off. I wish he was still here, Brother, don't think I don't. But his death, and the votes of the members has given me a chance at something I didn't have. Having someone worthy to take over the club."

I'm dumbfounded. I hadn't expected that. I'd thought I was a poor second choice.

"I was burying my head in the sand like the proverbial ostrich, hoping I could wish my problem away, but it doesn't work like that, does it?" Brick shakes his head. "Fate stepped in and somehow gave me an option, one that I think the members would accept."

I purse my lips. "It's one thing voting me in as VP, but as the prez?"

Brick nods. "Bit of a leap in one day, isn't it?" He leans forward, elbows on the table, chin resting on his hands as if needing the support. "Which is one of the reasons why we're going to keep this secret. We've got a bit of time to work on this together. You'll shadow me, work closely with me. Learn every fuckin' thing about how I run this business, and that's what it is, okay? It's budgets, insurances, and a lot of HR thrown in. You'll let the members see you're up to running this club. Then, when I need to... step back... they'll look to you to take my place." He stares at me, his eyes narrowing. "We can't show weakness. The vultures would start gathering if they thought I was going soft. We've dealt with Ringo and his gang, but there will be others coming onto our turf. You need to be seen by my side, deal with shit on my behalf. You need to become me even while I'm still living."

I'm having problems sitting here talking to a man about his death. It's unnerving. But like a deathbed promise, I know I'll give his last wishes everything I have. As he's said, what's the alternative?

"I'll do it." I'll deal with the fact I'll become an MC prez later. Maybe, after we've done all he's said, I'll grow into it.

"I knew I could count on you, VP. I just need your word you'll keep my condition secret. I don't want anyone to know. No one in the club, no one outside of it."

"Drummer?" I ask, seeing as he's the mother chapter prez.

"No one," he rasps, fixing me with another stare. "This is our club business."

It's his call if that's the way he wants to play it. I give him a chin lift to show I understand.

"Just one thing. Rosa." Brick looks down as his breath catches. "This is so fuckin' unfair on her. Her and the boys." He glances back up. "Oh, don't get me wrong. She's a strong fuckin' woman. She knows what's coming. She's prepared for it."

As his mouth twists, I reckon there's been a lot of tears, a lot of recriminations, and a lot of what might have beens and many regrets. But Rosa is a practical woman, she'll know there's no running from it.

I jump to the conclusion as to why he's brought her up. "She'll always have a place in the club, Brick. If she wants it."

Relief floods his face. "You hear how Rosa and I got together?"

I can honestly shake my head. No one's mentioned it. I just kind of assumed they'd always been a pair.

"I met her on her first night on the street. She was looking for a john. Her parents threw her out because she was pregnant. Well, I couldn't leave her there, took her in, had some idea about her being a sweet butt in the club. At that time, I was just a member." He pauses to grin. "When it came to it, I wasn't gonna let any other fucker near her. When she lost the baby, I was as devastated as she was. Had been looking forward to having the little fucker around. That's when I realised what she meant to me, so I claimed her and married her. Best fuckin' thing I've ever done. Oh, apart from eventually giving those babies to her. Twins." He shakes his head. "Fuck. She took years to conceive again, but in the end, we were rewarded." He chuckles and adds, "Or punished."

Yeah, Prez is well aware what handfuls the kids are in the club.

"Club's her home." I state the obvious.

"You picked that up?" Brick smiles. "Yeah, her homelife was shit. When I took her in, she thought this place was a fuckin' palace. She loves me, loves the club. Once part of that is gone—"

"She'll still have us. Still have her home. And," considering I'll be unlikely to take an old lady as no one has yet crossed my path, "she'll still be queen of it."

A huge sigh comes out of him. He doesn't have to verbally give me thanks. It's written all over his face.

I decide to lighten the moment. "And it will help to have someone to keep me on my toes."

"Oh, she'll do that, Brother. She'll do that." He grins widely, but the effect is spoiled by his cough.

CHAPTER TWENTY-SEVEN

I suppose it's only natural once you've heard news like I had, that for the next few days I'm watching Brick like a hawk, waiting for any sign of weakness or a suggestion he can't cope.

But now I've agreed to take the mantle from him, he's rallied, so much so, I start to think the diagnosis was wrong. He still smokes, still coughs, but his complexion is ruddier, though that could be due to the hot Vegas sun.

He readily agreed to put my suggestion of Joker for road captain to the vote, and the whole club accepted it. It was more of a *why didn't we think of that before?* then any question we didn't need one or that the man put forward wasn't right for it.

Joker was over the moon and couldn't stop grinning. Watching him carefully, I wondered whether the man had been uncertain of his acceptance by the club, and this promotion had cemented it. Whatever, he appeared to be more settled and happier.

He's a strange one, I think to myself. He leads us to believe he has a honey in town which is why he never goes with the sweet butts, but he never brings her to any of our parties and isn't even forthcoming on her name let alone any other details. Still, each to his own. As long as he doesn't put her needs before the club, it's nothing for me to worry about.

I've more concerns than his love life or lack of it to deal with. Brick's as good as his word, getting me to accompany him to meetings I'd only heard of before. I'd attended a meet with the prez of the local Wretched Soulz chapter, the dominant club all over the southwest. I wouldn't be able to deny Missile, the prez, gave me a warm welcome, but his eyes were narrowed as though summing me up. His VP, Debunk, was more reserved, his manner suggesting he'd reserve judgement until such a time as I'd proved myself.

You and me both, Brother, I'd thought to myself. Unless Brick defies medical science, it's me they'll be dealing with in just a few months. Unless, of course, the club chooses another, but as Brick had said, no man comes to mind. In my assessment, Crash would make a great second, but he's not a leader. Same goes for Twister.

The only other contender is Indian. The man's impressed me, but as he's not in an officer role yet, and raising an as yet unknown quantity to run the club would be unheard of. Though it's hard to think in terms of a future without the larger-than-life Brick in it, I do wonder about the make-up of the team I'd like around me.

Crash now, I'd like him as my VP, which would leave vacant the sergeant-at-arms spot. Indian, yeah, that's who I'd like to step up.

I bang the heel of my hand to my forehead, hating I'm thinking about stepping into Brick's shoes. I'd rather hide my head in the sand just like he's done. I've only just been made VP for fuck's sake. How can I get the brothers behind me to accept me, let alone help me to run the club?

But Brick's good. More so than he did with Rainman, he defers to me in front of the brothers. My business ideas with his clear approval get the go-ahead. His obvious show of confidence boosts my standing within the club.

Members start bringing their problems to me, matters they wouldn't have brought to the old VP. I take pleasure in finding routes to resolve them.

Soon, I'm wearing the VP mantle as though it's always rested on my shoulders. I get comfortable, and if most times I forget about the future, who could blame me? Brick looks strong as an ox. I start to doubt a little thing like cancer can bring him down. As a month passes, followed by another, then a further one zooms past, I start to think the future isn't mapped out as clearly as Brick had set out.

Four months have gone by since that first meeting between prez and new VP. As I stride across the clubroom, heading toward church, my phone vibrates in my pocket. My lips curve up as I see the caller. Deciding I'll tell him I'll call him back after the meeting, I answer.

"Hey, Brother. Good to hear from you, but—"

"Red." Just the way Wraith says my name pulls me up.

Pausing my steps, I enquire sharply, "What's up?"

There's an intake of breath, then, "Lefty hit the dust. Came off at speed, Red. He's gone."

Lefty? Dead? "Oh, fuck, Brother." He was a solid man for the Tucson chapter. They'll miss him like fuck.

"His funeral's on Monday. Wanted to know if you can make it, Brother."

Of course, I'll move heaven and earth to be there. I'd spent my formative MC years in that club, and Lefty had a hand in making me the man that I am. "I'll be there, Wraith. You don't need to ask."

"Everyone else is invited. We want to give him a good send-off."

Shit. Brick won't be able to make it. While I try to ignore the life sentence he's got, an eight-hour ride is too much to ask for a man who's standing beside, if not quite yet lying on his deathbed. Quickly, I think of an excuse. "Brick will be tied up, but I'm sure we can bring a good contingent."

"Tell Brick no worries, Brother. It's short notice. It's come as a shock."

"I'm heading into church. I'll bring it up there." While I've been speaking, brothers have been walking around me, and with a hand gesture, I've been indicating I'll join them shortly.

"Everyone's welcome, Brother."

"Take care, Wraith." I know this must have hit them all badly. "I'll see you in a couple of days."

"Want me to warm Pussy up for you?" His tone, which had understandably been sombre, lightens.

I snort. Trust Wraith. But the thought of sharing Pussy just like old days? Fuck yeah. I end the call having answered in the affirmative.

I'm the last to enter church. As I take my seat, Brick is watching me carefully.

"Problems?"

I tap the table and grimace. "Tucson's lost Lefty, their VP. Came off his bike, apparently."

"A hit?" Indian queries.

"Nah." I'm basing that on the way Wraith told me. "Accident. Anyway, the funeral's Monday. We're all invited." I catch Brick's eye and hold it. "I've given your apologies already."

"Whatcha up to, Prez?"

I round on Titch. "He's got a meet with Missile."

Brick raises an eyebrow at me and gives a nod showing he's caught on quickly. "In turn, I'll give your apologies to the Wretched Soulz. You're right, one of us should be there."

"I'm up for a shindig," Rope says.

"Me too," Cuff joins in, not surprisingly.

I bite my tongue to stop myself growling that they'll be going to pay their respects, but they hadn't known Lefty, and wouldn't know how much the man meant to me.

As it turns out, with the exception of Titch, most want to go. Lefty was a Satan's Devil, and he'd get the send-off he'd have been right to expect.

After our normal business is sorted, Joker gets his instructions to make sure everyone gets their bikes ready for the ride. It's decided Sarge will be coming to drive the crash truck.

I start to look forward to returning to Tucson, even if it's for a reason I wouldn't have chosen. The Arizona chapter started me on my MC journey. I've a lot to be thankful to them for, including Lefty, of course. Fuck, but it will seem odd without him there.

Joker proves I was right to suggest him for the role, and thanks to his diligence, our ride to Tucson goes without incident. He's planned every detail down to all the fuel stops, taking account of the various sized tanks. The crash truck was loaded with spare tyres and parts, thankfully none of which were needed.

Having set off in the small hours, it's one in the afternoon when we arrive. There's not much time to do anything other than take our place in the escort following the hearse. Then, as always, we all stand with heads bowed as we remember our fallen brother while he's being laid into the ground.

There but for the grace of God, or of Satan, go I, goes through my head and I don't doubt the majority of others. A turn misjudged, a slick of oil on the road, a spoke through a tyre could happen to any of us at any time. There's a reason why bikers pledge their lives so readily. Just riding means they're already living on the edge. Any person who mounts a two-wheeler knows they take their life in their hands each time they ride.

It doesn't mean the loss of a brother is made easier. It's always fucking hard and serves to remind us all of our own fragile longevity.

Honours done, we again fall in line and ride back to Tucson. On the compound, we meet with a variety of people. Colorado, Utah and San Diego have turned out in numbers. As the highest-ranking member from Vegas, I have to exchange pleasantries with the prezes of the other clubs. Hellfire and Snatcher are both old-school, gruff, but clearly good at their jobs and have a ton of respect from their members. Bird from San Diego also seems alright. It's the first time I've been greeted as a fellow officer, and I don't feel I let myself or my club down.

Thank fuck. If Brick's health declines, I'll soon be their equal. That's still hard to get my head around.

Eventually, my duties as Vegas's representative are done, and I catch up with Wraith.

"You fucker!" I pull him in and slap his back. "I've heard your news. You kept that quiet."

Wraith looks in no way contrite. "It's Lefty's day."

"True. But congrats are also in order. Hey, Brother. Look at us now." I stab at the brand-new VP patch on his cut.

He can't hide his pleasure and he gives a wide grin. "Puts all that back-breaking work into perspective," he agrees.

"What's it like working with Drummer?"

"Give me a fuckin' chance." He chuckles. "But it will be fine. Prez and I have similar views."

"Proud of you, Brother."

"Back atcha."

"You heard we lost Digger?"

I go blank for a moment, search my brain, then remember. "Fuck, I'd forgotten about him. Thought he'd have been in the ground a while back." He was occasionally around while I was prospecting. "He die a patch?"

Wraith chuckles. "Doubt he'd come around the club in a few years. He was one of the original members, loyal to Bastard, so no, Drum never took his patch. We kinda overlooked that he couldn't ride. We had a funeral but kept it local." He shrugs. "Not sure people would have known who he was anymore."

"Red!" a voice bellows out. When Drummer approaches, I raise my chin. "Where the fuck's Brick? I thought he'd be here."

"Meeting with the Wretched Soulz, you know how it is." I shrug, hoping he doesn't take the subject further.

"Yeah, fuckers think they pull our strings." Drummer gives a sympathetic shrug as he swallows my line without question. "I suppose we do have to dance to their tune when it suits us. Hey, look at you two." Standing back, he offers one of his uncommon grins. "Who'd have thought you two reprobates would rise to the top?" In truth, he looks as proud as fuck, and I feel warm as though I'm getting approval from my father.

But the answer is he had foreseen this outcome, I'm sure he had. Or something of the like, way back in the day when he originally sent me to Vegas.

We drink, socialise, catch up and listen to stories of Lefty and the shit he got up to in the past. Mid-evening, Wraith catches up with me.

He leans in. "Pussy's in the crash room waiting for us. Girl thinks she's won the fuckin' lottery being fucked by two VPs."

"Yeah?" I smirk. "Well, we better go and prove her right."

Half an hour later, I'm sliding into Pussy's cunt with Wraith slipping into her ass, and I have the feeling of having come home. We adopt our old rhythm as if it's been days, not years, since we've taken a girl together. I slide in as he slides out, and if Pussy's sighs, moans and cries are anything to go by, we haven't lost our touch.

Using my fingers on her clit, I ensure she reaches the peak at just the right time, and the room is filled with one scream and two grunts as we all find our release together.

"Jeez, boys," Pussy gasps out when she's able to get enough breath to speak. "I think you two just about wore me out."

Wraith, like me, is busy tying his condom, but he pauses to slap her butt. "Got a club full of visiting Brothers, Pussy. Think you'll need to get your stamina back."

She pretends to pout but her giggle gives away that she's not at all put out. "Oh, I think I can manage that." Biting her lip coyly she adds, "I've done two VPs, do you think I can do two prezes?"

I snort. "You're not playing a fuckin' card game." Through my laughter I add, "Drummer, Snatcher and Bird are your only options, sweetheart. Hellfire's tight with his ol' lady, or so I've heard."

"He's a silver fox, isn't he?" She looks unperturbed and flutters her eyelids coyly. "Maybe I can tempt him to stray."

If she can, then that's on him, not her. Either way, whether men stay faithful or not is none of my business.

Girls are few and far between tonight, so having got laid, Wraith and I keep to our own company. I notice Wraith keeping an eye on the rowdiness. It might be his club, but I help him out. We break up a couple of alcohol-fuelled fights, and when Pussy says no and means it to a man who's not taking that for an answer, we step in and send her back to the sweet butts' house.

Fuck, those girls have worked overtime tonight. There comes a point when even they can't take it.

"Hey, Brother." Heart comes over to me, his arm around a very pretty young woman. "Meet Crystal, my old lady."

I raise an eyebrow. *Old lady?* From the way he's staring down at her, it's clear to see he's a sucker deep in love, and she's returning his gaze with stars in her eyes. They make a good pair, and what can I do, but wish them good luck? As they walk off, I find myself envying him for having something I never had.

"She's pregnant, you know," Wraith informs me quietly.

"That why—?"

My brother laughs. "Why they got hitched? No. What you're looking at is a love match made in heaven, Brother. There'll never be another woman for him but her. Don't have to be an expert to see that."

"You envious, Bro? You looking to take an ol' lady?" I don't let him into my secret that I often have, though the chance has eluded me.

"Me?" Wraith snorts. "Fuck no. I'm surrounded by pussy, and I like the variety. I won't ever be settling down." He punches my arm. "What about you?"

I bark a laugh. Unbeknownst to him, I'm looking at wearing the prez patch shortly. "Got no time, Bro." I watch Heart so proudly walking around and introducing his wife to everybody. "It takes a special woman to come into this life, and good for Heart if he thinks he's found it. Me? I never have." Maybe once, but she left me. Now when I think of her and what I might have missed, I believe I'm blowing our brief connection up and out of proportion. Maybe it's because she's the only woman who's ever turned me down. Though, at the time, I didn't have much to offer. Even less now, perhaps. Who'd want to be hitched to the prez of an outlaw club? Only someone like Rosa, hard as nails, or Moira, Hellfire's old lady, who by all accounts, is even worse.

"You're right there, Bro," Wraith says, thoughtfully. "I really doubt the right woman is just going to walk into the club. We only get whores and hangarounds, and I've no fuckin' time to meet any civilians."

That ends that particular conversation. I go to get another beer, find myself catching up with my old friends, spend awhile joking with Beef, Rock and Dart. I find Peg's his old self, morose and grumpy as normal, and Blade, well, he's not changed one bit. Despite the reason why I'm here in Tucson, I enjoy catching up. And if I spend a moment looking up at the stars and relishing the fresh pine-scented air blowing down from the mountains, who can blame me? This was my first home after leaving Vermont.

When the party slows down, or more accurately, the participants have passed out, I follow Wraith up to his room on the compound where I'll be staying. We've just fucked Pussy together, won't be much different sharing a bed for the night. As old friends, there's no awkwardness between us.

I thought I'd be envious seeing he's still got what I lost, a suite with a bathroom and a balcony which, if it wasn't dark, would give views to die for. But if tonight's taught me anything, it's not the facilities which make a club, it's the members.

While I've enjoyed catching up with everybody, it was those chin lifts I'd shared with the likes of Twister, Indian, Crash, Shadow, Joker and all the Vegas members which had taught me home's not so much a place, but the people who make up your family.

Much as I love Wraith, sometime over the past few years, the Vegas members have become just as, if not more, important to me.

I'm right where I want to be, and I have no regrets.

Whether my club will, when I take over the prez mantle, remains to be seen.

CHAPTER TWENTY-EIGHT

"Rosa." I speak into my phone as I glance at the screen checking the time. No one rings with good news at o'shit o'clock, or to put it more accurately, just going on three am.

"Brick's gone."

Sitting up, I throw off the covers and growl, "What do you mean he's fuckin' gone?" He seemed fine earlier today.

"The ambulance has just taken him to hospital. He… he can't breathe, Red."

I feel a wave of relief go through me. He's not dead. Yet. "He'll be fine, Rosa. They'll get oxygen in him, then he'll be right as rain—"

"Red, don't be an asshole. You know as well as I do, this is the end. He left it too late."

Fuck it. I think of the sealed envelope he left for me, his final instructions. Is it time for me to open it? Hell no, I don't want to do that. I'll hang on to hope.

"I need help, Red." For the first time, I hear the catch in her voice. It's unusual to hear anything other than strength in it. "I need to be with him, but I've got the boys—"

"You need someone to watch them?" I'm thinking fast. Asking would bring the person I'm requesting into the knowledge there's something wrong with Brick. But maybe it's time. "I'll ask Tiff."

"No," she contradicts. "Get Titch. The boys respect him."

"You don't think they ought to go in and see their dad?" It could be the last opportunity they get.

"Yes, no. But I'd like to see how he's fixed first. So I can prepare them."

Only a few words, but it shows despite what she's said to me, she too is hanging onto hope. "I'll rouse Titch and bring him with me. Then I'll drive you to the hospital." My phone now on speaker, I'm halfway into my clothes. "We'll be there as quickly as we can. Just hang on, darlin'."

Brick and Rosa have a family suite at the club, but more recently they've spent most of their time at their house. The excuse was with the boys growing older they needed more space to themselves, the truth being, it was easier to hide Brick's illness when he wasn't always in sight.

"Red, I don't know if I can..." Rosa lets out a sob which twists my guts.

"You can do this, Rosa." I put my own pain to one side as I try to convince her. Over the past few months, I've really gotten to know her. We've shared a secret after all. Rosa has to be the strongest woman I've ever met, but everybody has a point where they break. And losing Brick will doubtless be hers.

"Please, Red. Hurry."

And there's the betrayal that Rosa's not optimistic. She wants to get to say her goodbyes before he leaves this earth.

Hoping we've all got more time with him, that this is an interlude and not the final fall of the curtain, I end the call, pull on my boots and go down the hallway where I try the handle on Titch's door. It's unlocked so I enter, go to the bed, and shake the old man by his shoulders.

It takes a moment to rouse him. When he comes to, he's got a gun in his hand.

"What the fuck? Who's there? Are we under attack?"

"Relax, Brother," I tell him. "Need you to come with me."

"VP? What's up?"

"Just get up, Titch. I'll explain on the way. I'll meet you downstairs."

Knowing he won't disobey an instruction from his VP, nor, despite his grumpy ways, a request from any member, I go down to the bar and put on a pot of coffee. It's brewed by the time he's reached the bottom of the stairs. Making a to-go cup ready for him, I drain the one I'd poured for myself, grab the keys to the club truck, and lead him outside.

Once he's seated in the passenger seat, I make my way out of the gates and start driving into Vegas.

"Prez has cancer," I tell him, as he'll find out soon enough. "He's been taken to the hospital. Rosa needs someone to keep an eye on the boys while she finds out what's happening."

"Fuck," Titch says quietly. Then he slaps his hand against the dashboard. "Fuck," he repeats, this time more loudly. "You knew?"

"Only recently," I reply, truthfully. "Brick didn't want anyone else to know."

"Well, hopefully they'll be able to treat him. Brick's as tough as a fuckin' ox. He'll beat this." Titch gives a dramatic nod of his head.

I don't disillusion him or say it's unlikely. He'll find out the truth soon enough, best ease him into it gradually.

Sensing he needs time to process, I drive on in silence, turning onto Brick's road, then pulling up outside his house. The front door flies open, showing Rosa was waiting for me.

"Titch. Thank you for coming. The boys are still asleep." Her eyes examine him worriedly, knowing he'll have been told the secret.

"They know?" Titch asks, clearly wondering what to tell them when they awake.

Rosa's face grows tight. "Not in so many words. They know Brick's not been feeling himself lately. But..." *They don't know he's on his deathbed*, I think to myself. "Soon as I know what's happening, I'll call you, Titch, okay?"

"I got this, Rosa." Titch's stern face softens. "You go be with your ol' man. Don't you worry about anything else. And Brick's a fighter. He'll beat this."

Rosa grabs for my hand, and I put my arm around her. Holding her, I help her to the truck with just a chin lift over my shoulder to Titch. Brick's time for fighting has long passed. He's lost the battle. Whether it's today, tomorrow, or in a month's time, his days on earth are almost over.

The drive is conducted in silence once again. At the hospital, Rosa immediately races off to find a doctor to speak to. When I catch up with her, I discover she's being allowed back to sit with her old man.

Returning outside, I harden myself to what I now have to do. My first call is to Crash.

The sergeant-at-arms sounds sleepy, and not happy to be disturbed. "Fuckin' hell, VP. You know what time it is? This better be a matter of fuckin' life or death."

"'Fraid it is, Brother." I pause to take a deep breath. "Prez is in the hospital. It doesn't look good."

"What the fuck?"

"He's got cancer. It's in his lungs and spread." They'll know that soon enough, no point now holding anything back.

"Jesus," he breathes. "You sure?"

"Yeah. I'm at the hospital with Rosa."

There are sounds that suggest he's getting out of bed. All sleep has gone from his voice now. "You want me to pass the message on?"

I do. It's time to bring in the club. "I'll call Twister and Fox, if you could—"

"I'll do the rounds. Rouse everyone here, and we'll meet you there."

I don't tell them to stay away. If the presence of his brothers can only bring enough positive vibes, they'll all want to come for

Brick. And if this is our last chance to say goodbye, no one will want to miss it.

I make the other calls as I promised, getting a similar reaction as I had from the sergeant-at-arms from the enforcer and secretary. Fox, surprisingly, sounded more prepared. Maybe he's more observant and had known something was coming. Within an hour, the waiting room has filled up, and the hospital, wary of men in cuts, has found us a relatives' room which we all crowd into.

It's too small, but no one complains.

"He's conscious." Rosa comes in, timidly for her. Her eyes are red-rimmed, but she's keeping it together. "He wants to speak to you, Red, and then Twister, Crash and Fox."

"He'll be alright though, won't he?" Hammer asks.

Rosa's mouth twists. She looks at me, and I raise my chin. Unless she's being given more positive news, it's time that they heard.

"He's in a lot of pain. He's been refusing morphine, but he'll soon be getting that. He can't breathe well, so he'll be ventilated. It's..." she chokes up, and we all give her a minute. She clears her throat, and her voice strengthens. "It's unlikely he'll wake up."

"Fuck!" Hammer breathes out, while others sit stunned trying to process.

"The kids?" Cobra asks. "If this is true, Rosa, shouldn't they...?" He can't bring himself to say, *see their dad for one last time.*

I make the decision for Rosa. Young they might be, but they'd want to be here. "Call Titch, get him to bring them."

She nods at me gratefully. I only hope Brick can hold out. Fuck me, eight years old, this is one hell of a lot to lay on them. But even at that age, if it had been my dad, I'd have wanted the chance to say goodbye to him.

It's a setback, I tell myself, following the directions I'd been given to Brick's room. *He's beaten this so long, they'll give him some meds and help him.* But when I enter and see him, all hope is swept away. He looks fuckin' awful. The only time I've seen worse was when I saw my father's dead body. The weight loss I'd noticed but disregarded is more evident. He looks shrunken lying in the hospital bed as if the effort it's taken for him to hide his illness for the last few months has all at once caught up with him. Every breath he tries to take in is a struggle. His brow is creased in evidence of terrible pain, and I suspect it's only sheer determination that keeps him from giving in.

He doesn't acknowledge my presence but continues to scrawl his signature on something. When he's finished, he collapses back and holds out his hand to Rosa. They clutch hands while he fights for breath. Then, with an effort, he opens his eyes and fixes them on me. They look dull, not bright and sharp as I remember.

He speaks to me, but his words are meant for both me and Rosa. "I'm not going on a ventilator. I've signed a do not resuscitate order."

"Brick, love—"

"Rosa." Fuck, how he gets the strength he's put into those words, I'll never know. "I don't want to drag this out. A few more days as a vegetable ain't gonna help anyone. Let me go, girl. Let me go."

Rosa's eyes meet mine; I try to telepathically send strength back. It's hard hearing, but Brick's right. If the end is coming, why prolong it?

I see her struggle, trying to find some argument that would let her keep her husband a while longer. She's fighting internally with herself, but knowing Brick so well, ends up not arguing with him. Pain is radiating off her as she straightens her back, then, plastering a fake smile on her face, she turns back to her man, leans over and kisses him. "You always said you'd know when it was your time."

"Never wanted to leave you, darlin'. This wasn't the way I planned it." Brick tries to raise his hand, but his strength seems to have gone.

"I know." She chokes back a sob. "Darlin' husband, I know."

She sinks into a chair, leaves her hand in his, and rests her head next to him. He half turns his head so his lips can nuzzle her hair, but his eyes land on me.

"It's time Red. Time for you to step up." It's an effort for him to get the breath to speak.

I raise my chin and broaden my shoulders.

A few more attempts to get air, then he continues, "You've got this, Brother. I'm leaving my club in good hands."

I don't argue, don't say I'm not ready. Now it's come to this, I think that I am. I'm also aware he's got others waiting, and not much time. So, I keep it simple.

"Shiny side up, Prez."

"Always," he gasps. "You keep the dirty side down."

His free hand lifts, only an inch or two, but it's obvious what he wants. I go to clasp it in both of mine, his grip is weak.

I've no more words, just put what I can't say into my expression, then I take one last look at the man I've been proud to call Prez before I leave him and his wife together.

I don't know what he said to Twister and Crash, but they return to the waiting room, and stand for a moment with their arms around each other. Fox is equally distraught when he emerges. Then Titch turns up with two scared-looking boys. As he disappears with them, I realise it's time to step up and abide by my promise to Brick.

Rosa, if she wants it, will always have a place in our club, and those boys won't lack for a father figure. They'll have all the damn members setting them on the right path. It's all I can do for my soon-to-be-fallen brother.

Rosa, Tom and Trist don't appear again, but when Titch comes out, he sends Hammer in. One by one, the brothers disappear for a few minutes. When the last, Joker, comes out, all his normal levity is gone.

"He couldn't speak." Joker leans up against the wall as if needing its support. "Why's he not fighting?" He turns and slams his fist into the drywall, tears openly falling down his face.

"He's fought, Brother." Approaching, I rest my hand on his shoulder. "He's fuckin' fought this. Battled on until there's no fight left in him anymore. Let him go in peace."

"His choice," Twister agrees, making me wonder if he, too, questioned the DNR letter Brick had signed.

"He's come to the end of the road," Fox adds, sagely. "It's his time."

"Well, it's not fuckin' ours." Cobra copies Joker and puts another hole in the wall. "What the fuck are we going to do now?"

"We wait." I start, in my best VP tone. "We'll be here until he's gone. Then we take Rosa and the boys back and make sure they're comfortable. After that, we'll raise our glasses to him and trust him to find his way safely on whatever journey he's on now. Only then will we think of ourselves and the club."

"We'll ride on," Crash offers, in his reasonable tone. "Might not be the same route as we thought we were taking, but the destination remains the same. Satan's Devils will ride on, together. We've got the VP to guide us."

I give him a chin lift. Yeah, if I have my way, this is the man I want riding beside me. Crash would make a fine VP, as long as the brothers vote the way Brick had planned.

If they don't, who the fuck will steer this club in the right direction?

Minutes, hours, days later, time seems to have stood still, but also speeds by too fast, Rosa appears with her arms around two sobbing boys.

She waits by the doorway, looking stoic, but I see her shivering, though the room isn't cold.

She doesn't have to tell us, the atmosphere already seems heavier. Tiff pulls away from Fox, and somehow envelopes the trio in her arms.

I don't need the words to know, Brick is gone.

CHAPTER TWENTY-NINE

Losing Brick is, in many ways, like losing my father all over again. Since I took the VP slot, he'd been my mentor, and I couldn't fault him in any way. In some things we hadn't seen eye to eye, but I'd gotten where he was coming from. It had been the education I'd needed to slip into the top spot, assuming I'd be voted into it.

Over the past months, he'd reminded me of Manny, subtly grooming me for a role which in those days I hadn't wanted, and which never once have I regretted not taking. Now though, it's different. Prez of an outlaw MC is not where I thought I'd ever be but know I won't turn down the chance if it's offered to me.

I'd never have wished to receive such an honour this way. I feel like I've been punched in the gut by the events of today, never having expected losing him so quickly and with such little warning. Fuck, I thought he'd spend weeks fading away, but it had happened in hours. Brick must have been hiding his suffering, and for that he had my admiration. It was love of the club, of his wife and his boys that had given him the strength to carry on for so long.

Now it's down to me to take care of his family, both blood

and those linked by patch. Whatever the outcome of the vote, until it's taken, I've got responsibility for this club.

I drive the truck back to the compound with Titch seated beside me, and Rosa and the twins in the back. Glances in the rearview see the boys looking like they're in shock. Trist has tears freely flowing down his cheeks, and Tom's face is blank. My soul hurts for them. They'd gone to bed last night expecting to get up and wake to a normal school day. Instead, they've witnessed the death of their father. It's something I can relate to and wouldn't wish on anyone. At least I had been older and better prepared, not fuckin' eight years old.

Tom and Trist can be pests, let's be straight about that, but I'm determined to do the best I can for them, as a surrogate dad.

As for Rosa, well, I'll be there with a shoulder for her to lean on.

Seated in the middle, she has one arm around each of her boys. Her mouth is fixed, and her eyes are staring. I wonder what she wants to do now.

"You want to go to your house, Rosa? Or come to the compound?"

"Home," she states, as though her mind is already made up. "But I won't be staying there, not without Brick. I'm taking the boys to their grandparents."

It's probably a good idea, but I'd expected her to stick around. Rosa organised Rainman's funeral, and I'd expected her to do the same for her old man.

Her eyes meet mine in the rearview, and she must see the question written on my face. "I can't, Red. I just can't. You do it on my behalf. Tell me where and when and I'll be there. I can't liaise with other chapters, can't get in the food Brick would have liked... Not yet. I just can't."

I totally understand it. "Leave it with me, Rosa." It's an easy promise to make. "I'll give him a send-off he'll be proud of."

"I know you will, Red. He told me if our boys grow up to be half the man you are, they'll be doing okay."

I swallow to get down the lump that's risen into my throat. That's high praise indeed and coming from beyond the grave. Or the steel coffin in a hospital mortuary if I'm to be exact. Whatever, it's good to know Brick thought of me that way.

I drop her off, going inside to make sure she's going to be okay. It breaks my heart when I see her look around her home as if suddenly realising her husband will never be there again.

"Go check the boys. Maybe get them to pack a couple of bags?" I suggest to Titch who's followed me in.

Then, I put my arms around Rosa, forcing her cheek to rest against my chest. "Cry, darlin', let it out."

She takes a shuddering breath but holds in her tears. "I need to stay strong for the boys."

"Titch has got them. Just let it go, darlin'."

She moves slightly, still connected but making a gap between us and stretches out her hand. "We…we sat there last night, watching TV. Brick looked pale, but I believed him when he told me everything was okay. He made me make popcorn, poured us both whisky, and we watched a film. He must have been in such pain, but he didn't let on."

That sounds like him. "He'd want you to remember him like that, Rosa. One last normal day."

She raises her now tear-streaked face to me. "Do you think he knew?"

How could anyone know? "Darlin', who knows? Do I think he knew it was his final day on earth? I've no idea. He knew it was coming though, he'd accepted it. Do I think he'd have wanted that last moment of normality, to give you pleasant memories to remember him by? Fuck yeah, that was Brick all over. Rosa, I know this is a fuckin' nightmare for you, but you are going to get through."

She does that shudder again. "I knew it was coming. I thought I was prepared. Now I'm lost and I don't know what to do."

"You'll muddle through," I tell her. "You'll get up each day, putting one foot in front of the other. You're a strong fuckin' woman, Rosa. Brick knew he could depend on you." I don't tell her I wasn't prepared either. However you can try and get ready to accept what's coming, when it arrives, the reality of it's a shock. I'd been through that with my dad.

"Mom? Can we take the Xbox?"

Rosa pulls away from me, wipes her eyes and gives me a sad smile. She turns toward the stairs and calls back, "Sure. Just choose a few games."

Tom hesitates before going back to his room. He stares at his mom, then comes running over and throws himself into her arms.

"We'll be okay," she tells him, rocking him as though he was still a baby.

"Dad said we had to look after you."

Rosa swallows a sob. "We'll all look after each other."

Tom takes her comfort for another moment, then with the resilience of children, pulls himself together. He shoots me a look, but can't seem to find words, then turns and makes his way back upstairs.

A family torn apart, that's what they are. My heart bleeds for them.

"When you're back," I tell Rosa, "come back to the club. There'll always be space for you and the boys there. It's what Brick wanted."

She tries a small smile. "I know, he told me." She closes her eyes for a moment, then visibly steels herself. "I've got stuff to do before we leave. I better get on with it."

"Want Titch to drive you?"

She considers it for a moment, and I hope she accepts. She's been through hell today, and I wouldn't want her to break down while she's behind the wheel.

"Do you think he would mind?"

I'm VP, I can instruct him if necessary, but I think he'll help. As I recall, Brick's parents live in Baker just under an hour and a half away. They have to be the grandparents she's talking about, according to Brick, she'd not seen hers since they'd thrown her out.

I grimace realising they'll have lost a son today. Christ, one death affects so many.

The boys come down the stairs, Titch laden with bags following behind them. Rosa starts fussing about packing a bag for herself, then remembers she's got to tidy up the glasses and stuff from last night.

"Don't worry, Rosa. I've got it." I'll get Sarge to come around and tidy the house, change the bed, wash the dishes, make it straight for when she comes home. Having been in the Army, he's good with shit like that, and an ace at making things neat and tidy. Sure, it's probably OCD, but we do make the most of it at times. Along with his PTSD, the man's a walking acronym.

She doesn't ask if I'm sure, just takes me at my word, just as she would as if Brick had spoken.

When she emerges from her room, trailing a suitcase in her hand, she nods at Titch who corals the boys and rushes them out.

"You call me, Red. Date and time, remember?"

"I'll call and tell you, Rosa. I'll speak to you, keep you up to date on the plans. We'll give him the send-off he deserves."

She glances around one last time, her eyes landing on the whisky glass sitting next to an unemptied ashtray, where presumably Brick sat last.

"I'm not sure if I can come back."

"You will, Rosa. But there's no hurry. Take your time. You've always got a home at the club, and we'll help with the twins. You've lost Brick, but you haven't lost us."

Some of her tension leaves her at the reminder we'll still be there waiting for her. She reaches up and pats my cheek. "Take care of my boys when I'm gone. They'll need you now."

Taking boys in this context to be the club members, I don't hesitate to make her a promise. "I'll take care of them, Rosa."

"His bike—"

"Leave it to me. I'll take care of everything. You don't need to make any decisions until you get back."

She bites her lip and looks more vulnerable than I've ever seen her. "I feel I'm running out on you."

I give an exaggerated shake of my head. "You're not. You're taking care of yourself and your sons. The other boys you can leave to me."

"You're a good man, Red."

And she was a great old lady to an amazing Prez, I think to myself, as with one final look at the home she shared with Brick, as if soaking in his presence for one last time, she turns to go, leaving me to lock up.

The clubhouse is sombre when I return. All brothers are here. Our businesses are closed. No one's got any inclination to keep things going. While they all seem to have a glass or a bottle in their hands, conversations are kept low and subdued. I remember it was more of a shock to them than to me. At least I knew it was coming.

As I walk in, I whistle, grimacing when I realise I sound like Brick. When they all turn around, I update them.

"Titch is driving Rosa and the kids to Baker. When he returns, we'll have church."

Then, waving off Twister's offer of a beer, I go into the prez's office. *Brick's domain*, which, if all goes the way he was planning, might soon be mine.

I stand for a moment, eyeing the Satan's Devil's insignia hanging behind the desk, recalling the day I vowed myself to be loyal to the patch. I never dreamed of how much it would ask of me.

Then, I move to the rear of the desk, but avoiding Brick's seat, open the second drawer down. I extract the sealed envelope. Taking it away with me, I go to my room, pour myself a vodka, then settle down to read the missive he'd left me. The last words from Brick.

After reading, I place four phone calls. The first to Drummer, the second to Hellfire, the third to Bird and the last to Snatcher. Annoyingly and strangely, it takes Utah a moment to get their prez on the line, enough time to wonder about the quality of their prospects if along with the title I had to state the name of the man I was after. In each call, I said the same few words and received the same commiserations. To say all were shocked is an understatement.

Drummer, with the sixth sense he's known for was the only one to question how long I'd known. I'd hedged my answer, but he'd guessed.

"Brick was stubborn to the fuckin' end. Okay, Red, let me know if there's anything you need from us, and we'll talk more at the funeral."

Nursing the one drink I'm allowing myself, I stand at the window and look out. The sky is blue without a cloud in it, and the sun blazes down. It's a reminder that life goes on even when there's one man less breathing.

I challenge myself. *Do I really want to do this? Am I ready?* I could propose someone else, another VP perhaps willing to move to Vegas and take over. But who is there? Demon from Colorado, perhaps? Thor from Utah? I shake my head. Such a backward club, I doubt anyone would put his name forward. Snake from San Diego? I shudder. I've never taken to the man, not that there's anything particular I can put my finger on, but he's too arrogant for my likes.

I chuckle as I think of the other option. Wraith. How would it feel for him to be prez and me to be his VP? Workable, perhaps, but in that situation, I'd prefer to be boss. We'd clash, we're too alike. Equals, I think, which is why he's the perfect balance for Drummer at the mother chapter. And against him is he's only been VP for a number of weeks, while my experience is at least measured in months.

I snort. Put like that, there's little between us.

Except for the note I'd left on my desk.

If Brick's right and his words count, he'll have his way, and I'll get the votes to become the new prez.

That's why I'm using this alone time to question what is in my grasp to become reality. Until today, it wasn't certainty, just a notion voiced.

I ask myself again, *am I ready?* Well, if I'm not now, I never will be.

Do I want to do this? Fuck yes. It's the realisation of a dream ever since I joined the MC. I thought I'd reached the pinnacle when I was made VP, but to have the top role within my grasp? I'll be fucked if I'm not prepared to reach out and grab it.

"Red? You in there?"

I go to open my door to Crash. "Titch back?"

"Yeah. Just arrived. We need to sit and talk about what's happened."

"We do," I agree. "Tell everyone church in ten."

"Will do, VP." He mock-salutes and then leaves.

I take a piss, change into a fresh shirt, brush my hands back through my hair, then picking up the letter Brick had left me, proceed down the stairs.

In the meeting room, I leave Brick's seat empty, having no right as yet to sit there. As men walk in, all eyes go to the vacant chair as if acknowledging the ghost sitting there. There's an air of despondency, as there would be, and a time for mourning necessary and will be allowed. But men also need help and guidance.

Brick had instructed me not to delay, his view being feeling adrift and abandoned wouldn't help anybody. Someone has to take the reins, to show the gavel could be transferred quickly and smoothly.

Fox is both our treasurer and secretary. He records all the important decisions of the club. As he'll be recording this one, I feel he's the man who should read aloud Brick's final words rather than myself. How could I properly give voice to the sentiments in Brick's letter, written not just to me, but to them? I'd stammer, contradict his words, and my damn pale skin would betray me. Especially already knowing his final words to the club.

When everyone's seated, I pass Fox Brick's missive, his last chance to influence the club, his legacy for the Vegas Satan's Devils.

Fox looks at what I've handed him, scans briefly then clears his throat. No one else speaks, and all eyes stare his way.

Brothers, if you're reading this, I'm no longer with you. It's hurts like fuck to think that way, but the grim reaper got me. I'd rather have had a bullet or come off my bike, but that choice wasn't mine.

Red knew for the past couple of months, but I swore him to secrecy. If you want to place blame, place it on my head, not his. I wanted to leave this chapter strong, feared and respected, the way it's always been. I didn't want people feeling sorry for me or trying to sort through the pickings while I was still breathing. Drummer would have been all over this shit, and I wanted the final say to be left to me.

I'm not arrogant when I say I know you'll be hurting. A ship is adrift when its captain is missing, and whatever else you'll be thinking of me, I was at least that, a steering presence directing this club. In my own way, I'll grieve the loss of each and every one of you. I've known some for many years, some for a few less, some just for months, but I love you all equally, Brothers. You're more than a club, you're family to me.

Drink, bemoan my loss. Celebrate my life, shed a tear for me. But then, buckle up and hang on for the ride. Nothing changes at the Satan's Devils MC. We live to ride and we ride together. The club isn't about one man, so after the mourning, move on. You'll do just as well without me.

Take care of Rosa and my boys for me. I know they have a place in your hearts, and if you let her, Rosa will do right by the club. Those boys of mine are strong willed as fuck, people say they take after me (pause for a laugh).

Fox clears his throat. "Yeah, the old man really wrote that."

As a few chuckles sound, I reckon it's not just me hearing Brick's voice saying those words.

Then Fox continues.

They'll need a strong hand and guidance to stay on the right path. I know I can count on you, Brothers, which means I can die a happy man.

"Sure you can, Brick." Titch thumps the table, and his vow is echoed around.

Now I'm aware me leaving has left an empty chair at the head of the table, and if I know my men, it's sitting vacant now. However much you'd prefer it, and maybe you don't, I'll never be sitting there again. As a ghost, I promise I won't haunt you.

An empty chair needs filling, Brothers, and I can only think of one man. A man who you had enough faith in to make my second. A man who's got a better head for business than I ever had, and a man who sees the future clearer than me. The man who I hope is your future, Brothers, and the man who sat to my left. The man I trust my life and club with, the man known as Red.

At this point, I want to sink under the table. I'd known those words were coming, but it's still ultra-embarrassing to hear them read out. Blood rushes to my cheeks and I flush bright red.

Now Red isn't a man who knows his own worth, who projects what he thinks of himself onto others. But that doesn't mean he doesn't have faith in himself, or doubt in his ability to run this club.

I know, I've groomed him since the day he stepped up as VP. I swore him to secrecy for the reasons aforesaid, and it worked as a test of his loyalty. And that loyalty he'll show to you in return, if you show you've got faith in him.

I can't think of better hands I'd wish to leave my club in, but we're no autocracy, we're a democracy. Discuss it all you like, but let me have one final vote and record it for Red.

If you can't settle on someone, speak to Drummer.

I could ramble on. I could reminisce about the good times, pick over the bad, talk about men we've lost and men who'll no doubt come along. I could express all my hopes for a future in which I won't take part, but somehow, I know you'll be doing that with no need for input from me.

So, this is my final goodbye. I'll miss you, Brothers.

Stay the shiny side up, keep the dirty side down and ride on proudly as Satan's Devils. The club rides on and depends on no one man.

Yours in love and forever

Brick. President of the Satan's Devils MC, Vegas Chapter.

There's an exhaled breath, a few open mouths, but Fox waves them down. My lips curve knowing he hasn't quite finished.

P.S. And if you do nothing else after this meeting, patch the poor fucker Sarge in. He's done his time.

There are snorts all around. No one could disagree, and as our only prospect for a while, Sarge has had a hard go of it. But he's proved himself time after time.

Fox still hasn't finished. He holds up his hand. *"P.P.S. Take my advice. Give up the fags."*

Cobra snorts and laughs, Hammer chuckles, but others briefly close their eyes as expressions of pain cross their faces. Silence descends at the sombre reminder of what took our prez's life. I reach into my pocket, take out the packet of cigarettes, crush them, then throw it down. Indian does likewise.

"I'll try," Twister states. "Don't know if I can. But I'll give it a shot or at least cut down."

As VP, I've got some power here. "I propose to help us all out, we no longer smoke at the table."

"I can cope with that," Keys states, seeming happy to be able to do something even if he can't promise to totally give up.

His sentiment is echoed around.

I spare a thought for our missing brother, hoping that whether he's looking up or down, he'll be happy with how things have turned out. Then, knowing they've other business to discuss, I push my hands against the table and start to stand. "Guess I'll leave you to have your discussion."

"Sit your ass down, Red," Twister snarls. "I don't see there's anything we need to talk about. Anyone disagree?"

Crash shrugs. "Not me. Seems quite clear cut."

"We going to rubber stamp Brick's wishes?" Fox calls out. "'Cos Red's got my vote."

"Mine as well," Hammer says just as Cobra says, "No shit."

"Show of hands for Red?" Twister asks.

I'll be fucked, but every hand shoots up.

"Any against?" he asks for the record.

This time, all hands stay down.

Crash grins at me. "Then get your ass moved, Red. Er, Prez."

Snorting at the audacity from the sergeant-at-arms, overwhelmed by the support from the rest of the table, this time I do make it to my feet, but only to take one step to the right before sitting my ass back down.

Faces which moments ago were sombre and down, now look optimistic, showing me Brick was right. The club needs direction. Sure, we'll mourn, but me taking this seat shows the future is still in our hands. Safe hands if I've got anything to do with it.

I pick up the gavel and bang it. "Right. I want to make a proposal. I want Crash as my VP, and Indian to move up as sergeant-at-arms."

We vote, and Fox records it, but no one objects or puts forward counter proposals. I have my top team, and I think it's a fucking strong one.

There's only one thing I can do now. I bang the gavel again.

"Church dismissed. Get out of here and go remember Brick."

There's a scramble to get out of the room, but Crash, Indian and Twister stay behind. For a moment, we stand just looking at each other.

"We got this, Prez." Crash breaks the silence and uses my new title for the first time.

"Sure fuckin' have." Twister loops his arm over Indian's shoulder. "Good calls you made there. Crash for VP, and Indian as sergeant-at-arms."

Indian looks shellshocked. "I won't let you down."

"Know you won't, Brother," I tell him. Then I pinch the bridge of my nose. "We've got our work cut out for us, Brothers. But I know Vegas is strong and we'll go far."

"Six months back we had a different VP and Prez," Crash observes. "That's gonna hit the men hard."

"Up to us to lead them through it," I state. "And failure ain't a choice."

"Too fuckin' right," Twister vows.

CHAPTER THIRTY

Funerals are best over and done with. The sooner a body is laid to rest, the sooner survivors can start to mend.

Despite bikers' send-offs being an excuse for a get-together and a party, for the principals involved, they can cause an inordinate amount of stress. I've been to funerals before but have never been responsible for hosting one. At Rainman's, I did my duty but only as a lowly member. At Lefty's, I was a guest and had no responsibility myself.

The loss of an MC prez is, of course, a huge occasion. Everyone wants to show their respects.

While I didn't want to bother her, I've had to have contact with Rosa to make sure what I'm planning complies with her preferences, and, in doing so, took the opportunity of drawing on her experiences. She didn't have a long list of priorities. Her only wish was for him to be buried wearing his wedding ring, and that her property cut was to be placed in his coffin, a part of her that would always be with him.

Tiffany proved to be a godsend, organising catering and block booking rooms at nearby hotels for those who wanted overnight comfort. As it is, our clubhouse is going to be filled to overflowing. All chapters are going to attend with only a skeleton crew left at base. The local Wretched Soulz, led by Missile and Debunk, will also be in attendance.

When the day arrived, I knew this was my first test of being seen as the rightful prez of the Vegas chapter.

It seemed odd to be greeting Drummer, Hellfire, Bird, and Snatcher as equals, due deference still given to the foremost of course, as mother chapter prez he'd always take precedence. But as I rode directly behind the car carrying Rosa and the twins, I felt a strange nervousness. I wasn't used to riding alone and heading a vast column.

The funeral itself was short. Rosa held her boys, and I had my arms around her, lending her my support. She'd cried silently, tears streaming down her face and shudders racking her body. Then when the clods of earth fell on the coffin, she dried her face, straightened her clothing, and turned away. As becomes a prez's old lady, she then proceeded to do the rounds, thanking the other prezes for coming.

She's so fucking tough.

Fox and Tiffany looked out for the boys who looked completely lost. Despite Rosa's ability to hold herself together, I knew their route to healing would travel a long road. You don't get over the loss of a presence like Brick in a short while, or even in a lifetime. I should know, I often feel my father still with me.

The clubhouse, packed to the rafters, is mayhem, and only this side of organised. I rotate around, unable to linger to chat with any one person as I accept equal commiserations and congratulations from every side. At the end of the night, I'm relieved and so fucking tired. I consider making a declaration, that members are forbidden to fucking die, as their send-off is exhausting.

I fall into bed with my mind racing. *Had I spoken to everyone? Had I given a good show of myself or was anything lacking?*

Brick might have been the star attraction, but all eyes had been on me. *Would Red stack up?*

The next day it seemed I'd passed muster. Drummer asked

me into a meeting with the other prezes and spent a few moments reiterating his views on the future of the Satan's Devils. I was onboard with all his plans, and we all bought in to maximising our legitimate businesses and keeping off the radar of the cops, while, of course, keeping to our rules in our own houses. In other words, taking no shit from anyone, and exacting our own forms of retribution.

When all the visitors leave, I heave a sigh of relief, and relish the thought of getting back to normal. But at first, I've no idea what that is.

Despite my worries, it comes naturally.

During her time away, Rosa had decided the boys needed to get back to some form of routine, so she, Trist and Tom return to the house they shared with Brick. But they continue to make regular appearances in the clubhouse. And if Rosa was continuing to act as if she was still the first old lady, I wasn't going to interfere. I had no mind to put anyone else in that role, and she fit it fine. She organised the kitchen and kept the club girls in line.

Sarge is patched in and not before time.

The club moves on. Our security business grows and becomes our main money winner, and I become comfortable sitting in the top seat and being addressed as Prez. The lustre wears off quickly as I settle into the job. There's an always present tension of being the man who has the last word, the man everyone looks up to. If sometimes at night I go to bed questioning some decision I've made, I'm the only one who knows it. I'm so busy I'm barely aware of how the months turn into a year, and then another goes by. It's not long before I can barely remember a time when I was simply a man called Red.

Two years later, I'm attending yet another funeral of a Satan's Devil prez, this time for Bird from San Diego. His successor, Snake, still makes my skin itch when I'm around him, but I can't put my finger on why. Snatcher, well, he's old-fashioned as fuck, but still a solid guy. Hellfire, equally set in the old ways is at least open to new ideas, but Snake? He's only a little older than myself, and something about him rubs me up the wrong way. But his club voted to promote him from VP to the top spot, so who was I to argue? It was only the same move as I'd made myself.

I've got enough to worry about, building up my own club in Vegas. It's not all work though, a boy's gotta play sometime. Some of the decisions I get to make are more fun than others.

"Prez? Can we have a word?"

Glancing up from a security report Keys had asked me to look over, I wave Rope and Cuff in. "What can I do for you?" I fold my arms and sit back.

"We—"

"You," Cuff interrupts, glaring at Rope. "You. I'm just along for the ride."

"You thought it was a good fuckin' idea," Rope turns on him. "You can't back out now."

"I said—"

I slap my hands down. "Whether it's you Rope, or you, Cuff, spit it out. I'm too busy for fuckin' games."

Cuff snorts. "I'll remember you said that later."

I roll my eyes. "You've got five minutes," I warn them.

Rope sits forward and clasps his hands. "You know we belong to a BDSM club in town?" It's a rhetorical question. We all do. Knowing that, he assumes my response and continues, "You ever been to one, Prez?"

"I can honestly say I have not." Sure, I've toyed with hand-cuffs and tied a girl up once in a while, but that's the extent of it. Girls seem to like it, and I see nothing to complain about when having someone at my mercy.

"We'd like you to come with us. As our guest," Rope spits out fast.

"Whoa." I hold up my hands. "Much as I love you, Brothers, I'm not having your hands near my dick."

Cuff snorts and turns to Rope. "He thinks we want him to be

our submissive." He turns to me and in a very gay mock, half sings, "Sorry, Prez, you're not our type." He adds a limp hand gesture in a flourish.

Despite myself, I laugh. If it's tinged with relief, then I'm keeping it quiet. All we know is that Rope and Cuff are quite deviant types.

"Got a request to make of you, Prez."

"I think you've already made it. And the answer is no. I don't want to go to a sex club."

Rope rolls his eyes. "That wasn't our request. But before we put that on the table, we want you to see some things for yourself first."

"Like you beating on Cuff?" I shudder slightly. "No thank you."

"Oh, but Prez, I like it so much." Cuff again uses his singsong voice.

Rope, however, looks at him sternly. "Will you be fuckin' serious for once or shut the fuck up?" When Cuff mimes zipping his lips, Rope sighs and again fixes me in his sights. "There'll be no guy-on-guy action from us, but there's some shit we want you to consider. And, I think, you might enjoy it."

Going to a sex club is not a thing I've contemplated in my life. To my mind, it's like going to a brothel, and with the sweet butts on tap, why should I pay for it? But what's life if not to have a few experiences?

I point to Rope. "If I come, it's our secret." I'm not going to be the butt of the joke with brothers yanking my chain about how I spend my free time. "And you're not putting me in a leather harness and dragging me around on a lead."

Rope and Cuff high five each other, while I look on with a suspicious frown.

Later that night, I'm rethinking my hasty decision as the club's SUV draws up in a parking lot next to a discreet building. Instead of the glaring signs that decorate most parts of Vegas, there's barely any indication outside that this is actually a business.

As we enter through the doorway, it's into a smart reception area. Rope steps forward and signs in himself and Cuff, and then introduces me as a guest to the receptionist. I feel slightly uneasy even if the dude behind the desk doesn't seem to think anything of it. Soon, I'm sporting a white wristband around my wrist.

"Brothers?" I hold it up once we're out of earshot.

"Newbie," Rope explains.

"This better not fucking suggest I'm available," I rasp, my stare promising sudden and painful death if they mislead me.

Cuff snorts. "Come on, this way."

They're both carrying bags I notice. The first room we enter is a posh men's changing area. I avert my eyes from the freely swinging dick I see as one man's already in the midst of changing. Then wait while Rope and Cuff swap their jeans for leather pants and waistcoats hanging open leaving their chests bare, then both tie back their hair with leather thongs.

"Can you at least loose the shirt, Red?"

And walk around half naked? I shrug, well, why not? When in Rome and all that. At least I can keep my jeans on. I slip off my t-shirt, not afraid to show off the hard worked for six-pack under it. At least it's a chance to show off my tats.

I have to admit, I enjoy the next few hours. Mostly I stand on the sidelines, watching my brothers tie various victims, submissives they call them, on to different equipment. I listen as they explain the Dom/sub relationship to me and see it at work when the girls seem to get lost in their heads. I even pick up a flogger and get a lesson on using it. The girl I'm working over seems to love it. *Would Cheryl have liked it?*

I get instructions in how to properly tie a girl up.

I do all this, walking around with a raging hard-on. Fuck, I thought the club girls dressed sexily, but they aren't a match on the clientele here. Corsets, bra and panty sets so brief as not to be necessary, some girls parading naked, some with short skirts with nothing on underneath.

What impresses me is the expressed need for consent, and that all activities are carefully observed by aptly named dungeon monitors.

To my surprise, Rope and Cuff are obviously looked to as experts, and Cuff gives a demonstration of something called Shibari, which involves cocooning a girl in rope.

It's a heady evening, and yes, I enjoy myself. Not to the extent that I want to join the club, but it's definitely opened my eyes. I thought Wraith and Pussy had been good tutors, but they were just high school, this is degree level.

It's at the end of the night when Cuff is cleaning down the last piece of equipment he used and Rope has an exhausted and sleepy sub on his lap, that he at last broaches the subject he's been dying to raise.

"You have a good time tonight, Prez?"

I did. I might have found it unusual to sink my dick into an unknown woman who was completely restrained, but she was all for it. And if someone wanted to enact a fantasy by me covering their tits with my cum, who was I to deny them that pleasure? An odd night for certain, but not an unenjoyable one.

"I did," I reply, but looking around me, add, "I see the attraction but it's not for me. I prefer one-on-one in private." Or two-on-one, but behind closed doors. Not like the orgy I watched earlier.

"Each to their own." Rope grins. "But private is kind of what we wanted to talk to you about."

"You asked him?" Cuff, having finished his job, flops down beside Rope, taking a moment to look at the girl who seems fast asleep now.

"Getting around to it. Take her?" Rope passes the comatose girl over. "Prez, we wanted to see if we could use part of the club's basement. Put some equipment like this there. We could then play at home."

I frown. It's a big area, and unused most of the time. Our only use for it is that it's soundproofed and excellent for when we want some quiet time with a person we're questioning. It's equipped with all kinds of tools for encouragement, and a big drain hole in the middle for any blood.

"Don't you torture women enough here?"

Rope doesn't respond, but simply observes. "We could fit a nice St Andrews Cross in one corner, a spanking bench and have room for whips and floggers."

I snort, imagining it. "You want to turn our basement into a fuckin' dungeon?"

"Just part," Rope confirms.

"And you had to bring me here before you asked me?"

Cuff chuckles. "Well, first, we thought you might enjoy it. And we wanted you to see what we do for yourself. You'd have thought we were perverts if we just came out and told you."

I still think they're perverts, but maybe I understand them and their proclivities better. "One of those cross things?" I jerk my head toward what I think he's talking about. "And a bench?"

"And a table," Cuff puts in. "For wax play and the like."

We've got the space. What would it hurt? And the brothers might find it amusing.

"You're proposing all brothers have the use of it?"

"If they want," Rope confirms. "Though they'd need some guidance. Can't tie a girl up then forget her."

I snort and find myself agreeing to them having a dungeon. And you know what? I might even see me using it myself. Without an audience, of course.

Cuff winks at me. "See, Prez? You do have time for fuckin' games."

He'd told me my words would come back to haunt me. I shake my head as they bump fists.

CHAPTER THIRTY-ONE

As I'd predicted, the installation of Rope and Cuff's equipment caused quite a bit of amusement, and all hands were on deck to help get the newly delivered equipment assembled. Twister, in particular, was fascinated by the new possibilities of the apparatus, leading to threats from Rope and Cuff that he'd be the one tied up and whipped if he got blood on any of their new shit.

Pixie, Jinx and Angel were intrigued, and volunteered to help the brothers demonstrate the correct ways of restraining a sub, and how to pleasure them. In fact, it became hard to keep the girls away from the basement.

But as any nine-minute wonder, things soon settled down. Rope and Cuff would bring their conquests back and disappear downstairs, but most of the brothers forgot it was there, or only used it occasionally for their own entertainment.

The downside was that I had a furious Rosa on my hands. Did she object to having a sex room in the basement? No, though that was what I'd expected. Instead, she ranted about members getting everything, and that there was nothing for the ladies.

Rope had contradicted her, saying he was more than willing to take her downstairs and show her just what their new toys could do for the female sex—and once I'd sent him away to get an ice pack for his jaw, I'd sat her down and questioned her.

"Rosa, discounting the club girls, there's only you and Tiff here. What accommodations could the two of you want?"

Still rubbing her fist and glaring after the man I just sent away, she sits, and raises an eyebrow. "There's just me and Tiff now, but who knows what will happen in the future, and who will take an old lady? I want a space set up for females."

While I can't see any of the Vegas members in a rush to take an old lady, she's got me interested. "What are you thinking of?"

Her face falls and she swallows. "Brick and I used to discuss it. A room, with a bar to ourselves, sofas, a TV." She pauses. "A *safe* room."

I'm just about to laugh when I realise the emphasis she's put on one word. *Safe.* Instead of showing my mirth, I settle back and fold my arms.

Have I gotten lazy and complacent? Just because there's been no direct attack on the compound for years, I can't discount it. And the last thing we want is our women, and that includes the sweet butts, or our kids being unprotected. It sounds like Brick was more forward thinking than I gave him credit for.

"I'll bring it to the table," I say, firstly to appease her, and secondly to buy me some time.

I do start to think about it. There's an old, and big, storage room off the kitchen that could be emptied of all the crap kept in it, and with a lick of paint and fresh drywall could easily be transformed into something she wants. But as a safe room it wouldn't work, there are dual aspect windows.

"What you doing here, Prez?" Crash comes upon me as I stand in the space mulling things over.

I swing around taken off guard, then let him into my thinking. "Rosa's asked for a women's room."

He snorts. "She's still on about that? I thought she'd forgotten it." I raise an eyebrow. He shrugs. "Brick and I discussed it."

"And?"

"It's a good idea to have somewhere secure. We'd thought about partitioning off part of the basement."

"Ah." Pennies start dropping. "The part that now houses sex club equipment." No wonder Rosa had gotten her panties in a twist about it.

"Yeah." Crash looks around, shaking his head. "As his sergeant-at-arms, Brick asked me to think about it. But where I thought about planning to send the women, kids and injured down to the basement, I realised there was a problem." He raises and lowers his shoulders again. "They'd be trapped. Especially nasty if there's a fire."

I can see his point. I start to move around the area, pulling boxes away from the walls. My eyes narrow as I find something. "What the fuck's this?"

Crash comes over to stand next to the door I've just revealed. Together we exchange puzzled glances and try to open it. It's jammed, having been unused for years. When our joint strength eventually opens it, we both stand back and stare.

"Laundry shoot?" Crash's brow creases.

Maybe. But it goes down, to where? We're already at ground level. "Got a flashlight?"

He has, and he passes it to me. I lower myself down. "Not sure what the fuck it is." My voice echoes in the darkness. "But it leads somewhere." It's a narrow corridor running under the building, high enough for me to stand up.

I hear a thump as Crash lands behind me.

"Let's explore."

He's crowding me as I'm the only one with a light. Cautiously, hyperaware of the cobwebs hanging down, and the fact there might be snakes or rats down here, I proceed.

"What was the old warehouse used for?" I ask him.

"Fuck knows. Word is, it was derelict when the Devils bought it. Before my day, man."

We make slow progress but cover about thirty yards before

our way starts to slope up, and we come upon another door. This one jammed and sealed just like the last one, but neither Crash nor I can open it.

"Where are we?"

Closing my eyes, I estimate the direction we've travelled and the distance. "I reckon we're near the garage."

Catching his eyes in the beam of the flashlight, I see they're burning with excitement. "Let's go check it out."

It takes a while, and a lot of moving of racking, to the amusement of the brothers fixing up their bikes, to find what we're looking for. But eventually, we do find it.

Crash high fives me. Then I find myself leading Joker, Shadow, Cobra and Hammer in the reverse direction, seeing their bemusement when we climb up into the storeroom off the kitchen.

Hammer looks around, his brow furrowed. "I reckon something dubious went on here back in the day. Drugs? Guns?"

"Liquor?" I put in, wondering how old the bones of the warehouse structure are. It's quite possible it was built over some illegal distillery.

"Don't think it's as old as that, Prez." Cobra, like Hammer is taking in the surroundings. "But I'd say some nefarious activity took place here."

Crash's eyes are gleaming. "Whatever, this is fuckin' ideal. The women can have their room, and if we're under attack, can escape straight to the garage."

"Women getting a room?" Joker creases his eyes. "What the fuck's that all about?"

I leave it to Crash to enlighten them, while I walk around, eyeing the space again, and what needs to be done to it. In truth, I'm like a kid with a new toy. None of the other chapters, to my knowledge, have a setup quite like I'm envisaging. I'm already thinking about the pat on the back I'll get for forward thinking.

By the time I'm ready to bring it up in church, I've got Keys onside, and Indian brimming with ideas.

"Moving onto other business," I start, then can't hide my grin. "The women's room, or rather, our safe room."

By now, all members have seen the escape tunnel for themselves, but haven't been let into the rest of our thinking.

Indian reaches under the table and brings out the rolled-up plans which he flattens and lays out.

"The room needs new sheetrock. We'll just reinforce the walls behind it."

Fox leans forward. "Yeah, but the windows leave us exposed." He rolls his eyes as if he can't believe we've missed that.

"Bulletproof shutters." Keys is as excited as he sounds. "Anyone in the room will be able to control them."

"And the door will be reinforced steel," Indian informs them. "Keys is going to put cameras around the club and monitors in the room so anyone in there can see what's going on."

Titch snorts, sits back and folds his arms. "You expecting a fuckin' invasion, Prez?"

Indian leans forward, and angrily rebukes him, "You saying we're not? You got a fuckin' crystal ball I don't know about? If you have, you're welcome to take over as sergeant-at-arms for the club."

"I like the idea." Fox uses a more reasonable tone. "I'd like to know should anything happen, that Tiff will be safe. And, she'll have somewhere to go while we're here."

"Set it up with game machines too, keep Tom and Trist from being under our feet all the time," Hammer suggests.

In the end, after a bit of toing-and-froing, the plan was agreed.

With all brothers pulling together, the work was quickly completed and furnished by Tiff and Rosa of course. In no time at all, the Vegas chapter had a women and child-friendly safe room.

Time moves on. We pick up a new prospect, a guy called Scott Flintstone who's immediately given the nickname Fred. As the months pass, I'm impressed by the man who, while looking like a strong gust of wind would blow him over, is solid, and not to be underestimated when we put him into the ring. Showing MMA skills that we didn't expect, he can take down men far heavier. The only drawback seems to be an animosity directed at him from Joker.

I delay bringing him getting his patch to the table, having the notion I'd get Joker's vote so it wouldn't be unanimous. But as Fred had done his twelve months and then some, there are grumbles from other members who can't understand the hold up, and not a little unease from the man himself.

I've no option but to bite the bullet and face it head-on. At the next church, I put it starkly. Fred gets his patch, or we part company. As I expected, Joker objects, but when challenged can't come up with a reason why he shouldn't be patched in. It's obvious Joker hates the man for reasons even he can't put a finger on, but in the end, even he votes yes. Fred, now becoming known as Lady's Man, joins us at the table.

But Joker's hatred of him appears to be deep seated and doesn't come to an end. When they're pitted against each other in the ring, it's like he wants to kill him.

I can't have this. Having two members at each other's throat for no apparent reason goes against our code. How can we swear to have each other's backs under circumstances like these?

In the end, I have to take action. Joker and Lady will have to sort whatever there is between them. To force the issue, I admit I pushed them together, the term sink or swim being in my head. Either Joker would overcome his objections to calling the man brother, or the weaknesses that only he perceived in Lady would become common knowledge.

I made the right call. The job I'd sent them on did indeed reveal Lady's strengths, but only at the cost of Joker getting a concussion and breaking a few ribs. His injuries would have been far worse had Lady not been there to have his six.

The timing of that was unfortunate, our road captain out of

action when we most needed him. The Tucson chapter had lost a prospect under circumstances which meant the man, Hank, was posthumously patched in. The kid had given his life for the club, and due respect would be shown. The Vegas Chapter would be putting in an appearance at the funeral.

A sad occasion for sure, but visiting Tucson to pay my respects led me to reconnecting with Wraith once again. To my equal shock and delight, he'd found himself an old lady.

It had made me cast my mind back to years prior and a conversation we'd once had, about how we could meet a suitable civilian girl and bring her into our life. The only way, we'd joked, was if one turned up at the club. Which is exactly what had happened in his case.

When I saw his Sophie, a woman who needed protection from the Devils, I mentally called him a lucky fucker, then repeated that to his face. She was like a little blonde pixie. If he hadn't seen her first, I'd have stepped in myself.

Sophie, though, was broken. Physically because she'd lost a leg, mentally as she couldn't accept she was still a whole woman in a man's eyes. On that memorable occasion, I'd shared a woman with my best friend again, but for the last time. I was happy helping Wraith to prove a point but knew I'd never again cross that line. If ever there was a better match, I hadn't seen it. Sophie was his old lady and would be for life.

It had been the Rock Demon's that had taken Tucson's prospect out. Shortly after the return from the funeral, I had news from Drummer that the Demons were again stirring shit. This time, they were travelling through our territory as well as coming for Tucson. I took out a team comprising of Twister, Sarge, Hammer and Cobra and took those coming into Vegas out, while Crash, Rope and Cuff went to assist Drummer and his crew, blowing up the Demons' clubhouse in Phoenix.

It was while we were celebrating the end to our enemy when we got news that Adam, a brother from Tucson, had been killed protecting Wraith's old lady. Thank fuck she was okay, but it meant we were off to yet another fuckin' funeral.

There was an unexpected consequence of Tucson's loss to the Vegas club. Feeling his club was exposed and wanting to boost their ranks, Drummer requested me to transfer one of my members. After a bad experience with a San Diego transfer who'd tried to rape Sophie, and who was obviously now dead, Tucson wanted to make sure any new members were solid and dependable.

Unwilling to lose anyone, I'd already asked around, and had had two men approach me individually. I'd had to laugh. Unbeknownst to each other, Joker and Lady had put in separate transfer requests.

While I was loath to be down a road captain, I knew Shadow could step into Joker's shoes. When I recommended both men to Drummer, I was amused to keep the information from him, that Lady and Joker tolerated each other, but were far from being friends. I suppose it was cruel of me. Joker would have been happier either staying here while Lady went or going alone. But something told me they'd mend their differences if they were both newcomers in a different club.

Petty and Roller were already on board as promising new prospects, so it hadn't hurt to lose two men from the club.

Two surprising things happened shortly after Joker and Lady transferred. Drummer, the man who got his name from banging every woman in sight, settled down and took an old lady. It sent a ripple of shock through the whole club, in a good way for once. Many a glass was raised in his honour. But when you met Sam, you could easily see how she'd ensnared him. She was a true one-off. How many women could rebuild a Vincent Black Shadow from the ground up?

The other event, one which unsettled every man wearing a Satan's Devils' patch, was Snake's betrayal of the club in San Diego. As Prez, I witnessed his torture and demise. If any man ever deserved to be dispatched to Satan, it was him. He'd turned a number of members against the club. One, his fucking sergeant-at-arms, shared his death sentence. Seven others were sent out bad. That a prez could turn on the club was something we all had to recover from.

My boys are solid, but many a church meeting immediately after was spent reassuring each other that we were all on the same page. If it went down hard in Vegas, fuck knows how the San Diego club could recover from it. Kudos goes to Lost who stepped up as their new prez, along with Dart, a transfer from Tucson who became his VP. Somehow, they managed to hold that chapter together. I doubted that was an easy job.

The Vegas chapter doesn't operate in a vacuum, we're all Satan's Devils at heart. Over the years, we ride to support the other clubs, and host their members and old ladies when they need to get away for a while. As Prez, I okay the arrangements, accompany my men, or sit back and let Rosa take over the organising when we give harbour to those from other clubs.

Apart from the odd skirmish with those stupid enough to want to bat heads with the Devils, the chapter begins to settle back down. Before I know it, another six months have passed, and Crash takes me aside to talk to me.

"What is it, VP?"

"Petty and Roller." Crash raises his beer. "They've done their prospecting time. Shouldn't we patch them in?" He shrugs. "Or kick them out." The way he says it shows either option would be okay with him.

Fuck me, he's right. Time passes so fast, one day blurs into another. "Bring it to the table. We'll vote on it." Like him, I wet my throat with my beer, then interested, ask, "What's your opinion?"

He doesn't immediately answer. His brow furrows, and his hands pick at the label on the bottle. "They're both as hotheaded as each other, but I think Roller's more sound."

"They're pretty tight, aren't they?"

An up and down of his head, then he gives me the words.

"They served together, so yeah. Not sure how it would work if one got in and one was out."

I tend to agree that could cause problems. Leaning back, I link my hands behind my head. "There could be an issue if Joker was still here."

"Yeah. I picked up on that."

But Joker's not, and as far as I know, none of the other brothers are of the same persuasion. But who the fuck am I to know? And furthermore, it's none of my business. Nevertheless, I'm driven to shake my head. "Joker and Lady, hey? I never saw that coming."

"You didn't?" Crash raises an eyebrow.

"You did?" My brow furrows.

"Fuckin' obvious when I saw them kissing one day."

"You did?" I repeat my question, my own eyebrows rising. "You didn't say shit."

"Wasn't my business, Prez. I judge a man by his deeds not who he's doing."

Crash is one hundred percent right. I tilt my beer bottle toward him. "I hear you, Brother. I fuckin' hear you."

The next church, Petty and Roller are patched in when all hands are raised in their favour. And if I have a small doubt in my mind, I remember the VP's wise words, to judge a man by his actions. On how Petty has fulfilled his prospecting duties, well, there, I can't fault him.

Which leaves us on the lookout for new prospects, but there are always men in the wings wanting their chance to ride with the Devils. Only weeks later, two drop into our hands, a scrawny lad who wears thick-rimmed glasses, and who immediately picks up the handle, Owl.

His complete opposite, a brawny fella, stocky, almost as wide as he is tall, also comes to our attention. His trade? He's a butcher for fuck's sake. He soon comes to be known as Meat.

CHAPTER THIRTY-TWO

I'm sitting at my desk, discussing the latest takings with Fox when my phone rings. Annoyed at the interruption, I glance down to identify the caller, then shooting a look of apology toward the treasurer, pick the device up. It's the new prez from Colorado. Hellfire had not long ago stepped back, and his son had taken his place. A man so it happens I've got a lot of time for, and none of the reservations I'd had about Snake.

"Demon, what can I do for you?"

Fox pulls the paperwork together and gives me a wave of his hand. In return, I offer a chin lift confirming we'll get back to this later. I settle back with the phone to my ear and listen to what becomes an incredulous story.

"We've got a missing member, Red. Had given up on him as he disappeared months back, thought he was dead. But his ol' lady's friend just sent her a picture. He's been spotted alive and living it up in Vegas."

My eyes widen incredulously. "What the fuck? He run out on the club?"

Demon sighs heavily. "Not that we suspected it, nor his pregnant ol' lady. There was no fuckin' reason for him to have left. One day he was here, the next he and his bike were missing."

"Pregnant?"

"Yeah. She's fuckin' cut up as you'd expect. Truthfully, it would have been better if he'd stayed dead. As it is, well, we want to fuckin' find him." Demon's voice hardens. "Him being alive raises too many fuckin' questions."

It sure does. A member does not just walk out on the club. During prospecting, there's a chance for a man to walk away if they don't feel a good fit, but once you put on that patch it's for life, unless there's a fuckin' good excuse. Even then you'd leave with a beatdown at the least. Most times, you'd forfeit your life. You have to be one hundred percent trustworthy to walk away with the secrets of your club.

"Who is this fucker?"

"Name's Skull. He'd not been patched in that long, but he'd done his time and we thought he was solid."

Him being new is why I don't recollect him. "Send me the pictures, Demon. I'm presuming you want me to keep a look out?"

"Yeah. But there's more. Brothers and I thought he was fuckin' dead. Him strutting around carefree has caused a fuck ton of bad will as you'll understand. I got members here itching to get their fists on him. I want to send some brothers to Vegas, so I'm calling to see if we can partake of your hospitality, and if so, have you got room for Judge, Wills and Sparky?"

Fists? "Man's a fuckin' traitor whichever way you look at it. I'll gladly hang, draw and quarter him for you." Having snarled that out, belatedly I answer his question, "Yeah, of course they can stay."

"You can do what you like with him after I've finished," Demon states firmly. "What I want, Red, is him alive so I can talk to him. There's a reason he turned his back on the club and his ol' lady, and I want to know what the fuck that is."

The way Demon growls makes my lips curve up. I can understand him completely. "You got whatever help I can give, Brother. And of course, we'll put anyone you send us up."

I end the call and don't have to wait long for the ping that tells me that the photos have been sent on. Examining them carefully, I see a young man and don't have to look twice to see why he was given his handle. His face looks like a skull with skin stretched over it. But he's still handsome enough, I suppose, at least sufficient to attract an old lady. Though it's his companion in the pictures that I settle on longer. She's pretty, the kind of woman that appeals to a man like myself. She reminds me a lot of Cheryl. She's pushing a stroller with a kid in it. *Hers? Hers and Skull's?* If so, I could be looking at a man leading a double life, and if I'm right, she's not got a clue about it.

He doesn't look like a biker. Sure, he's wearing jeans, but no cut. He looks just like any man you'd pass on the street.

I wonder if learning his biker momma was going to spit out a brat made him run back to his first love. Maybe she's his wife. If I'm right, there's one hell of a lot of pain coming his way and the fucker will deserve it.

Bikers aren't the most loyal creatures, I know that. But most of us remain single if we want to have a good time. Satan's Devils tend to treasure their old ladies, and not many step out of line once they've claimed a woman as theirs. It's part of the reason I'm so particular about settling down. Temptation is always around me unless I can be certain the woman I choose is enough for me to be faithful to for life, and so far, I've found no one who'd hold my attention for long.

Brick had had that with Rosa, Fox with Tiffany. As far as the others in my chapter are concerned, they're much of my mind. Why give over your balls and independence when you've got pussy on tap? But I've seen examples in Tucson and Colorado how much the members are devoted to their old ladies.

Skull had claimed Melissa, and then he'd walked out. Whether he was fed up with his old lady or with the club is the big question mark. Whatever the reason, he abandoned her, and worse, disrespected his brothers. I can't think of an excuse that would allow him to escape with his life.

The following day, the three Colorado members duly arrive. When I greet them, Sparky comes up with an extra request, asking sheepishly if we could provide space for Pyro and Melissa, the woman who thought she was Skull's.

While I question the judgement that puts a pregnant woman in the stressful situation of being faced with an old man who not only is unfaithful but could have another family, I have to admire her spirit. It was her, as well as the club, who was wronged. Consequently, I'm eager to meet her. Her plight calls my protective instincts to the fore. When I hear Pyro and Melissa are on a plane, something makes me want to be the one to meet them.

Already gutted on her behalf, I wait outside the terminal, watching as the damaged woman and Pyro approach. My eyes widen as she draws closer, and I can read her expression. To my astonishment, she doesn't look sad or destroyed, in fact she's giggling.

"Christ. And I was led to expect a demure pregnant woman." I'm relieved in many ways that the woman is smiling and joking, and notice the pair seem close. Very close. Fuck, but this situation is complicated. If Melissa and Pyro have paired up thinking her old man was dead, who could blame them? Now his reappearance opens a whole new can of worms as an old lady is off-limits to any other brother. But who could fucking blame them?

Melissa's looking from me to Pyro and trying to control her laughter.

My eyes narrow. "Anything I should know, Brother?"

Pyro looks at Melissa who mouths something to him. My lips quirk when he shrugs. "Mel was just saying…" there's a gasp from the woman at this point, and I suspect she thought Pyro was going to say something very different as he innocently adds, "…that she's never been to Vegas."

There's something about her which means I immediately take a liking to this clearly spirited woman who's managing to survive such hurt. "Well, then, let me welcome you on behalf of the city."

I find I admire her even more as I drive them through the city. Pyro's asking me for updates, and telling me he's going to join the search, while Melissa, who I understand prefers being called Mel, seems intent on going looking herself. While I'm impressed with her determination, I'm not enamoured by the suggestion.

Pyro, though, he seems to know how to handle her. "Mel, we find him, we'll bring him back to the compound. You'll have your opportunity to speak to him face-to-face. You deserve his explanation."

"Same as the club," I add fast. "Fucker walked out, and he better have a fuckin' good reason for that."

I'm not doing the guided tour so avoid taking them along the strip, instead taking the fastest route to the clubhouse. Once we arrive, I leave them to catch up with the Colorado members but ask Rosa to show them to their room. Rosa, I know, will go into mother-hen mode, looking after Mel and making sure she's sorted.

Finding a man in Vegas sounds hard, but we lucked out seeing as the photos turned out to have been taken on his home turf. Finding him was one thing, holding on to him another. Brothers had chased him, but he'd escaped through a back entrance. All was not lost though, Wills and Cuff had taken off after him.

The rest of the search party had returned to the club, expectant that we'd soon have the absconder in our hands. I'm standing by the bar checking the inventory when I hear Pyro shout.

"Fucker's gone!" he screams at the top of his voice.

My attention shifts from the paperwork fast. "What do you mean, he's gone?" I snarl. "Wills and Cuff lost him? One of them come off their bike?"

Pyro stares at the phone he's still holding, shaking his head in disbelief. "Nah. Skull had help. Two cars intercepted and prevented them from following. It was stop or be run off the road."

He had help? That Skull's not a lone wolf starts alarm bells ringing. "They get ID on the cars?" I cross the room over to him.

Pyro's face falls as though he realises he's forgotten to ask.

"Trail's not dead," Keys shouts from the other side of the room. "I've tracked that licence plate Cuff called in." Thank fuck for techno freaks and men on the ball.

"Then let's get moving. Text me the address." I want this man now. It's more imperative now I know someone's aiding and abetting him. There's something wrong about this situation, and I need to find out what. I take my bike key out of my cut. "Coming, Twister?"

"Try and stop me," my enforcer replies.

Feeling adrenaline rising through me, it's been a while since I was involved on the front line. I lead the group that's heading to the destination Keys had come up with. I want my hands on this Skull, now more than ever. Demon's got a prior claim on him, but for all that, this is my town.

When we reach the locality, I give the signal for them to slow down and pull over, whistling to gather them around me.

"Place we're headed to is a couple of roads over," I tell them, pointedly looking at Pyro, the stranger to our town. "Any sound of bikes and he'll be off."

"He won't get away from me next time," Cuff growls a promise.

He didn't get away without help. Question is, how was the fucker able to summon assistance so fast? I'm certain stopping the chase was no accident.

Leaving that to be answered once we've got our hands on him, I lay out my plan, which is for me, Pyro and Twister to take the crash truck and scope the place we assume is his home address out, then call for reinforcements dependent on what we find. Pyro voices my fear, that Skull, having recognised the Satan's Devils were after him, won't have come back to his home, but will have left town.

What we feared seems confirmed when we get to the house, but oh, the surprises we find inside. There are pictures of Skull with the woman and child which definitely point to the kid being his as we'd expected, but the man in those photos was dressed in a suit and tie and looking nothing like a biker. Furthermore, the bills were addressed to a Donavan Jordan, and not the legal name, Kris Cox, that Colorado had known him to go by.

Something stinks.

Despite my gut feel that our rat has run, and this house, prestigious as it and its contents is, has been left abandoned, I nevertheless agree to some brothers and Pyro staking it out in the vain hope that Skull might be back.

I return to the compound, trying to make up some bullshit about where her man Pyro, is, but Mel, clever woman that she is, isn't having it. I settle for my go-to excuse, *club business*, which works. Leaving her swearing after me, I go tend to some of my own work.

With one thing and another, eating in my office, I'm still hard at it when hours later, I get a call from Pyro. His words cause me to punch the air. Skull's woman has turned up, and they've got her.

I quickly agree to send Crash to bring the woman to the compound, feeling like we've made a breakthrough. Now, at last, we might have some answers.

When Pyro appears, I wonder whether we're on the same wavelength about questioning a woman. While we might not use precisely the same methods we'd use on a man, if a woman's got information, in my view she needs to be interrogated, and that means using all the tools at our disposal. But when he mouths basement to me, I know he's in the same ballpark.

It's clear Pyro intends to use fear and intimidation, but he's gentle with the bound woman when he removes the gag from her mouth. I harden my heart when I see she's terrified and looking around frantically, her eyes going wide.

Yeah, she might be confused. This place has been witness to torture, and on occasion, death. But there's also Rope and Cuff's spanking bench and St. Andrews Cross occupying one corner, and a wall where whips and crops are hanging. The variety of restraints on show also has to be admired. I've used them myself from time to time. That part of the basement tends to have more willing victims.

The woman doesn't seem to see any positive possibilities in the arrangement. "What the hell is this place?" she cries out. "It looks like a torture chamber."

I again glance around, taking note of my deviant brothers' enhancements, and chuckle. "It does, doesn't it, doll?" Of course, some torture might be pleasurable, but I doubt she sees that at present. I step in front of her. "It's Clare, isn't it?" Pyro's just used that name. When she nods, I point to Twister who's followed us down. "You know what an enforcer is, Clare?"

She swallows rapidly and shakes her head.

"Well, he's the man who gets information by whatever means necessary. I happen to know Twister is very good at his job. No one leaves here alive without telling him what he wants to know. You know how he got his handle?"

Another shake.

"I'll give you a clue. People who don't talk, quickly find out how twisted he is." My face shows I'm completely serious. If I can get her to spill any info she has without bloodshed, so much the better.

"I don't know what you want to know," she cries out. "I don't know who you are or why I'm here. I'm a part-time librarian, a housewife, and a mother. I don't know anything."

"To be honest, Clare, you look like a nice lady," I tell her honestly. And she does. I try to ignore the resemblance to the woman I remember from my past. "And we have no beef with you. But we'd like to have a talk with your husband. Now, you can start by giving us his phone number."

Of course, it isn't as easy as that. She holds out, worried we'll hurt him, even though I try and impress on her we just want to talk. Pyro tries his best to coax the information from her, but her lips are sealed tight.

Fuck it. Pyro's getting frustrated, as am I. As there's no indication she's other than another innocent caught up in Skull's web, I can't justify hurting her, even though a little voice inside me suggests part of my reluctance to use force is down to how much she resembles the woman I had so briefly and lost.

Deciding the truth might persuade her, I tell her there's a woman who's five months pregnant upstairs, and that her beloved husband's the father. She denies it, at first, then I think a little doubt sneaks in. Whatever, she finally gives me Skull's number. Thank fuck. I was close to letting Twister loose on her.

We're able to contact the fucker at last. Whatever Skull is, he proves he really loves her, or at least enough to agree to come to the compound. While we're waiting, Pyro continues to question her.

Each word I hear chills my spine and puts another nail in Skull's coffin.

The bottom line? Skull was a fuckin' undercover cop who'd infiltrated the Devils.

Clare knew the basics, but not the details, and definitely not the important ones. Pyro takes the opportunity to explain exactly what her husband had done while fooling the Devils he was part of the club.

"He decided to take a woman as his own. Claimed her, which in our world is as good as marrying her. He lived with her. Slept with her every fuckin' night. Forgot to use a condom, twice. Then he up and left, leaving her pregnant." What Skull had done makes his voice harden.

She's now hanging onto his every word, her mouth agape in disbelief and horror.

"He come home and fuck you? After he'd been with his old lady without a condom?" Her widened eyes suggest yes. "And what about her? What about the woman he said he loved, the woman he'd promised to spend his whole life with? He never came back, left with no warning. She found she was pregnant with no man to tell. You've got a kid, Clare. What if your husband left for a job and never came back? Disappeared off the face of the earth and you never had any answers. Can you imagine that, Clare? Can you imagine the fucking hurt?"

"No." Her hands cover her face. Her denial, I suspect, more that those things had actually occurred than her answering Pyro's question.

"Yes," Pyro insists. "She's five months pregnant with your husband's baby. It's a boy. Your little girl will have a brother. What about her, Clare? What about the innocent woman he used and discarded? What about her?"

Has he gotten through to her? As I watch, she sits up straighter.

Movement behind me makes me turn to see what's caught her eye, and I wince when I see the woman heading straight for her.

"What about *me*?" Mel screams, spittle landing on Clare's face.

Clare makes the connection easily, her eyes flicking to Mel then dropping to her stomach. A myriad of expressions appear on her features—anger, disbelief, sadness. It's hard to predict what she's going to say.

Finally, she settles on denial. "I don't believe you. The baby can't be his."

"You don't believe me?" Mel scoffs. "Well, in about four and a half months I'll have proof. Do you know what it's like, Clare, to be in love with a man you then find out doesn't exist? To mourn the death of a man who's still alive? To be carrying the baby who came into being through falsehood and deceit? Can you even begin to imagine it?"

She focuses on my eyes, as though trying to find something she can use to disbelieve Mel's words and her expression which is telegraphing pain and hurt.

"If what you're saying is true, you're right, I can't begin to imagine it," Clare says at last. "But if what you say is the truth…" She swallows. "I don't know." Her voice drops to a whisper. "It was his job… Maybe he had to—"

"Job?" Mel rasps back, interrupting. "I was part of his *job*?"

It's clear Clare doesn't want to believe her, and to me, some of her words don't make sense. She tries to justify Skull was hers first, and then retreats to the explanation that Mel must be lying. They go back and forth for a while, until we're interrupted.

"Clare, oh my God, Clare. What have they done to you?" Her husband, Mel's old man, Skull has arrived. He's been escorted down to the basement and is running straight across to Clare, examining her, running his hands over her as if to see whether she's been hurt.

I draw in a breath, ready to take over. *This man is a traitor to the Satan's Devils.* He deserves every ounce of pain he's going to get. Then I hear someone calling me urgently.

"Prez, VP. Come quickly, we've got company."

What the fuck?

Annoyed I'm being called away, I pause only a moment to satisfy myself Pyro's got this under control and then climb the stairs leading out of the basement.

"What the hell is it?" I warn Indian, "This better be fucking important."

"I think you'll find it is." He points to Keys who's staring at a monitor.

"Jesus," I breathe. "They're here for Skull." I blink, but it doesn't make the sight any different. Right outside the gates there are police cars and cops, and what I think is even a SWAT team. "Damnation! Fuck it!"

I turn and take the stairs back down to the basement two at a time to stop Pyro from making a mistake we'll all regret.

"Skull, here, brought company," I hiss when my hasty reappearance gets their attention. "Cops. They're outside the gates. His insurance policy to make sure he, and she, walk out unscathed."

Knowing he's prevented from using his fists, Pyro blasts him with words. We get the confirmation we knew already. That he's a plant.

"You working for the cops or the feds?" I ask, knowing the difference is vital. One could see a few men behind bars, the other could close the club completely.

He refuses to comply and his answer as to why he disappeared was simply, "Job done."

Which, quite rightly, sends Mel off the handle. I step back. She's the one most hurt.

To my disgust, he doesn't try to deny that he used her, doesn't even gloss it up by saying he couldn't resist her, and as to why he left without a word, he repeats, "My job had ended so I returned to my wife."

His concern and eyes had been on his wife. He hadn't the decency to even look at Mel, so she had to spell out that she's pregnant. When she does, Skull, Donavan, or whatever he's going by now looks like he's going to be sick. He staggers back and then staggers again when Pyro's fist in his stomach winds him.

Then what happens next means I have to hide my grin. Never, ever, underestimate a scorned woman. I'm full of admiration for Mel and for what she says after Pyro informs him, he'll never be seeing his kid.

"He won't be seeing him from behind bars."

Doing his job isn't a crime, so Mel must be on to something. I can see it in her intelligent eyes. "Whatcha saying, Mel?"

"He raped me. He misrepresented himself. If I'd known who he was, what he was doing, I'd never have given my consent. I didn't give my body to a cop, I gave it to the biker he was pretending to be."

My eyes gleam. *Too fucking right.* I turn to Skull. "You were sanctioned to fuck for information?"

Skull's eyes widen. "What?" For the first time, his voice isn't steady.

I raise my eyebrow in challenge. When Skull doesn't say more, I probe further, "Your superiors know? Or is this something you did on your own? Did you want an old lady to get information, use her in some way to strengthen your acceptance into the club? Or did you just want a handy fuckin' companion?"

"Don?" his wife asks, almost hesitantly, as though she too wants clarification but is afraid of the answer.

But instead of answering her question, he rounds on her, accusing her of being caught and him being put in this position.

I'm sick of the man. Enraged the cops waiting means I can't hurt him. But there's one thing I want. One thing that's important to every Devil. I demand his cut. The cut that according to Demon, he'd disappeared wearing.

Skull shakes his head. "It's in evidence."

"You're building a fuckin' case against us?" Pyro's face is bright red.

Mine is a likewise colour as I work through the implications. Cops waiting or not, I'm about to put my hands on him when there's a commotion in the room above—shouts of "Put your hands up!" and another yell of, "Jordan, time's up."

Skull jerks his head upward as if acknowledging the faceless voice, then looks at Clare apologetically and demands of his ex-old lady, "I want a DNA test, Mel."

The atmosphere could be cut with a knife. After all he's done to her, after the pain he's put her through, he's now calling her a liar.

I get up into his face. "You don't trust her? You have the fuckin' balls to question the woman you raped and impregnated?"

"It wasn't rape. She consented."

"I don't fuckin' think so," I tell him. My face is glowing but for once I don't mind it betraying how angry I am. "We're going to see you in court, fucker."

"Bikers taking a cop to court?" He scoffs. He turns to look at one of his colleagues, who's bravely descended the stairs. "I've said all I'm going to. Now I'm taking my wife and we're both going to walk out of this compound. You're going to do nothing to stop me."

He looks toward his wife, gesturing she's free to go. Which she is. With the heavy presence of cops, our hands are tied. But she doesn't make a move to go to his side.

I watch her carefully. I've only once before seen a woman fall apart while struggling to hold herself together, and that was the night Brick had died. Loss and betrayal war on the features of Clare's face now, and it would take a harder man than I not to feel sorry for her. In one night, she's had her world torn asunder. Her defence of the man had been blown wide open by the very words that had come out of his mouth.

He's a liar, a cheater, and uses women as if they mean nothing. She must now be questioning all that they'd had, and what they'd really meant to each other.

Something drives me to offer her a chance. Putting myself between him and her, I address Clare. "You don't have to go with him. We've got no argument with you. If you need help, we can give it to you."

Clare looks astonished. Her eyes widen, and her hand goes to her head.

"She's coming with me," Skull states angrily.

Clare looks from him to me, then back again, then sighs. She eyes the mob of angry bikers with disdain in her eyes, then again shakes her head and finally steps closer to her man.

She's made her choice and thrown away the escape route I offered to her. My jaw clenches. Fucking civilians stick together.

Skull, Clare, and the cops who came to their rescue, disappear up the stairs. The non-climax leaves us in stunned silence.

But now we've got to deal with any possible fallout to the club. "Church in half an hour," I announce, then my eyes fall on Mel who's gone completely white. "Pyro, see to your woman."

CHAPTER THIRTY-THREE

The aftermath of that incident continues for days. Mel's distraught and first pushes Pyro away from her, and I spend time trying to give sage advice when what do I know about women? Then, it's counselling my club and Demon's about what knowledge Skull could have taken with him.

Were we facing a RICO investigation? The circumstances that first brought me to the Vegas club all come flooding back, with brothers worried we were going to be harassed by the cops. Expecting an imminent raid has all brothers on tenterhooks.

It all hinged on the question, had he found anything to take down the club? That it had been months since he'd left Colorado seemed to suggest he had nothing on us. But having had a plant in one of our chapters hit us all hard.

When Demon and his VP, Beef—a man I knew from my time in Tucson—arrive in Vegas, they're full of remonstrations about what they could have done to prevent the mess. But when I questioned Demon how Skull had come to them in the first place, I honestly couldn't see what he'd done wrong. And that's what I told him.

It was a fraught few days. All my prez's diplomacy is called into action in the numerous meetings and discussions.

Not one member wants anything other than to see Skull meet Satan, but with his connections, any attempt on his life would fall back on the club. In the end, I persuade them that Mel had the right idea, and that while the legal route was long, it was the right path.

To top it all off, and down to the stress, Mel had a miscarriage. A world of hurt summed up in a few simple words.

It hadn't mattered to her and Pyro whose baby it was. It was hers. It was theirs. It was already loved and cared for. Skull had murdered that kid just as much as if he'd taken a knife and cut it out of her. We all knew who was responsible.

We had another fucking funeral, this time for a kid that had never known life. Then, it wasn't my problem any more as Pyro took Melissa home to Colorado, and the clubhouse was back to being ours.

After such an emotional time, it took a while for us to settle and get back to normal. The threat that Skull was only the vanguard for the feds to swoop down on the MC was always on our minds, but as days, then weeks went by, I made a concerted effort to put it behind us.

No member was pulled over and searched, not here, nor in Colorado. While we took extra care and precautions, the danger seemed to have passed. Then there came a time when a whole day would go by, and Skull's name wasn't even mentioned.

The only thing of note was when I got word Tide had been shanked in the penitentiary, and that this time, he hadn't survived. Despite us getting him protection, it was far from the first time he'd been attacked inside. The mood was sombre when I announced the news at the table, but only Titch seemed genuinely upset. For myself, it was a problem solved. While when I'd first discussed him around this table many years back, his ever getting out seemed so remote and distant it wasn't worth worrying about. But now he's served half of his twenty-year sentence, it's possible his remaining time will pass just as fast. Now we won't have to worry about stripping his patch and there would be no appetite for anything else, the legacy he'd left on the club had caused too many problems. His death means he's now firmly in a box labelled never again to be worried about.

I'm busy enough that I like a quiet life, one where I can concentrate on making money for the club, and even, when I've time, tinkering with cars and bikes in the shop, never having lost my love of working with engines and such shit.

Brothers seem to have settled down, and I only have to manage minor disputes between them.

But when you've reached stasis, the universe likes to throw in a curve ball, and that came to our door one day in the shape of a tall, willowy blonde.

"What the fuck?" Crash angrily exclaims when the clubhouse door had opened to reveal her standing there. "What the hell is she doing here?" He takes a step toward her before I can move myself. "Is *he* with you?"

I notice Crash's hands on his gun, so I move in fast, getting in front of him and moving him back.

"Clare."

She looks down at the floor, then seems to brace herself. Her eyes rise to meet mine, and shyly she asks, "You offered to help me?"

"I did." But as I confirm it, my eyes crease and I take a step forward. Raising my hand, I touch her chin and gently move her face so the light falls on her. My jaw clenches. "He hit you?"

Her eyes blink away tears. "I don't know who he is anymore," she starts, then corrects, "Or whether I knew him at all. But I'm scared, Red. I've nowhere to go—"

"Where's the kid?" I ask tightly.

"She's outside, in the car—"

"In the fuckin' car?" I push past her and am out the door hearing footsteps following in my wake. I breathe a sigh of relief when I see the car's parked so the backseat is in the shade. The engine's running and the air-conditioning going full blast, and in a child carrier, there's a kid asleep.

"I only left her for a moment." Clare sounds defensive.

"I was watching out for her," Owl, our prospect states.

I go to the driver's side, open the door, turn off the engine and take her keys out. Then return to the passenger side and open the rear door. Hell, that's a cute little kid. Carefully, I unbuckle the belt. She wakes as I disturb her.

I pause, I'm a strange man, is she going to cry? But instead, those eyelashes flutter, and I silently laugh, knowing in the future she'll be breaking a few hearts. When I lift her, she makes no murmur. And when I try to hand her to her mother, she protests and turns her head toward my cut.

Clare stares, as if surprised.

"What can I say?" I tell her, grinning widely. "All girls love a biker." Then to Owl, I instruct, "Bring any bags she has in."

"Does this mean we can stay?" Her face is now full of hope.

I jostle my burden to make sure I've a tight grip on her. "It means we'll give you sanctuary. For now."

Do I trust her? I have to consider that she could be following in her husband's footsteps, infiltrating our club to dig up dirt. I have to consider it, but it won't take much to dismiss it. The authorities might plant one woman perhaps, but not a woman with a kid in tow.

"I figured here is the one place he won't look for me."

I can't totally suppress my snort at her explanation. Yeah, a fed wouldn't expect his civilian wife to run to an outlaw MC for help. Alternatively, though, as we couldn't seek revenge on him, he might wonder if we've taken his wife to punish him. But a problem can't cause much harm, as long as I can see it coming and mitigate against it.

Still carrying her daughter, I lead the way back inside. As we do, I casually ask, "This a temporary reprieve to make him come to his senses?"

"No." Her footsteps stop, making me spin around. "As God's

my witness, no. I'm going to divorce him, Red. This," she points to her eye, "was the last straw. That business with the woman, he didn't care that he'd fathered a kid. Didn't care what happened to it. If that's how he feels, what if he decides he doesn't want her?" She gestures toward the squirming bundle I'm carrying. "What if he hits *her?* He's not the man I thought I married." I start walking again, and she comes up beside me. "The truth is, with his work, he's been working away most of our married life. My husband was someone who didn't exist. When he'd come home, having been away for months, I'd notice he'd seemed different, less interested in me. When I challenged him, he'd say he was tired, and needed to recuperate. When the truth is, I was no longer exciting. Not when he could fuck whoever he wanted while he was working."

"Hey, Rosa?" I call out when we reach the bar.

With a smile, she turns and hurries over, reaching out her hand to touch the babe in my arms. "And who do we have here?" She beams, all her focus on the kid, and none on the woman.

But that doesn't matter to Clare, who, seeing the motherly figure, seems to relax. There's pride in her voice as she explains, "This is Cordelia, though we call her Delly."

"She's a cutie." Rosa now spares Clare a glance, her eyes fast narrowing as she seems more eagled-eyed, but she doesn't pry, just turns her attention back to her daughter. "Look at those long eyelashes."

I grin. "Yeah, and she already knows how to use them."

Delly, sensing another person interested in her, holds out her hands to Rosa who delightfully removes my burden from me.

"Clare and Delly are staying for a while," I tell Rosa.

Her brow furrows. "There's not a suitable room free." Then she brightens. "They can have our rooms. We don't really use them anyway."

When Brick had died, I hadn't wanted to move Rosa out, though his president's suite was much larger than mine—two bedrooms, a private bathroom, and a living area. It's true, Rosa's not using it much anymore. Her grief at the loss of her husband might not be fading, but is becoming easier to live with, and she doesn't mind living with the memories in their house.

"You sure?" I don't want to pressure her into anything.

"It's time, Red. It should have been yours anyway."

What would I need two bedrooms for? But in the current situation, it's the ideal solution.

"I don't want to put anyone out." Clare seems anxious.

"Don't you worry," Rosa says firmly. "It's time. Trist and Tom are getting older now. They need more space and will enjoy more room to have their friends over more often." She winks at me. "Some parents don't see the MC as a suitable playground."

I frown. I don't want strangers' kids running around either.

Clare looks like she's been put in an awkward position, and I mark her up that she's not selfish to expect everything handed to her. "I won't be here long."

Rosa's face hardens. "You'll be here at least as long as it takes for Red to sort out the man who blackened your eye for you."

But that I can't do, though there's nothing I'd like better. He's a fed and my hands are tied. If the Devils take him out, we'd be the first under suspicion. My only comfort is that Pyro's got a far more personal reason for wanting him dead, and eventually Skull will be six feet under. Won't be today, won't be next week. Maybe not for months yet. But one day, he'll stop breathing and then both Clare and Mel will be free.

Of course, I don't say that to Clare. She's a civilian. Her way to get him out of her life is to get a divorce and receive a settlement.

Loud voices get my attention. Turning, I grin as two exuberant teenage boys run in.

"Hi, Mom, we're starving."

Them permanently living off compound might lower our food bills.

"Hey." Reaching out, I grab them both by their collars. "If you ask your mom nicely, you might get something." I gaze at them sternly. Hell, it seems like only yesterday they barely reached up to my waist, now I only have to lower my head slightly to glare at them. "How was football practice?"

"We made the try-outs," Trist says, high fiving his brother.

"That's great." Rosa gives a fond mom smile. "Got some news, boys, we're moving back to the house, permanently."

Tom, the quieter of the two, narrows his eyes, and doing an impression of his father, turns to me. "You kicking us out, Uncle Red?" His eyebrow rises as he awaits an explanation. But just like Brick, he doesn't dive in and make an assumption.

"F… No." I refute that immediately. "You're always welcome, you know that. But we do need the space for a while, and you might like a bit more freedom."

Trist elbows his brother. "We could have girls around."

Rosa looks horrified, while I chuckle. "You could bring your girlfriends here."

"Here?" Trist looks around. "What if we want some privacy?"

What the fuck? They wouldn't get a chance. They'd have a dozen biker chaperones' eyes on them all the time.

"There won't be any privacy in our house either," Rosa tells them, firmly. And the look she gives to me is to suggest forewarned is forearmed.

At least I've already had the discussion with them about condoms. There are some things best said man-to-man.

"It could work," Tom says cautiously. "At least we'll have our own rooms, and I won't have to put up with you snoring."

"Don't snore."

"Do."

Fists are raised, and I step in between them. "Why don't you two go raid the fridge, then go get your stuff packed?"

"Can I invite Marvin over tonight?" Trist isn't slow to pick up on the opportunity.

Rosa purses her lips. "If we get packed and home in time, then yes, you can."

"Yay! Come, Tom, let's get packing."

"I thought they were hungry," Clare muses, as two pairs of feet stomp up the stairs, sounding like a herd of elephants.

"I'll swap you." Rosa looks down at the cherubic baby in her arms who'd been watching the boys' interaction. "This little angel for the pair of them."

Clare chuckles. "She has her moments, but somehow I think I'd be getting the worst of that bargain." She reaches out her hands and takes her daughter back. "Now if I'm staying, what can I do? Can I help with your packing? I'm kicking you out, I need to do something."

Again, she goes up in my estimation.

"No need," I tell her. "The boys will get their shit together, and the prospects will do the heavy lifting."

"You okay in the kitchen?" Rosa asks, seeming to realise Clare has a need to do something. "Because I could do with some help getting these boys fed."

Boys, in this instance, meaning me and the crew.

"I can do that, yes." Clare brightens at the thought of being helpful.

I catch Rosa's eye. She gives me a chin lift reminiscent of Brick. As I telegraph a request for her to take Clare under her wing, she signals back, *will do.*

CHAPTER THIRTY-FOUR

I've been the prez long enough that while my brothers might raise their eyebrows and shake their heads, they don't come right out and ask what the fuck I'm doing without giving me the chance to explain.

Once Clare takes the lovely Delly and disappears into the kitchen with Rosa, the vultures descend.

"What the hell?" Crash is the first to reach me. "You know who she fuckin' is, don't you?"

"Heap of trouble right there, Prez," Twister observes.

Looking around, I see we've gathered quite an audience, including the sweet butts who are blatantly listening. "Let's discuss this in church." As I lead the way, all present follow me.

When they take their seats, I count up the ones who are missing—Titch, Cobra, Cuff and Petty. Most are here, the rest I can fill in later.

I note the curious stares pointed my way. Taking a breath, I begin to set out what's on my mind.

"You all know who that is?"

All of them nod. Even if they hadn't seen her last time around, they've been updated.

"She's the bastard Skull's woman," Cobra spits out.

My mouth curves. "Not any longer. She's seen the light and left him."

"Why the fuck has she come here?" Hammer seems particularly unimpressed with her presence.

Twister answers for me. "Red made the offer for her to stay when she was last here."

I raise my chin toward him in thanks. "Look, Skull's a cop with all the resources that go along with his job. She needs a place to hide out where he won't come looking for her."

Roller starts nodding his head. "Cops fuckin' stick together. If she goes anywhere else, he'll be able to find her."

He's right. I recall it happening to one of the Arizona guys, Dart, who's now VP in San Diego. His old lady was a cop's wife. When she left him, it wasn't long before he found out where she was. The thought makes me frown. Not only did he find her, he half killed her. Luckily, Dart found her in time. Of course, he was soon put underground.

"What made her come to her senses at last?" Fox asks, his brow creased.

"Skull hit her."

"Fuckin' bastard."

Fox's comment is echoed around. There's one thing that's an anathema to Satan's Devils, and that's violence toward the fairer sex. Sure, there are some women who can take care of themselves, but normally men have more brawn, and unfortunately, usually the upper hand. To my mind, using that strength is a sign of weakness.

Sarge raps on the table to get my attention. "You take in a broad who the cops will be looking for, where's the benefit for us? I can only see downsides."

Rope's nodding at him. "And don't forget she could be a plant. Skull might like to keep it in the family."

"Why do we owe her anything at all?" Crash asks.

"Good points," I say loudly, getting the attention back to myself. "Who I'm thinking about is Mel. You all saw how it destroyed her to lose her baby? Well, by keeping Clare and his kid here under wraps, he gets to feel just a bit of the pain of losing something."

"Rather he was six feet under," Indian complains.

It seems everyone agrees with him. "He'll get his. Eventually. In the meantime, though, how about we cause him a bit of pain?"

To be honest, I'm clutching at straws. I can't really explain why I have this urge to keep her under my roof. There's just something about her, something that drove me to make the offer in the first place weeks back, which was amplified today once I saw the injury Skull had caused her.

"How about one of us fuck her? Let him know what it feels like to be cheated on?"

"Good fuckin' idea, Rope. She's a good-looking broad."

Rage rises fast. "No one," I glare at Hammer, then repeat myself, "no one is touching her. Got it?"

Cuff nudges Rope and says loudly, "Prez is keeping her for himself."

I send my best prez scowl toward him. It works as he pretends to slide under the table. I'll be keeping my hands off. Won't I?

"We gonna vote to let her stay?" Crash catches my eye.

I suppose we ought to. "Anyone got any objections?"

"Nah. If it hurts Skull, it serves us."

Twister's sentiment is echoed around the table while I'm just pleased they accepted my lame excuse.

Dismissing the meeting, I go to check on our new adoptee. Walking into the kitchen, I hear laughter, and smell something tantalising.

"Prez." Rosa beams at me, and points to Clare. "You should keep this one. She's got good spicing skills. This fried chicken is going to be the best you've ever had."

Clare blushes red and gets back to what she was doing.

I should tell Rosa not to get dependent on her as she won't be here long, but something holds me back, unable to put a time limit on how long she's going to stay.

It's her, I decide, leaning back against a worktop and folding my arms. Despite having a baby, she's slim, tall—not my height, but enough so a man wouldn't need to fold himself in half to kiss her. Her long hair is tied back in a ponytail, showing off her shapely face. Her nose is small and perks up at the end, and her mouth, well, I bet I'm not the first man to imagine my dick going there.

Someone should fuck her. Rope's words echo in my head.

Nah, not going there. Clare wouldn't be up for casual sex. She'd want something to last. While my dick wouldn't object to giving her a trial run, it wouldn't be fair.

Seeing me watching her, Clare gives me a shy smile, then goes back to what she was doing. She and Rosa seem to work well together, I notice, anticipating each other's needs. When Clare looks around for a spatula, Rosa's already handing her one. All the time, Clare keeps one eye on her daughter, who's asleep in the stroller she must have brought in from the car.

As plates clatter, the sound brings the brothers swarming in. I tense, wondering how Clare will take the men crowding her, men who'd she'd last seen when she was tied up in the basement, and not on one of Rope and Cuff's toys.

But she seems unfazed, simply turns her head, purses her lips, then reaches for more plates.

Rosa and she seem to have a conveyor belt going, and soon full plates are being handed around. More than one brother puts their nose to the chicken and inhales sharply, looking up with raised eyes.

"If ya'll like it, you've her to thank." Rosa grins at Clare who blushes and shrugs.

The sound of utensils hitting porcelain wake the child. Clare picks her up, takes a vacant seat at the table, and balances Delly on one arm while she feeds herself.

The kid reaches for a piece of chicken, which Clare gives to her. Rosa produces a sippy cup from somewhere, and places it down.

It's so natural, it's like they've always been here.

Twister walks in and comes to an abrupt stop. "Whoa. That's a kid." He starts moving again, his face softening as he gets closer. "Well, ain't you just a pretty one."

Delly looks up at him and giggles, offering him the chicken she's holding in her hand. My hard-as-nails enforcer bends his head and pretends to take a bite. Giggling, Delly snatches it back.

"Want me to hold her so you can eat?" Cobra offers, holding out his arms.

And that's the start of it. That poor kid starts getting passed around from brother to brother. Not that she seems to care at all.

"Sends me back," Rosa says fondly.

"What you talking about, Mom?" Tom and Trist, having just appeared, ask.

She turns around and grins at them. "About back when you were babies."

Yeah, a lot of the men in the club are used to having babies around, or were, a decade and a half ago. Seems like they haven't forgotten the touch. But Delly is easy to fall for, a happy kid who so far always seems to be smiling, big blue eyes and a curly mop of blonde hair. Luckily for her, her looks don't favour her dad. She's all her mom, and that makes it easier to forget why she's here.

"You grow up with a big family?" I ask Clare a few days after she's arrived. We're alone in the clubroom. Brothers are either out working, or sleeping last night off. Our security business keeps us active at all hours.

Clare settles Delly in a playpen, making sure she's surrounded by toys. "I was an only child, why?"

Raising and lowering my shoulders, I explain why I'm surprised. "You just seem comfortable having this rabble around you."

And she does. She ignores the off-colour jokes like an expert, doesn't turn a hair when an argument turns physical. In fact, at least once I've seen her expertly breaking such an altercation up with a coy look and a *"why don't you two make up?"* Her gentle teasing approach seems to work. She's become the mistress of the first aid box, brothers going to her first when they've got themselves a cut. She'd strapped Shadow's wrist up yesterday when he wrenched it doing something with his bike.

She fits in here. She doesn't seem out of place. And rather than being a spoiled princess expecting to be waited on hand and foot, she throws herself into any job which needs doing.

The sweet butts? Well, she's taken them in her stride. Taking her cues from Rosa, she directs their tasks. I've heard rumblings from the girls about what exactly is her place here. Truth is, I'm still wondering that myself.

Having made sure her daughter is occupied, Clare takes a seat on the couch opposite the chair that I'm sitting on. Wiping strands of long hair from her face, she takes a breath. "I can manage the boys. I used to be a teacher in an elementary school. Believe me, being here isn't much different."

I snort, noting she's picked up on Rosa's terms for the brothers. "You saying we're a bunch of oversized kids?"

She chuckles and shrugs. "If the cap fits."

I find I'm grinning. "Even Titch?"

She winks at me. "I got him eating his greens yesterday. Well, I shamed him into it to encourage Delly to eat hers, but the end was the same."

A snicker of laughter escapes me. Titch is a man who likes his meat.

Clare continues with a chuckle, "Pre-pubescent boys and bikers have a lot in common I've found. Keep them fed and watered, don't take away their toys, and they're happy."

There is quite a lot of truth in that, but there's one thing she's missing. "I can assure you we've all passed puberty." She surely can't have missed the X-rated activities which go on after Delly's been settled for the night. Though she does make use of the women's room and doesn't stay long to take in the sights.

"Of that I'm well aware," she replies with a smirk.

And that's another thing I'd thought she'd find hard to ignore, open sex in the clubroom. But it seems she's capable of disregarding it without censure.

"It's your house, Red. I'd be a poor visitor if I complained about the way you live your life."

"But you don't approve of it?"

She grimaces. "If I'd known, I'd have doubted Don was faithful long before it was thrown in my face. How could he have pretended to be a biker and not have gone with the girls? He'd have stuck out like a sore thumb."

"Not really," I correct her. "While he was prospecting, the girls would have been off-limits. And even when he was patched, he'd not have to put on a show. We don't grade men on their sexual prowess. There's plenty that don't partake of the free sex, and we think nothing of it." In particular, I remember how I was always fooled by Joker having "a woman in town", when women were not his preference. Of course, a lot of things had come together when Joker and Lady had come out. As prez, it had hurt most that they'd thought they'd be censured for their sexual leanings. I'd wished they'd trusted me. It was the secret they'd kept to themselves that had upset me, not the reason behind it.

She listens to my explanation, then flinches. "So, Don was an ass. I just wish I'd seen it earlier. Of course, he didn't want me when he had the likes of Mel, and the club girls to tempt him."

"Skull was fuckin' blind," I growl. Her words give me an excuse to make a visual assessment of her, reminding me once again of the woman I'd lost. She's everything I'd be looking for in an old lady if I were on the hunt.

When she shrugs, not believing me, I want to convince her. Convince her by showing her exactly what her presence here does to my cock. I'm mostly hard when I'm around her.

But she's a guest here. And she's married to an enemy of ours.

The devil on my other shoulder whispers into my ear, *she's getting divorced. And she'd make a fucking great old lady.*

The devil's words slam into me. The way she is with the men, the way she fits in with Rosa, why shouldn't I take a chance on starting something with her?

I'd given up on having my own family, so why shouldn't I take Skull's? Wouldn't that be the most fitting punishment?

Acting impulsively had got me nowhere with Cheryl, so I decide to take things slow.

Once the idea gets lodged in my head, it seems to get stuck there. I find myself in the clubroom more often. When she's seated, I try to sit beside her. When I'm leaning forward to get my beer one day, I put my hand on her thigh, and a sideways glance shows me she's blushing, but she doesn't evade my touch.

When I talk to her and a strand of hair escapes from her hair tie and falls over her face, more than once I've brushed it back, noticing how she's shivered as my fingers brush her skin.

She's been here at the clubhouse for a couple of weeks now. It's no longer a surprise to see her in the kitchen cooking along-side Rosa or playing with Delly in the clubroom. Twelve-month-olds seem to have a lot of toys, I've found, and brothers seem unable to resist bringing more back. Rope turned up with a plastic ride-on motorcycle the other day, even though she's too young to ride it as yet. But Delly loved to sit on it and screamed with delight when she managed to roll it a couple of inches with her chubby legs.

Yeah, my brothers are softies when it comes to kids.

CHAPTER THIRTY-FIVE

When Delly took her first steps, the brothers took the opportunity to have a party, while I relished the fact that Skull was missing all of this. It was at that party to celebrate the achievement of her child—as if she was the first kid to ever learn to walk—that I decided to test the waters.

Naturally, the party continues long after Delly has been put to bed.

I sit, beer in hand, watching Clare and waiting for my chance, which comes when she walks into the kitchen to get herself a glass of water. She'd had a couple of glasses of wine, but having responsibility for her daughter, was clearly restricting herself. I'd followed her in.

As she holds her glass to the tap, I come up behind her, leaning against her and imprisoning her body between my arms, hands resting on the counter to either side. She jumps and turns her head, then seeing it's me, she sighs.

"Skull was an idiot." I speak quietly, directly into her ear. "He had no fuckin' idea what a prize he had."

"I'm nothing special."

"I disagree." Turning her around, I take the glass out of her hand and place it down safely. "You're an amazing mom, and an incredible woman. You take everything in your stride, and you take no shit from anybody. You're also," raising my hand I brush it down her cheek, "beautiful."

"Red—"

As she goes to protest, I stop her. "I'd like to kiss you, Clare. You gonna be okay with that?" I hope she fucking is.

Her teeth worry those lips I hope mine will soon be touching. "I'm married."

I tense. "You going back to him?"

"Never, but still—"

My voice hardens. "He fuckin' hit you, Clare. And as for keeping marriage vows, he obviously didn't care about his."

"You're right." She considers my words for a moment, then takes me by surprise, going up on her tiptoes and brushing her fingers through my hair.

She might be the one bringing her mouth to mine, but a second is all it takes for me to come to my senses and take over, pressing my lips to hers, insisting she open, and when she does, I sweep my tongue inside. Firmly, I hold my hand to the back of her head and position her just right. Her taste is so damn sweet, I could kiss her all night.

Instead of trying to evade me, she presses against me, showing she wants more. I don't try to hide the erection that's digging into her belly, leaving her in no doubt about where I hope this evening will end.

She moans softly, her fingernails digging into my skin as she takes as much as she's getting. She's not shy and presses herself against me.

My nostrils fill with the scent of her, and my hands run through the lengths of her silky hair as I slip it out of the tie that's keeping it back.

All I can think about is getting closer, removing our clothes and sliding into her. Forget taking things slow, I'm getting drunk on her taste, on her touch, and can only think about speeding this up.

Not here. I come to my senses, knowing I was only seconds away from having my way with her in the kitchen where any brother could walk in. I start to wonder whether I can issue a blatant invitation to come to my room when a sudden cry interrupts us.

Clare pushes at me with her hands, and when I release her, she takes hold of the baby monitor she had clipped to her belt. She frowns as she sees Delly awake and crying.

Her face is full of apology, regret, and maybe a little of a coming to her senses. "I gotta—"

"Yeah, go." Frustrated, I watch her leave, raking my hands back through my hair, my eyes resting on the ass that I'd thought I'd soon make mine. I can't be angry at a kid, but hell, who wouldn't be annoyed? What a cockblocker.

Maybe she'll come back.

Returning to the party, I hang around, drinking slowly, wanting to stay sober in case she gives me another chance, but she doesn't return down the stairs. I socialise, make conversation, but fuck knows what I'm talking about. Eventually it becomes clear that she's not going to reappear, so I take myself off to bed.

Or that's my intention. Rather than opening my own door, my footsteps take me on until I'm outside hers. I hesitate. *She'll be asleep.*

Or she might not be. She might be awake. I pause before I knock. If she opens the door, am I really going to take the next step? Now I'm away from her influence, I start questioning myself. Is it really her I want, or is she a substitute for a memory that should be lost in the past? Clare doesn't deserve to be a fling, and am I really prepared to take a ready-made family on?

Deep thoughts, ones I should think on. Ones that don't deserve to be driven by my dick which is telling me it doesn't care about any consequences, it just wants to be inside her.

Fuck it. For years I've kept myself on a tight rein, never allowing myself to act upon impulse. As a prez I can't afford to be other than always on my guard, else it won't just be me that suffers from a knee-jerk reaction. I've got the reputation of being measured in my approach, and never reacting without thinking.

Maybe there was always going to be a point where I'd break and give into temptation. That Clare tempts me beyond reason is a given.

All logic seems to be lost as my hand seems to rise of its own volition, and with just enough sense to make sure my touch is gentle, I tap on the door—loud enough for her to hear me, but soft enough not to disturb her sleep.

Expecting the door to remain firmly closed, I'm shocked, but delighted when it opens. Then my heart sinks.

"What's up with her?"

A drawn-looking Clare is holding Delly in her arms. I notice the kid's face is red and blotchy.

"I don't know. She's running a temp." Clare's drawn face shows how harassed and worried she is.

Even my cock knows not to argue with a concerned mother and immediately deflates. "She need a doc?"

Her mouth twists, showing she's thought about it. "I don't think so. It's probably just one of those childhood things. I've given her some infant Tylenol, and at least she's stopped screaming. She wakes when I put her down though."

I feel utterly useless. "Can I do something?"

Clare shakes her head. "Nothing. Hopefully she'll sleep now."

I place my hand on the doorjamb and lean in. "You know where I am if you need help with her. Anything, you hear me? If she gets worse, let me know."

She looks up gratefully. "Thanks, Red, I appreciate that."

Placing my hand on her cheek, she leans into it for a moment. After receiving sufficient tactile comfort, she backs into the room. I close the door for her, then continue along to my own.

Wraith's got a kid, I remember, and another on the way. For a moment, I wonder about ringing him and asking advice from Sophie.

But does Clare need suggestions on how to deal with her baby? It hadn't seemed that way. Maybe it is just a kid thing and moms automatically know what to do.

And what could I say to Wraith anyway? How could I explain Clare away? *Hey, I met a woman who resembles a chick who ran out on me. I'm thinking of making her my old lady.*

Am I? Am I, really?

I pace my room. If Delly hadn't gotten sick, there's a good chance I'd be balls deep inside Clare right now, if she reciprocated my feelings of course, and the only indication is how she responded to my kiss.

Sure, she's great with the club, and the club accepts her, but that's on the basis we're harbouring her temporarily. Would they vote her in, knowing her connection to the law? A connection that's yet to be broken.

What's really driving me? Is it just my dick? A chance to go with a woman who's not a sweet butt or hangaround. Is it my head who's building her up into a reincarnated Cheryl? Or is it the revenge I could get by going with Skull's woman?

Perhaps Delly has done me a favour tonight, stopping my dick's impulse to just get inside her. I shouldn't let this go further without being able to answer the questions I've just asked myself.

Maybe it's best for a prez to remain single. Though Demon and Drummer don't seem to be less than they were now they've taken their old ladies, Snatcher and Lost seem to be doing fine remaining bachelors. I'm lucky in that Rosa takes charge of the social aspects of the club. In that, I don't need an old lady.

My dick can get release anytime it wants it. Even now I could march along the corridor and pull one of the sweet butts out of their bed—they'd suck me off or spread their legs or whatever my preference was.

Would my life be better with a woman in it?

Would my life be better with Clare?

Can I really say I can't live without her, or that if she left, she'd still be on my mind years later?

Could I ask her to compete with a ghost?

Oh, I know the Cheryl I've built up in my mind doesn't exist. Had it been the great love affair, I'd have gone after her, or would have tried harder to persuade her not to leave. However much I look back on that time as me having made a mistake, I know my head's twisted the image I have of her, making her out to be such a paragon, no one else can live up to the picture my brain can't forget.

Perhaps a therapist would say I'm using her memory as a way to protect myself from falling for anyone else. Even with Clare, I wouldn't be able to give all of me.

It's not fair to measure any woman against my idealistic vision that I've made Cheryl into. Hell, I don't even know if she wanted kids, or whether she'd be a good mother to them. Why is it that she seems to be perfection to me?

Though I tell myself what I could have with Clare could be the real thing, will my preconceived notions convince me she's a poor substitute?

Am I fated to ride through life alone?

I stop pacing, sit on the bed, and put my head in my hands. *Why won't Cheryl leave me alone?* It's been fifteen years since I last saw her. She's probably happily married to a man from her Podunk town, with kids of her own.

Does she ever think of me?

I fucking doubt it.

I snort, knowing I can never let my brothers know how fucked up I am.

Grabbing a whisky from the stock I keep in my room, I down a shot, hoping it will relax me. When I shower, my hand goes to my cock and starts sliding up and down my shaft. It doesn't take long before my practised motions have the desired effect. But when I come, is it Clare's face I see?

No, it's the image of Cheryl who's in front of me.

Fuck my life.

Still, the whisky and my release have relaxed me, and I have no trouble getting to sleep. I wake still undecided whether I want to pursue Clare, and whether I'm serious about having her in my life, or am I just using her to replace a woman I'll never have?

I'm sliding into my cut when there's a knock at my door. Opening it, I see a tired-looking woman standing there, the baby in her arms agitated and screaming.

"I think Delly needs a doctor, Red."

It turns out she's already made an appointment with the paediatrician. I drive her there, with Delly crying nonstop in her car seat. I'm worried as fuck, though Clare seems calmer than I.

In the waiting room, I watch as Clare's immediately led in, probably due to the volume of Delly's screams.

I fidget as I wait for news. What's the worst a kid can get? Fuck, I hope it's not serious.

It seems to take hours, but by the clock it's only minutes before Clare returns to me, a still upset baby in her arms.

Clare tiredly smiles at me. "It's an ear infection. He's given her meds."

I stand and look down at Delly. "Poor little mite. Earaches sucks. No wonder she's screaming."

"Kids are pretty resilient, Red. Once those meds kick in, they'll hopefully work quickly."

Proving mothers know their children better than a man who's never fathered a kid in their life, Clare's quite correct. Back at the compound, Rosa takes charge, allowing Clare to catch up on her rest. By the evening, Delly's almost back to normal, and thankfully has stopped her incessant crying.

But once her daughter has recovered, it's Clare who now has a problem. Leaving Delly in Rosa's more than competent hands, she asks if she can talk to me privately. Concerned by the troubled expression on her face, I usher her into my office.

Clare takes a breath and enlightens me without waiting for me to ask what she needs to talk to me about. "Don knows where I am."

"How the fuck?" In the action of seating, I reverse my direction and stand, resting my hands palms down on the desk.

"The visit to the doctor's flagged him. He got one of his cop friends to follow us back."

Now I do flop into my seat and drop my head into my hands. Christ, I fucked up. So worried about Delly and distracted by her screaming, I hadn't considered Skull was still looking for her. How the fuck had I missed a tail?

"I'm so sorry." I take it all on my head.

"No, don't be." Clare takes the seat opposite me and links her hands in her lap. "He got in touch with my lawyer, who asked me to give him a call."

"And you did?" I wish she'd come to me first so we could have discussed it.

She shrugs. "The damage is done, isn't it? He knows where to find me."

That's true. "What did he say?" I'm wondering whether we need to batten down the hatches and be prepared for a visit from the cops.

An unladylike snort comes from her mouth. "He told me if I thought he'd have me back again after I'd been in your bed, then I'd have another think coming."

I bark a laugh. "Bit rich, that, isn't it?" It was him who'd taken the opportunity to get his dick wet.

"That's what I said." Clare grimaces. "But to be honest, I don't think he really cared. He told me he's left the house, moved all his stuff out of it and that if I wanted, I could go back."

"It's a trick," I say quickly.

Her brows pull down. "I'm not so sure. Of course, I want to check it out. But he said he's moved on, that he's got a new assignment."

I frown. "With another MC?"

She shrugs. "Even if I asked, he'd never tell me."

Mentally, I note that we need to find out.

I lean back, folding my arms, and eyeing her carefully. Things had gotten pretty heated between us last night. Do I want to pick up where we left off? Does she? Cautiously, I pose the question, "And what if he has vacated your house?"

She looks down at her hands, bites her lip, and tells me in a soft tone, "Then it's time Delly and I went home."

<hr>

CHAPTER THIRTY-SIX

It's time she went home.

The words echo around my office. That she and I weren't meant to be together was the conclusion I'd kind of come to myself last night, but it still fucking hurts when it feels like I'm facing yet another rejection. Maybe Cheryl and Clare are even more alike than I'd thought.

Perversely, while I'd been doubting Clare and I getting together was a sensible move, I find myself on the defensive. "I thought we were getting along well together."

She blushes. "We were, and it would be easy to start something with you, Red. I like you, I really do. But for now, I'm still married to Don, and I'd feel guilty. And there's Delly. I worry about the future. I love the club, but it's a bit like being on vacation. If something happens between me and you, then I know it will change. I fear it will become a prison, not a welcome break anymore."

"You wouldn't be trapped here. You could still pursue anything you want to do."

"And have Delly looked down on as a biker brat?" She shakes her head. "I can't do that to her."

"Tristan and Tom don't have problems."

"How would you know?" she snaps back. "According to Rosa they do, but there's the two of them, and they've got the reputation of their father to back them up, and the manpower that reputation can call on."

I bite back saying if I was Delly's stepdad she'd also have that. Her words have made me think. It's one thing to take on an old lady, but her daughter will always come first in her life, as she should. While I look at the MC as having brothers who'd have my back, whether or not I was wearing the prez patch, to Clare it probably doesn't mean that. Hell, she's lived with a lawman. How can I ask her to live in a world totally different? Would she run at the first sign of trouble?

She seems to realise she's been harsh on me. She leans forward, stretching out her hand. "I like you, Red, I honestly do. If it was just me, I'd take a chance. But Delly deserves a life without fear and without being embroiled in all that comes with an MC."

Moving to meet her halfway, I take her hand in mine. We sit like that for a moment. "Whatever you need," I start to make my promise to her. "Whatever you need, day or night, you call me, and I'll be there. If Don ever comes back to bother you…" My voice trails off, but I can promise I'll have brothers queuing out the door to put an end to him.

"I'll call, Red. I promise." She bites her lip again, then asks, "Will you come and check out the house for me?" I was going to anyway, to make sure the bastard's really gone. I wouldn't put anything past that man. I give a nod. "And can we make a stop on the way?"

"Sure." I'm suspecting it's to stock up on groceries.

For a second, Clare's hesitant to say more, but then she reclaims her hand and sits back. "I'd like to go and see Mel's baby's grave. Lay some flowers out of respect."

What? My brow creases. "Why the hell would you want to do that? What happened to Mel had fuck all to do with you."

"I know that. Speaking to Don, though, well, it reminded me

of all the damage he's done. And that poor baby, he's the victim in all of this. He never got to know life because of what Don did."

"Miscarriages happen, Clare." Though I've fuck all doubt it was the stress that had caused Mel's, the fault lies all at Don's door, and she's no blame in this herself.

"Do you think Mel would talk to me?"

I can't see why she would, or how it would help. "I don't see the point."

"I need closure, and so does Mel."

This day certainly isn't turning out like I expected it to. I stare at her for a moment, her impulse to grieve for a child who basically fucked up her marriage shows what an amazing woman she is. I have to bite back a request for her to reconsider our relationship.

But talking to Mel? I'm not sure Pyro would go for that.

She's fidgeting, glancing up at me through her eyelashes as I consider her requests. Now she's made her decision, it seems she wants to act on it.

"I'll come with you to your house. And I'll take you to the cemetery. And if you really want, I'll ask Pyro about you speaking to Mel."

"Thank you." She glances down, then asks shyly, "Can we go now? I'll ask Rosa to look after Delly."

I was going to suggest that, if, as I suspect, Skull's laying a trap to get her back, having the kid here on the compound will be a form of insurance. As to the timing, why should either of us prolong this? She's clearly not going to change her mind. When she leaves my office to make the arrangements, I go find which of my brothers are around. I end up with Twister and Cobra and hastily give them some instructions.

While I take Clare to Melissa's baby's grave, they'll go scope out the house and check whether anyone's there.

We buy flowers, take them, set them down. I wait a respectful distance as Clare wipes a tear from her eye and places a hand on the headstone. "It's not fair," she says quietly, then takes a moment to gather herself.

Me? I hate coming here. It just serves to remind me of Mel's distress and Skull's culpability, and that for now, I'm powerless to do anything.

He'll pay, I vow quietly. *In time, he'll pay.*

Then we go to her neighbourhood, rendezvousing with Twister and Cobra.

"No one seems to be home," Twister assures me. "There's no car in the drive, and I've peered in the windows. If he's in there, he's hiding."

"That's not Don's style," Clare, overhearing, tells me.

I tend to agree but am not prepared to take risks. Leaving Clare in the car waiting, I beckon to my brothers. "Let's go check it out."

Twister and Cobra take the lead as we head to the house. Soon, I notice Twister was right. There's an air of the place as if it's been vacated, as if Skull moved out weeks before. The flowers in the front yard are dead from neglect and the windows look dusty. We walk to the front door. Using the keys Clare had given to me, I turn them in the lock, then Twister's hand lands on my shoulder.

"I'll go first, Prez."

I shake my head, but allow it, knowing it's his job to protect me, but am right at his back, weapon in my hand ready. "Wait out here." I catch Cobra's eye and he raises his chin to me. He'll know what to do. If Skull is here, he'll get Clare back to the compound.

Once the door's ajar, Twister leans in and listens. It's deathly quiet. Then he takes another step in, allowing me to come up beside him.

He's got an odd look on his face as he leans into me. "Last time I was here, it was to kidnap Clare."

I remember he's been here before and that could prove helpful. "Skull said he cleared out his shit. Does it look different?"

Twister looks around, then grimaces. "Sure fuckin' does. No TV, look." He points in one direction. "There was a Lazyboy recliner there," he indicates another, "that's gone. Half the bookshelves are empty."

Quickly, we search the rest of the house, then satisfied Skull had been truthful, I send Cobra back to get Clare.

When she enters, she makes her own inspection. "His PC is gone. His Xbox too, and his games." She shakes her head as she catalogues what's missing.

I jerk my head toward the stairs. When Clare enters the bedroom, she goes to the closet and opens it, pausing and straightening her back as though things are as she'd expected, but I don't doubt it still hurts. "He's taken all of his clothes."

She sits on the bed, bowing her head. I leave her alone and descend the stairs to find Twister riffling through drawers.

"Find anything?"

I know he'll be looking to see if there are any clues as to where Skull might have gone to, but he doesn't find one. It was worth a look, but the result was what I'd expected. Skull's a man used to covering his tracks.

When Clare finally comes down, I can tell she's been crying. Seeing I've noticed, she explains, "I don't miss Don. I miss what I thought I'd had with him."

This suburban house has affected me. It's a lifetime away from anything I've ever had, or like any place I thought I'd be. It's so domesticated, with no room for me. It cements my thoughts that Clare and I weren't destined to be together.

"You'll be fine," I tell her, sure that she will. She's been used to living without Skull and has her own life to step back into.

She belongs here, unlike me.

"You moving back today?"

When she nods, I give Twister and Cobra instructions to get Clare and Delly's shit moved from the compound.

Then I take her back, help her gather Delly's things together. I have a final cuddle with that cute little kid, then I watch her drive out of my life.

I'd half expected to feel the same sense of loss as I did when I'd driven off leaving Cheryl in my rearview, but waving Clare and Delly off just left me with a feeling this is how things should be. She's not another one who got away. It wasn't meant to be. We'd parted as friends.

To my surprise, Pyro had agreed that Mel would like to speak to Clare, so after a few days, she returned to the compound. It was gut wrenchingly sad to see Mel again and being back in Vegas had brought back old memories. But she and Clare seemed to clear the air between them, settling on them having both been deceived by a mutual enemy.

I took the opportunity to advise Pyro that Skull had gone undercover again. If he can be found, it won't be long before he pays the final retribution.

My life settles back into a routine and continues with nothing out of the ordinary for the next couple of years. While the Vegas chapter seems immune, other chapters suffer from the same affliction, collecting old ladies, and almost everyone seems to have hooked up in Tucson. There's a standing joke as more and more kids are born there, that any woman visiting the Arizona chapter should avoid drinking the water.

In San Diego, Lost's got himself hitched, and so has the eternal bachelor, Grumbler.

The most interesting thing that happens is when the truth comes out about Utah. And didn't that knock us all for a loop? Instead of being the backward country folk we'd always taken them for, they ran their business based on top-notch information technology, and earned their money foiling kidnappings or rescuing kidnappees. And that, though bad enough, wasn't the only thing that they'd deceived us about. Snatcher only acted the prez and was just the figurehead for our benefit. Behind him was an ex-spy who couldn't fucking ride a bike as he'd lost both his legs.

I, myself, was initially inclined to shut down the chapter. But after sit-downs with my fellow prezes, and under the guidance of Drummer, we'd agreed to let them keep their charter.

On that, we'd been proved right when the Crazy Wolves MC came onto our radar. I was incensed to learn they were running a prostitution ring in Vegas, one where the girls were neither paid nor willing. And I wasn't the only club with a grudge. The Crazy Wolves had taken one of San Diego's members and his woman.

For the first time in years, all chapters had banded together to defeat them. Colour me impressed at the almost military precision with which Utah ran the operation.

Once the Crazy Wolves were all underground, life returned to normal again.

I never regret becoming the MC prez, and it must be age creeping up on me, but sometimes I look into the mirror and see the lines etched on my face and wonder where I go from here.

I'm not unhappy per se, but something seems to be missing. At times I wonder whether I'd have felt more fulfilled if my life had proceeded along the lines I'd expected. By now, I could have a wife by my side, and kids in their teens. Instead, I get my sexual needs catered to by sweet butts and hangarounds, and my pinnacle of excitement is when I use the BDSM equipment Rope and Cuff installed in the basement.

Then I shake the doubts out of me. Here is where I'm meant to be, and if I lack offspring, well I've got a whole damn club depending on me, and at times they themselves resemble rowdy teenagers.

"You take that fuckin' back." Petty's on his feet swearing at Roller, while Twister's got his hands linked behind his head and is rolling his eyes.

Crash is looking on, his brow furrowed as he assesses whether he should break up the argument.

The other brothers seem to be minding their own business.

"What the fuck's going on?" I ask, as Petty takes a swing at Roller who blocks him.

I land a hand on Petty's shoulder. He turns, fist raised, sees it's me and swiftly drops it.

"I asked you a fuckin' question." Waiting, I raise my eyebrow.

Petty shrugs. "Nothing, Prez."

I change my attention to Roller. "Well?"

"Like he said, nothing."

I look at Crash who holds up his hands. "They were going at it when I got in here."

"I saw nothing," Twister says.

"Anyone?" Those who know decide not to say.

"Fuckin' hell." I let go of Petty, waiting to make sure he's not going to go for Roller again. "Just kiss and make up, you two."

My words seem to get Petty riled all over again. "I ain't no perv."

"I never fuckin' said you were," Roller holds up his hands and states.

"You said I was like Joker—"

"I never said—"

"Fuckin' stop it now!" I shout. "I don't fuckin' care. Now sit down and shut up."

Petty is a fucking homophobe, and for that reason I was glad Joker and Lady had transferred out of the club when Petty was still a prospect. Though the truth hadn't come out for another year after that, when it had, the man couldn't hide his disgust. It was as though he'd been contaminated.

I couldn't care one way or another where any man found love, and when I see Joker nowadays, he's more contented than I've ever seen him. I don't bother confronting Petty about his, as I see it, shortcomings, deciding it would only be a problem if another gay decided to join the club. I doubt any of the others would judge a man on who he prefers sexually, but I can't be certain on that. If the time comes, maybe I'll have to face it.

Roller and Petty are tight, same as Wraith and me. Their friendship had developed even before they shared trials of their prospecting time as they'd serviced together. The only occasions the two men fall out is if there's any comment or aside that could put Petty's own sexuality in doubt. As has clearly happened just now.

The two men are still glaring at each other, so I know I haven't completely shut that shit down. There's one way of dealing with it. "If you two want to continue this after church, you can do it in the ring."

"Too fuckin' right," Petty growls.

"Bring it on," Roller snarls back.

"Can we get this fuckin' meeting started now?" Fox, clearly with something on his mind, scowls at the two men, then turns to me with his eyebrow raised.

Agreeing it's time, I sit down. "Meeting in session," I announce formally, bringing the gavel down. "You want to kick off, Fox?"

Normally he'd start church with a rundown of how our finances are looking, so I expect him to click on his tablet and start reading figures out. Instead, he pushes it away from him and seems more animated than I usually expect.

But it's Crash who beats him to it. "Hey, Brother. Settle down. Let me set the groundwork." He eyes the treasurer for a moment until Fox gives a sulky nod. He then turns to me. "There's a new casino that's opened up. Not on the strip, on one of the streets that run off it."

I raise my chin thinking I've heard of it. "Lucky Fortunes?"

"That's the one." Crash nods enthusiastically.

"We going to try it out?" Cobra looks up excitedly. He does like playing his hand at the slots, but he's got no gambling problem and knows when to stop.

Back before I transferred, the club had had a problem with gambling, so it's something on which I keep a close watch. People come to Vegas for the casinos. Those of us who live here have been there, done that, and in truth, losing money soon becomes old.

"Might do." Crash grins at Cobra, which makes Sarge start shaking his head. The loud sounds can set off his PTSD, as we've found out to our cost on a club night out before. "But that's not why I'm raising this. We've been approached with a job offer."

That makes me sit up. "Yeah?" I frown, wondering why it hadn't come direct to me.

"Yeah," Crash says. "One of our customers put our name forward, and as I was his contact, they got in touch with me first."

I shrug it off. No matter if there's more money coming our way. "What kind of job?"

"Providing security for the casino."

Now I frown. "Sounds like a fuckin' big job, Crash. We'd be spread thin if they want full-time bouncers."

Crash shakes his head. "They've got their own security team, but they want us to oversee them. Check who they're employing, shit like that. Be there to be called on should they have any problems and show our faces occasionally to make sure everyone behaves."

I feel a glimmer of excitement. It's taken years to build up our security business from the bottom up. Okay, this isn't one of the major casinos on the strip, but if we do a good job, it could be a boost to our reputation.

"Hey, I like the sound of that," Rope offers.

So do I. It means the rep we'd gained when our previous members had tried to rob a casino has at last been forgot.

"The figures look great." Fox can no longer contain himself. "Crash gave me their proposal to look at. It could mean a lot to our bottom line."

Again, I wonder why I'm only now hearing about it? I frown at Crash, and don't have to explain my confusion.

Crash shrugs. "You were tied up in dealing with the fallout from taking the Crazy Wolves out."

I suppose that I have. "Shit's sorted," I tell them. "Now, how far have you gotten, Crash?" I don't need to worry he'd have committed to anything. It's one thing checking it out, but only I can sign on the dotted line, once all the members are in agreement of course.

"Not far. I've told them we're capable and interested. They've invited us in to look around and to talk."

Nodding, I throw a grin at him. "I like the sound of that."

CHAPTER THIRTY-SEVEN

I'm not the only one who likes the idea of us picking up new work, and one which could put our security business on the map. Everyone starts talking, though most are more interested in having an evening out and wanting to know if they'll get free tokens to play at the table. All except for Sarge who throws his hands up in a gesture clearly meaning he'll leave it to everyone else.

Titch leans back, his hands in his belt. "I'm willing to sacrifice some of my time."

"They got a buffet? Entertainment?" Hammer's definitely looking interested.

Crash grins. "Buffet, yes. Entertainment, no. Unless you count the scantily clad ladies serving drinks."

"Oh, I count that," Petty says with a loaded look toward Roller who rolls his eyes.

"I didn't mean anything, man," Roller again says to him.

I speak fast, not wanting to get pulled into their argument again. "Crash, Fox, Keys and I will meet with the management." There's a chorus of groans until I add, "And whoever wants can come with us. You'll stay on the floor, look for weaknesses, check out the security personnel they've got, and report back to me with any observations."

"Ah, fuck, Prez. Can't we just go and enjoy ourselves?" Cuff looks disappointed.

"You can enjoy yourself and still work." Indian looks at him sternly.

"Will we get drinks on the house?" Shadow asks optimistically.

Cobra cuffs him around the head. "We're there to drum up business, not to get drunk."

"So?" the road captain retorts without rancour. "I can do both."

"Want me to set it up, Prez?"

Grinning at my VP, I confirm, "Might as well. Keys, can you take a look at how secure their systems are?"

"On it already, Prez." Keys points to his laptop where he's clearly been jotting down notes. "Would be good to go in with some ideas for improvement."

Christ, I love this team I have around me. And I love the idea of having more income coming into the club, all legit and above board.

"I'll leave it with you to set up the arrangements." I turn to my VP. "We'll go check it out, then meet back around the table to confirm it's something we want to take on."

A couple of them are still joking about letting Devils lose in a casino, but most of them seem to be on the same wavelength as myself. It sounds a good deal, and I'm wary of looking a gift horse in the mouth, but it wouldn't do without making sure. There's a warning at the back of my mind that letting an outlaw club take over security could be a way of fucking us up, of us being convenient fall guys if all goes to shit.

Why are they coming to the Satan's Devils for help? That needs checking out.

"Okay. Let's move on."

Church then gets back on its normal track. When we wrap

up, Petty and Roller seem to have made up. Either that or they've both decided their argument wasn't worth risking getting their faces smashed in.

Crash had spoken to his contact and arranged for us to go to Lucky Fortunes the following Thursday. A day when it would be busy enough as usually is the case in Vegas, but not so crammed it would hinder us getting a good look at what could be a lucrative job.

While I, my VP, and Keys will be meeting with their management team, Twister and Indian will be keeping an eye on the rest of the members who all want to go with the exception of Sarge, and the prospects who have no choice.

We arrive at the casino at ten o'clock. Walking in, I notice the tables are busy. The décor still looks relatively new and fresh, and even welcoming. Whoever decorated knows their shit. The cacophony of sound which greets us is not unexpected. Machines chime and play stupid tunes, balls crash around wheels and even the snap of cards being shuffled reaches my ears as I pass by the croupiers dealing. There's a rumble of conversation, and beneath everything else, background music playing.

Crash, having been here before, leads us through and toward a staircase at the back. A uniformed man is standing beside it. When Crash approaches, he uses a two-way radio, then getting an answer, unhooks a rope and gestures we should proceed up.

The casino certainly doesn't rival its biggest competitors in size, but from what I've seen it makes use of the space it has got. There are no frivolities like a fairground, or gondolas. It caters to people who want to chance their luck, rather than pulling in all sorts for the entertainment.

We're led to a room which overlooks the floor. Having not seen it from below, I gather it's one-way glass, but it offers an uninterrupted view of what's going on below. Staff are watching both the physical action and that transmitted by cameras and viewed on monitors.

I watch, interested. Key steps up beside me and seems to be checking out what views people have on their screens. After a few moments, Crash taps me on the shoulder and jerks his head in the direction of an office I haven't yet seen.

Dragging Keys away, I follow Crash. We end up in a small meeting room with four men inside, one of whom stands to greet us.

"I'm Jordan Crossman, and these are my partners, Clancy Rodgers, Austin Carson, and Trent Greaves."

"Colt Masters," I introduce myself. "Otherwise known as Red. Peers West, or Crash, I think you've already met. And this is Gabe Hickson, otherwise known as Keys."

"Your security guy." Crossman shakes Keys' hand, then takes mine and gives it the same treatment. "Crash, good to see you again." He stands back and gestures toward the empty chairs. "Please sit."

We do. The next hour is spent going through what the partners of the casino want from us, and them listening to some ideas that Keys has come armed with. I start to relax as I realise we can provide all the services they're after, and on their part they're satisfied with what we can provide. Keys will take a look at the technology, do extra background checks and provide suggestions for upping the security. We can arrange to have a brother here during opening hours, with others in the club on call for backup if it becomes necessary.

Apparently, our anti-protection racket work has gotten a good reputation, and Crossman thinks it will stop trouble from gangs if the Devils are in this from the start.

We talk figures, the tally of which makes me more than happy. Once hands are again shaken, and the Satan's Devils have one more legit business to line our pockets, Crossman suggests we descend to the bar and raise a glass to celebrate our new partnership.

As we relax and try out the bar, I keep my eyes moving around, now taking in the place with more interest, knowing we'll have some responsibility here. Once we've all got drinks in our hands, Crossman takes his leave of us.

I nudge Crash. "I'm going to have a walk around."

"Sure, Prez. Try not to lose your shirt."

I roll my eyes as I walk away from him. One thing I've learned since living in Vegas is that you can't beat the house. Of course, some people get lucky, but they're few and far between. Far more fortunes have been lost rather than made in Sin City, and I'm rather partial to my shirt.

Rather than getting involved, I want to soak up the atmosphere. See if the customers are happy or not, and if it's the latter, how the full-time security staff are dealing with it. I watch a game of roulette for a while, turning down the offer of another drink from one of the servers, then move on.

I've walked the room almost from one end to the other when I stop at a table where the croupier is dealing hands of Blackjack. I admire her dexterity with the cards and also take a moment to admire her blonde hair perfect for twisting my fingers into as I feed her my cock. Then I berate myself, *haven't I learned my lesson*? Why is it every blonde reminds me of Cheryl?

Raising her face from the cards for a second, her eyes meet mine, deep blue eyes which look familiar. A nose shaped just how I remember. Sure, there are the beginnings of crow's feet and a few wrinkles that weren't there before, but that face? To this day, I've been unable to forget it. She's still as beautiful as she ever was.

For a second, the ability to breathe leaves me.

She, too, looks like she's having difficulty. She pauses mid deal, and her mouth drops open. Her eyes widen. A flush comes to her cheeks as though she's recalling the heated nights we spent together. Her expression is blank for a moment, as though she's not sure whether she's pleased to see me or not, then a tentative smile starts to form.

A man coughs, getting her attention back to the task at hand.

With a little shake, an apologetic smile, in a professional manner, she gets back to her job.

I just stand there. It's been years since I've stopped hoping to bump into her, knowing seeing her again was beyond all odds. Now she's in front of me and I've actually found her, wild horses couldn't make me leave.

I guess, in this case, you could say the house just lost.

When a customer throws down his cards and walks off in a huff, I take his place at her table. While I watch her working, I note there's no ring on her finger. Doesn't mean fuck, she could still be married but doesn't want to advertise it at work or had been and is now divorced. She's lived half her fucking lifetime without me. I hadn't been waiting for her, so why should she for me?

I take the card she deals me, fuck knows why, my head's not in the game. I do it just to be closer to her. I wait, without actually knowing what I'm waiting for. If I find out she's single, would I give it another shot? Would she want to?

Telling myself I'm just curious about what happened to her, and how she's here and not in Illinois anymore, I linger, not even moving when Crash comes up, bending his head to speak to me. I carry on a conversation with one eye on that dealer, determined this time, she won't escape.

"Keys and I are heading out, most of the rest are ready. You coming?"

"Nah," I tell him, still with my eyes fixed on the apparition in front of me. "You go on."

"Seen something you like, Prez?" Crash looks from me to the table, then leans in close. "I can see the attraction, but perhaps you shouldn't shit on our doorstep. We've just landed this job."

I'm not upset that the VP has sanctioned me, but I do seek to reassure. "I'm not going to jeopardize shit." I lower my voice. "I know her, from way back, that's all. Just want to catch up."

"Okay, Prez." He slaps my back. "You have a good night, you hear?" He winks at me and then walks off.

It's not long after he's left that I get the chance I was waiting for. Another croupier comes up to relieve her. I immediately stand ready to chase her, but she doesn't try to sneak away. Instead, she comes around the table and straight up to me.

"Is it really you?" She gazes at me, an unreadable smile on her face.

I don't bother answering. "You finished for the night?"

"Yeah." Her voice sounds hesitant, as if she's in two minds whether she wants to speak to me.

I feel tongue tied like a schoolboy, but manage to ask, "Can we go somewhere and talk?"

She grimaces, and there's a moment's hesitation. "I should go home. I'm dead on my feet. But, okay, I'll have one drink with you."

I notice she doesn't sound particularly enthusiastic. Buy hey, maybe I should just be pleased she's remembered me after all this time. It's not been her fault that she's remained on my mind, that's my aberration. Though it would be nice to know she'd thought of me from time to time and regretted leaving.

I follow her to the bar, not failing to notice she's still got a shapely ass. When I step up to order our drinks, it puts her behind me for the first time. I hear her indrawn gasp and swing around.

"What's the matter?" I glare in the general vicinity to see who's put that sudden look of fear in her eyes.

"You're in a motorcycle gang," she accuses me, quite rightly. But it's the tone of her voice that has me taking a step back.

Of course, I'm used to the reactions of civilians when they meet us, but somehow, I'd expected better of her. "Worse," I tell her through gritted teeth, picking up that she's clearly not enamoured with my chosen way of life. I tap the patch on the front of my cut, which she'd obviously not noticed until now. "I'm the prez."

Another night, another woman, and they'd be begging me to

take them to bed, or to the nearest wall and fuck them. But it seems, not her.

"I expected better of you," she tells me, primly, accepting her vodka and tonic from the bartender. "I thought you were a mechanic."

"Still am." I narrow my eyes. "I don't remember you being this quick to judge."

She shrugs. "People grow up." She casts an eye at my cut again, her mouth twisting with distaste. "Well, at least some of us have to."

I glance up at the ceiling while I gather myself. If I needed proof that instead of losing the love of my life, I'd had a happy escape, this is it. My only regret is that I wasted years measuring other women up to her.

I should just walk away, but I've a drink in my hand, and while I feel she's been rude to totally dismiss my chosen way of life, I don't. Though I don't feel the need to explain myself to her, I can't bring myself to leave without satisfying my curiosity.

"So how did you end up in Vegas?"

She moves from one foot to the other, obviously uncomfortable. "My feet are killing me. Do you mind if I sit down?"

Of course not. I shake my head, then follow her over to a table. Placing my beer on a mat, I wait for her to seat herself, then prompt her again. "Vegas is a fuckin' long way from Illinois."

She takes a sip of her vodka, licks her lips then puts the glass back down. "I left Illinois years ago. We, *I've*, been travelling around."

I notice her correction. "We? A partner?"

"No. I was alone," she says fast.

There's something about the way she says it that has me not completely believing her. But how is it my business? I've spent the last fifteen years trying to replace her. I couldn't have expected her to remain celibate all that time, nor judge her for not wanting to share information about her partners.

She's aged well, I consider, as I take another sly glance at her. Her figure is more mature now, but at her thirty-five years she could easily pass for someone younger. Though that sense of girl-next-door innocence I'd seen all those years before has become jaded. I try to read the expression on her face. It's hard to tell whether she's pleased to see me or not. That she'd recognised me and remembered my name suggests I'm not a ghost lost in the past. *She remembers.*

Thoughts of our few nights together come into my head. There's nothing about the way she's aged that would stop me wanting to go there again and show her the lessons I've learned over the years. *She cried out my name in the past. I bet I could have her screaming out now.* My cock twitches, and I make sure to refrain from adjusting it.

She doesn't seem to want to fill the silence with conversation, so I start talking instead. "I'm in a motorcycle club, not a gang. I ride with the Satan's Devils MC. Have done for the past fifteen years. We wear the one-percenter patch, but what we do nowadays is mostly the right side of the law." I gesture to the club still bustling around us. "The reason I'm here tonight is that my club is taking on some of the security."

"You are?" That seems to surprise her. "You'll be around here a lot?" Now that thought seems to worry her.

I feel annoyed. If she doesn't want to see me, then I can stay clear. "I'll mostly leave that to my boys, but yeah, as boss, I'll be popping in to check how they're doing, and if there are any problems of course."

She bites her lip, then takes another gulp of her vodka. A large one as though she wants to drink it fast.

"I suppose you must have done well for yourself if you're the prez." She takes another, smaller sip, before placing her glass on the mat. "Are you married? Kids?"

"No to both questions." I don't add that no one has measured up to her, nor that I've recently decided to give up looking. But I do explain part of it. "The club takes up most of my time, I wouldn't be able to do a relationship justice."

As I pick up my beer and drink, it occurs to me in all the times I've thought about bumping into her and all the ways I'd expected it to go, I never dreamed it would feel awkward. Those few nights which I've never been able to forget are possibly just an embarrassment to her.

I decide to test her on it. "Do you ever regret it? Turning back? As I've often wondered what would have happened."

She doesn't ask me to clarify my meaning, she immediately understands. "We can never go back, Red. Whether I did or didn't, life's dealt us hands, and we've got to play them."

"And what's yours?"

"My hand?" She glances around the club much like I had a few moments ago. "I've no education to speak of, so I worked unskilled jobs to get by. Worked in a casino in Reno, got the hang of it, and moved here when a vacancy opened up."

"How long have you been in Vegas?" *How long have we been living side by side and I knew nothing of it?*

"Only a few months."

For some reason, I feel satisfied. Though it's crazy talk, somehow, I'd think I should have sensed her if she's been around.

"And what about you? Are you married?"

She looks up with a start. "Me? No, I have not."

"Partner?" I push, thinking someone must have picked up on what I'd missed out on.

Biting her lips, her eyes look to the side, before coming back. "I've had no time for relationships."

No time? What the fuck has she been up to? I open my mouth to pry when we're interrupted.

"Cher? I've been looking for you. You ready to go?"

She looks up at the man who's spoken and smiles. "I'll be ready in two minutes."

He nods. "I'll wait outside for you. Could do with a smoke."

She wiggles her fingers as he walks off.

"No partner, huh?" I ask, gritting my teeth, this time for a truthful answer.

"Jed? No." She seems surprised that I asked. "He's part of the security around here, lives in the same building where I've got an apartment. As we work the same shifts, he gives me lifts." She shrugs. "It saves money and means I don't have to drive home alone."

On the face of it that's wise. She's an attractive woman. But some possessive feeling inside me doesn't like it.

"I'll take you home if you want. I've only got the bike." I wink. "But that never bothered you before." As I say it, I realise what a big deal that is. No woman but her has ever ridden behind me.

"No." The way she says it suggests I'd be wasting breath if I tried to persuade her. She drains her drink and stands. "It's been nice catching up with you, Red. I suspect I'll be seeing you around."

I've got no hold on her. I can't prevent her leaving or call her back when she stands and walks away. And proving I never learn, I realise, fuck it, I didn't even get her number.

As I watch her wind her way around tables, customers, and slot machines, I narrow my eyes. That's not the last I'll be seeing of her. I'll make sure of that.

There's always tomorrow, I remind myself. And I'll have time to prepare and not be taken off balance.

I'm not stupid, there are things she's not telling me. She barely said anything about her life.

And what better place to get those secrets out of her than in my bed?

As for me, another fuck might prove my memory false and there's nothing to go back for. Maybe having her one more time would mean I could finally move on.

CHAPTER THIRTY-EIGHT

I ride back to the clubhouse torn between pumping my fist in the air and feeling my soul sink in regret.

I've seen and spoken to Cheryl. Something I've wanted to do for literally years. I don't know what I expected but seeing her was anti-climactic. It's not that I expected her to fall into my arms and declare undying love while declaring leaving me had been the worst mistake of her life, but I'd expected something.

Initially she'd seemed pleased to see me. But all those little glances and half-smiles as she was dealing my cards disappeared when she got sight of the cut on my back. Hadn't she guessed from the patches on the front? It seems not, but if she hasn't been involved in our lifestyle, maybe she'd just thought it was a fashion statement, the word Prez added as an embellishment to flatter my ego. Whatever, when she found out, it certainly hadn't impressed her.

I scoff at myself for ever thinking she could have made a great old lady. Hell, I'd had a lucky escape the day she'd walked away. If she's got such a downer on MCs, how long would it have been before she'd convinced me to sell my bike? If I'd have met Wraith, her influence might have ensured we'd never have become friends.

What would I have been? A fucking mechanic slogging my guts out for the man day after day.

She's got no idea of my club or what it means.

Having ridden on autopilot, I find myself at the clubhouse while thoughts are still whirling around my head. I back into my parking spot and turn off my engine, then rest my hands on the gas tank for a moment.

I guess this is it. My club's my family, my bike my old lady. I'd made my mind up on that when what I thought I could have had with Clare had disappeared like a breath of air. I'd been hanging onto a dream, something I know I'll never have.

All this time I've wondered about Cheryl, built her up in my head to be something more. If I misread her that badly, it doesn't say much about my instincts or at least when it comes to women.

I've been lusting after something which doesn't exist. Now it's time to put her behind me, once and for all.

Filled with new determination, I swing my leg over my bike, and enter the clubhouse. The first person I see is Crash, gesturing to me from the bar.

"Hey, Prez. Didn't fuckin' expect you back. Or not this early. Thought you'd be getting your dick wet." His voice is not at a level that can be considered discreet.

It gets the attention of Twister. "You been dipping your wick, Prez?"

"No, I fuckin' have not." I approach them, sending them warning glances.

"Pretty little bitch you were talking to. I wouldn't mind getting to know her better if you're not going there."

I tense, then shrug my possessiveness off. "I thought you were the one telling me not to fuck up our business?" I raise my eye in challenge, then shrug. "Anyway, you'd flake out, VP. She's got a thing against bikers."

"Yeah?" Crash narrows his eyes. "She had a bad experience, like that girl Vengeance hooked up with? Maybe she's come across her own version of the Crazy Wolves."

Now that had never occurred to me. Vengeance's ol' lady had been kept prisoner and abused for years, and it was no wonder she didn't like MCs. Hell, we'd gotten to the Wolves' den to rescue her only weeks back. I should have remembered. Not all MCs are like the Devils, and some are exactly as bad as citizen's fear.

"I didn't get that vibe from her," I admit, my tone thoughtful. "But she seemed pleased to reconnect until she saw the patch on my cut."

"Old friend you said," Crash remembers. "Or old fuck buddy?"

"Bit of both," I tell them, gesturing to Meat to bring me a beer. I pull up a stool and settle in. "Met her on the road when I first left Vermont. We gelled, and she rode bitch with me for a bit. But her home called to her, so she left me on the road. I always wondered what had happened to her."

Twister nods sagely. "It's the ones who get away that leave the most mark on you. Those you have to fight off, you never give them another thought."

I raise and lower my shoulders. "That must be it. I've often wondered about her, whether we could have made it. She went back, and I've often speculated whether I should have gone with her."

"Lots more bitches in the sea." Twister jerks his head pointedly toward the club girls who are still up, albeit yawning, and wondering whether their services will be required.

Meat places a beer in front of me and also pushes a full shot glass over. When I raise my eyebrow, he shrugs it off.

"Just thought you could do with a pick-me-up, Prez."

"Prospect shows promise," Twister remarks when Meat's gone back to polishing the bar and is out of earshot.

"I look that bad?" I huff, thinking I've got to brush up on my poker face. Mind you, with my skin liable to flush at the first sign of emotion be it excitement or anger, I've long learned not to try my luck at the card table.

"You look like a dog that's lost its bone," Crash puts eloquently for him. "This bitch meant something to you, didn't she, Prez?"

I drink the shot and chase it down with the beer. Maybe it's the alcohol loosening my tongue, or maybe it's that I'm among family, but I find myself becoming loose lipped.

"Crazy as it might sound, I've always wondered what would have happened if we'd stayed together. We clicked, you know?" I pause for Crash's nod and Twister's shrug. "I suppose I've built it all up in my head, but I never found anyone to match her."

"She resembles Clare a bit."

Crash noticed? I feel my cheeks glow red as I admit, "Yeah, well. Anyway, fifteen years is a fuck of a long time, and when I saw her again, the magic wasn't there." Maybe if she'd given me a chance it might have been resurrected.

"Must have been a hell of a shock, for both you and her." Twister looks sympathetic. "Now I'm not the one to give relationship advice, but why leave it there? Why don't you meet up with her again? She could have been tired as fuck after her shift and reacted without thinking."

Glancing toward Twister I frown. I had surprised her, hell, her being there had surprised the fuck out of me. Perhaps once she's gone home and thought about it, maybe she would be amenable to another chance to catch up. I wanted the girl. On my part, I'd like to see if a spark remained now she was a mature woman.

Maybe it had been a mistake approaching her at work. Idly I massage the bottle I'm holding with my fingers. Perhaps it would be a good plan to go back to the casino again, this time not to confront her, but to ask her to go for a drink or a coffee sometime when she's not rushed off her feet or tired.

If nothing else, I'd like to have closure. If she doesn't want anything to do with me, then so be it. But I'd prefer to think it's because of something other than the cut that I wear on my back. It's possible if I spend more time with her, I'll see the woman she's become is nothing like the image of the person who's haunted my mind, and I can totally rid myself of her.

Time moves on, and maybe we both have.

I slap Twister on the back and then to the same to Crash. "Thanks, Brothers, I'll go back tomorrow and see if I can get her to meet me on neutral ground."

This is why being a Devil is so important to me. They're my family, always there to have my back even when the only weapons likely to be used are words, and when that support comes as advice rather than action.

The next day seems to pass slowly. When we convene for church the main discussion circles around what brothers had observed at the casino. Indian had spoken to a few of the security staff and found most had a suitable background, but a few could do with some additional training of how to get the upper hand in a fight.

Titch and Fox had spent a bit of time seeing how money was controlled and had some suggestions for the cash handling, while Keys had focused on the technical side and had a list of locations where he felt more cameras could be situated. His suggestions included inside and out.

Fox offers to put together a rota so a brother is always there on the grounds, after a bit of discussion we agree there should be two for starters, until we've got a better idea of the lay of the land.

Keys then mentions he's started to review the background checks on all the employees.

When we agree who's going to go back there tonight—Shadow and Cobra volunteering—I tell them that I'll be going along to have another chat with Jordan Crossman. While the bulk of them accept that as perfectly natural, we've already got a few things to discuss with them, Crash gives me the side eye, and Twister's openly smirking.

I'm like a teenage boy out for his first date as I choose my clothes for the evening, not that there's much of a choice, and to wear anything but my standard t-shirt, jeans and cut would raise a hell of a lot of raised eyes and questioning. I put the smarter white button down back on the rail and select a black tee which at least doesn't have holes in it or oil stains.

I trim my short beard making it neat, then ask myself what the fuck am I doing? It's not a fucking date I'm going on, but a business meeting. And if I do speak to Cheryl again, it will only be to invite her to meet up elsewhere. No fucking need at all to put the aftershave I'm wearing on.

When I ride out with Shadow and Cobra behind me, I realise I'm as nervous as fuck. Me, a badass prez of an outlaw MC. The thought makes me scoff at myself. The sooner I can put Cheryl out of my head the better, I've got more things to worry about, and definitely more opportunities for getting my dick wet.

We arrive. I walk past the table where she was based last night, ready just to give her a chin lift until I get the meeting with her boss over with. But she's not there. I feel a flicker of disappointment, before it dawns on me, she's not necessarily always at the same table. But a security guard has seen me, and waves me across, so deciding to track her down later, I go over to see him.

As I'm expected, I'm led to the stairs and this time there's nothing to impede my progress up the stairs. Instead the man working security is quite deferential, tipping me a respectful nod.

"I'd like to see your written proposals. And costings for the cameras," Crossman says after I've finished speaking. "But I've got to say, I'm impressed with the Devils so far."

I stand at the large glass window overlooking the casino. *I still can't see her.* I try to bring back my attention to the matter in hand. "I'm glad you're happy with us." I respond politely. *Can I ask him where she is? Fuck, she might have had the night off.* It's on the tip of my tongue to ask him for her schedule but I stop myself in time. Why would the fucking casino owner know which of his staff are going to be here at any time?

When I'm able to take my leave of him I descend to the casino floor. There I wander around, but don't find the woman I'm seeking. I walk around again just in case she left for a moment for a bathroom break, but finally I reach the conclusion that she isn't here tonight.

I'm surprised at my level of disappointment, and the frustrated anger it draws up inside. I try to console myself by promising to return the next night.

But Saturday she's not there either.

When I arrive back at the compound, I've one target in mind. And if Keys has gone to bed already, I'll drag him back down. It's eating away inside me. *Had my appearance upset her so much she jacked in her job?* Though the more sensible side of me reasons, she might work part time, and has had these two days off.

Nevertheless, I'm at the end of my tether and want answers now.

"Keys!" I bark, thankful to see him standing at the bar. "A word."

"Prez?"

"My office now." I'm so worked up politeness is beyond me. What makes me even madder is that I can't understand why.

After fifteen years I've found her. If she's taken lengths not to see me again, why should it fucking matter? But the reasonable side of me seems to be drowning in the part of me that never wanted to let her go in the first place, and now she's returned, I want to hold on to her. I'm not even sure why.

I'm a logical man, and I'm acting illogically, and even that makes me mad. She's unsettled my equilibrium by reappearing, and I want her back. If she leaves again, it will be my choice, not hers.

"What can I do for you?" Keys enters and closes the door.

"I want you to hack into the casino's databases and find out when a croupier named Cheryl is working next."

Momentarily he looks at me as if I've gone totally mad. Then some sort of penny drops as his mouth opens in an O of understanding.

"And you know her…?" he prompts.

I wave my hands dismissively. "From way back."

"Right," he says, all business like. "Got any more details about her? Like her family name?"

Just like her number, I hadn't asked. When I shake my head, Keys frowns.

"And you know she's bad news. I'll get onto it, dig into her background, assuming there's only one Cheryl. If I find something, you want me to come to you, or warn Crossman?"

My eyes widen. "She's not a fuckin' criminal."

"Whoa!" He rears back defensively. "How the fuck was I to know what you wanted her for. Care to enlighten me?"

"It's personal," I snap back. My cheeks are burning and the red-headed rage I normally manage to keep in check is starting to surface now.

Keys does not deserve to suffer the brunt of it, so I clench my hands and try to push my temper back down. Fucking woman has gotten under my skin, making me act out of character. I pride myself on being a man in control and just look at me now.

Keys stands. "I'll go see what I can dig up."

When he disappears as fast as his legs will carry him, I grab a bottle of whisky I keep in a drawer and without bothering with a glass, put it to my lips. *Fuck Cheryl.* Why's she got me so tied up in knots? Can't she see I just need to see her again to end our relationship properly, all tied up in a fancy ribbon and bow? Then that will be the end of it.

I've drunk about a third of the bottle when Keys reappears. He bravely drops back down in front of me, his laptop resting on his lap.

"You ready to hear this?"

I wave an unsteady hand. "Hit me."

His mouth quirks, then he starts speaking. "There's a Cher Samson listed as an employee."

Cher. That was the name the man giving her a lift had called her. In my head I try it out. *Cher. My Cher.* A drunken smile starts to curve my lips before I remember where I am, and what I'm doing.

"It's her." I confirm.

"I went to look at her schedule, she works Monday through Friday. But there's a note on her file that she'd called in sick yesterday."

Sick? My ass. There was nothing wrong with her on Thursday.

Keys is watching my reaction carefully. He taps at his keyboard, and a moment later my phone pings. I ignore it.

He nods my way. "As this is personal, and you're so worked up about her, I thought it best to keep it out of the casino. You go in like a bull in a china shop you could fuck shit up. So, I got her address for you. That's my text you just received."

My temper dissipates so fast I feel dizzy, instead I want to laugh. *Why the fuck hadn't I asked him for that earlier?* It makes so much more sense. I attempt a smile which might have come out as a leer as a thanks for his help.

Keys stands. "My work here seems to be done. Just one other thing, Prez. In case the alcohol made you forget, it's Sunday tomorrow and she's not on the roster."

I know the grin I'm giving him is cheesy. But he'd done well to remind me, I'd forgotten what day it was.

Tomorrow. Well, that gives me a chance to get rid of the inevitable hangover and go confront her on her home turf. At least, there'll be nowhere for her to run.

CHAPTER THIRTY-NINE

Sunday dawns and as daylight breaks, so does my head. Or that's what it feels like. Regretting, as I knew I would, the amount of whisky I'd drunk last night, I pull myself out of bed.

My head might be pounding, my legs as wobbly as a newborn foal, but on my phone is Cheryl—*Cher's*—address. Today I'll be going to see her, and I won't be letting her get away. Not until we've had a chance to have a decent conversation. And if that ends up in bed, so much the better.

After a shower, copious amounts of coffee and a huge plate of one of Rosa's special breakfasts, by lunchtime I'm feeling partway human, or enough to get on my bike and ride.

Keys gives me a smirk and a wave of his hand as I head outside. I check my phone again, reminding myself of the direction in which I should head, then wasting no time I start my engine, ride through the gates and soon hit the pavement. I grin to myself anticipating the look on her face.

She'll be as surprised as fuck when she sees me. Happy, I hope. If not, then now's the time for explanations. If she tells me to get lost, then I'll take it like a man. Or, more likely a biker. I'll head off, get roaring drunk, and forget all about her by losing myself in a faceless woman's cunt.

On the way I ask myself if I know what I'm doing, and why I didn't take the hint with her first brush off. I'll be fucked if I know why, but I'd felt there was something being left unsaid. Call it a sixth sense if you want, but something about our encounter was off.

I arrive at a pleasant enough apartment block on a well-maintained street. Not overly expensive, but in Vegas it won't come cheap. I park my bike, put my gloves in my helmet, then check her apartment number again. It's on the second floor, so I head for the stairs.

As I take the first step, I'm practicing my opening gambit. *Hey, babe. We need to talk.* Lame, but what else can I start with?

There's a bell, I ring it, listening to it chiming inside. I hear footsteps and feel my heart leap, with my luck lately, I'd expected her to be out.

A chain rattles and then the door is swung open.

That it's not Cheryl standing in the opening takes me a moment to process. It takes me a further few seconds to digest what I'm seeing. It's like looking in a fucking mirror or would have been two decades and more back.

The youth staring back at me is equally open mouthed, and I take a moment to analyse exactly what I'm seeing. He's got green eyes, his nose is mine, as is the way his mouth curves. Fuck, but he's got the same freckles which immediately makes me feel sorry for the kid. His cheekbones, though, are more pronounced, and his face on the whole is more slender.

A tide of rage rises inside me. *This is my kid.*

He's the first to speak, just two words out of his mouth confirms the situation and damns us all on new paths.

"You're Red."

"Who's at the door?" Cheryl's voice sounds light as if she's no idea her whole world's about to turn upside down. "Is it Sue? If it is, tell her I'll be ready in a bit."

"It's not Sue," my mini-me says, but adds no further explanation.

I'm yet to speak, I've not recovered from the shock.

"Then who is—" Cheryl's head appears, and hell, her face goes completely white. Her hand grasps the doorjamb as if she knows she needs it to support her. "Zeke, go to your room."

"Mom?"

"Zeke. Your room. Now." Her voice takes the sternest tone only a mom can.

Taking one last look at me, the kid reluctantly turns. I notice Cheryl giving him a supportive squeeze to his shoulder as he walks past as if to comfort him. *What the fuck has she told him about me?* That I'm the Devil personified? What excuse has she made for me not being in his life? *And why the fuck didn't she try to find me?*

It's that that I start with. "Were you ever going to tell me?" I snarl, pushing my way in through the door.

She doesn't try to deny that she knows what I'm talking about, doesn't say his looks are just coincidence. Instead, she says what I know is the truth.

"How the fuck could I? When all I knew was your name was Red, and that you were heading south?" She accompanies her statement with a roll of her eyes. "Anyway, it doesn't matter. We've done just fine. Now you can turn around and forget all about us."

Fuck. She never knew me at all. "I can't do that," I spit out, trying to keep a rein on my temper, conscious *my son* is in the next room. "If I'd known then, I'd have come back and supported you. Fuck, Cheryl, I had no idea. I didn't even think —" Wraith's words come into my head. *Never assume a woman's protected.* And that's exactly what I'd done. Not that I think it was any trick, it was just a stupid mistake, by a pair old enough to know better, but who didn't.

I'd never broached the conversation, but neither had she. And she was left carrying the burden for fifteen years.

"If I knew where you were, I would have told you." The positivity in her voice tells me what she's said is the truth.

I go to the window, lean my elbow on the wall, and gaze outside through unfocused eyes. My other fist I pump against the wall. "All that damn wasted time," I say half to myself, half to her. I hit the paintwork a couple more times, then swing around. "All these years I've been wondering whether we would have made it. You, Cheryl, have always been on my mind. Cheryl, my fuckin' peril. My downfall." Shaking my head, I scoff, "You have no idea how I've thought about you, dreamed about you. Had visions of us being together, raising a family. Can you imagine how I feel knowing you've had my kid all this time? A kid I knew nothing about, didn't see born, didn't see take his first steps…" My voice trails off, and hell, I have to wipe my eyes.

MC prezes don't cry. I'm sure there's some unwritten law about it, but I'm doing a good approximation now.

Cheryl doesn't speak, doesn't say a word, but I can tell I've astonished her. There's a wealth of sadness in her eyes. Then, in front of me, she seems to gather herself together.

I'm not sure what I expect, whether she's going to welcome me with open arms and suggest somehow we'll try to make up for lost time. Or, at the least, she'll call her, *our* son, and introduce us properly.

What I don't anticipate is for her to stand, go to the door, and open it. "Well, you know now, Red. We've done great without you. We don't need you in our lives. Please go."

Go? Is she fucking serious? My temper flares, I do indeed approach the door, but only to wrench it out of her grasp and slam it shut.

"You want me to go? Walk away, pretend this never happened?" I rake my hands through my hair, the action stopping me from using said appendages to throttle her. "You think I can just turn my back now? You won't even give me a chance to know my *son?*"

She visibly flinches but holds her ground. "You're in an MC, Red. Hell, you're the fucking man in charge. Believe me when I say you'll be no good for us. All you'll do is hurt our child."

"I would never hurt him!" I yell.

Her voice is deathly quiet. "Oh, you will. You won't be able to help yourself."

What the fuck? "Who the hell do you think I am, Cheryl?"

She tosses back her hair and places her hands on her hips. "Oh, I know exactly who, and what you are, Red. You're the prez of the Satan's Devils MC."

To be continued *in Red's Peril Part 2*

RED'S PERIL

PART 2

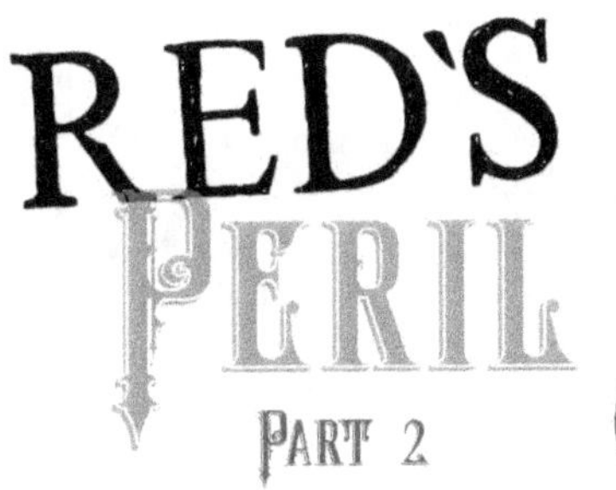

Pre-order https://books2read.com/u/m2l2nR

Red's Peril Part 2: The Prez's Old Lady

Oh, the decisions we make when we're young, which with age we come to regret. If I could have a do-over, I'd never have walked away. But I did. It was done, and my actions couldn't be taken back.

I was only twenty, and I believed I had time to find my special one. Then life threw me a curve ball that altered all my plans. The result being I could never forget the man I'd met so briefly on the road.

The question of what would have happened if I stayed with him is constantly on my mind. What would my life have been like if I'd been braver? What if I hadn't walked away?

Would I have ended up a weary thirty-five-year-old croupier in a Vegas casino with no man by my side?

When fortune offers me a second chance, it comes with strings attached. The man I'm attracted to is the prez of the Satan's Devils MC, whereas I'm a law-abiding citizen who's never broken a single rule in my life.

Is there any way we could make a future together? Or should I run and never look back?

Pre-order: https://books2read.com/u/b6vpZ0

Warts an' All

Toad

I've seen her around with her airs and graces, making out she was better than the rest of us. Head held haughtily high, nose in the air as if everyone else was beneath her. She had it all – a rich daddy, a fine mansion, fast cars. Yeah, that princess wanted for nothing.

I've seen her, but she's never seen me. Until she needs my help, that is. Then she comes crawling, words sticking in her throat as I make her beg.

Grovelling to a biker obviously hurt, and every word out of her mouth was a lie. She said she'd thank me with no thought to paying her debt.

But I know not everything in her perfect life is what it seems. I've got the power to bring this snooty princess down to my level. I've got her daddy in the palm of my hand.

She owes me, but his debt is bigger. He won't think twice, giving her to me as payment.

Love? Nah, that doesn't come into it. I'll show her who gets looked up to around here, and it's not her.

ACKNOWLEDGMENTS AND AUTHOR'S NOTE

Oh what a tangled web I started to weave when I wrote what was originally going to be a one-off novella. Turning Wheels became a full-length book and spawned the Satan's Devils MC.

The Tucson chapter was the club's mother chapter, and some of the other chapters were introduced. One man stood out in particular, the prez of the Vegas chapter – a man called Red.

Red's had cameo roles or mentions in almost every one of these books, and seems to have captured the imagination. For a long time, I've been asked when I'll get around to writing his book.

He'd prospected with Wraith as we already knew from *Turning Wheels*. I didn't think I could write his book without at least some mention of that, which led me to thinking it would be fun to revisit the club in its very early days. That led me to considering how Red got involved with the MC, and how he went from being a man who loved riding his bike to rising up through the ranks of the MC.

I'm often asked what inspires me to write a book, and it can be any number of otherwise insignificant things. A news story, a comment, or, as in this case, a song. I wasn't ready to write Red's book until I was listening to Bob Seger one day. Suddenly, the beginning of Red's story came to life. Can you guess which song it was? If you know it, you'll probably guess immediately as the lyrics really fit.

I don't like writing two-parters – as a reader I'm impatient and want to know how the story ends, but I'd spent so much time on Red's history, I'd either have to rush the second half of the book or take time and do it justice. I decided I'd take my time and give him the end to his story that he deserves. To readers who hate cliffhangers, I offer my apology. It's not so drastic a cliff edge as it was in *Avenging Devil*, so I hope you'll forgive me.

I do hope you've enjoyed the first part of Red's story. I was very conscious that you all have high expectations and hope that I didn't disappoint. I was nervous about how it was going to be received until my amazing beta readers assured me they liked it.

I am so lucky with my beta readers, especially Sheri who picked up on things that were inconsistent with the previous books. During the previous twenty-six books, I'd occasionally mentioned the history of the club, and Sheri corrected me on some of the details I hadn't remembered correctly. Sheri – you are worth your weight in gold!

Danena, once again a massive thank you to you. You know how much your opinion means to me, and I'm so glad you didn't think Red or Cheryl were like dry toast.

Jo – I honestly don't mind you criticising anything or pointing out where my math has gone wrong. I'd rather someone corrected me at an early stage than have readers scratching their heads. Thank you so much for being the newest, but valuable member of the team.

Tami, Tera, Alex and Zoe, thank you once again. As I've said, I was worried about how the book would be received and your views were important to reassure me.

Once again a huge thank you to Maggie Kern my long-suffering editor. I high-fived myself when I actually made you cry. You're a tough nut to crack, but apparently I did it with Brick. (Admission, I cried myself when I was writing that part.)

Thank you for your comments, which made me laugh, and for all your invaluable input.

Darlene, thank you again for proofreading this book. I know I was late getting it to you and rushed you to complete it, but you came through for me again. I really am very grateful.

It was hard trying to find a model that fit my image of Red. I know Andrew Flanagan might not be everyone's vision of what Red is to them, but to my mind, he's pretty damn close. The images were brought to you courtesy of Golden Czermak of Furious Fotog, and the cover was again brought to life by Dar Dixon of Wicked Smart Designs.

Finally, last as always, but definitely not least, thanks to all of you, my wonderful readers who've taken a chance on this book. If it wasn't for your encouragement, I wouldn't keep writing. I have recently received messages and emails telling me how much you like my books, and I love reading every one. A positive message inspires me to write more.

This book, like all of my works, has been to beta readers, through editing twice, to a proofreader and then to ARC readers, but there could still be the odd typo that's crept through. Please message me if you've found anything, so I have a chance to correct the book. I love to hear from readers, even if you're pointing out something I've got wrong.

If you've enjoyed this book, please consider writing a review. Reviews are essential to us authors, and I appreciate and read them all.

Part 2 of *Red's Peril* will be in your hands very soon.

I'm also writing a much shorter book as part of the *Bleeding Souls Saved by Love* anthology, a collaboration of some great authors. Each book is a standalone and based on a fairy tale. My contribution, *Warts an' All* is based on the *Princess and the Frog*. My chapter of the Wicked Warriors MC has its home in Arizona. It will be published on Jan 3, 2022 and is available to be pre-ordered now.

And after that, another Devil will be coming along.

OTHER WORKS BY MANDA MELLETT

<u>Blood Brothers – A series about sexy dominant sheikhs and their bodyguards</u>

Stolen Lives (#1) Nijad and Cara

Close Protection (#2) Jon and Mia

Second Chances (#3) Kadar and Zoe

Identity Crisis (#4) Sean and Vanessa

Dark Horses (#5) Jasim and Janna

Hard Choices (#6) Aiza

Satan's Devils MC - Arizona Chapter

Turning Wheels (Blood Brothers #3.5, Satan's Devils #1) Wraith and Sophie

Drummer's Beat (#2) Drummer and Sam

Slick Running (#3) Slick and Ella

Targeting Dart (#4) Dart and Alex

Heart Broken (#5) Heart and Marc

Peg's Stand (#6) Peg and Darcy

Rock Bottom (#7) Rock and Becca

Joker's Fool (#8) Joker and Lady

Mouse Trapped (#9) Mouse and Mariana

Blade's Edge (#10) Blade and Tash

Heart Mended: A Satan's Devils MC Novella

Truck Stopped (#11) Truck & Allie

Satan's Devils MC Boxset 1 Books 1-5

Satan's Devils MC Boxset 2 Books 6-8

Satan's Devils MC Boxset 3 Books 9-11

Satan's Devils MC - Colorado Chapter

Paladin's Hell (#1) Paladin and Jayden

Demon's Angel (#2) Demon and Violet

Devil's Due (#3) Beef and Steph

Devil's Dilemma (#4) Pyro and Mel

Ink's Devil (#5) Ink and Beth

Devil's Spawn (#6)

Satan's Devils MC - Next Generation

Amy's Santa (#1) Wizard and Amy

Hawk's Cry (#2) Hawk and Olivia

Twisted Throttle (#3) Throttle and Gwen

Satan's Devils MC - San Diego Chapter

Being Lost (#1)

Grumbler's Ride (#2)

Avenging Devil Part 1 (#3)

Avenging Devil Part 2 (#4)

Satan's Devils MC - Utah Chapter

Road Tripped (#1)

Stormy's Thunder (#2)

STAY IN TOUCH

Email: manda@mandamellett.com

Website: www.mandamellett.com

Sign up for my newsletter to hear about new releases in the Satan's Devils and Blood Brothers series.

Facebook reader group: https://www.facebook.com/groups/mandasbadboys/

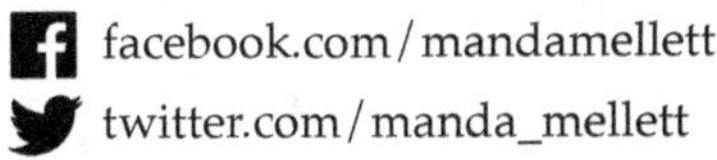

facebook.com/mandamellett
twitter.com/manda_mellett

Manda's life's always seemed a bit weird, starting with a childhood that even today she's still trying to make sense of, then losing her parents in the late teens. Going from the tragic to the bizarre, who else could be unlucky enough to have had two car accidents, neither her fault, one involving a nun, and another involving a police woman?

There isn't enough space to list everything that's happened to Manda, or what she's learned from it. But by using the rich fabric of her personal life, psychology degree, varied work experiences, and amazing characters she's met, Manda is able to populate her books with believable in-depth characters and enjoys pitting them against situations which challenge them. Her books are full of suspense, twists and turns and the unexpected.

Manda lives in the beautiful countryside of Essex in the UK, the area's claim to fame being the Wilkin's Jam Factory at nearby Tiptree. She can usually find jars of jam which remind her of home wherever she goes. As well as writing books and reading, Manda loves walking her dogs and keeping fit. She lives with her husband of over 30 years, who, along with her son, is her greatest fan and supporter.

Manda is thankful that one of the more unusual, and at the time unpleasant, turns her life took, now enables her to spend her time writing. Confirming, in her view, every cloud has a silver lining.

Photo by Carmel Jane Photography